It Never Happened

A Novel by Ron Tell

FORWARD
Ron Tell

I would like to take this opportunity to thank several people without whom this book would never have been possible. Primarily I would like to thank my wife, Kathy, who put up with me spending hours writing the book when I should have been taking care of the dog or doing chores around the house. I would also like to thank my daughter, Rachel. It was her idea and encouragement that started me writing the book. There are also many friends that helped proofread early drafts and encouraged me to continue, despite the horrible use of the English language that I had displayed in the first few drafts. I would also like to give a special "thank you" to Bob Armistead for allowing me to include his poem *HERE LIES A SILENT WARRIOR* in the book.

I remind my readers that this book is a work of fiction. While some of the historical characters are actual people, what they said and did in this book are pure figments of my imagination. Some events are actual historical facts, but details may have been modified to fit into the storyline.

It has been noted by several of the early readers that some of the places and things that happened in the book fit very well into my own life story. True, I was in the Air Force. True, I was assigned to the Air Force Security Service. True, my military records say that I was stationed at Lackland Air Force Base, Keesler Air Force Base, Clark Air Base and Iraklion Air Station. True, I was assigned to the 6922nd and the 6931st Security Groups. True, some characters mentioned have names that closely match my friends and relations. True, that during the time of the Vietnam War, some politicians and military leaders adamantly denied that we ever had troops in North Vietnam, Laos or Cambodia, when history has proven that we actually did. True, I did go back to Crete for a military reunion. However – just like the characters in this story say quite often - IT NEVER HAPPENED! That's my story and I am sticking to it.

So having said that – characters in this book are fictional and any resemblance to actual persons, living or dead, or actual events is purely coincidental.

If you need more information about the author, some of the acronyms or the weapons used in the book please check out my web page at www.RonTell.weebly.com   There are even a few photos of places mentioned in the book. Thanks for reading my book.

Ron Tell

DEDICATION

This book is dedicated to all the Silent Warriors, past, present and future of the United States Air Force Security Service (USAFSS). After its creation in 1948 as the United States Air Force Security Service, it has had many names over the years: Electronic Security Command; Air Force Intelligence Command; Air Intelligence Agency; the Air Force Intelligence, Surveillance and Reconnaissance Agency and is currently designated as the Twenty-Fifth Air Force. No matter the name of their unit, the members of these commands are the Silent Warriors of USAFSS who have kept, and will continue to keep, America safe and free.

They are called the Silent Warriors because, unlike the characters of this novel, the vast majority of the personnel whom performed COMINT, SIGINT, COMSEC, and other intelligence missions as members of USAFSS never fired a physical weapon at an enemy combatant, but they have always been in the front lines to keep America safe. Many members of USAFSS did indeed die of wounds during the Vietnam War and/or had other fatal mishaps performing their missions. It is to those that have fallen and those who have served that I dedicate this work.

HERE LIES A SILENT WARRIOR
by Bob Armistead ©2009

We served in silence, never breathing a word,
Of the things we'd seen, or that which we'd heard.
We worked by a code that few have ever known,
And we served in countries that were far from home.

We left all our friends and families behind,
To perform the work to which we were assigned.
We manned our positions – every hour of every day.
Our work never stopped, and we never did sway.

We did all that was asked and we did it with pride;
We stood shoulder to shoulder and worked side by side.
If I'm ever asked, "Would you do it again?"
I'd just smile and say, "How soon can I begin?"

The time which I've served, I'll never regret,
And the men whom I've known, I'll never forget.
Now time has passed and our hair has turned gray,
And our ranks are thinning with each passing day.

So when my bell tolls for the final time,
And the echoes fade from the very last chime,
And my eyes are closed and I've been laid to rest,
Just be assured that I've served with the best.

Please drape my coffin with the American Flag,
And on top of my casket lay out my dog tag.
With my dog tag as my I.D. and the Flag as my shroud,
I'll go to my grave...an American...and still proud!

I'll trek to that place to join all the others,
My comrades in arms: My sisters, my brothers.
I'll be with my friends who have gone on before,
And are waiting for me beyond Death's door.

So, when I'm gone, shed no tears for me,
For I've died as I've lived – an American and Free!
And once I've traveled to my eternal home,
Just carve the following on my gravestone:
"HERE LIES A SILENT WARRIOR"

CONTENTS

Ron Tell

CHAPTER 1
May 9, 2018
Hersonissos, Crete, Greece

Some heroes of ancient conflicts are remembered in fables and lore; the stories of some are forgotten in the sands of time. Some heroes of the more modern conflicts are documented in our written histories, but some heroes are never named because they are lost in silence.

* * *

The hotel's meeting room was buzzing with the chatter of four veterans, all in their late sixties, and three of their wives. The veterans had not seen each other in over 45 years but they were chatting away like the years had never passed.

As the door opened just enough for him to see who was entering, one of the veterans immediately shouted, "Attention!" Magically the veterans became instantly quiet and as though they had never left the military, they "almost" assumed a posture of attention. They didn't quite pull it off due to a few having a lot more stomach than they had during their prime. The ladies, not having had the experience tutelage of the kind words and sweet inspiration from a military Training Instructor pounded into their heads, continued chatting for a bit before they realized something was up and turned to pay attention to the person that had walked into the room.

Major General George Straight took his place at the head of the table and said, "Could everyone please take their place." As the group moved to the seats that were labeled with their names, the General scanned each of their faces with a penetrating stare but a soft smile kept growing upon his lips as he looked at them. Even though he was in his late 70's he stood ramrod straight in his U. S. Air Force dress blue uniform. He was a tall man with many rows of "been there, done that" ribbons pinned on his chest. His gray hair was still clipped short in the military style even though he had retired many years ago. Seated around the table were the four veterans and their neatly-dressed wives. One man stood out wearing the uniform of a Chief Master Sergeant. The other three veterans wore civilian clothing varying from a tailored three-piece suit to a denim vest decorated by patches displaying motorcycle gang colors. On the side of the table to the general's right was an empty seat with a place setting on a black placemat.

The general picked up a glass of white wine that had been waiting at each place setting then turning to the empty seat he said, "Before we begin our unit's reunion, I would like to propose a toast to those members of our unit who are no longer here."

1

Everyone stood. He continued, "Please raise your glasses to the thirty-seven of us who lost their lives 50 years ago in the hell holes of Southeast Asia, and to the four who were fortunate enough to have passed in their own beds. To the fallen!" Before taking a sip of their drinks, the others echoed, "To the fallen." A few of the words were mumbled through throats suddenly constricted by dark remembrances.

The General, after taking a second to clear a frog from his own throat, said, "I would like to welcome all of you to the 50 year reunion of Detachment Eleven of the 6922nd Security Group. Of course, you guys all know each other very well." Hearing a few snickers and seeing a few knowing smiles pass between the men, the General continued, "Perhaps too well. But for the sake of the ladies and all the time that has passed since we were last together, why don't we go around the table and re-introduce ourselves. I am George Straight and have had the honor of being the creator and commander of this group of lying, cheating, conniving, brave, unknown bastards. Let me give you the Readers Digest version of my life. I was born in a small town in rural Georgia about 40 miles from Atlanta. I attended the Air Force Academy. I was then cursed and had to work with this group of misfits. I commanded them through specialist training, our time in Southeast Asia, and here on Crete at Iraklion Air Station. I spent a total of 31 years in the service, retired, and went to work for the NSA. When I retired from NSA, I decided to spend my golden years back here on Crete." Pointing to the other man in uniform to his left as he sat down, he said, "Bill, why don't you take it from here. And keep it brief!"

A lanky six foot one inch tall, still red-headed, Chief Master Sergeant stood and said, "First I want to say a thanks to the General, for putting this together and helping out with the finances to get me and Mary here. I'm William, Wild Bill, O'Rourke. I am from Moscow." He pronounced the city name Maas-co. "The one in Idaho, not the Russian *великий город Москвы в Союзе Советских Социалистических Республик* (velikiy gorod Moskvy v Soyuze Sovetskikh Sotsialisticheskikh Respublik)." Pronouncing the last part with a flawless Russian accent, he continued, "I stayed in the Air Force for 20 years. Fortunately, most of the time was spent working for our general, otherwise I most likely wouldn't have all the stripes that I do."

He smiled broadly when someone interrupted him with, "Judging by past experience, more than likely, you wouldn't have any."

Nodding yes, he continued, "True. Thank goodness the General is a glutton for punishment, because just about every other duty station I was back with him again. After being stationed all over the world, I finished my last tour at Fort Mead, retired and moved back to Moscow where I managed an RV park for a while. Mary and I are still living in a trailer at the Snake River RV Park."

As Bill sat down, Mary stood. She was a plump five foot nothing in gray slacks and a dark green gingham patterned shirt. Her pixie-cut hair was white with a few red highlights still remaining. Just by looking at her turned up, freckled nose you could instantly tell she too was of Irish descent. With a mischievous grin she began, "Hi, I'm Mary, Bill's wife. I met Bill while he was stationed here on Crete and I was on vacation. We were married on the base and were fortunate enough to have lived here for close to three wonderful years. I was a camp follower and went with Bill to all but one of his postings. We have two boys and four granddaughters. And ladies, if you want to know all the bad things that your boys did while they were here, I have some outrageous tales I can tell you later."

To sounds of a few groans from the men, and snickers from the women, Harold stood up. Harold was the man dressed in a motorcycle vest over a white T-shirt and well used blue jeans. The vest had a large patch from the "Minotaur Motorcycle Club - Iraklion Air Station" on the back and patches of flags from several places around the world, along with a few Harley and other motorcycle logo patches on the front. He was about five foot nine with a bushy white Fu Manchu mustache and long white hair pulled into a ponytail. The first words out of his mouth were, "Don't believe anything Mary says. It never happened! Right, guys?"

All the men said almost in perfect unison, "It never happened!"

"I'm Harold Vinter. I escaped from the Air Force the second my four years were up and went back home to Boulder, Colorado. I got a mining job and worked for several companies around the Rockies until I retired. Now I spend my free time riding the roads on my Harley and getting as much clean air into my lungs as I can." He quickly sat down.

While all the others were in their 60's and 70's, next to Harold was a very attractive woman in her late thirties with long blonde hair, just a tad shorter than Harold, dressed in a dark blue pantsuit. She stood with a big smile and said, "Hello everyone, my name is Joan. I have the misfortune to be Harold's third and final wife. I know I will be his final wife because he knows I will kill him if he goes back to his old ways of chasing tourist skirts again like he told me he did when he was stationed here on Crete." This brought a laugh from everyone including Harold. Joan began to sit down but popped right back up and said, "Oh yeah, I'm a kindergarten teacher. We have one boy and one girl. And Mary, I'd believe anything you would tell me." Then she sat back down.

Next up was a man wearing aviator glasses with neatly groomed pure-gray hair and a pot belly. "Harold, you cradle-robber, and the rest of you gentleman, and I use that term loosely, I thank you for bringing your lovely ladies to this gathering. I am John Porter from Everglades, Florida but I am currently residing in Miami. I am a retired civil engineer that specialized in building demolition."

He was interrupted by Harold who blurted, "Johnny, you always did love to blow shit up."

With a grin, John when on, "And I finally got paid well to do it too! What more can a guy want? After I got out of the service I used the G. I. Bill to attend college at Florida State and got my engineering degree. It was there I met my wife Linda. We got married right out of college and moved to Miami where she worked for an insurance company while I was starting out with a large construction firm. My boss finally figured out I was better at knocking things down than putting then up, so I got lots of experience destroying stuff all over the world. After a few years, I started my own company. Things were great until Linda died of cancer a few years back. I sold my company and now I just play with the two grandkids.

Next to Johnny sat Kathy. She was a good looking, petite brunette with just traces of gray at the temples. Dressed in a floral printed summer dress and white sandals, it looked like she was going to a garden party. "Hi, I'm Kathy, Ron's wife. I too want to thank you, George, for arranging this reunion. Ron and I have been here on Crete a few times before but I always love returning. Ron has told me a lot about what you guys did on your time off ... chasing the tourist girls. So I will believe any story you tell us, Mary. But Ron has never talked about what he did in the military, other than chasing girls. So perhaps at this reunion I can learn what you guys actually did."

Ron stood as he took off the coat that went with his three piece blue pinstripe suit and hung it on the back of his chair. He loosened his gray and red striped power tie. Finally, running his hand through his hair, a shaggy mess of silver with just a few dark brown highlights, Ron began, "So to keep the introductions short and sweet. I'm Ron Lafayette. I retired from IBM and now live in southwest Louisiana. Back to you, General."

The general said, "Let's get this party started."

He then rattled off a few words in Greek to the waiter who had been quietly standing in the back of the room. The waiter opened the door and spoke to someone in the hall. Seconds later, several waiters filed into the room and proceeded to serve the kind of meal the men had learned to love when they were all based at Iraklion Air Station. Instead of one plate with a full meal they were given what seemed like hundreds of small appetizer dishes, served family style. The group talked among themselves about the food, their children, and grandchildren - not necessarily in that order. As they chatted, the waiters rolled in a desert cart and brought the traditional serving of Raki to the table.

As the tiny Raki glasses were distributed to everyone, Harold said, "For the ladies who may not know better, this is Raki. It should be quickly consumed, just like a shot of tequila. The toast that goes with it is Yiamas."

Everyone raised their glass and said "Yiamas!"

Upon tasting the liquor, Joan's face screwed in an expression that was a combination of biting into a lemon, pain, fear, and total shock. After a few seconds she finally managed to gasp, "What the hell is that stuff, liquid fire?"

As everyone laughed at the look on her face, Ron explained, "Raki is a Cretan moonshine made with the distilled remnants from grapes once they have been pressed for making wine. Good Raki is superb and bad Raki may remind you of turpentine. But good or bad, drinking it after a big meal always helps the digestion. Also, given the high alcoholic content, it also greatly helps a post-meal conversation."

As another round of the clear Raki was poured into everyone but Joan's liquor glass, from the mini-carafes spread around the table, General Straight spoke to the lead waiter for a few seconds. Immediately a cart with a large selection of liquors, wines, and beers was rolled into the room. The waiters left and the doors were closed behind them.

After the General poured himself a triple shot of Jack Daniels over ice he said, "Everyone help yourselves to your own poison because it's time to pay for this vacation by listening to what I have to say."

After a few stage groans (and a lot of good nature elbowing at the drink cart), everyone returned to their seats. The General began by thanking all for coming and started going over some of his plans for the remainder of their reunion. The group murmured approval, and judging by the consensus, it was going to be a fun-filled two weeks.

After he explained the plans, the General turned to face Kathy, "During the introductions, Kathy wondered if she was going to finally learn what we did besides chasing girls. Well, there was a good reason the guys never talked about what we did. Up until just last month, everything they did was classified Top Secret. They were warned while they were still in the military that if they ever spoke a word about what they did, I would hunt them down and shoot them like rabid dogs. And I meant it."

He shrugged and gestured with his drink. "But time has passed. It seems that the powers that run Washington have agreed that since none of them were in office when all of this took place, they couldn't be hurt if the information was declassified now. Since their butts were covered, it no longer makes any difference to them if the world knew about a lot of the stuff that went on during the Vietnam War and the Cold War. One of the benefits of having been a general is I still get some information a little early. I heard the declassification was going to happen last December, so I started a few balls rolling down the long corridors of the Pentagon. Naturally, it takes a crisis to move anything faster than a snail's pace in the Puzzle Palace but I was promised by a mobile crisis on two legs called General Frankes, aided by my son George Jr., the Honorable Senator from the state of Georgia, that we would get a few of my requests answered in writing by the end of this week. We will get back to that later, but for now I can officially say that what you guys did for our country can be talked about without anyone having to be shot."

"So grab another drink and I'll tell you about how our little band of bastards got started."

CHAPTER 2
May 9, 2018
Hersonissos, Crete, Greece

The room became totally quiet. All but one of the men sat with open mouths at the shock of the news that what they had done during their time in Southeast Asia was no longer a secret. It was a deep secret that they had kept suppressed for so long that they sometimes had difficulty remembering what was real and what was their invented "cover story." Sitting with a smile spread across his face, instead of shock, was Wild Bill. Wild Bill's mind ran off on a tangent that perhaps now he would finally be able to join the VFW since they had a much nicer bar in their hall than the American Legion did. But he too was snapped back to reality when General Straight began to speak.

"For the sake of the ladies, I will try to explain some of the military jargon I use as much as I can.

"It all began Thursday, February 1, 1968, the day after the start of what later became known as the Tet Offensive. I was a captain working at the Pentagon for the Air Force Chief of Staff, General John P. McConnell."

* * *

February 1968 ~ Washington, D.C.
As told by General George Straight

That day, I along with most of the staff were scheduled to be off as part of a long five day weekend because of a ceasefire scheduled for Tet, the Vietnamese New Year. But I had gotten a call during the night to come into work that morning. Very early in the morning General McConnell came into the office in a super big rush and yelled at me to bring him some coffee as he breezed past me and went into his personal office slamming his door. Being the good assistant dog robber that I was, within just a few seconds I brought him in a large cup of coffee in a blue china mug bearing the logo of Second Air Force which he had since he was stationed at Barksdale Air Force Base. After he took a quick sip he said, "The Cong have broken the Tet ceasefire and all hell is breaking loose in Vietnam, there are attacks being reported from bases and cities all over. The Cong may have even gotten into the U. S. Embassy. We have Air Force bases getting hit too. Somehow they have managed to launch hundreds of coordinated attacks throughout South Vietnam. The information is rather shoddy since this mess started but it sounds like the thousands of troops that Westmoreland had already reported killed are alive and kicking ass over there. The president is going to be raising hell and screaming for someone's hide. And I don't want it to be mine!"

McConnell then began to shoot orders at me like an M16 on full auto. Requests for reports on the operational status and casualties suffered at air bases that had been attacked. Requests for statistics on the air support packages that were being flown to counter the Cong offensive. Requests on logistics for the supplies on hand and what will be required to support the defense of units still under attack and for the eventual counter attacks that we would be launching. My mind was reeling from trying to remember all the details of everything he was requesting when he dropped the big bomb and said, "I need a draft report on all the excuses we can concoct to explain why the Air Force was not responsible for this offensive and for not having already bombed North Vietnam and their Cong buddies back into the stone age."

Normally the duty I was about to do was handled by the general's aide-de-camp but the colonel was in the hospital due to an emergency appendectomy - so the job fell on me. I dashed back into the outer office and started to round up as much staff as I could get my hands on. I started divvying up the report requests to the staff and I called in all kinds of favors to get the communications lines opened to the staff in Vietnam so we could get the answers and statistics required. The office became a madhouse with everyone pecking away on their manual typewriters with one hand, taking longhand notes with the other, all the while with a black telephone handset tucked between their ear and their shoulder. The troops in Nam may be taking fire but the troops at Headquarters were scrambling as well. We knew that perhaps something we were doing could just possible save some lives where the danger was real.

Everything, except the bombshell excuse report, was well on its way to the general's desk. I was just not ready to allocate a task like that to the others on the staff. I didn't think that I would want to have them get such a disgusting job when there were so many other positive things they could be doing. I was actually quite shocked that the general even asked for it. But once everything else was in progress I had no excuse to put off that request any longer.

I had a sneaky suspicion as to why the general wanted the report. He was going to need it as ammunition to protect his own ass when the shit hit the fan at the White House. But I knew darn well that I could not put the real reason down on paper. I knew the real reason, just like almost every other thinking man in a uniform – the reason was that the A-hole local politicians were too busy trying to look good in the press so they could get reelected and the politicians in Vietnam were corrupt idiots. That was why! Our local officials were busy playing politics instead of actually waging a winnable war. I remembered sitting quietly in the back of meetings I attended with the Air Force Chief of Staff as the President, the Secretary of War and the Joint Chiefs discussed the war. It had been a real education on how the politicians were waging the Vietnam War. They were all too busy dodging potential bullets from the press and they could care less about the men being killed by real bullets they weren't able to dodge. The kind of bullets that killed and maimed, not the ones that cost a vote or two.

For a few seconds I toyed with the idea of typing one word on a piece of paper – POLITICS and hand that to General McConnell so he could have his excuse report. But I really did want to have a career serving our country in the military and quickly dismissed that idea.

Finally I decided to put on my big boy pants and grabbed a yellow legal pad and began to jot down notes I could use to build my report. I put down a header – Why we haven't just bombed North Vietnam into the Stone Age. I then began to list reasons, for example:

- Most war materials come from the Russians and Chinese so there are limited war material manufacturing targets. Bombing the real manufacturing plants would escalate the war into a global conflict.
- War materials entering and leaving North Vietnam via Haiphong Harbor also could not be bombed because destruction of Soviet and other communist bloc country shipping could cause an escalation to the war.
- Mass bombing of the civilian population centers rarely achieves a military objective. For example, city bombing during World War II did not significantly lower war materials production and it increased the civilians' determination to fight on.
- Carpet bombing of city centers generates news releases only showing destruction of schools, hospitals, and other soft civilian targets such as children and never military targets. This generates negative feeling toward the war effort both in the U. S. and abroad.
- The inaccuracy of carpet bombing means that many munitions strike non-military targets and collateral damage of civilian targets only cause a greater resolve of the civilian population.
- Complicated airstrike routes caused by detours due to placement of enemy anti-aircraft defenses, as well as, lack of visual navigation points due to the thick jungle cause some air strike missions to miss their targets.
- Thick jungles make it difficult to see targets to strike.
- Bombing missions to interdict supplies along inland routes produce little results since they are not using railroads or hard surfaced roads but jungle trails which are difficult to find from the air.
- Bombing jungle trail routes only cause rerouting of supplies and just some minor destruction of war materials and forces.

- Except for when our intelligence enables us to locate enemy troop concentrations, conventional bombing only destroys jungle and not enemy troops.
- ...

* * *

The day and night streamed by in an unending string of tasks fueled by the reams of paper filled with the transcriptions of the voice, encrypted teletype, and Morse code radio reports coming from halfway around the world. I was kept busy delivering the fresh logistics and status reports, receiving fresh requests, sending out orders based upon the reports, then getting more requests for additional details and up to the minute data updates, not to mention keeping the general supplied with what must have been a hundred gallons of coffee. In the infrequent and short breaks I worked to expand and refine the list that I had started. After I built the list of about 30 or so items, I definitely knew that conventional mass bombing had a lot of limitations when it came to achieving military success in a low-tech, highly rural and jungle area like Vietnam. Many of the reasons had to do with the fact that it is difficult to win the hearts and minds of the civilian populations by dropping high explosives on their families.

I wasn't exactly sure how detailed the general wanted this excuse list so I waited until he'd had sufficient time to view the meaningful reports before I asked for a few seconds of his time to show him the draft excuse list I had created.

It was close to 4 AM when I walked into the general's office with the draft list in one hand and another steaming mug of coffee in the other. The general was sitting slumped down on the black leather sofa in the seating area of his office. He had abandoned the gray metal standard military desk for the more comfortable sofa. The last mug of coffee I had brought him still sat balanced on his belly and his puffy eyes were at just about half mast. His normally razor sharp creased uniform looked like a pile of laundry heaped on the sofa. I had never seen him so tired and disheveled. I guess I wasn't looking too sharp myself when the first words out the general's mouth were, "You look like hell, George. Have I been running you that ragged?"

My reply was a slurred, "Yes, Sir."

He looked at my hands and said, "If I have another cup of coffee I will burst. Why don't you grab a seat and drink it yourself. You look like you need it." I put the mug on the table between the sofa and the black leather chair I had flopped into. Reaching out for the report still in my hand he asked, "What do you have for me now?"

I pass the five page report over to the general but I began to explain before he could start reading the report. "Sir, to be totally honest with you I was not so sure what to do with this request. I was not even sure that I wanted to commit it to paper, but since you asked for it, here is my first rough draft of why we haven't already blown North Vietnam back into the Stone Age."

A pained look appeared on his face as he accepted the paper. "I'm sorry that I asked you to do this but I am very sure that I will need some talking points readily available in my mind when it is my turn to be the target of LBJ's rage at tomorrow's, oops, I mean this morning's meeting at the White House." He took a few minutes to read through the report, nodding a few times and "uming" at a point or two. As he got to the bottom of the list he closed his eyes for a few seconds and thought of what lay ahead.

He rose slowly from the sofa and walked back to his desk, stacking the report with several others in an open briefcase. "Great job, George. But right now I am totally bushed and we both need to get a few hours shut-eye so we can be fresh to begin the battle again tomorrow without making a lot of mistakes. I'll have my driver pick you up here at oh-nine-thirty so you can go with me to the White House for the great finger pointing meeting. Hopefully we will be able to walk out of that meeting and not need to be carried out. Get a few of the still warm bodies outside to stay on top of the radio reports from Nam and contact me if necessary. Have them throw together an abbreviated, updated casualty report and a list of the number of sorties flown since this mess started. That way I can have the latest information for the meeting, and then get yourself to bed. We have another big day ahead of us."

When I finally got back to my apartment I set my alarm so I could get three hours sleep and flopped down on the bed still dressed. It seemed like I had just closed my eyes when the stupid alarm clock started ringing. Fumbling to turn off that damn ringing I dragged myself out of bed to take a shower and get a fresh shave.

I rushed through my morning ablutions and put on a fresh uniform. I managed to get back to the office by 8 and started going through all the fresh information streaming in from Vietnam. The next hour and a half went by quickly but I had the latest updates in hand when the general's car picked me up. On the ride to the White House the general quickly read through the reports, made a few notes on them, and closed his eyes to visualize what he was going to report at the meeting. The news wasn't all that bad. Each and every air base was up and functioning. Sorties were being delivered in support of beleaguered ground troops throughout South Vietnam. So all in all, the Air Force didn't look too bad. Also, judging by the reports we were getting back, the counterattacks and airstrikes were causing a lot more casualties than we had suffered during the attacks.

At the meeting, I tried my best to become invisible and shrink into the back wall of the situations room, just like the rest of the aides, as the powers around the central conference table did a wonderful job of finger pointing, blame shifting and twisting the facts to make themselves look good. The people seated around the conference table were a who's who of the Washington military power elite. Besides President Lyndon B. Johnson there was Vice President Hubert Humphrey, White House Chief of Staff W. Marvin Watson, Secretary of State Dean Rusk, Secretary of Defense Robert S. McNamara, Chairman of the Joint Chiefs of Staff Army Gen. Earle Wheeler, Harold "Johnny" Johnson Chief of Staff of the United States Army, Chief of Naval Operations Thomas Moorer, Commandant of the Marine Corps Leonard Chapman, and my poor boss John McConnell.

Since he wasn't there to protect himself, General Westmoreland took the brunt of the heat. Especially since the statistics that he had been reporting for the last few months to the White House said that the Viet Cong had already been all but destroyed. Army General Johnson was doing his best to support General Westmoreland but judging by the way LBJ was yelling into his face you could tell that he would not be in the army much longer, at least not if LBJ had anything to say about it. (General Johnson did retire from the army in 1968 and didn't last another 5 months as the Army Chief of Staff.)

General McConnell didn't take as much heat as he was expecting. He kept his report to currently known numbers of Air Force casualties suffered during the initial attacks and the fact that all Air Force operations in Vietnam had already recovered and were back to running close air support missions for those units still under attack.

The first words out of his mouth as we got into the car for the ride back to the office were, "I'm damn glad that I didn't need to start reading off the excuses you had prepared. But there are a few of those that caused me concern and I want to see what we can do to rectify them."

"Which ones are those, Sir?"

"The one that I was definitely not going to present at that Witch Hunt was the one about air strike reroutes caused by avoiding anti-aircraft defenses and lack of visual navigation points due to the jungle causing some air strike missions to miss their targets."

"I'm sorry I put that one in there, Sir."

"No problem, it is true, but I believe we better fix that before it comes up again. Also the ones about missions being wasted because of not having worthwhile targets along the North's supply routes into the south."

"Yes, Sir."

"What I want you to do, in all your spare time, is to come up with some solutions to those problems. I also don't want any fixes you come up with to get us into any hot water if they don't work."

With those final words, he leaned back, closed his eyes, and I believed he started to dream up other ways to make sure I never had a moment of free time for the rest of my life.

* * *

The next few weeks were spent analyzing the results of the Tet Offensive. Militarily we actually were quite successful. All Vietcong gains were neutralized. They lost far more men when compared to the limited casualties that we suffered, but the liberal anti-war press was having a field day. I don't remember any positive press being presented on TV. If you judged by what the press was presenting and not by what had actually happened, we already lost the war, by the end of the week the Viet Cong would be raising their flag over the U. S. Capitol Building in Washington D.C., and the NVA were soon to be having a victory parade down 5th Avenue in New York.

While I spent some time keeping the General up to date on reports coming out of Vietnam, I was laboring away at what I had code named the Detachment Eleven Report. The personnel in Detachment 11 and some fancy electronics could very well be an answer to the question of how to solve the problems of missing targets and finding more worthwhile targets. It contained a justification for creating a form of Special Forces for the Air Force. I knew that I could not call the group anything like "Special Forces" or the Army contingent on the Joint Chiefs would scream bloody murder. The Green Berets were their baby and they would not allow anything to steal the thunder and glory they were getting in the press. Ever since Barry Sadler's "The Ballad of the Green Berets" hit the airwaves, the Army was soaking in the good karma and recruiting potential that it generated. At that time they were even working on a John Wayne movie where he was a Green Beret. The Navy had their Seals and between the Army and Navy any idea of trying to create an Air Force version of Special Forces would be quickly squashed by the Joint Chiefs. I knew we would have to keep the unit a total secret, therefore it became known covertly as Detachment 11. As another way of keeping it hidden I decided it should be cloaked under the cover of the Air Force Security Service.

The United States Air Force Security Service (USAFSS) was a little known unit whose primary job was cryptographic intelligence, sometimes referred to as a Signals Intelligence (SIGINT). The signals or radio intercept intelligence that they gathered was analyzed and forwarded to the National Security Agency (NSA) for further analysis and reporting.

Before being assigned to General McConnell's staff I had been assigned as a commander of one of the 24/7 shifts of SIGINT workers at a base in Japan. I knew that one of the SIGINT intercepts and the analysis that my team generated was a large contributor to getting my job on the General's staff.

Another reason to place Detachment 11 as part of USAFSS was that the personnel assigned to these SIGINT units were usually the cream of the crop. The airmen destined for USAFSS were skimmed off the top of all the recruits as they came through pre-enlistment testing and Air Force basic training evaluations. Many had degrees or at least some college education and almost all higher than average IQ's. As an added bonus they were all thoroughly screened because they had to get Top Secret Cryptographic clearances. Because of the nature of SIGINT work the special Top Secret Cryptographic clearances were actually higher and harder to get than normal Top Secret military clearances. The process of getting the clearances started early in their training process so I knew we would not need to be delayed in the Detachment 11 recruiting process waiting for security clearances.

I determined that the enlisted personnel for Detachment 11 would come from two places. We would get the Airman from those who were in the early phases of radio intercept training. And we would get the NCOs from combat experienced Army and Marine personnel who had transferred services into the Air Force and perhaps a few from the Air Force Security Police that protected our air bases.

Training would be the hard part. I knew that the best training schools would be Navy Seal or Army Special Forces training. Since I didn't see any need for the specialized water aspects of the Navy training it had to be the Green Beret training. That left trying to figure out a way to get the Detachment 11 men through training at the Army's Special Forces Qualification Course sometimes called the "Q Course" or Snake Eater School, and the Basic Airborne Course. The parachutist course should be the easy part since the Air Force did supply the planes they used and we had several qualified jump masters that I could get to create our own mini-course. However, I noted the parachute jumping qualification as something of very low priority. I could also lay my hands on several other key instructors to create mini-courses for Forward Air Control training and to work with the other specialized equipment I had planned on using.

I was lucky in that I had generated a friendship with Frank "Ski" Bronski. Ski was on General Wheeler's staff, and with both of our bosses on the Joint Chiefs of Staff, we got to know each other very well. He was also a combat decorated officer who was an alumnus of the 5th Special Forces Group during his two tours in Vietnam. Early one morning at breakfast in the Pentagon cantina I saw him sitting alone and asked to join him.

Breaking the ice with an insider breakfast joke, I asked, "How are things going so far today, Ski?"

"So far today, fine. I think things are finally settling down in Nam but they would be a hell of a lot better if we could get the G-damn press to shut the F up."

"You're preaching to the choir, Reverend Ski. I got a quick question for you. We want to train some of our guys that go in to rescue downed pilots to be far better qualified if the shit should hit the fan big time and their ride home gets broken. What is the best school for combat and survival training you guys use?" Considering his background I knew what his answer would be, but I wanted to set this up right so I could later use this to get some of our guys into a Green Beret school.

"I learned more going through Snake Eater School than I did all the advanced infantry or other specialty courses I ever took, especially how to survive if I were ever stuck in Indian Country."

"I wonder if I could a get a few of our rescue guys trained."

Laughing he responded, "I doubt that any of your guys have the background to even get into the school much less survive the course. I damn near didn't survive it. Not to mention that it would take a hell of a lot of horse trading to grease the wheels to get non-Army personnel into the course. We are keeping those facilities full ourselves."

I shifted the subject back to sports and started plotting ways to build up favors for the horse trading that lay ahead.

* * *

I was ready to pitch Detachment 11 to General McConnell. I had the Detachment's first missions planned. I knew what specialized equipment the missions would require. I had a targeted group of combat experienced NCOs that we could transfer into the unit. I had a list of potential officers to run the unit and well over a hundred potential airmen that had already started their SIGNET training with their clearance investigations well underway. I had a training plan. I even had some leverage ready to get them into Snake Eater School. All I had to do now was give the plan to General McConnell. My opportunity came that very day when General McConnell came back from a meeting with Chief of Naval Operations, Admiral Thomas Moorer.

It seems as if an Air Force bombing mission over North Vietnam diverted to a secondary target that the Navy was already in the process of hitting themselves. The secondary target of both the Air Force and the Navy strikes was the same potential NVA training camp. Both strike groups had diverted from their primary target. The Navy because of weather and the Air Force because they couldn't find their primary target and had to divert to a target they could find. Due to the confusion of both flights arriving at the secondary target at the same time there were some very near midair collisions. Luckily two of the planes missed each other with only inches to spare. But the Navy Commander that was leading their strike force had been raising holy hell ever since one idiot Air Force pilot on the strike said over the radio that they wouldn't have been there if they could have found their primary objective.

After General McConnell told me about his meeting with his naval counterpart he asked me how we stood getting the missed target problem fixed. I excused myself for a second while I bolted back to my desk to fetch my Detachment 11 plan.

I started off by asking what seemed like a stupid question to an experienced fighter pilot like him. "How do you find an airport you have never been to?"

He gave me a look like I had just crawled out from under a slimy rock, but he knew I was not a pilot and giving me the benefit of the doubt responded, "Ever since 1946 we have been using VHF Omnidirectional Radio Range or VOR which is a type of short-range radio navigation beacon. The pilot then uses equipment in the plane to home-into the VOR for his destination airport. Why do you ask?"

Putting the Detachment 11 report in his hand, I responded, "What if we put battery powered VORs in known locations in North Vietnam and briefed the strike team to fly to the VOR location on frequency X, and exactly 10 kilometers due north of the VOR is the target? Do you think they would ever get lost and miss the target?"

"If they did, I would pull their wings and have them painting rocks around an air base in Alaska for the rest of their military careers!" The second it came out of his mouth he knew the solution I had planned.

I sat quietly as he read the first three pages of the report that contained the overview of Detachment 11. He ruffled through the remaining 100 plus pages and said, "I assume the rest of this has enough detail to get this done?"

"Yes, Sir."

"George, we are playing with fire if anybody finds out about this before we can do it, prove it actually works, and declare it a great success."

"Yes, Sir. In the details, I cover how we keep it a secret."

"Let me read this tonight and we will review it tomorrow. Clear a few hours on my schedule for tomorrow after lunch."

The next day we settled into the general's conference room to go over my plan. Attending the meeting with General McConnell and me were

General Bruce Holloway, the Vice Chief of Staff of the Air Force, and his aide, Major "Trigger" Burns.

"OK, George. Bruce and Trigger have not seen this yet so why not give us a quick synopsis."

"Yes, Sir. The plan is to create a small specialized unit with the purpose of clandestine operations in North Vietnam, Laos, and Cambodia. They would be responsible for placing portable VORs in locations to aid in strike navigation. They would also be used for on the ground scouting of potential targets and providing first hand Bomb Damage Assessment."

Pausing briefly to scan the faces of General Holloway and Trigger I continued, "We would in effect be creating an Air Force Special Forces unit to allow us to have greater accuracy in locating and destroying enemy material."

Upon hearing the words "Special Forces," General Holloway interrupted with, "No way is the Army going to let us get away with having a Special Forces unit."

"I understand that, Sir. That is why the unit will initially be hidden under the cover of the Air Force Security Service. All personnel will be assigned to the 6922nd Security Wing based at Clark Air Base in the Philippines. The unit will stage out of Clark, perform their missions and immediately return to Clark to prepare for their next mission. Nothing on paper will indicate that the unit ever left the Philippines. It will all be kept under the Top Secret Cryptographic umbrella of the Security Service. Once the unit has proven itself we can then bring it out from undercover as a *fait accompli*."

"That might work but we better be 110% sure that no-one, and I do mean no-one, finds out anything about this until you have so much proof that it works that the Army can't say a blasted word against it."

"I understand, Sir."

I then spent the next hour going over all the details of logistics, personnel, and training. After getting several suggestions for improvement from the other attendees I wrapped it up by going over the list of officers I had compiled and asking, "If you agree with the concept, whom should we get to command the unit and when should we schedule them to start?"

The two generals looked at each other and seemed to have a full conversation without ever saying a single word aloud. General Holloway gave a small nod. Then General McConnell looked at a calendar on the wall, glanced at his watch, and said, "There is only one person who can put this together and keep it a secret. That's you, George. As of February 22, 1968 at fourteen hundred hours you are hereby promoted to Major and are in command of Detachment 11. Make it happen."

Inside my head I heard a loud knock which I am sure my jaw must have made as it hit the top of the conference table. I never - ever - had the thought that I would be in command of the unit. A million and one thoughts rushed through my head, as I imagined the enormous task that lay ahead. Then a small voice forced itself to the top of my conscience and I realized that I was just promoted to Major and that I was suppose to say something aloud. I finally blurted aloud, "Thank you, Sir. I will do my best."

"I'm sure you will, George. Now go get the paperwork started. And I guess you should send in my new staff assistant, Captain Austin. I would think we would want him to know about his new job. And one more question, George. Where are you taking us after work? I need to pin on your new oak leaves and have you buy us a few drinks to celebrate and officially wet them down."

* * *

May 9, 2018
Hersonissos, Crete, Greece

For a few seconds, the only thing you could hear was the soft murmur coming from the air conditioning vent in the Hersonissos Royal Hellenic Hotel meeting room. After his brief pause the general said, "And that is how Detachment 11 came to be."

The room was totally quiet as General Straight finished telling about the origin of Detachment 11. After another second of silence, with a gentle astonished look in her eyes, Kathy Lafayette turned to Ron and asked, "Does that mean you were actually a Green Beret in Vietnam?"

Ron shook his head and took a sip of his beer. With a deadpan face responded. "It never happened! I have never worn a froggy hat my entire life."

That caused a few chuckles from the guys. But then the general cut in, "Ron, I am not sure by froggy if you meant a French style beret or if you are referring to the color of the Army Special Forces headgear. What you said is basically true, Kathy, although there was never any special uniform or insignia that was associated with Detachment 11. The need to keep everything secret overrode the *esprit de corps* that something like special headgear would generate. However, I had envisioned them having sky blue berets when and if the unit ever became an official Special Forces unit."

"But while they never had berets, if what they did was ever told to a member of the Green Berets, he would take off his beret and proudly give it to any man sitting here."

When the last sentence that the general said sank in, the silly smile on Ron's face disappeared. He took a look around the table, his eyes landing on the empty place setting on the black placemat. Looking earnestly at his friends through eyes very close to tears, he said, "There are a few people that I would love to see taking a green beanie away from some Army guys."

Taking a deep breath to control his emotions, he continued, "This has been great guys. But I have been up since 8 AM yesterday traveling just to get here. Between the beer, the raki and the jet lag, I'm wiped out. When and where do we meet tomorrow for our tour of the old base?"

No one missed the look on his face and where he was looking. There were a lot of nodded, unspoken agreements.

"Let's meet after breakfast at 09:00 in the hotel lobby. I have a mini-bus picking us up then."

CHAPTER 3
May 10, 2018
Iraklion Air Station, Crete, Greece

The reunion group trickled into the breakfast area and started to get reacquainted. After breakfast they gathered in the hotel lobby chatting away as they waited for the bus. By the time the bus arrived to take them to the first stop on their tour, the old Iraklion Air Station main gate, everybody knew the names of everyone's children and the ages of their grandchildren.

The old guard shack at the gate of the base was still there. In 1972, when they were stationed there it was manned by both U. S. Air Force Security Police together with hired Greek nationals working as security guards. Fifty years ago the sign above the gate read, Iraklion Air Station, U. S. Air Force in English and ΑΜΕΡΙΚΑΝΙΚΗ ΑΕΡΟΠΟΡΙΑ in Greek. Now above the same unmanned guard shack was a sign for the Ενυδρείο Κρήτης – the Crete Aquarium. Their bus stopped at the old guard shack so the group could take photos.

The base was an Air Station which meant that it did not have an air strip like a normal Air Force Base would. No military planes were ever stationed on the base proper which officially began operations in support of activities of the 1603rd Air Transport Wing and other USAFE liaison operations in Crete on 5 October 1954. During the time the guys from Detachment 11 were stationed there in 1971 it was the base for the 9631st Security Group which was a part of the United States Air Force Security Service (USAFSS). The base closed and was turned over to the Greek government in 1994. For a long time, the old base was practically unused and suffered a lot of looting and vandalism which damaged many buildings.

Today the group found the base to be a mixture of new facilities like the Crete Aquarium along with a dinosaur park and exhibition center. Some of the buildings had been repurposed as a school and other viable businesses, as well as, many dilapidated vandalized buildings like the old operations center. The field that had once held a wide array of antennas that supported the SIGINT functions performed in the operations center building had been totally stripped for scrap metal.

As the group stopped and examined some of the buildings they frequented during their tour most were depressed at the state of the dilapidated buildings and remembered how beautiful and well-kept it was when they were stationed there. The base was on the north shore of the island of Crete and had a beautiful white sand beach that all the guys remembered using during their time at the base. The beach was still there, although some of the sand had eroded away and it appeared a lot grayer then it did then. When they drove through the old dependent housing area Wild Bill's wife, Mary, asked to stop by one of the buildings in particular.

They got out of the bus and chatted with the people who were currently residing in Bill and Mary's old apartment. They were quite pleased to find out that there was now a Greek military family living there. As with most of the Greeks, the new residents of Bill and Mary's old housing were super friendly. They even invited the group for a drink. Lemonade and of course Raki were produced while the veterans and their wives chatted away with members of several Greek military families who now lived in the housing area. The conversations were carried out just as they were when the guys were stationed there – a combination of Greek and English words with lots of exaggerated hand and face gestures used by everyone. The brief impromptu party was the highlight of the group's base tour.

After touring the base, the bus left for Agios Nikolaos which literally translates to Saint Nicholas but all the guys remembered it as St. Nick's. St. Nick's was a beautiful little town on the north coast of the island of Crete. There is a wonderful little lake harbor that the town is built around, as well as a large harbor for sea going ships. The group stopped for lunch at one of the outdoor restaurants along the waterfront of the small lake harbor. The harbor's water was slightly darker than the fabulous blue as the Aegean Sea and there were many small fishing boats and pleasure craft docked along the lake's seawall. As they were eating lunch Ron and Harold started wisecracking and verbally tearing each other apart.

During a short break in the conversation, as drinks were being delivered to the table, Kathy quietly asked Ron why they were speaking so sharply to each other. Ron just smiled and loudly repeated Kathy's question to Harold. His response was, "We did this constantly from the day we met in basic training until the day we separated. And now that we are back together and have each other's addresses, we will continue fighting with each other to the day we both die and more than likely even after that!"

Ron said, "I can fight with Harold all I want – I know that we could never hurt each other with words and I also know that while we may fight with each other, we will always fight together against anyone else."

They looked at each other, exchanged knowing grins, and fist bumped as Harold responded, "Amen, Brother!"

Observing Herald, Ron saw a very fit, trim, 68 year old man wearing a light blue denim vest sporting his Minotaur Motorcycle Club logo, with long white hair and a mischievous grin. But his heart saw the eighteen year old, mustached, muscular G.I. covered in camouflage grease paint, camo fatigues, armed to the teeth with that same mischievous grin that would go to hell and back, twice, for a friend.

Likewise, Harold didn't see the gray haired 69 year old portly, well dressed retired IBM computer consultant, but a young, brown haired, 19 year who was as skinny as a rail, a bespectacled friend that could run all day and never seem to get winded.

21

Ron began to tell the group the story of when he and Harold met by saying, "Our friendship began January 12, 1968 the day we started Air Force Basic Military Training at Lackland Air Force Base in San Antonio, Texas."

* * *

January 1968 ~ Lackland AFB, Texas
As told by Ron Lafayette

I arrived at the San Antonio Airport with six other recruits from New Orleans on a Trans Texas Airways DC-3, an old twin engine propeller airliner that had been around since World War II. It was the first time I had ever been on an airplane and I had really enjoyed looking out the window at the world passing below me. It was also the first time I had ever been away from my home in the New Orleans' infamous Lower Ninth Ward. The trip began early in the morning when after saying goodbye to my family, I took the bus to the city's recruitment center in the Customs Building. The seven of us were given physicals and were sworn in to the military. We were then given a thick stack of papers which was actually many copies of the same two-page order assigning us to basic training at Lackland Air Force Base.

When the flight arrived around 8 PM in San Antonio we were met by an Air Force sergeant that herded us towards a staging area along with many other recruits. With the aid of several screaming sergeants we were queued up to get aboard one of a long line of what looked like the common yellow school buses used everywhere, except these were painted a dark blue. I was first in line of the recruits from Louisiana but I was separated from them when I was the last person to board a bus. The others were shepherded to the next blue bus in the queue and I never saw them again.

When we arrived at the air base, the people from my bus joined a line of recruits made up of a group from a previous bus. A sergeant, wearing a Smokey the Bear hat, herded our group of long haired civilians off to a barracks to create a new training unit, one that was destined to train together for the next six weeks. It was just the luck of the draw and the order in which you arrived that determined how individuals were assigned into a unit that the Air Force called a "flight". The flight was a small part of a larger group called a training squadron.

Before we entered the barracks we were lined up in front of the barracks and given our first basic military instructions by one of the two sergeants that would be our T. I.'s, Training Instructors. We stood in our brightly colored civilian clothes with our bags by our sides as another group of trainees all dressed in their sickly green, olive drab, utility uniforms marched past us. As they were marching past they started singing a marching cadence song.

Rainbow, Rainbow don't be blue.
Our recruiter screwed us too.
Sound off, One, Two
Sound off, Three, Four
Sound off, One Two
(pause) Three, Four.

I started thinking that compared to the group in their matching utility uniforms and us all in various colored civilian clothes; we did look like a rainbow. I was quite amused and started laughing aloud. The guy next to me started laughing when I did. Wrong thing to do!!! One of the sergeants in the Smokey the Bear hat that had introduced himself as Staff Sergeant Jones quickly walked up and stood square in front of me. He put his rather large red bulbous nose approximately one inch from mine and yelled, "What in the world is so funny that you have the nerve to laugh while I was speaking? What's your name, Laugher Number One?"

I responded, with a meek, "Ronald Lafayette."

"I asked you, what is your name?"

A little louder I said, "Ronald Lafayette."

"I can't hear you. What is your name? And the first and last words out of your mouth better be 'Sir'!!!!"

With shaking knees, I responded in a much louder voice, "Sir, Ronald Lafayette, Sir!"

Still yelling to such an extent that I could feel small specks of spittle hitting me in the face, SSgt. Jones raged, "Well Airman Basic Ronald Lafayette, I can see where you and I will be having a lot of these little private conversations! Now shut the fuck up and the next time you laugh better not be until six weeks from now!"

He then turned his attention to the 5 foot 9 inch, broad shouldered, muscular, blond haired guy standing next to me.

"OK, Laugher Number Two! What the fuck is your name?"

Laugher Number Two had been listening attentively and responded, "Sir! Airman Basic Harold Vinter! Sir!"

"OK, Vinter. I will be having my eye on you too. But apparently you learned something from your friend here. You stay close to him and teach him to listen!"

"Sir, Yes, Sir!"

SSgt. Jones then moved back to the front of the group and began to give us instructions on what to do once we entered the barracks.

We then filed into the barracks. The barracks had light gray walls, a very shiny maroon vinyl tile floor with a row of double-decked gray metal framed beds down each side of the open bay building. One in front and one behind each set of bunk beds were gray plywood footlockers. There was a two-foot walkway between the wall and the footlocker behind the beds. And a five-foot wide aisle down the middle of the barracks. The open chipped gray painted wooden footlockers were about 30 inches by 16 inches and about 15 inches high. There was a shallow 2 inch tray laid tilted across the top in each so you could look below the tray to quickly see that the footlocker was empty.

I put my small travel bag on a lower bunk and Harold put his bag on the bunk above mine. With a scowl on his face the first words he spoke to me were, "Thanks for getting me into trouble, Asshole!"

I quickly defended myself with, "I just laughed because I thought their cadence was funny. I didn't make you laugh; you did that all on your own, Asshole!"

I grinned, put my hand out to be shaken, and said, "I'm Ron Lafayette. Nice to meet you, Laugher Number Two."

The tough guy look immediately left his face to be replaced by a big smile as he shook my hand saying, "I'm Harold and I sure as hell hope that we will get a chance to laugh more than once in the next six weeks or I think I'll die."

At that introduction we saved Harold's life by laughing out loud together.

* * *

Minutes later, the T. I. yelled "lights out" and plunged the barracks into darkness. It seemed that I had just laid my head on my pillow when I was awakened by a loud crash. That was the sound of a metal trash can being thrown down the aisle of the barracks by our T. I., Staff Sergeant Jones. He then proceeded to yell at us, giving us instructions to "fall in" by getting into two lines in the aisle between the two rows of bunks, with each man standing in front of their bunk. Once we had accomplished this task, we were given the basics of what we had to do to make our bunks. After making our bunks, he then yelled for us to run outside and get into two lines facing the street. The sun had not yet risen as we lined up in the area before our barracks. We were given basic marching instructions. Several airmen were given reflective web harness and flashlights with long red tubes over the lenses. They were told that they would be our Road Guards and were given quick instructions by our other T. I., Sergeant Billings. Finally, after a few more minutes of marching instructions, we were marched to the mess hall to have breakfast.

The Road Guards would run to block the intersection each time we came to a cross street then quickly rejoined the flight as we continued marching to breakfast. As we lined up to get our meals we were told in no uncertain terms we were to only take what we would eat and with great threats of what the T. I. would do with any food remaining on our plates, we were told to eat everything we had taken. The remainder of the morning we were given basic training on how to march, and then we proceed to practice by going together as a unit to various places on the base to take more medical exams, fill out in-processing paperwork, and take a battery of tests.

After lunch we were marched to a large barber shop. There had to be at least 20 green vinyl barber chairs in a long row. We were told we would have to pay the barber $1 for our haircut. We were lined up to get our haircut, or should I say, have our heads shaved. The thing that really stuck in my mind was the large piles of multicolored hair around the barber chairs. As freshly bald recruits, we were marched off to get uniforms and other basic supplies, and then it was back to the barracks where we learn how to fold our new uniforms and put them away. Followed by some more basic military marching instructions, finally we marched off to supper.

I didn't have much trouble with marching since I had been in a marching band in high school. But Harold had a very difficult time trying to keep in step. I showed him a trick of doing a quick skip every time he saw he was out of step. He then managed to get back in step with the flight, at least for a little while, before he had to do another skip to get back into step once again. The Training Instructor heard me give Harold the tip and noted my face, but luckily didn't give me hell for speaking in ranks. When we got back to the barracks, it was more instructions on how to keep the barracks in military order.

The next morning before the sun rose we were told to fall out in our P. T., Physical Training, uniform which consisted of blue shorts, yellow T-shirts and combat boots. The sergeant then put us through a long, long, long, series of calisthenics. There was lots of verbal abuse heaped upon those that didn't do an exercise correctly, or were not able to perform the required number of repetitions of each exercise. The poor recruit that suffered the most abuse was the guy from the lower bunk next to mine, Sam Talbert. Sam was overweight and wore rather thick glasses. Before his head was shaved, he had dark curly black hair which emphasized his pasty white complexion. Just by looking at his white legs you could tell that he spent little or no time in the sun. When Sam would do an exercise wrong the T. I. would yell and proceed to make the whole flight redo it again. Sam did not win any friends that morning.

Following the exercises, we rushed in for quick showers and to clean up the barracks before breakfast. As we lined up in preparation to go to the

Mess Hall, SSgt. Jones asked if anyone had any military training before arriving at Lackland. I was the only one who raised my hand and explained that my high school had just introduced Air Force Junior ROTC during my senior year and I had just a little training. He then told me to march the flight to breakfast. He followed along behind me to see how I handled the task. Between my one year of AFJROTC training and four years of playing in my school's marching band I had little trouble marching the guys to the mess hall and back to the barracks.

Sgt. Billings took over and we were given more instructions in close order drill and how to act as proud members of the military. Sgt. Billings then marched us to get more medical screenings and take a whole lot of shots. We were lined up single file and marched through a double line of medical personnel who each had a kind of gun in their hand with a vial of liquid attached. You would stop at each set of medics and get a shot in each arm and move to the next set. The guy six people ahead of me in line dropped to the floor like a water balloon from the top of a skyscraper the second he got the first shot. A little confusion occurred as the medical personnel got him up and over to the side to check him out. But the delay caused the pairs of medics to have to speed things up by giving both shots simultaneously instead of one at a time. When I went through the second pair of medics they were a little off their rhythm and I got one shot a split second sooner than the other. As I jerked from the first shot the second shot caused a long cut instead of just an injection. The dirty look I gave the medic just rolled off of him like water off a duck's back. When we got back to the barracks Sgt. Billings gathered up the belongings of the guy who passed out getting his shot and we never heard about him again except in rumors. The rumor mill ran wild, things like he died or he turned into a zombie. But the main rumor was that he would get a medical discharge. We never did find out.

That night was the first free time that we had. As we shined our shoes, four of us started a bullshit session. There was myself, Harold, Sam Talbert, and Terrence "Terry" Garcia in the conversation. It started out when Harold asked, "How in the hell did we get ourselves into this nightmare? If it wouldn't be for the damn draft, I sure as hell wouldn't be here."

I began by saying that I had to be a little crazy because I wanted to enlist, and that I didn't need to worry at all about the draft. I had grown up the fourth child of a working class family and I had been working each summer and sometimes after school all through High School to build up some savings for college. When I started college I managed to get through my freshman year with fairly good grades but between school and work I had no personal life which was just starting to drag me down. I figured enlisting and getting the GI Bill's educational benefits would be the thing to do and allow me to continue college without having to work at the same time. So I went off to see the Air Force recruiter. However, the first time I tried to enlist, because of the physical, I was turned down. At the time I was 5'9" and weighed a whopping 111 pounds. I was a skinny nerd who wore glasses and didn't have much going for me physically except for one thing. I was skinny mainly because I loved to run. I would run ten or more miles every morning and along with the outrageous Louisiana heat I was continuously burning off every calorie I ate.

When I went in for the physical the first time I tried to enlist, they said I was way underweight and my draft status was reclassified to 4F. A draft status that basically said I was medically unfit for military service. At that time, due to the Vietnam War draft, most guys my age would have killed people to get that draft classification. But I waited until I thought that I had put on some weight and tried again, I was up to 112 and a half pounds. This time the recruiter told me about getting a Medical Exemption Waiver which allowed me to enlist and stay in the military if I got up to 120 pounds by the time basic training was over.

At this point Sam cut in and said he too joined for the GI Bill's education benefits and he was also in on Medical Exception Waiver, but in his case he had to get from 210 pounds to less than 180 pounds. We all started laughing when he volunteered to give me all the weight I wanted.

Sam went on to explain that he was from a poor family just south of San Jose, California. And that he too had to dropout of college because he could not afford to go, even though he had received a scholarship that covered books and tuition from Stanford University. He told us that he burned through all of his savings by the end of the first semester and couldn't afford to continue because his scholarship didn't cover room and board.

Terry Garcia then told us that he was from the same area as Sam and that he lived between San Francisco and San Jose. Terry was a little shorter than the three of us, but he was built like a brick wall. Terry had a rusty complexion and was a third generation Mexican-American from a family that had always been itinerant farm labor. He loved sports and played as the first string fullback on his high school football team and was on the first string team even when he was just a freshman. He went on to explain that he enlisted so he could get out of picking fruit for the rest of his life.

Harold had a different story. His dad was a foreman for a mining company so his family was fairly well of. He was from a small town in Colorado and his great love was riding and racing motorcycles. He had dropped out of college to get started as a professional motorcycle racer and even won a few cross country races. Then when his buddy got drafted and sent to Vietnam he figured it was far better to enlist in the Air Force and get a nice comfy job as opposed to getting drafted into the Army, headed straight to Vietnam. He told us about his brother who had just been

27

discharged from the Air Force and since he was in some sort of intelligence job he spent his full four-year enlistment in a nice air conditioned office in Maryland. At that point we all agreed that getting a nice intelligence job would be a lot better than slugging through the jungles of Vietnam.

The next morning after calisthenics, I was told to march the flight off to breakfast. I was on the side of the flight while the T. I. followed along in the back of the unit. Marching next to me was Tony Catalano. Tony was one of three guys in the flight that were from the same neighborhood of the Bronx. He was almost 6-foot-tall and had the "I don't take-no-shit-from-nobody" attitude of a big inner city brute. When I told him he was out of step, his response was a whispered, "You don't tell me nutten, ya skinny four eyed twerp."

I then said loud enough for everyone to hear, "You are out of step, Catalano. Listen to the cadence count. Your left foot is supposed to hit the street on odd numbers." He tried to get back into step as he gave me a look that could kill. I think trying to do the two things at once, think and walk, caused him to stumble. This got a laugh from some of the guys around him and a bellow from SSgt Jones of, "Quite in the ranks. Quit screwing up Catalano!" I made an enemy that morning.

That night after I had fallen asleep I was awaken when my blanket was pulled from my bunk and thrown over my head. Two people, one on each side of my bunk, held me down by pulling down on the blanket while a third punched me repeatedly on my face and upper body. As I started to struggle and rise, the blanket was quickly wrapped around my head and all three assailants fled back to their bunks in the dark. I didn't see anyone but I sure knew who the three guys were – Tony and two of his Bronx cronies.

The ruckus awoke Harold, Terry and Sam. They help untangle me from the blanket and went with me to the latrine to wash the blood off my face. Harold confirmed my suspicions when he said he saw Tony getting back into his bunk. Terry then wanted to know if we should go return the favor to Tony now. I put them off saying I would take care of it later.

The next morning as we lined up for calisthenics, SSgt Jones got a look at the cuts and bruises on my face and asked what happened. I said that I must have fallen out my bunk. He knew what must have taken place but just gave me a several second-long knowing look, but he accepted my answer and started our morning calisthenics.

That afternoon we were running the obstacle course or as our T. I. called it, the 'confidence' course. I had just gotten to the top of the wall of the rope climb obstacle when who should be coming up the rope right behind me but Tony. Just as Tony got to the top, his upward moving nose met my downward moving fist. The impact caused Tony to fall off the obstacle. As he got up he started yelling that I had sucker punched him and caused him to fall. SSgt Jones magically appeared and looked down at Tony lying on the ground with a bleeding nose and up at me grinning on the top of the obstacle. The only thing Jones said was, "It never happened."

Tony proceeded to continue to rant about me sucker punching him. SSgt Jones got directly in Tony's face and quietly said, "It never happened. Just like it never happened that Lafayette fell out of bed. And it better never happen again."

* * *

The next five weeks flew by with Terry, Sam, Harold, and I becoming the very best of friends. Though we were constantly bickering with each other, we never had any issues with Tony or his gang again.

With only two days left in basic training Sam and I went to get our final weigh-in physical. With not running as much as I did back home and the starchy mess hall food I got up to 121 pounds. Sam having started to exercise for the first time in his life lost weight and actually got down to 175 pounds. We were both quite happy that we had passed our Medical Waiver requirements. When we got back to the barracks we saw all the guys standing around the flight bulletin board. Terry came running out of the crowd and seeing us; he began to beat us on our backs all the while grinning like the Cheshire Cat. We were joined by Harold when Terry announced that all four of us were going to continue our training together at Keesler Air Force base in Mississippi at something called Intercept Operator Preparatory Course 3AQR29222.

Harold said, "What the hell is that?"

I responded, "Harold, you ass, who cares! We will all still be together so you and I can piss each other off some more." This caused us all to laugh as we head back into the barracks.

* * *

May 10, 2018
Agios Nikolaos, Crete, Greece

Just as Ron was at that point of the story the waiter brought the group our bill. Our lunch had been a marvelous souvlaki, small cubes of lamb that had been marinated in lemon juice and oregano seasonings, grilled and served on a skewer, French Fries fried in olive oil, and a Greek Salad. Of course he also brought us a complimentary glass of Raki and a dessert with the bill. Ron raised his glass and said, "To Lackland Air Force base, where we learned to be airman but not soldiers."

After the toast General Straight told us we were leaving the coast to go up into the mountains to the Lassithi Plateau, known as the valley of the windmills, with a stop at Dikteon Andron, the cave where Zeus was supposedly born.

CHAPTER 4
May 10, 2018
By the Harbor in Iraklion, Crete

The group decided to go into Iraklion for supper that night. The bus dropped them off at the Ιπποκαμπος. The Ippokampos which translates to Seahorse is a wonderful restaurant that the guys used to visit quite often when they were stationed there. It is located on the waterfront with a gorgeous view of the sea and the old Venetian fort. Seeing the harbor, the lighted seawall, and Koules Fortress brought back many memories of their frequent trips from the base to the city. They selected tables along the waterfront across the street from the main part of the restaurant. That way they could have a better view of the fortress which was built to protect the harbor in the early 16th century. With the General's assistance and with the guys slowly starting to remember their Greek again, they again ordered a meal of about 20 different small appetizer size servings of various foods to go along with a seafood main course.

As the group was eating their fresh seafood course Wild Bill remarked that living in Idaho didn't provide him the opportunity to get fresh shrimp like the ones he was eating now. Turning to Ron he asked, "What was the name of that restaurant in Biloxi right on the Gulf of Mexico that we used to go to where we had the fried shrimp dinners?"

Ron clarified by asking, "You mean the one just east of the lighthouse by the beach on Highway 90? If so, it was the White House, I'm not sure if it is there any more, one of the hurricanes may have destroyed it."

"Yea, that's the one. I remember the night we almost got thrown out of the place before we even sat down just because we were a little 'scruffy' after that fight with those local guys. Good thing Ron's grandfather came in with us and spoke with the waiter. He had known why we were rather disheveled, since he had just stopped the local cops from arresting us earlier that night."

Joan, who had been a little busy putting another serving of octopus on her plate asked, "When were you guys in Biloxi and what is this about a fight?"

Bill then told the story of when he met the group at Keesler Air Force Base. "I believe it was the very beginning of March 1968 that I first saw this motley crew."

* * *

March 1968 ~ Keesler AFB, Mississippi
As told by Wild Bill O'Rourke

31

We had all just been assigned to the 3408th training squadron to begin our Intercept Operator Preparatory Course, affectionately known as ditty-bop school. From what I remember almost all of the guys that were airmen when Detachment 11 was first organized were part of the 3408th attending ditty-bop school. Harold, Ron, Johnny and I were all in the same class.

In basic training we learned a little about military chicken-shit. We called all the little stupid things that you need to do, like fold your underwear in a certain precise manner "Chicken-shit." In basic training at least they had a reason to be chicken-shit. I remember asking my T. I. why we had to be so picky about how we folded our socks. He told me they were trying to instill patience and methodology in us. He said that if we were not methodical enough to fold our socks properly how could we be methodical enough to find a short circuit in the hundreds of miles of wire in a jet fighter. I bought his reasoning and never griped about it again, but at Keesler they turned chicken-shit to an exact science.

There they were so picky about our appearance that we even had to use extra heavy starch for our fatigue work uniforms. The starch would be so heavy that we had to run reformed coat hangers down the pants legs to "break" the starch. As you ran the hanger through the pants leg, you would leave about a half inch worth of the starch unbroken along the crease. That way you kept a very razor sharp crease in your pants. And they had us do this even in the hot humid southern Mississippi weather that seemed to melt a person, much less melt the starch in our pants, even though it was only March.

Every day we would be lined up for inspection by fellow airman that we called "the ropes." The ropes were students just like us but were given the responsibility to be sure that we made a good appearance. To distinguish the ropes from the rest of us poor slobs, they were given a dark green aiguillette to ware. An aiguillette is a braided cord worn on the shoulder of your uniform. Most of us didn't even know how to pronounce aiguillette much less know what one was, so we just called them ropes for the cord used in the braid.

The ropes use to do a super nitpick open ranks inspection before we were marched in parade off to school. They were far tougher than the meanest first sergeant I ever met. About the only thing they ever did to justify their existence was at the end of each inspection they used to ask, "Is there any gravity?" At which point we would all answer, "There is no gravity, Keesler sucks!"

The course itself was not that tough. It was really made up of three parts. The first part was basic radio technology, the second part was how to type, and the third part was learning how to copy or "take" Morse code. The radio technology portion of the class was spread through the entire course. They taught us the basic typing portion before they began to teach us Morse code. We were taught "to take Morse code" by typing the corresponding letter on an old manual gray typewriter as we heard the coded character. For several hours a day we sat wearing headphones plugged into a jack at our desk, listening to pre-recorded tapes of Morse code and pounding away on a typewriter.

Morse code is a technique of representing text information as a series of short and long tones. For example, the famous SOS signal is made of three series of tones, one for each character. The character S is represented by three short tones and the O by three long tones. The short tones are known as dots or 'dits' and long tones are called dashes or 'dahs'.

After a while, if you heard a *dit dah* the little finger on your left hand would automatically move to type the A. They taught us using random strings of characters and numbers so that we were never typing real English words. That way you almost instantly forget the last character received as soon as your finger smashed the typewriter key. As the sound stream of the Morse code characters was transmitted to you faster and faster you would begin to type the corresponding typewriter keys faster, never knowing what letter or number you were typing.

The Morse code portion of the class was self-paced and as you got proficient at one speed they would attach your desk headset port to a faster speed recording. One of the two guys that did the best was our friend at the end of the table, Johnny, and a person we first met at Keesler, Steve "Sonny" Borns. Johnny and Sonny would kind of bounce in their seat a little to the rhythm of the code and pound away on their typewriters. It even got to the point that they would hold a conversation with each other as they were taking the code and never miss a character. Scary!! Before the class was over those two were taking almost 40 words per minute. That equates to over three characters every second. Back then, to me at that speed, the dits and dahs of the code were one continuous blur where I couldn't even hear the individual dits.

Class was only eight hours a day so we got a lot more free time than we did in basic training and our weekends were wide open. That was when I got to know the guys that were in Ron's basic training flight better. Ron's maternal grandparents lived in Biloxi and he invited about ten of us over to his grandparent's house for a barbecue. Mr. Trochesset worked for the city of Biloxi and lived in a section of town called Back Bay. It was by a lake that was about three miles from the Gulf of Mexico. There was a baseball field right across the street and we made use of it most of that afternoon before we gathered under a pecan tree in their backyard to chow down on burgers, chicken, and homemade smoked sausage.

Steve Borns brought his wife, Cheryl and his guitar along. Steve was from Eastern Tennessee and when he started to play his guitar and sing is when he earned his nickname "Sonny." He was playing music from Sonny

and Cher and darn well too. He and Cheryl started singing together and
aside for a slight southern accent it was difficult to tell them from the real
Sonny and Cher. Even though Cheryl had short blond hair, from that
moment as far as our group was concerned they were no longer Steve and
Cheryl but Sonny and Cher.

The barbecue hadn't been going on that long and perhaps all the beer I
had been drinking, while we were playing baseball, started to get to me. So
it seems my Irish side took hold and I continued to consume a little more
beer than I ever had before. At one point I smashed a beer can against my
head and challenged Sonny to do the same. Cher said, "Hold your horses
there Wild Bill, Steve's head is a lot softer than yours." That sentence stuck
in the guys' heads and they started to call me Wild Bill. I have been stuck
with that nickname ever since. Perhaps I was lucky and they didn't start
calling me Hard Headed instead of Wild Bill. But I must admit that Mary
has called me hard headed a few times since we were married.

I think it was the next week when Sonny came back to the barracks on
Thursday night as mad as a wet cat. Because we were still in training we
could not live off base. So Sonny spent the weekends with Cher but had to
sleep on base in the barracks during the workweek. It seems as if there were
a couple of the local neighbors giving Cher a bad time. We didn't make
much money as airmen, so they were staying in a rather bad part of town
and sure didn't have the best neighbors in the world. That Friday at lunch
he told us about how his neighbors were intimidating Cher and frightening
her badly. So Terry, Ron, Harold, Sam, Johnny and I decided we would go
with Sonny back to his house and see if we could intimidate their neighbors
enough that they would leave Cher alone.

The seven of us got there a little after 5 PM but there was nobody
around. We broke out a couple of six packs of beer and sat on the porch of
the duplex Sonny and Cher were renting as we waited for the offending
neighbors to show up. About six, two of them arrived in an old rusted '53
Ford pickup. Cher was sitting on the porch with us and pointed out that it
was these two guys who were giving her the verbal abuse. As they were
getting out of their truck the seven of us walked around them and Sonny
said that he wanted to talk to them. He expressed his dissatisfaction with
their attitude and said that if they continued to bother Cher that they may
perhaps come to some bodily harm. They may have been redneck hicks but
they knew better than to start something with that many of us standing
around backing up Sonny's play. They didn't even go into their house but
instead got back into their pickup and drove away after very unconvincingly
saying they would not bother Cher anymore.

We went back to sit on the porch to finish our beers before going out
for supper. However, about a half-hour later four pickups with several guys
in the back of one pulled up in front of the house. The two neighbors with

an additional ten of their friends piled out and stood in the yard in front of us. Two of the new arrivals were impatiently thumping the palms of their left hands with baseball bats. Their twelve to our seven, and two with weapons, the odds were not looking good. But our fearless little group stood up and waited on the porch which was about two and a half foot above street level where the locals stood.

The locals started talking to each other, ignoring the fact that we were right in front of them, saying that perhaps they should send a few of the damn Yankee G. I.s to the hospital. Then perhaps they would stay out of our town where they are not wanted. When they started walking toward the porch Cher ran inside the house. I can't say that I blamed her, I wanted to run away myself but I would not desert my friends.

One of the locals shouted, "Let's kill the Yankee bastards!" That started them moving toward us, with the two guys carrying the bats leading the way. As they put their feet on the first step Terry threw a plastic cup half filled with beer right into the face of first guy carrying a bat. As one of his hands went to wipe away the beer that was burning his eyes, Terry snatched the bat right out of his other hand. With his hands around the thick end of the bat he lunged forward poking the handle of the bat right into the belly of the second guy that had been carrying a bat. Harold, whom had been standing next to Terry on the porch at the top of the stairs, took one step down and just as quickly as Terry did, disarmed the other guy that had a bat as he was doubled up desperately trying to get some air back into his lungs.

Things kind of froze in time for a minute, the locals realized that their two leaders with the baseball bats were no longer leading the way and that we were now in position of the two bats. Sonny said, "We don't want any trouble just leave my wife alone and you guys go home." Ron said in a whisper that only we could hear, "Hold the high ground, stay on the porch, and let them come to us." The standoff held until Sonny, trying to broker a peace, took the bats from Terry and Harold and tossed them to the back of the porch and returned to stand at the front of the porch by the side of the stairs. I wish he hadn't done that. As soon as they realized we no longer had the bats they decided to rush us.

Ron immediately proved his high ground strategy by kicking a local on the point of his chin while he tried to climb up onto the porch. The guy was knocked out cold and the momentum of him falling back knocked the guy behind him to the ground. Terry and Harold who were standing at the top of the stairs took the brunt of the attack. They managed to get in a few good swings at the original bat wielders. Just a few punches from Harold and Terry took their previously partially disabled opponents totally out of the fight. Good thing they took them out quickly otherwise the other locals swarming up the steps would have Terry and Harold outnumbered, but that didn't happen.

Though never having done any fighting together before, we worked like a team. Ron and Sonny, our two smallest guys, held our flanks by holding the high ground on the side of the stairs and using the two and a half feet of height to their advantage to keep the others off the porch, while Johnny, Sam and I rushed in to assist the hard pressed Terry and Harold. With the limited width of the stairs still blocked by the two fallen batters, the numerical superiority of the locals was neutralized. Having just finished basic training, the seven of us were in the best physical shape of our lives and the results of the fight quickly show this as two more of the locals were knocked out of the fight.

Ron did a 'kamikaze' with a flying leap off of the porch right into the chest of the largest of the two neighbors that had been bothering Cher. The impact knocked him off of his feet with Ron landing on the chest of the fallen local. Straddling him with his two knees holding the local's arms blocked against his own body, Ron proceeded to use both fists to quickly smash six blows into the redneck's face, breaking his nose in the process.

While Ron was engaged with one redneck, the other neighbor took advantage by kicking Ron a glancing blow to the side of his head, knocking him off of the redneck he was straddling. The kick left the other neighbor off balance allowing Ron enough time to regain his feet and get into a defensive boxing stance. Even with some blood from a cut opened by the kick running from his hairline to his neck, the grimace on Ron's face was enough to stop the larger neighbor from rushing in to take the 121 pound Ron on immediately, and the two stood in a frozen standoff as the fight proceeded around them.

Two locals had pushed Terry up against the door. But Sam grabbed one by the shoulders and swung him around like a rag doll back towards the stairs. His backwards momentum caused him to stumble back and fall over one of the previously bat wielding locals that was still clutching his stomach and lying at the top of the stairs. Falling over his friend, he lost balance and with his arms flapping like a bird, fell back off the porch with his head hitting the sidewalk. His head bounced once or twice and he lay there dazed and out of the fight.

That kind of took the fight out of the remainder of the locals and they retreated back to the lawn, panting and giving hard looks to our group. A few moments later two local police cars with lights flashing and sirens wailing pulled up behind the pickups, blocking the street. Two cops got out of each patrol car and advanced on the group with billy clubs in their hands.

One of the police officers was an overweight corporal with his belly hanging over his belt. He was the first to speak using a Mississippi accent so thick that you could cut it with a knife, he asked one of the locals what was going on. The local, using an expletive ever other word, began to tell the corporal about how these damn "blankity-blank" Yankee G. I.s had threatened their friends.

Cher had come out by then and jumped right in with a Tennessee accent that was just as thick as the corporal's and said, "First of all we ain't no damn Yankees!" Then pointing at Ron she said, "Heck, Ron's grandparents are from right here in Biloxi."

Ron was fast on the take up and said Charlie Trochesset was his grandfather. Perhaps they knew him. The corporal knew the name all right and told the youngest of the policeman to go get Mr. Trochesset.

At that time, the local who's nose Ron had broken, started yelling at the cops pointing at me and said, "That skinny ... (expletives deleted) ... knocked out Bryan and broke my darn nose!"

Perhaps that was the wrong thing to point out to the cop because he looked at the 121 pound Ron and at both of his over 175 pound victims and started laughing. He said, "He might just be Mr. Trochesset's grandson."

The neighbor with the broken nose said, "Oh she-it, I w'rk for Mr. Trochesset."

The cops started to take everyone's names and statements. A few minutes later the other police car returned with Ron's grandfather. Mr. Trochesset looked at the blood running down Ron's face and spoke to the corporal and asked what was going on. As the corporal was explaining the situation as he knew it, Mr. Trochesset was glaring into the faces of each local while only giving our group the briefest of glances.

Ron's grandfather turned to the broken nose neighbor that worked for him and asked, "Randy have you and these G.I.s settled your differences, and do you promise that nothing else will happen like this again?"

"Yep."

Turning to Sonny, remembering him from the barbeque he asked, "Are you and Mrs. Borns O.K. now?"

"Yes, Sir."

He then spoke privately to the corporal for a few seconds. The corporal said, "Y'all stay away from each other and we'll forget all about this."

Harold winked a now blacked eye at me and speaking for our group said, "It never happened."

While Mr. Trochesset was talking to Cher, the pickup trucks with the locals and the cop cars pulled away and Johnny asked Ron, "Who is your grandfather and why does he have so much pull around here?"

Ron responded quietly that he had been a city councilman for many years but was now the head of the city's maintenance department.

Sonny said, "Now that this mess is over why don't we go to the White House and get a nice shrimp dinner like we were originally planning. Will you join us Mr. Trochesset?"

"Sure let's go."

$$* * *$$

It was the next Monday that things really changed. That was the day we first met the General but at that time he was still a Major. Major Straight entered our classroom that morning after our first radio technology lecture of the day. He walked in and spoke quietly into the ear of our instructor, SSgt Murry. Our SSgt introduced the Major by rank and name only and quickly left the classroom. The major didn't say anything for a while. He just looked around the class staring into the eyes of each student. His eyebrows coming together as he squinted a little looking at the bandages, cuts, and bruises on our little group. He looked right at me, read the name tag on my uniform and asked me what happened. I assumed he was here about our fight and I didn't know what he knew or what the police may have told him so I told him the truth about the seven of us getting into an altercation with a dozen of the locals.

He pointed to the bruise on my face and asked, "Who won?"

I proudly said, "Sir, We did, Sir! We put six of them on the floor and the others gave up right before the cops got there, Sir!" That caused a few chuckles from many in the room who were not at the fight. Those of us who were in the fight sat up a little straighter as we saw the looks of respect coming from others in the class.

"And what did the police say?"

"Sir, it was mutually agreed to at the time that the altercation never happened, Sir."

The Major laughed and just said, "Very good." This caused another round of laughter from the class. He looked around as the good humor was spreading around the class; he then proceeded to tell us that he was not there because of the fight.

"I am here to look for some volunteers to start a new elite intelligence gathering unit that we are forming. If you are interested could you please stand up and I will take your names so we can schedule a one-on-one interview this afternoon."

I didn't even think about it and was the first to stand up. Harold who was looking for a cushy job in intelligence like his brother had also stood up. With two of the gang of seven already standing, the rest of our little gang stood also. Seeing us stand caused almost everyone in the class to stand as well. Apparently there were four guys who were smart and knew better than to volunteer for anything, and they were the only ones to remain seated. The major wrote down the names of the volunteers and for the rest of that day and the next we each got to have a private meeting with the major.

Since I was the first to volunteer, I got to have the first interview. Because the meetings were private I don't know what went on in the other guy's interviews but the way I remember mine went something like this:

As soon as I walked from our classroom next door into the classroom Major Straight was using for the interviews, I snapped to attention and said, "Sir, Airman William B. O'Rourke reporting as ordered, Sir."

Looking up from the personnel jacket he had been reading he said, "Relax and take a seat, O'Rourke. Let me tell you about the unit that is seeking volunteers. The unit and what it will be doing is highly classified, and as such what I can tell you will be very limited. It will be an elite intelligence gathering unit that will require you to undergo a lot of additional training. The unit will be headquartered in the Philippine Islands but will operate throughout Southeast Asia."

I should have gotten the hint right there since the hottest place for military intelligence in Southeast Asia was Vietnam, but I guess I was dwelling on the words "elite intelligence ... unit" and pictured myself as James Bond and I missed a big clue as to where the unit would actually be operating.

Major Straight continued, "The tasks of the unit will potentially be physically demanding and perhaps quite dangerous. The duration of the volunteer assignment will be 18 months. After the 18 months, if you no longer wish to continue to be assigned to the unit, I can guarantee that you will be assigned to what I consider the best European duty station in the Air Force, or at your discretion you can be assigned to any base of your choosing in the continental United States. I repeat. The tasks to be performed by the unit will potentially be physically demanding and quite dangerous. Are you still interested?"

I guess my mind still had the James Bond image in my head and I totally skipped over the word "dangerous" as I was considering. I did hear best European duty assignment but not the word dangerous. So I replied, "Sir, yes, Sir."

"Very good, O'Rourke. Tell me what you were doing before you entered the Air Force."

I went on to tell the major about my education, and how the majority of my free time was spent hunting and fishing in the Idaho panhandle. I also talked briefly about the construction work I had done when I graduated high school.

He then said not to worry about getting in any trouble but he wanted to know more about the fight we had been in. I was still a little swell headed about how well we'd done and all the "attaboys" we had gotten from the rest of the class upon hearing of how we had taken care of the locals. So I got into telling the major all about how we got into the fight, how Ron come up with the plan of holding the high ground, how Terry and Harold had quickly disarmed the lead attackers before the fight really got started, and perhaps even exaggerated a little about my personal part in the combat.

The major smiled and nodded while I was telling the story. When I finished he stood up, reached across the table extending his hand to be shaken and said, "Congratulations O'Rourke, you are officially the first airman assigned to the unit upon the condition that your security clearance is approved."

I popped up like a Jack-in-a-box and shook the major's hand. My mind was running a mile a minute about getting into an elite unit. I was so puffed up, it was a wonder that my head was able to fit through the door as I exited the room after he told me to send in Airman Vinter in 10 minutes.

I went back into our normal classroom just as the class was going on break. I couldn't wait to tell them that I was "IN" and how they should all try to get in too. I quickly checked my watch and told Harold that he was the next to be interviewed in six minutes.

* * *

May 10, 2018
Iraklion, Crete

At this point Wild Bill looked around the table at the reunion attendees and said, "I sure am sorry guys that my over enthusiasm and selective hearing helped to get us into so much trouble."

Harold looked over to Bill and said, "Your attitude back then did initially make me want to join up too, even before I heard what General Straight had to say. But I have ears too and I heard what he said, so as to you being the cause of my volunteering too – It never happened."

The General had been listening to the story and he shook his head morosely as he said, "I'm sorry too, guys, but I was very restricted in what I could tell you."

To which Harold responded, "Όχι μεγάλο πράγμα. And for the ladies who don't know any Greek that means no big thing."

Ron quickly changed the subject by saying, "You guys remember my Cretan friend, Niko Sfougaras? He was the DJ at the Disco Piper in the basement of the Astoria Hotel."

After a chorus of yeses, Ron continued, "He now DJs at a club just off of Lions Square. He is still playing the kind of music we listened to at the Piper, of course now that music is considered oldies. Are you fellow 'oldies' game to listen to some good music?"

CHAPTER 5
May 11, 2018
Knossos, Iraklion, Crete

After a late breakfast the group took a tour of Knossos, a Bronze Age archaeological site on the outskirts of Iraklion which is said to have been the heart of the Minoan civilization. The site of the palace, which was constructed somewhere around 1700 and 1400 BC, is a combination of traditional archaeological excavation and rebuilt sections. The restored portions of the palace, which made use of replicas from the ancient murals unearthed during the excavation, helped to bring the site to life. So many ancient excavations are nothing but vague outlines of stones on the ground where visitors without a PhD in Ancient Greek & Roman Studies see nothing but old rocks. But the restorations at Knossos allow today's visitors to almost picture the glory of the Bronze Age palace. When most of the world was living in huts and squatting behind bushes, the residents of Knossos had water that was distributed around the palace using gravity to flow through terracotta pipes with destinations of fountains and spigots. There was even sanitation drainage that went through a closed system leading to a sewer.

After the tour, the group stood in line to pick up a gyro for lunch. A gyro is a wrapped pita bread sandwich made using thinly sliced meat, which can be a combination of lamb, pork, or beef, that has been shaved off of a vertical rotisserie. When the guys were stationed on Crete, the gyros were the staple of their off base diet. It was available almost anywhere and always filling and inexpensive. While they were standing in line Harold started telling Joan and Kathy and the rest of the group how he and Ron use to bring tourist to Knossos. He explained how they give very unprofessional tours of the site, quite often mixing facts they had learned with totally made up tales, just to impress the tourist girls.

Ron said, "Harold had so much bull manure in his tourist stories that he must have been the fabled Minotaur, half man and half bull." Harold's response was to take a very slow motion swing at Ron, which he easily ducked, again in slow motion.

Ron teased asking, "Where did you learn to fight like that, an all-girls finishing school?"

Harold chuckled and responded, "I wouldn't call Eglin Air Force Base an all-girls school. Nor do I think Ducky would be a teacher at a lady's finishing school."

They sat at picnic tables shaded by a pergola, which was totally covered by a grapevine, to eat their gyros. Harold said, "We thought we were tough in Biloxi at Keesler, but we really learned how to be soldiers at Eglin Air Force Base in Florida."

With a worried look on his face Harold quickly looked at the General and asked, "Everything is declassified now. Right?"

As the General nodded, Harold said, "Good! Let me tell you all about it."

While they eat their gyros, Harold began to tell the story of their time at Eglin Air Force Base.

* * *

April 1968 ~ Eglin AFB, Florida
As told by Harold Vinter

The General managed to get 50 guys from Keesler to volunteer and even though they were in different classes and in different phases of their education, somehow they all seemed to magically complete their ditty-bop class on the same day. The very next morning the group was loaded onto a couple buses and was taken for a drive that lasted around three hours to a remote section of Eglin AFB in Florida.

As we departed the buses, we were met by Major Straight, standing with a group of other officers and NCOs. One of the NCOs told us to get into two lines by drawing imaginary lines in the parking lot with his finger. Major Straight then gave us his welcome speech.

"Welcome to Special Training Detachment 11 and Eglin Air Force Base. If you do well, you will be here for the next 5 weeks, receiving a crash course in some of the things you may or may not need as members of the new elite intelligence gathering unit we are forming. If you do not do well, or you want to quit, you will be returned to Keesler for another technical school. Which tech school you would attend has not yet been determined."

"Everything you see and do here is classified as Top Secret. You are not allowed to discuss - with anyone - anything that goes on during this training. If you do you will be prosecuted to the fullest extent of military justice. Understood?"

The major watched closely as everyone responded with a, "Sir, Yes, Sir!"

"I and the rest of the staff here only have a very little time to turn you gentlemen into the finest unit in the United States Air Force. I will now introduce you to the staff. First, my executive officer, Captain Joseph Cummings."

A short, 5' 6 and a half broad chested officer wearing Air Force camouflage leaf pattern fatigues and a boonie hat stepped forward and quickly stepped back into line with the other officers and NCOs.

Major Straight continued his introduction of Captain Cummings by telling us that the captain was a recent transfer to the Air Force and that the captain had come to the Air Force after having served a year tour of duty in Vietnam as a Green Beret.

Next in line was Second Lieutenant Nicholas Washington. Lt. Washington was a large black man that seemed to dwarf the shorter Captain Cummings. He was wearing the same short sleeve tan colored 1505 uniforms we were all wearing. The major didn't tell us anything more about Lt. Washington but went directly to Master Sergeant Raymond Briede who was also wearing 1505s and had the diamond of a First Sergeant in his rank insignia. The major told us that if we had any personal issues we were to bring them to the attention of First Sergeant Briede.

Next introduced was Technical Sergeant David Brown. TSgt Brown was a slightly taller version of Captain Cummings. He too was in camo fatigues and was also an ex-Green Beret but with two tours of duty in Vietnam. Then he introduced Staff Sergeant Robert Ellingson. SSgt Ellingson was an ex-Air Police NCO who had been stationed at Tan Son Nhut Air Base in Vietnam. SSgt Ellingson who was a little heavier than the others was also in camo fatigues but he was the only one of the group that had a smile on his face as he stepped forward when acknowledging his introduction.

Major Straight turned us over to TSgt Brown. TSgt Brown bellowed in a parade ground voice, one that was capable of scaring children within a 50 mile radius of the base, that when we were dismissed, the first rank was to go to the barracks on the left and the second rank the barracks on the right. He told us to get into the barracks, grab a bunk to dump our stuff on, and get the heck back out there in 15 minutes dressed in PT gear.

What a welcome! Fifteen minutes and one second later we were off on a welcoming run that had us all wondering what in the heck had we gotten ourselves into.

After the first mile we were all, and I do mean all including the officers and NCOs, perspiring and breathing heard. SSgt Brown then started singing, if you can call yelling offkey at 30,000 decibels singing, an extremely modified form of the lyrics to John Philip Sousa's "Stars and Stripes Forever" march. It was similar to the version that was sung at the end of the '60s Mitch Miller TV show.

Be kind to your web-footed friends,
For that duck may be somebody's mother
She lives in a hole in a swamp
Where the weather is always damp
You may think that this is the end:
Well it is,
... but to prove that we're all liars
We're going to sing it again,

43

But only this time we will sing a little louder.

He sang it the first time alone then he shouted for us to sing along and to jog in time with the music. We sang those silly words over and over and over. By the time we were nearing the end of the third mile we all hated those lyrics and TSgt Brown. Several of the people were really dragging now, but it was surprising that the lyrics of that damn song kept the guys going. But into mile four we started losing men who just couldn't run that far. The rest of us just kept singing and cursing those same lyrics over and over until at the end of mile five when we arrived back at the barracks.

When we got back TSgt Brown dismissed those of us who had finished the run for the day, then hopped into a deuce and a half truck to drive back and pick up the dropouts. When the truck returned to the barracks area, the dropouts got out of the back of the big 2.5 ton truck and were formed into ranks by TSgt Brown. As soon as they were in ranks he made a pantomime of shooting them with an imaginary machine gun, he yelled loud enough for those of us already in the barracks to hear, "Rat-a-tat-tat-tat-tat! I'm the Cong! Every one of you sorry ass fools is dead! Today is Wednesday. We are going to go on this little run again tomorrow and the morning after that. The difference will be that this Friday I will be caring a real gun and I will actually shoot anyone who falls out of our little warm up run!"

Several of us were in the latrine showering off the grime from our welcoming run when a guy I hadn't met before started whistling "Stars and Stripes Forever." There were a few groans but I just threw my wet face cloth at the whistler. The dark ruddy skinned and dark black hair whistler said, "Ah! Come on, lighten up. I liked Ducky's little song."

Laughing at the nickname Ducky for TSgt Brown, I picked up my face cloth, stuck my hand out, and introduced myself, "Hi, I'm Harold Vinter. And to be honest with you, I think getting mad at the song, and Ducky too, helped me to keep going."

Whistler watched my face closely as I stared at his hooked nose and coloring; he beat me to the punch by saying, "Hi, I'm Michael Begay. And before you ask, yes, I am a full blooded Navajo."

"I'm cool with that, Chief." And I stuck my hand out even further.

This time Michael shook my hand and responded, "I'm not a chief, I'm a warrior."

"You and Lafayette over there," nodding my way, "were the only two not dragging ass after Ducky's little run. That makes you the 'chief warrior' in my book."

"OK, I can live with that, but if you ever call me Tonto, I'm going to scalp your ass one night while you are sleeping."

I had kept my hair shaved just like it was in basic training so I ran my hand over my almost bald head and said, "Mighty slim pickings there, Chief."

That caused the whole bunch of us to start laughing. At that point Chief instantly changed our Biloxi group of seven to a group of eight.

* * *

The next morning Ducky took us for another five mile run. Again at the end he mimicked shooting those that had fallen out during the run adding that tomorrow he will really shoot anyone who falls out. The look on Sam Talbert's face was none too happy since he had been the first to fall out both days. Then to add insult to injury, Ducky added a half hour of calisthenics before we were dismissed to clean up for class.

The first day of class was Major Straight teaching us how to use several types of radios. The first one he taught us to use was the AN/PRC-25. This radio was about the size of a case of beer, and weighed around 20 pounds. He explained that this radio was an FM line of sight broadcast with an operating distance of about three to seven miles with the standard antenna. He said that we would not be using these but he wanted us familiar with their use as he phrased it, "just in case."

Next he covered in detail the AN/URC-64 radio. It was a survival radio used by Air Force pilots in case of emergencies. It was approximately 10 inches by 5 inches by 4.5 inches and weighed only 7.5 pounds. Its range was limited not because of its size, but because of the fact that many Air Force planes would monitor its frequencies, it would be used as our backup emergency radio.

He then introduced a custom made version of the PRC-64 that had been modified by Air Force technicians. The PRC-64 was different from the URC-64 in that it was designed as a spy radio set and not a rescue radio. The custom version had a bug type Morse code keyer for faster hand transmissions. It also came with a burst encoder. The burst encoder allowed rapid transmission of a recorded message. The burst transmission was necessary to keep on-air time to a minimum reducing the possibility of enemy interception and direction finding. The main modification performed by the Air Force technicians was a greatly increased transmission range for Morse operations. This would allow the users to operate much further from friendly units. The radio had voice as well as Morse capability so it could be used for communicating with recovery, forward air control, or attack aircraft. The radio was approximately the same size and weight as the URC-64, but due to the modifications it had a far greater transmission power. The radio even came with a couple of metal Slinkies, the coiled wire kids toy, that could be connected to the antenna jack to provide even longer range communications. The compact shape of the Slinky allowed for ease of transport and it could easily be tossed up into the foliage of a tree for higher antenna placement.

The major then passed out the "bug" Morse code keyers with a small custom buzzer attached so we could practice sending code. We all knew how to take Morse code on a typewriter but now we had to learn to take it by hand, remember what we had received, and sent messages in it as well. A bug Morse key allows the user to swing a paddle sideways as opposed to up and down like the original telegraph keys worked. Pressed to the left the key makes a dash, pressed to the right a short pulse or a dot. A right handed person used the bug by pushing to the right with their thumb for a dit. Most found it easier to use the middle finger for pushing to the left to send the dah. I would assume it has to do with the better leverage for swinging your wrist back in forth when using the bug. The class generated quite a bit of noise for the rest of the morning as we practiced sending and receiving Morse code messages with each other. But it was not close to as much noise as we made that afternoon.

After lunch two large deuce and a half trucks pulled up to the training area. Everyone pitched in to get them unloaded. The trucks were full of weapons, ammunition, equipment and clothing. The majority of the weapons were CAR-15 carbines and Mk22 handguns. The Colt CAR-15 Commando assault carbine is a smaller version of the famous M16s used by the Army. This version had the full automatic feature unlike the ones that were only semi-automatic known as AR-15s. The weapon had several aliases, the Air Force ordered it as a GUA-5/A and the Army called it a XM177 during development. The pistols were Smith & Wesson Model 39, 9mm handguns, which had been modified to allow for the attachment of a noise suppressor. But they were officially classified as the Mk22. There were also a number of M79 Grenade Launchers and a case of Israeli made Uzi Submachine guns with the 10-inch barrels chambered for 9mm rounds, the same round used by the Mk22s.

We were all issued a couple sets of camouflage fatigues, boonie hats with mosquito netting, jungle boots, a large variety of web gear, and two weapons, the CAR-15s and the Mk22s. It became very obvious at this point that we were really going to go to war and not to sit in nice air-conditioned offices in Maryland. That afternoon we were all taken to a shooting range very close to the training area and taught how to use our weapons. We were also taught to use the Grenade Launchers and the Uzis.

The conversations in the barracks that night were interesting to say the least. Seven guys even went to see the first sergeant that evening to see what they had to do to "un-volunteer". The Biloxi seven plus our new addition, Chief, all decided to stick around a little longer.

The next morning, Friday, we fell out of the barracks and lined up for our Ducky run. However Ducky wasn't there when we lined up. A few minutes later we nearly jumped out of our skins as Ducky appeared firing off a full twenty round clip from his CAR-15. He then went to great emphasis to show us that he had loaded another clip. He bellowed, "This second clip is for those who fall out in today's little run!"

This time he just whistled "Stars and Stripes Forever" as we jogged the first two and a half miles. Then he started us singing his version of the lyrics. At approximately four miles Sam started to get into trouble. He was keeping up but you could tell he was getting pushed close to his limit. Ron and Chief got on either side of Sam and continually urged him on. About a half mile later he stumbled and fell, Ron and Chief picked him up and with one on each side they carried him along with them. Not more than twenty meters later another guy fell. A few of his friends followed Ron and Chief's example and helped their friend along too. Back at the barracks area when we finished the run, it was difficult to see if Ducky was pleased or disappointed that he didn't get to shoot anyone. However, Major Straight did give Ron and Chief a big smile as he went to assume his position for the calisthenics. After calisthenics Ducky told us that for tomorrow's run we should fallout in our new camouflage fatigues and our CAR-15s instead of just PT shorts and T-shirts.

The rest of the morning was again practicing our Morse code skills and using our bug telegraph keys, in conjunction with the PRC-64's burst encoders. The afternoon was split between lectures on the proper procedures for calling in air and artillery support followed by more time on the firing range.

The next two weeks were pretty much the same – the morning runs with Ducky slowly adding more and more gear for us to carry and increasing the distance until we were running ten miles every morning with full backpack, weapons, and ammunition. The runs were always followed by some form of communications training and lectures. We learned about using one-time cipher pads to encrypt and decrypt our communications. They even had us practice using the equipment, both the radios and our weapons, loading and cleaning our guns while blindfolded. The afternoons were always weapons training and practical experience in calling in air and artillery support. Our training was incorporated into the training of some of the fighter units stationed at Eglin AFB. We practiced calling in air support strikes and they practice by actually flying the close air support strikes as we called them in.

Doing these live exercises with the fighter units was very good practical practice for all concerned. Early during the training there was one incident where two guys from our unit were injured when the dummy napalm canister the fighter dropped fell way too short and it slid right into the trench we use to practice our radio calls. The results were one man with an ugly bruise on his leg, and one guy with a dislocated shoulder and a cracked rib. But there were some positive results of the incident; we were all made well aware that if it had been an actual napalm bomb instead of a practice canister, the results would not have been bruises and cracked bones but dead humans. That made us a lot more diligent and careful in all of our studies. The other positive result was the next weekend the pilots from the unit that caused the accident showed up at our training area with a couple kegs of beer and a whole bunch of T-bone steaks for supper.

The Monday after the beer and steaks weekend we began spending our time in field training. We learned how to move and fight as small units. We worked in units of ten or four, most of the time with three airmen and one officer or NCO in each unit. We always worked carrying a full load of gear. The extra elements of the loads were distributed among the team's equipment. The officer or NCO team leader carried the PRC-64 for quick access, another person carried the URC-64 radio as backup, the third carried the M79 Grenade Launcher and ammunition, and the fourth carried an additional M18 Claymore mine.

We usually learned a lot more when we were training with Ducky or Captain Cummings. But to allow for cross training and experience sharing, the team compositions were always changing. One of the important things we learned was that our job was not to engage in combat, our job was to pass through territory and never be seen or heard. Because of this we started to do most of our training at night. To aid us in nighttime operations one set of AN/PVS-5, dual-tube night-vision goggles was available for each team.

We also started to do a lot of training using helicopter incursion and extraction. There was one HH-3E stationed at Eglin for training. Most days it worked with our team, though it also worked with the fighter pilots stationed at the base for air rescue training. The HH-3E is a modified CH-3E helicopter, which was commonly called the Jolly Green Giant. The HH-3Es were updated for use in combat rescue missions with armor, defensive armament, self-sealing fuel tanks, a rescue hoist and in-flight refueling capability.

Because of our abbreviated mode of study and selective topic specialized training, we were more extensively trained for the job we were to do than many army or marine recruits ever were before they were first shipped off to Vietnam. We even developed a few tricks that were not used by any other groups. We started to communicate with each other when we were in the field by waggling our hands like we were using a bug telegraph key. We got to be very good at communicating visually using this technique. We also communicated in total darkness by using our fingers and touching another team member's arm and sending code using our bug technique. On one of our exercises Ducky pointed out the fact that when signaling our right hand got too far away from our weapon's trigger so most of us became ambidextrous with our hand signals.

On the last day of our fifth week we met in the classroom and were told by Major Straight how proud he was and how well we had done during our initial training but we still had a few more classes to complete. He told us that the next class was a three week abbreviated course at the Green Beret training area in North Carolina. After the Green Beret special class we would return to Eglin to pack up all of our equipment. Once our equipment was ready for shipping we were to be given a two week leave. Hearing that caused a lot of cheering. After leave we would reform the unit at Clark AFB in the Philippine Islands for additional training. As Major Straight finished his presentation, he turned us over to TSgt Brown. TSgt Brown also complimented us and shocked us all by saying, "Since I now considered you to be semi-trained warriors, you no longer need to address me by saying 'Sir, Technical Sergeant Brown, Sir'. You are welcome to call me: David, Sergeant, or you may even call me Ducky to my face." This cause a lot of laughter and an even bigger round of cheering than when Major Straight had said we would be getting two weeks leave.

* * *

At Fort Bragg, a U.S. Army training camp in North Carolina, we were met by a Green Beret Major, Wayne Phillips, and a Sergeant First Class, James Smith. The Major wore a Class A, dress uniform and the Sergeant First Class was in olive drab fatigues. Both were decked out in their Green Berets with the pants legs tucked into their highly shined combat boots. Major Phillips stood tall and straight but his face looked like he had just eaten five lemons. The way he looked at us, you could almost feel the contempt he had for us radiating from him like heat from the sun. Sergeant First Class James Smith looked like he was stamped from the same die as Ducky. He was also a short fireplug of a man with a booming voice. The only difference you could see in the two was that SFC Smith was black.

We had disembarked from the buses with everyone dressed in camouflage fatigues except Major Straight, who was wearing his tan 1505s. Everyone else was wearing boonie hats, scuffed jungle boots and camo fatigues which definitely did not have any razor sharp creases. The rest of our officers and NCOs were lined up interspersed with us with no distinction of rank evident on anyone.

Major Phillips was definitely unimpressed by what he saw standing in front of him. He gave a short 3-minute welcome to Fort Bragg speech and turned us over to SFC Smith. SFC Smith just looked at us while Majors Phillips and Straight jumped into a jeep and drove away. Once the majors were out of sight he began his own welcome speech but at a volume that could be heard by deaf people a mile away.

"What a sorry looking lot of Zoomies this is. I have no idea why in the hell they are wasting my time by having me work with you. If the upper brass wouldn't have forced this down our throats you sure as hell wouldn't be here. You have no right even being alive, much less coming to a school that only the very best of the U.S. Army ever attend."

He moved forward and stood toe to toe with Terry and asked him, "Have you ever attended Advanced Individual Training or Basic Combat Training courses? What kind of combat training do you have?"

Terry answered the questions semi-truthfully since we were told that our training at Eglin was classified and was to only appear on our service records as a radio technical school. He responded with a straight face, "Sir, No, Sir. I have only attended Air Force Basic training and two radio technical schools. Sir!"

Smith responded to that answer by rolling his eyes so far back into his head that it appeared as if he had no pupils. He then bellowed back at Terry, "Don't call me 'Sir'! I am not an officer, I work for a living!"

He walked back a few steps so he could see the entire unit, he was mumbling about his whole training plan going out the window. He got positioned and said, "OK, Zoomies. Let's see what you ladies are made of. Since you are dressed so nice in your Sunday go to meeting clothes, we will only take a short little run."

He gave orders for us to get into four lines and proceeded to double time us away from the barracks area. Was he ever surprised. I think he assumed we would start falling out after a mile or two. We were use to running ten miles wearing all of our gear and carrying our carbines so running without all the extra weight was a lot easier. His original plan was for a three mile run but he just kept going waiting to see when somebody was going to quit. After we passed the barracks area for the eighth time, each circuit being about a mile, SFC Smith was starting to suspect that something was amiss. In the ninth circuit someone started singing Ducky's Stars and Stripes ditty. When we all finished the tenth circuit he stopped us in from of the barracks and started walking up and down the ranks looking at each person closely. He came to a screeching halt as he looked into Ducky's face.

"I know you and your song."

Ducky responded using SFC Smith's nickname, "No you don't, Smitty. I am just a dumb ass Zoomie like the rest of these men. Continue your inspection."

SFC Smith knew better than to push it further and followed Ducky's suggestion to continue his inspection. He did a double take when he walked past Captain Cummings, backed up a step and said, "Hello, Lieutenant Cummings, Sir."

"I'm an Air Force Captain now, but don't tell anybody and treat me like one of these Zoomies."

"Yes, sir!"

Recognizing two of the group as ex-Green Berets and seeing how we had handled a ten mile run, SFC Smith knew beyond a shadow of doubt that we were not normal Air Force Zoomies right out of basic training. He dismissed us and told us to find racks in the barracks. And that we were to form up at oh-five-hundred tomorrow for a little light exercise.

The next morning at a few minutes before 5 A.M. we were all outside and waiting, in our PT shorts and T-shirts lined up with Major Straight when SFC Smith and Major Phillips arrived in a jeep. Major Phillips jumped out of the jeep and said, "Nice to see you ready and waiting. Let's go for a little five mile run."

You could tell by the way he said it he expected to run most of us into the ground. I guess SFC Smith had not told the major anything about yesterday's welcoming run. You had to give it to SFC Smith though; he just smiled and got in line with us in drag position. Major Phillips led the group at a pretty good pace. He didn't keep us double timing like SFC Smith did, but led us in a freestyle run. Everyone kept pace with the Major, and the first two miles were completed in around eleven minutes. He looked over his shoulder periodically to see if he had lost anybody yet. SFC Smith was running drag and he just waved his right arm, in a fist, over his head once every time the major looked back. It must have been a signal they were using to report on dropouts. The major started slowing down a little when we completed the fourth circuit. At this point Ron and Chief picked up speed and passed the major like he was standing still instead of running. This caused the major to pick up his pace but by the time he did so about a third of the guys were sprinting all out for the last mile and left the major eating their dust. As the guys finished the fifth mile they quickly got lined up and calmly awaited the arrival of the major and the rest of the unit. Major Phillips looked none too pleased with the results of the short run.

While the rest of us were led in calisthenics by SFC Smith, Major Phillips and Major Straight went into the barracks room, that was set aside as an office for Major Straight, to talk. We finished the exercises and SFC Smith dismissed us to shower and change into fatigues for breakfast and to begin our classes. As we were entering the barracks we heard Major Phillips loudly talking to Major Straight. He was really upset about our unit being in his training camp taking up precious resources that were better off teaching real soldiers rather than a bunch of Air Force Boy Scouts. Major Straight then tried to calm him down by saying that our unit was there only for a four week customized jungle survival course and the escape and evasion portions of the training and would not be taking the full curriculum. He also emphasized that the extra five C130 aircraft that were transferred to the Green Beret school for jump training more than offset what resources we would use while here.

The majors left the office shortly after that but the fact that Major Phillips had called us Boy Scouts ran through the ranks like wildfire. We didn't see Major Phillips for the next few weeks of training.

We attended classes and had practical exercises on jungle survival along with escape and evasion techniques. We were also given lectures on the military units and capabilities of both the North and South Vietnamese military. There was extensive training on things we could encounter while in Vietnam including the flora and fauna. We were even taught about various types of booby traps that we could potentially encounter. There were lots of exercises conducted at night but we didn't use any of the night-vision equipment we had taken with us for the nighttime training.

Several times during one class or another, the instructors would give us strange looks as it appeared that many members of our unit had strange hand twitches. They never caught on to the fact that we were talking to each other using our Morse code bug hand movement code. That, together with the fact that the entire time there we wore our uniforms without any insignia caused quite a few people to wonder who we were. As we would march from one class to another or to meals we would often sing a cadence that we knew would cause concern from Major Phillips if he heard it.

Everywhere we go
People want to know
Who we are,
So we tell them.
We are the Boy Scouts,
Mighty, Mighty Boy Scouts.
Sound off one, two
Sound off three, four
Sound off one, two
(pause) three, four.

As we neared the end of the training we were told that the course's final exercise was to be dropped off in a remote section of the camp in groups of four and the groups had to make it back to the base area, a lighted parking lot, by dawn the next day. The hard part was that there would be two Green Beret training units acting as the aggressors, their job would be to 'kill' or capture us. It was our mission to evade capture or being killed by the aggressors who would be firing blanks. There would also be several members of the training cadre participating as judges for the exercise. The night before the exercise the Major gave us a mini-briefing to be sure we did our very best, to use everything we had learned, and to use our AN/PVS-5, dual-tube night-vision goggles for the exercise.

The morning the final exercise was to start, in order to make it more real, they had us fall out in full gear, with weapons loaded with blank ammunition. Wearing face paint and our camouflage uniforms, we piled into the back of trucks and were driven along a dirt road in a remote section of their training area. We were dropped off in groups of four every few miles. The exercise rules gave us fifteen minutes from drop off time to get away from the road and then the exercise would officially start.

My group of four consisted of myself, Chief, Major Straight and Terry. As soon as we got out of the truck, Major Straight told the guys, "We have fifteen minutes grace time before the exercise officially starts. Let's not worry about sound conservation yet. Come on, we'll run like hell for the first seven minutes in order to cover as much ground as possible."

So we took off at a dead run crashing through the woods of the training area. The Major hand signed for a halt, implemented sound conservation protocol and moved off at an oblique angle from our original path.

We automatically followed the procedure we used when we trained at Eglin and augmented it with a few things we learned in the classes here at Fort Bragg. Chief walked point, followed by Terry, then the major, with me walking drag. The job of point man was to watch the trail for booby traps and the enemy. The point man was to concentrate in watching to the front, 45 degrees to his left and 90 degrees to his right. The second man was normally the person who carried the grenade launcher; his job was to back up the point man, provide fire support and to concentrate on watching the front, 90 degrees to his left and 45 degrees to his right. The third man was the team leader with the radio; his job was to backup the person walking drag and to watch front, 90 degrees left and 90 degrees right. The last person walking drag was to watch our 6 o'clock, meaning our rear and to do what he could to erase any signs made on the trail by their passage.

Two minutes later Chief signaled for a halt so we could listen to hear if there was as any pursuit. The guys immediately went to ground in a cross position, each person facing a different direction but close enough so they could tap the foot of the person next to them with their foot should they see or hear anything. We remained quiet in our cross position for the next fifteen minutes just making sure we weren't being followed.

We then changed direction and proceeded to slowly eat up ground towards our destination. Every few minutes Chief would raise his hand and all would freeze where they were to "Stop, Look and Listen." Having Chief working as point was great. He had grown up in the country hunting and tracking game. He put his field craft to use when we were training at Eglin and did what he could to pass his tracking skills to others. About two hours into our movement Chief raised his hand for us to stop. He pointed to the ground in front of him and signed to us that there were several sets of very fresh boot tracks. We immediately went to ground in our cross position to see if he could hear where the Green Beret aggressors were. We waited about 15 minutes and were just about to get up and proceed when our patience paid off and we heard a chuckle and loud whispers from directly ahead of us over a slight rise. Perhaps they had set up an ambush site and were just waiting for us to go over the rise. We stayed where we were for a while longer to see if they were in a static ambush position or if they were just moving through the area. Sure enough we heard more whispers from the same direction, so it was an ambush waiting just over the low rise.

Chief signed for us to quietly get up and move back about 100 meters. We did so, and then moved at a 90-degree angle to our original line of march long enough for us to be well to the side of the ambush site. We then shifted back to the direction of our destination. We cautiously advanced until we came to a ridge where the ambush was set up. Slowly belly crawling to the top of the rise we looked toward the place we thought the ambush to be. If we had continued on our original path we would have topped the ridge and been in a fairly open area. On the other side of the open area we could barely see the Green Berets as they waited in ambush. We were far enough away from the open area to bypass the ambush to the right.

Twice more during the daylight hours we came close to either ambushes or roving patrols. We held up at about 3 PM in an area with thick underbrush which would hide us well. We stopped there so we would not walk with the bright evening sun shining directly in our eyes. We would hide here for a while, eat some C-rations and take short naps, so we would be rested and continue our progress under cover of night. One person stayed awake on guard while the others napped.

When darkness fell we proceeded as we had before, making just as much progress in the dark as we had during the day. Unlike during our earlier training here, we used our night-vision equipment. This allowed us to make far better progress than would have been the case without them. Because using the night-vision equipment causes the user to potentially get headaches and some disorientation, every other time we halted for a Stop, Look and Listen we would swap who walked point using the goggles.

About ten at night we stopped when we thought we heard movement close to us. Whoever was making the noise froze just as we did. No one moved or made a sound. I was on point wearing the goggles with Chief walking second. Chief tapped me on the arm and coded that he though he may have heard something 120 degrees to the right of our line of march. I scanned the area with the goggles and just barely saw someone wearing goggles looking back at me. I raised my hand above my head and gave an exaggeratedly large hand signed the code for 'WHO' the other goggle wearer signed back 'RON.' After a quick tap conversation with the major, I signed for the other group to come join us.

We were now a group of eight. In the other group was Ducky, Ron, Sam and another airman nicknamed Ringo because he was a big fan of the Beatles' drummer and always 'air' drumming a trap set that only he could see. The group made good time and we were within 200 meters of our final destination and could see the lights from our parking lot destination. We knew that they would concentrate their defending force close to the destination to keep us from reaching our goal. We proceed by crawling forward in two lines with our two goggle wearing points leading. Very soon we spotted the ambush defensive perimeter they had set 25 meters outside the parking lot. Major Straight was point and tap touched coded us to shift to the right to see if we could find a hole in their defensive line. Each person passed down the tap touch code so we all knew the plan. With the aid of the night-vision goggles we kept shifting until we found a hole in their line big enough for us to slip past them. All eight of us got past their line and quietly gathered in the dark just out of the lighted parking area which was our destination.

Major Straight scanned the area and determined we were the first to arrive. He was a little mad that the aggressors had put so many men in such a tight defensive position around our goal. Then he decided that perhaps we should make it easier for the groups behind us. The plan was for us all to put the silencers on our Mk22s and 'attack' the defenders from the rear.

Before we began the major noticed one of the instructor judges leaning against a light post in the lighted area which was our goal. The major crawled into the light, slowly stood up, took off his boonie hat and walked up to the judge like he was just another judge greeting a friend. He quietly told the judge what we were going to do. He then wrote on a piece of paper. "You are dead. You were just stabbed or shot by a silenced handgun. Don't say anything or make any noise. Don't move." He gave the note to the judge to show to our future victims.

All of the aggressors were staring into the dark away from the lighted area because they didn't want to damage their night vision. This made it very easy for us to advance on the rear of our assigned targets. Four of the aggressors, one each, were assigned to Chief, Ducky, Terry and me. Ron, Sam and Ringo took cover in a position just outside the parking lot where they would be able to cover our retreat should we be detected. If we were detected or if our little plan fell apart, the fire support supplied by the three on the edge of the lighted goal area would be used to cover us long enough for us all to enter the area and successfully complete the exercise. Major

Straight had already completely entered the lighted goal area to talk to the judge so theoretically he was already out of the exercise.

Our four 'killers' quietly advanced on their victims. When we were within four feet of our targets we mimicked shooting them with our handguns. We back up a little and re-positioned to get the next four defenders along the line. After we backed away from our victims, the judge walked up to the 'dead' defenders put his finger to his lips in the time honored keep quiet signal and showed them the note. They all played fair, remained quiet and stayed where they were. We did this trick three more times taking out all of the defenders on the east side of the parking lot. Chief even managed to 'kill' a captain that approached down the line checking on his defenders. He was the only one to make any noise by very quietly saying something very unkind and unseemly about Chief, his mother, and many barn animals.

We then moved to a position where we could open fire on the rear of the defenders to the right and left of the opening we had made on the east side. Major Straight just stood in the bright light of the goal area and hand signed that the east side was wide open for entry and there were defenders on all other sides. In the next two hours five other teams approached the goal from the east. They were intercepted by Ducky before they entered the lighted area and joined us in positions behind the defenders. There were now twenty-seven of us behind the defenders. Ducky whistled loudly and we all opened fire with our blank filled CAR-15s into the backs of the defenders who were facing the dark. The judge declared all the defenders were dead and out of the exercise.

Before the night was over, three more groups entered the undefended goal area for a total of 40 out of 52 successfully completing the mission. Only three groups had fallen into ambushes during the course of the exercise. The judge, Captain Moran, told Major Straight that this was the best finish of any other class taking the evasion exercise. We were also the first class that ever 'attacked, wiping out' the base guards allowing other groups to get easily past the defenses.

The next day was the feedback session on the exercise. Both sides learned a lot from each other. Major Phillips was in rare form as he thoroughly chastised the captain of the base defending platoon. He gave him holy hell for having his entire platoon wiped out by a bunch of Boy Scouts. After class we lined up to march back to the barracks to get our gear and head back to Eglin for two more days to pack up all our equipment for shipment to the Clark Air Base in the Philippines. Just to give Major Philips one last jab we marched off to our buses loudly singing our "We are the Boy Scouts" cadence.

The sad part was that three of the guys that were in the groups that were 'captured' decided to leave the unit. Smart men.

* * *

May 11, 2018
Iraklion, Crete

General Straight interrupted Harold's tale here by saying, "I caught a little hell myself because of that damn cadence. It seemed Major Phillips complained to the base commander, who complained to the Army Chief of Staff, who complained to the Air Force Chief of Staff who called me when I was home on leave. But after I told him the story about Major Phillips calling you guys Boy Scouts and how bad we beat them in the evasion exercise, he was laughing too hard to do any more complaining."

The reunion group returned to the bus for the ride back to the hotel to spend the afternoon soaking up some rays on the beautiful beach behind the hotel. On the ride back Wild Bill started whistling "Stars and Stripes Forever." Then the guys all started singing Ducky's cadence over and over and over until Mary screamed, "Enough already!"

CHAPTER 6
May 12, 2018
Lions Square, Iraklion, Crete

Getting up earlier than had been the norm, the group met for breakfast the next morning. Apparently drinking only lemonade on the beach the night before instead of the beer, ouzo, raki, or some other potable was a little less trying on the guys' heads. There was nothing official on the schedule for today, but the minibus they had been using was available to take them anywhere the wanted. Today the ladies asserted their prerogative power and decided to go shopping in Iraklion. The plan became shopping until noon, then lunch in Lions Square, followed by another afternoon on the beach.

The minibus dropped them off in Eleftherias Square right by the Astoria Hotel. Everybody had just gotten off the bus when the General said, "This is the same place that the old Blue Goose shuttle used to stop. The Blue Goose was the base's dark blue 'school bus' shuttle that ran from the Air Station to here and back to the base. Rather than drive the old highway to town we would take the Blue Goose so we could have a few drinks and not kill ourselves along the coast road."

Mary expanded on that by remarking, "You can say that again. Back in the early '70s the road to the base ran along a section of the coast where you had a cliff wall on the landward side and a sheer drop to the sea on the other side. The old drive was along a narrow two lane road, with no lines painted on it, nor did it even have guardrails. The ride was scary, blind curves all along it and you could never tell if you would come around a curve to see some big truck hogging both lanes or come upon a flock of sheep being herded along the road. At least the new road we came in on today is a lot safer."

Mary continued, "On Sundays I used to love to come here to Eleftherias Square, of course we translated and called it Liberty Square. Back then there were outdoor tavernas all around the square. On Sunday afternoons it seemed like everybody in Iraklion would come here, all in their best clothes. Half of the people would be sitting at one of the outside tables watching the other half stroll pass looking at the people seated at the tables."

The General added, "Things were a lot simpler here on Crete than it was in the rest of the world back then. There were few automobiles and very little traffic. Heck, there was only one traffic light on the whole island in 1971. It was over by Market Street, I think."

Harold's wife, Joan, said, "Market Street, sounds like my kind of place. Let's go there."

Harold started laughing, "If it's anything like it was when we were here you will be very disappointed. Market Street was predominantly an open air food market in the '70s. There was some of the most beautiful and fresh produce you would ever want, but there were also lots of open air meat markets. The meat markets were not the nice clean refrigerated super markets you use at home. Back then the raw meat was just hung out in the open air for display. You would see whole skinned goats, head included, swinging from hooks hanging into the street."

An "Oooo yuck!" came from Joan.

"Don't worry, Joan. It is not like that anymore. They now have refrigerated markets there, as well as many other types of shops. Follow me." The General led them down a pedestrian only shopping street that ran from Eleftherias Square towards Lion Square and then a small left turn for a little ways and they were at the foot of Market Street.

They wandered around shopping and sightseeing until a little after noon and then headed into Lions Square for lunch. Officially called Eleftheriou Venizelou Square, the area gets called Lions Square because of the Venetian-era Morosini Fountain in its center. The fountain, built in 1628, has water coming out of the mouths of four lions giving the fountain and the square its name.

They sat at one of the outside tables and ordered a wide variety of lunches. Johnny got another gyro, even though he had one just yesterday. He said, "I just can't get enough of these things. The fast food here sure beats the hell out of what we could get in the Philippines. Do you guys remember eating a balut?"

This time it was Ron who said, "Oooo yuck! The Filipinos loved to try to get the G. I.s to try one. Just so you girls know - a balut was a fertilized duck egg that is incubated for 14 to 21 days, then boiled and eaten direct from the shell. I thought it smelled as bad as it tasted, but it was a rite of passage for any FNG, which is what we called the blanking new guys that just arrived in the Philippines."

Johnny said, "Wimp! I liked my time in the Philippines as much as I liked my time here. The only problem with the Philippines was the time we had to spend when we were away from it."

"What do you mean, Johnny?" asked Kathy.

"That's a long story, Kathy. It all started when we ended our leave after Eglin...." Johnny then proceeds to tell about their first time on the Philippine Islands.

* * *

June 1968 ~ Travis AFB, California
As told by Johnny Porter

Before we left for leave we were given orders telling us to report to Travis Air Force base on June 20, 1968. We were given vouchers enabling us to fly a commercial airline to the San Francisco airport. In the orders was information about a military transportation office at the airport that supplied us transportation to Travis AFB. We were to spend the night at Travis and the next morning we would fly together as a unit to Clark Air Base in the Philippines.

It was like the first day of your junior year of high school after a long summer vacation. Everybody enjoyed seeing each other again and swapping tall tales of what went on during leave. You would think that we had been apart for years rather than just the two weeks. The only people who had seen each other on leave were Ron and Terry. Terry's family were off working on a farm during the summer and since Terry had no one at home to go see, he had spent his entire leave with Ron and his family.

For some reason, it was arranged so that our unit had an entire transit barracks for our one night at Travis AFB. This worked out well since the only people missing were the officers and First Sergeant Briede. They went straight to Clark AB after Fort Bragg with only one week of leave in order to get things ready for our arrival. The rest of the NCOs were right there with us in the barracks.

SSgt Robert Ellingson and Airman Charlie Lee joined the conversation our little gang of eight from Eglin was having. The topic of the conversation was about what we were to expect in the Philippines. SSgt Ellingson was an extremely happy-go-lucky ex-air policeman whom had been stationed in Vietnam before he joined our unit, but his duty assignment before Vietnam was Clark AB. He told us nothing about the base and spent all of his time telling us about the nightlife in the city, Angeles, which was right outside the base. His biggest desire was to go back and get some San Miguel beer.

Joking around, Charlie Lee, a fourth generation Chinese American from Seattle asked SSgt Ellingson if he would show us all the places we should go for a good time. "Don't you worry, Good Time Charlie. I know all the best bars we should go into and all the places we should never get CAUGHT going into. You just put yourself into the hands of good old Uncle Bob, and I will take care of you."

From that point on the gang of eight became the gang of ten with the additions of "Good Time Charlie" and "Uncle Bob." The BS session went on until well past midnight with Uncle Bob telling us all about Angeles and its entertainment areas. Uncle Bob closed out the night by telling us to enjoy the company of the stewardess on our flight because that would more than likely be the last round eyed woman we would see for a while.

* * *

June 1968 ~ Clark Air Force Base, Philippine Islands
As told by Johnny Porter

We flew out the next morning in a leased commercial Boeing 707 aircraft. Our unit was the only passengers so the plane was well over half empty. The NCOs took over the first class portion of the plane and the rest of us spread out in the back. I am glad we had the extra room because with an added 4-hour layover in Hawaii, the flight seemed as if it lasted forever. When the flight finally ended, I got my first impression of the Philippines as I exited the air conditioned aircraft by stairs that had been rolled up next to the plane. The 100 plus degree heat hit me like a sledgehammer. Combine that with the 500% humidity it felt like I was trying to breath underwater. Which may have been the case since the 1505 uniform I was wearing for the trip was instantly soaking wet from my perspiration.

The duffel bags with our clothes were literally thrown into the back of a truck directly from the airplane and we loaded onto a couple of buses for a short ride to the 6922nd Security Group barracks area.

The unit was given half of the second floor of one barracks building. The three barracks were different from anything we had ever seen before. The first floors were used for a recreation rooms called the Cobra Den, offices, mess hall, and semi-private rooms for NCOs. The upper floors of the barracks were split into two wings with a central core dividing the halves. The central core contained the stairs, the latrines and more semi-private rooms for the NCOs. Each wing of the upper floors was one large open bay barracks without air-conditioning and with a unique feature of not having any solid outer walls on two sides. Those outer walls were composed of large movable wooden louvers that covered screens to keep the bugs out. With the louvers open across both sides of the long bays there was almost always a modest breeze. The breeze was augmented by the hum of large electric fans on metal poles moving the hot muggy air around. The sleeping areas had the standard gray double bunk beds but instead of foot lockers each person had a large gray metal wardrobe locker. Our group of ten less our one NCO, Uncle Bob, grabbed a section on the right side as you exited the central core. But Uncle Bob and Ducky were in a room right by the area we chose.

The rest of the day was settling in, making a run to the base Post Exchange, usually called the PX, the base laundry, getting haircuts and exploring the unit's area. The gang of ten spent the afternoon curing our jet lag by sitting in the Cobra Den sipping beer which we bought out of a vending machine that was right there in the recreation room. The next morning, I think we caused a major commotion that seemed to scare the entire 6922nd Security Group. That morning bright and early we were outside in our PT shorts and T-shirts doing calisthenics and going for our morning run. People actually crowded the screen walls of the buildings that comprised the unit area looking down at us, or stood by the assembly area between the buildings and watched us do our calisthenics.

We were to find out that once other members of the Air Force Security Service got past basic training they never did group exercises again. Heck, at Clark the guys didn't even shine their own shoes or make their beds, everybody had Filipino House Boys to do that for them. For all intents and purposes, they worked an eight-hour day and only paid minor attention to things military. They told us the only time they marched anywhere was about once every third or fourth month when it was the turn of one flight of the 6922nd to stand parade for the raising or lowering of the base flag and even then they didn't really march to the parade area.

When we got back from our run, one of the bystanders asked, "Where did you guys run off to?" Somebody yelled back, "Just a short ten mile run." We heard all kinds of comments to that, most of them wanting to know if we were nuts or something. One bystander even shouted, "Don't you crazy fools know - we are in the Air Force not the Marines?"

The first thing we did after breakfast was to have pictured IDs made that would allow us entry into the unit's restricted operations area. When we got into the area we formed up and the Major announced that every airman in our unit was hereby promoted to Airman First Class with a date of rank the 1st of July. That caused a round of cheering then we spent the rest of that day setting up our own mini-compound within the main fenced compound used for the SIGNIT operations of 6922nd Security Group.

The Group's main compound was an extremely large area surrounded by a 10-foot chain link fence topped with barbed wire. It had a single large T-shaped building which had to be over thirty-thousand square feet in size. The cinder block building had a flat roof with a few small raised areas on the roof. The unusual feature was there was not a single window in the building and the doors were all made of heavy metal. There were several small buildings, one used for burning classified material and a couple of guard shacks. The other unique feature of the areas was that it was right next to one of the largest, weirdest looking antennas in the world.

The antenna structure was several concentric circles of towers, wires, and what looked like a huge fence. The outside of the huge circle was about 1500 feet in diameter with white 20 foot tall round towers on the outside ring, then a fence looking ring which was about 120 foot high, then several other fence looking rings all surrounding a low round building in the middle. We were later to learn that this was an AN/FLR-9 antenna which was commonly called the "elephant cage." It was an extremely sensitive radio antenna configuration that, when working with other FLR-9 antennas, could pinpoint the origin of a radio signal which could be as far as 7000 kilometers away from the antennas.

Our little compound was a fenced off area inside the fence of the main compound. It consisted of a guard shack at the only gate into the area and only two olive drab colored Quonset huts. A Quonset hut is a lightweight prefabricated structure made of corrugated galvanized steel having a semicircular cross-section. One hut was used to store our gear and the other would be used as a classroom and assembly area. Thank goodness they were both air conditioned. We also had a large room that was inside the main operations center building. That room would be use for our classified planning sessions and as our command center when we had an operation in progress.

* * *

The next four weeks were spent in more training. Hand to hand combat training, jungle survival and night movement skills taught in a real jungle instead of woods and wetlands and a special escape and evasion class. The escape and evasion class was taught in an area close to the base and used some of the local Negritoes as the opposition force trackers. The Negrito people look a lot like Negrillos, or African Pygmies, but are genetically closer to the native Southeast Asian populations and were one of the first humans to settle the Philippines. The Negritoes were very good at tracking us down but had a difficult time of actually coming into contact with us. We usually managed to slip away right before they would physically see us. Fortunately for us, they were far better trackers than stealthy movers. But our group did learn quite a bit from them, especially in covering our back trails and removing any tell tale trails our movement through an area would leave behind.

One of the weapons the Negritoes used was the crossbow. After seeing their use first hand, I had my father back in Florida hit all the sporting goods stores until he came up with the best hunting crossbow on the market. I thought that I might use it in Vietnam but I never did. My dad spent a lot more that I thought he should but he sent me a compound crossbow that even had a scope. With a little practice I was able to put a bolt into a two inch bull's eye from over fifty yards away with enough power to penetrate several inches into one of the local trees. The Negrito trackers were quite envious; ten of them actually pooled all of the pay the Air Force gave them and gave it to me to have my dad send another one. How the ten of them shared it later, I'll never know.

One of the nice things was that we were now given weekends off and actually had some free time when not training. Uncle Bob lived up to his word and definitely showed us all the spots in town that we should never be caught it and a few that were OK to go into regularly. In the latter category was the local joint that was the main haunt for the 6922nd, it was a bar called the Little Brown Jug. That was usually the first place we would hit when we went to town. The San Miguel beer was always cold there. Many other bars in town only used ice chests to keep the beer cold, so if you got to a bar early in the day the beer may not be cold yet. After a night of playing tag with the Negritoes, a quick shower and a run into town for a cold San Miguel was just what Uncle Bob recommended to cure all our training aches and pains.

Part of the unit was about to leave for some more training that was actually going to take place in Vietnam when a particularly funny thing took place. At least I think of it as funny now, but at the time I was mortified. I was in town with Uncle Bob, Ron, Terry, and Harold. We were doing our best to drink enough San Miguel to suppress our fears about our upcoming excursion into Vietnam at a bar called Alma's Little Place. I was having some intestinal cramps so I went into the bathroom to relieve the pressure. I was just about to start the paperwork when an earthquake hit. Now you realize of course I am from south Florida and I had never experienced an earthquake before. The building started rocking and rolling which cause me to panic and freeze in place. But when the water and other elements in the toilet started splashing out all over me, the floor, and my pants – my panic really hit. Since my pants were still around my ankles, I waddled out of the bathroom into the bar like a penguin with a look of horror on my face. The quake didn't last very long and the other guys didn't even get out of the bar before it was all over. But they were quick enough to see me standing there, wet from the waist down, and eyes wide as saucers.

"What the hell was that?" I yelled.

Terry who was from California and had experienced earthquakes before said, "Just a tiny little tremor." Then pointing at my naked bottom, he broke up laughing saying, "What the hell is that?"

I had to look down to where he was pointing before I even realized that I still had my soaking wet pants down on the floor. I talked them into going back to the base with me so I could shower and change. But the entire trip back, I wish I hadn't, because all they did was make fun of the way I smelled and the way I looked coming out of the bathroom.

* * *

May 12, 2018
Lions Square, Iraklion, Crete

Ron had just taken a bite of his baklava dessert as Johnny told the earthquake part of the story. He started laughing so hard he was spraying filo crumbs from his baklava across the table. Harold trying to keep a straight face said, "I think for the next two years we harassed Johnny by telling him we thought we felt an earthquake, even the small fake earthquakes we invented scared the shit out of him." After he said it, Harold realized the words he just used, lost total control, and starting laughing as hard as Ron. Everyone else joined in, the group was laughing so loudly most of the people in Lion's Square were looking at us trying to see what was going on.

Trying to save Johnny a little embarrassment, the General cut into our mirth by suggesting we head back and enjoy some time at the beach.

Of course the guys wouldn't give Johnny a break. That night at the beach the guys recruited Kathy into their plan and they struck. Harold stood behind Johnny's chair and started shaking it with his foot while Ron and Wild Bill stood in front of Johnny and started to shake like they were in an earthquake, to add to the illusion, Kathy yelled, "Earthquake!"

Johnny's eyes almost popped out of his head as he leaped from his beach chair and looked around. Everybody started laughing with Kathy laughing the hardest. Johnny got instant revenge on Kathy by picking her up, running out into the water and dropping her in. When he did this he told her, "I expect this from those idiots but I expected better from you." At which point he and Kathy were laughing as hard as everyone else.

CHAPTER 7
May 13, 2018
Bus between Matala and Hersonissos, Crete

Today's tour was a bus trip to the south side of the island to visit Matala, with a stop at Φαιστός. Phaistos or as it is sometime called Festos, is the site of another Minoan palace. While it too was a major Minoan palace at the same time as Knossos, it is located high on a mountain quite a distance from the sea. The site had been inhabited from the Neolithic period 4000 BC until the foundation and development of the Minoan palaces in the 15th century BC. The palace was located such that it had views on three sides of the valleys below.

As they walked around the well-preserved ruins, General Straight provided a knowable commentary of what the different sections of the palace were believed to have been used for. The site has been under excavation on and off since the late 1800's AD, but it had not been reconstructed like Knossos. The group didn't spend near as much time there as they had at Knossos. Then they were off to Matala.

Matala is a small community which primarily survives on tourism. Its main claim to fame is the caves in the rock on both sides of a beautiful sand beach area. It the '60s and early '70s when the guys were stationed on Crete the caves were inhabited by many hippies. Harold joked that there were always three distinct smells coming out of the caves back then – BO, WC or MJ. After seeing the puzzled expression on Joan's face, he went on to explain BO from the unwashed hippies' bodies; WC for the smell that comes from a dirty "Water Closet" or toilet; and MJ, Mary Jane, is an old nickname for Marijuana.

At Matala the group had lunch in one of the restaurants that overlooked the sand beach then they spent the remainder of their time swimming, exploring the caves, or shopping in all the tourist shops that were not there back in the 70's.

On the bus ride back Joan asked who were the hippies that were living in the caves there. Ron explained that they were from a variety of places, Europe, Canada and the United States. The most famous was the Canadian folk singer Joni Mitchell, who made Matala famous with her song "Carey". Some of the American hippies were either Vietnam vets trying to get their heads back together or hippies who were spending their time on Crete while they were dodging the draft.

Joan responded to Ron's explanation, "A lot of Americans dodged the draft because of Vietnam, but you guys didn't. When did you guys first go to Vietnam?"

Ron then began the story of the team's first visit to Vietnam. "Though I have never spoken about it to anyone I remember Tuesday, July 23, 1968, like it was yesterday. It was the first day we went to Vietnam."

* * *

July 1968 ~ Da Nang Air Base, South Vietnam
As told by Ron Lafayette

We left Clark AB predawn and arrived at Da Nang Air Base around noon. The first impressions I had as we walked down the ramp of the C130 was the heat and smell of burnt jet fuel. Twenty of us were in the first group that was going to extend our training here in Vietnam. With Major Straight leading the way, we all exited the aircraft dressed in full gear and armed to the teeth.

There were trucks waiting for us just steps away from the plane. The last few out of the plane were not only caring their weapons and packs but also several crates that contained our communications gear and some training supplies. Everything else we needed would be acquired here on the air base. We loaded onto the trucks and were driven to a rather open area southwest of the air strip close to Hill 327. There were only a few tents with sandbags piled up four foot high around them, a few outhouses, bunkers and not much else there.

Since Terry and I were some of the first to get into one of the trucks we were the last to exit and got stuck with unloading our extra equipment into a tent that was to be used as our operations center. By the time we unloaded and set up the communication gear all the other guys had taken the bunks that were available in the other tents so we got to grab two of the four cots in the command tent. The way equipment and other gear was stacked around the tent split it into a work area and two semi private sleeping areas. We unloaded our gear in one area; Major Straight and Lieutenant Washington were going to share the other sleeping area.

We were given the nickel tour as to where the latrines, bunkers and slit trenches were located. We were also assigned defensive areas we were to man in the event of an attack. Since Terry and I were in the command tent we were assigned to guard the com-gear and equipment in the command tent from two small fighting holes on opposite ends of the tent.

Harold being the smart mouth that he is, asked if he and Johnny should guard the latrine. He said that they needed to be close to the latrine because in the event of an attack or an earthquake, they would have the shit scared out of them. The major got into the spirit by telling Harold and Johnny they were to swap places with Good Time Charlie and Chief so they were now assigned to a slit trench which guarded the open approach from the main part of the air base which was indeed closest to the latrines. He then added that he hoped they enjoyed the aroma of being so close to the latrines if we happened to get stuck in defensive positions for a long time. With that comment Harold got a punch in the arm from Johnny and chuckles from Charlie and Chief.

After getting settled in we were introduced to our instructors, two Kit Carson Scouts and two Montagnards, for this part of the training. Kit Carson scouts were recruited from experienced Viet Cong defectors, *Hồi Chánh Viên* in Vietnamese. They worked closely with Marine units as intelligence scouts and guides. These two were on loan from the 3rd Marine Division and were to teach us about how the Viet Cong moved through countryside and about Viet Cong tactics. The Montagnards are an indigenous group from the Central Highlands of Vietnam. They had a very good working relationship with the Army Special Forces and were affectionately referred to as 'Yards' by the Green Berets. These two were borrowed from the Green Berets to teach us how to move and remain hidden in the highlands of Vietnam.

The rest of the day was spent with the Kit Carson Scouts telling us about Viet Cong counter intelligence unit tactics. They told us in highly accented English about how these specialized units would stake out landing zones and follow Marine Recon teams until the VC could gather sufficient forces to attack the Marines. They also briefed us on other Viet Cong unit tactics and about what they knew about how supplies and regular North Vietnamese Army, NVA, units were brought down from the north.

That evening hot food was trucked in from the air base and we enjoyed a quiet afternoon and night until about 2 AM when all hell broke loose. We were awakened by a loud explosion from the air base area followed by the wail of air raid sirens. The radio that we had tuned to the Air Base's defensive net started warning of rocket attacks. The four of us in the command tent grabbed our weapons and ran out the tent. Lt. Washington and Terry were the first out of the tent and jumped into the slit trench closest to the tent flap. I was following just a few steps behind them, but I made a quick decision to head to the trench on the other side of the tent. I think I based my decision solely on the fact that I didn't want to hurt Terry by jumping in on top of him. Major Straight was right behind me and for some reason followed me to the other trench even though it was quite a few steps further from the tent entrance.

In the bottom of the sandbag rimmed trench, we hunkered down with our hands over heads since we were never issued steel helmets. I was staring into the major's eyes. He'd just glanced up to look at the sky and the glow coming from fires on the main section of the base when there was an extremely loud bang. We could feel the heat of an explosion wash over the top of our trench. Through the spots in my vision, from the blinding light of the explosion, I saw the major mouth the words, "Oh God, that was close. I hope no one is hurt." I could not hear if he said the words aloud because my ears were ringing like the bells of Notre Dame on steroids from the sound of the blast.

We both popped our heads out of our hole to see where the rocket landed. The sandbags around the command tent were all knocked down and the canvas of the tent was flapping in the breeze on the outside of the sandbags and on fire. I jumped out of the hole screaming, "Terrrrrry" and ran to the other side of the ruins of the tent. There was only a smoking hole where the trench, that Terry and Lt. Washington took cover, once existed.

I ran to the hole looking in to see if I could help but the only thing I saw of them was a smoking boot with part of a leg bone sticking out. Through tear filled eyes I searched all around the rim of the crater and several meters out but found absolutely nothing of them. I fell to my knees looking down into the hole and cried like a baby. I felt a hand on my shoulder and looked up at the major. He was looking down at me with tears running down his cheeks too, but not saying a word.

By now several guys had come running up from the bunkers by the other tents. While a few joined me looking at the crater, the majority ran to put out the fires caused by the burning tent canvas. Major Straight bent down placing a hand under my arm, lifted me to my feet and lead me a few steps away from the hole. Ducky came running up to the major asking if we were OK. The major composed himself by wiping his face with both hands and told Ducky that Lt. Washington and Airman Garcia were in the trench that received the direct impact of the missile. He also told him to assign a few men to excavate the crater, search the area, and collect any human remains that could be found.

I don't know how or when I fell asleep but I awoke to activity all around me in one of the other tents. Nobody was talking or horsing around as we normally did. I was still in a tee-shirt and camouflage pants that I was wearing last night but someone had thrown a clean set of fatigues, a new tee-shirt, and some toiletries on the bed as I was bending down putting on my boots. I joined a couple of guys who were washing up at a ramshackle table that had a large barrel of water with a spigot. After cleaning up we headed off to join the rest of the unit who were eating a hot breakfast that had been trucked in from a chow hall.

As I was finishing breakfast, Major Straight approached and crooked his index finger signaling me to follow. He walked a few meters away from the rest of the unit and he asked if I was OK. I told him about how Terry and I had been together since basic training and had even spent our two weeks leave together at my home. He nodded as I raddled on about Terry for about five or six minutes. He never said a word but looked at me kindly as I dumped my feeling out. As I paused a second to think about other stories I could tell the major when I realized what I had been doing. Then I blurted, "I'm sorry, Sir. Thank you for listening. I'm OK now."

The major gave a small smile and said, "No problem, Ron. Just let me know if there is anything I can do for you." I responded in the negative and we moved back to the rest of the unit. During the walk back I said to myself that the major sure was a nice guy and I was a bit surprised that he even knew my first name.

The instructors had not shown up yet but the major gathered us all together for a quick talk. He started off by telling us how sorry he was about losing Lt. Washington and Airman Garcia. That was followed by a minute of silent prayer. He continued by telling us the rocket attack last night consisted of sixteen rockets that damaged five aircraft but caused no other casualties on the base. He also explained that our presence in Vietnam was classified and that we were not to tell anyone about what happened here and that as far as the rest of the world was concerned our comrades died in a training mishap in the Philippines. He ended his little pitch by asking if there were any questions.

No one said anything until I blurted out, "We will miss Terry and Lt. Washington. But it never happened, Sir." This was echoed back by several of the guys saying, "It never happened." Upon hearing our response Major Straight snapped to attention, turned towards the location of the fatal rocket impact and held a hand salute. The rest of the unit did the same. After almost a half a minute he dropped his salute.

Ducky took over and broke us into four groups and had us gear up to go on field exercises with our instructors. He told us – no backpacks but to pack along a few extra clips of ammunition, just in case we came across anyone we didn't like. With anger in his voice Harold said, "There are a lot of people out there that I don't particularly like right now." This caused a chorus of agreements and muted conversations while everyone got their gear and waited for our transportation and instructors to arrive. Major Straight and Ducky and a dozen or so Da Nang full-time personnel went to put the command tent back into operational status.

Two trucks bracketed by two armored personnel carriers arrived to take us to where we would be conducting our exercise. The two Kit Carson Scouts and the two Yards were in different trucks. Eight of us got into each truck and we were driven off base to some rugged hilly area about a thirty minute drive from the base.

There were two trailheads leading from the road where our little convoy stopped. The two Kit Carson Scouts took their groups down one trail and the Yards took my group and another group down the other trail. My group consisted of myself, Harold, Uncle Bob, and Good Time Charlie. The other group took off going down the trail first and we waited about ten minutes and followed. As we were waiting the Yard leading our group, introduced himself but I can not remember his proper Montagnard name just the nickname given to him by a Green Beret, "Spot". He told us that for the first part of the walk we should listen and he would point out all the trail markers the leading group left behind. He said his friend was teaching his group how to cover their trail so this should be fun. He warned us that even though this area was considered pacified and thus safe, we should not let our guard down because the Cong could be anywhere.

The first thing he pointed out was the boot prints of the other group. He said Viet Cong and NVA did not have boots but Ho Chi Minh sandals usually made from worn out truck and motorcycle tires. He also pointed out the difference between the fresh prints just made and prints that were much shallower and less defined. He said the older prints were only a day or two old because they had not yet been washed away by the rain.

As we followed the trail he pointed out more telltales: exposed dark decaying foliage, fresh broken foliage, and a broken spider web. Suddenly to my eyes it looked like the trail disappeared. Spot went on to explain that they were now covering their trail. He was still able to see the brush marks of the bush that was used to spread the dust on the trail and cover the boot marks. He followed the trail for about thirty steps and returned and told us they were tricky. And started walking back down the path we had just taken looking closely to either side. He pointed to some disturbed elephant grass about a meter off the trail. He then pointed to a lot of fresh green leaves on the trail. He said they were very good by leaving a trail as though they continued using the path but then doubled back to use a low hanging tree limb to swing over the foliage right next to the path. Then they fluffed up the elephant grass they disturbed when they landed and along their trail through the grass.

We exited the path where the other team had and started along their trail. Before we exited the patch of elephant grass we were in, he then held up his hand for quiet and we just listened. He ever so slowly turned around four times alternating between sniffing and listening intently. He pointed to the north and said they are that way. When asked, he told us that the noises of the surrounding were quieter, less animal and more insect noise from that direction. He explained that as we pass someplace the animals either flush from hiding or become very quiet. When someone passes the insects get disturbed and fly around more. We thought we learned a lot during our time in Green Beret school and from the Negretoes but this guy was good.

The rest of the morning we became the recipients of a wealth of information on tracking and being tracked. The trail led up into a more rugged terrain with thinner underbrush. We came to a section of hillside where the ground was quite rocky. Here Spot lost the trail for a while and did another of his circling sniffs. He pointed and we followed about ten meters further down the trail where he pointed to a small damp spot on the ground. He got a little closer to it, sniffed again and said, "G.I. pee here." He explained that G.I. spore smelled different than Vietnamese because of our totally different diets.

After the second time he did the spin, with the way he used his keen nose, I had a very good guess how he got his nickname, Spot, from the Green Berets. The man was like a friendly hound dog. My thoughts were disturbed by the sound of a single shot in the distance. Spot suggested that we head back for a pickup now because that shot was a signal used by the Cong to warn others of the presence of enemy troops in their territory. We radioed our intentions to the other groups and to Ducky who was manning the radios back a base. Ducky said he would have the pickup convoy back to where they dropped us off in about an hour.

When we got back to base camp the group gathered together to share what we had learned. Each of the groups gave their feedback to the whole team. One team emphasized that we had to travel as light as possible; too much weight would be a killer if we ever had to do extensive movement in the jungle or highlands. Another team said we had to make sure our gear was silent when we moved and the Jingle-Jangle-Jingle of loose equipment could get us killed. Someone brought up that we should never smoke while on a mission since the smell of the cigarettes and the glow of the cigarette could be seen at night. When it was our group's turn I brought up two points – if we were going to spend a lot of time in enemy occupied territory there were two things we had to do. One, glue some Ho Chi Minh sandal soles to the bottom of our boots so we didn't leave footprints that were obviously made by American boots all over in places where we weren't supposed to be. And two, we had to eat Vietnamese food for a few days before any incursions and only Vietnamese food while we were in enemy territory so wouldn't stink like Yankee soldiers.

The major agreed with all of the suggestions and told Ducky to add them to our SOP, Standard Operating Procedures. He also instructed him to get his hands on some Ho Chi Minh sandals so we could work out the best way to affix them to our jungle boots.

The major then briefed us on our next operation, tomorrow morning we would go for a nice long walk in the highlands and practice blowing thing up. We would split into four teams again with one of our instructors as our guides. We would be doing helicopter insertions to set up four observation posts that we would maintain for three days. Our call signs would be Zebra Zero for command center, and Zebra One, Zebra Two, Three and Four for the teams. We were to call in artillery support for any enemy sightings for the first two days and on the third day each member of the team was to take turns picking spots to practice calling in artillery strikes.

He told us that we would be in a free fire zone, that is, we would be the only American or South Vietnamese troops operating in the area so anybody else we spotted was fair game. He emphasized that if for any reason our positions were compromised we were to call Zebra Zero for an extraction and that our job was to remain hidden and only engage the enemy using artillery and airstrikes. The Major also announced that since Airman Green sprained his ankle, today, he would be taking his place on team Zebra Three and that Ducky and Airman Green would be manning the Zebra Zero command center. Our standard radio procedure would be to check in every hour using Morse code but only sending a 'Z', our team number, and a '1' if all was well or a '0' if we were in trouble. Confirmation that our status update was received would be Z zero Z team number from command center.

Each of the teams then received folders that contained the information for their part of the operation. The packets contained radio communication frequencies and callsigns for the artillery battery that each would be utilizing. We also had callsigns and frequencies for a forward air controller who would be flying around our area of operation should we need air support. There were coordinates and aerial photographs of the Landing Zones, LZs, we would be using for insertion and extraction, as well as, two alternate extraction LZs. Just to make sure we didn't call in strikes on each other, we were also given the approximate location we should set up our observation posts, as well as, the approximate locations of the other teams. The contents of the folders were transferred into small pocket spiral notebooks we all kept in our shirt pockets.

Ducky and Airman Green moved into the rebuilt command tent. The teams swapped around locations in the other tents so tomorrow's teams could be together a little longer to go over their own plans. I would be on the same team I was on today but with a Kit Carson Scout and not Spot. Surprisingly, I slept well that night.

The next morning we all covered our faces in camouflage grease paint and geared up for our three-day operation, then the quiet of the morning was shattered as four UH-1 helicopters, commonly known as Hueys, landed not far from our tents. Two additional helicopter gunships, that were to escort us and provide landing firepower support, hovered to the south of us as we loaded one team on each helicopter.

The cool morning air blew into the helicopter as we flew a roller coaster, nap of the earth, flight to our area of operation. The four troop carrying helicopters did a dance over a potential LZ with the gunships shooting up the area and one or more of the helicopters faking a landing. Then off to another LZ and another dance, this time one of the teams actually landed. They flew to another LZ to once again dance around and another fake landing, and then on the next dance is when our team landed.

The helicopters were once again off to other locations to either fake or actually land a team. After all the teams were landed they even made a few more fake landings to confuse the enemy as to where we landed.

The helicopter that dropped our team, Zebra Two, off didn't touch down, it just hovered a few feet off the ground and we jumped down into the elephant grass that filled our LZ. You never can tell if the enemy had been watching that LZ or had an ambush just waiting for some group to try to land there. So the second we hit the ground we hit the dirt for a minute then sprinted 15 meters through the grass to get to the tree line. As we got into the tree line we assumed a defensive star position with each team member facing a different direction. We remained still and listened for any sounds that could indicate that we had been seen landing. Hearing nothing we quietly moved another fifteen meters deeper into the tree line and dropped to listen again. Hearing nothing we went back to clean up our initial landing tracks than quietly moved out in another direction. Walking point was the Kit Carson Scout, followed by myself, Harold, Uncle Bob, and Good Time Charlie, who was walking drag and cleaning up our back trail.

We moved about twenty five meters and again assumed defensive positions and listened. This time we remained where we were for over fifteen minutes, just quietly listening. We were clear so we once again shifted directions and moved off in the direction we needed to go to set up our OP, Observation Post. We moved up hill heading for a destination about four fifths up the slope. The spot picked for our OP was about five meters from the origins of a small stream that ran back down into the valley where we had landed. The proximity of the stream would provide us with fresh water for our three day stay. The exact location that was picked for us wasn't the best so we shifted over about twenty meters to the other side of the stream to a location that had good rock cover on the side looking down into the valley. It also had trees over us to provide shade and to prevent us from being seen should anyone walk along the ridge line above us.

We didn't just settle into the OP once we selected the spot, first we scouted to the top of the ridge and a little down the opposite slope. It was very rough going with dense underbrush so we had help to protect us a little from the uphill direction. We set claymore mines and trip wires to further protect us from that likely approach direction. Half the team then did their best to eradicate all indications that we had scouted the area while the other half dug defensive positions as best we could in the rocky ground. We re-planted a few bushes to give us better camouflage and sent a burst encoded message that we had settled in our OP and its exact coordinates.

Our OP had a good view of our original LZ, as well as clear views of portions of several trails that crossed the area. We did this all under the watchful eye our Kit Carson Scout. He never said a word while we performed these tasks, he just observed. We on the other hand were chatting away using our hand Morse code signals, but never saying anything out loud. When we were all settled in the Kit Carson Scout, Hoang, whispered in his poor, highly accented English to Uncle Bob, "Very good job. You well trained. Do job not being told. You seem to think alike. Each knows what other do. But why everybody hand shake?"

Uncle Bob gave a small chuckle and said, "We are talking in a sign language." Hoang saved face by knowingly nodding his head. He then began to scan the valley using a pair of high-powered binoculars. Two members of the team proceeded to take a short nap while the others remained on watch. Every six hours we shifted who was on duty and who was off. We didn't include Hoang in our rotation so he just adjusted himself by being on duty when Uncle Bob was off.

The first day was extremely quiet. At dusk we broke out the night vision gear. Hoang was very interested in our little toy and spent half the night playing with the goggles on as he scanned the perimeter.

The next day was more of the same until about 4 PM. Harold was on duty and was scanning the LZ where we landed when he noticed movement. He kicked Uncle Bob to get his attention and handing him the binoculars, he pointed to the north end of the LZ. There were four Viet Cong in their black pajama outfits looking around the LZ. One seemed to be pointing at various locations as the other three nodded at whatever he was saying. Uncle Bob got on the radio to the artillery battery that was to give us support and reported his sightings, he then reported to Zebra Zero while waiting to get confirmation from the fire support base. As he was waiting an additional eight Viet Cong joined the other four and started to take up ambush positions along one side of the LZ. Since we had the exact coordinates of the LZ in our notes it didn't take long for Uncle Bob to do the minor adjustment to set the strike to hit the tree line on the north side of the LZ where the Cong had taken up positions. Uncle Bob asked for the first round to be High Explosives, HE, rather than a Smoke round. The first HE round hit dead in the center of the Cong position. We watched as bodies flew into the air. Uncle Bob was instantly on the radio to the fire support base and told them they were dead on target and to fire for effect. The second they got the fire for effect order, three more rounds blasted the area exactly where the twelve Viet Cong had set their ambush. A few seconds later an additional four rounds shattered the tree line of the LZ, followed by a third set of four blasts. Uncle Bob gave the ceasefire request and things got very quiet once again.

We kept several sets of binoculars trained on that area for the next thirty minutes and saw absolutely no movement. Hoang whispered, "All dead. Nobody got away. Good shooting. Radio in twelve dead VC."

Uncle Bob radioed in the report taking credit for the twelve Viet Cong KIA. Several minutes later we heard artillery hitting the next valley over from us, in Zebra Three's area of operation. Hoang said, "Artillery scared someone in next valley, enough to get them to move. Bad idea for them. Very good we kill VC and not just teach school."

While we waited during the quiet of the rest of day two, we had all picked the spot we wanted to blast when it was our turn to call in our artillery training strikes. The morning of day three we started calling in our strikes. Then adjusting fire as if our first strike was off or the enemy was moving away from the strike area. I was the last to call in my strike. I had located our extraction LZ and used that as my test target. I called in the shots and redirected fire to travel toward the slope closest to the LZ.

Around noon we moved out heading for our extraction LZ. We stopped where we had a very good view of the LZ and scanned the area before proceeding. We radioed in for the helicopters to come get us and proceeded closer to the LZ while they were in transit. We approached the LZ through the clearings created for us by the artillery strike I had called in. When we got to the crater that was caused by the first positioning round I called in, we found two mangled bodies both with AK-47s near them. Luck had been with us. Apparently some NVA had set an ambush at this LZ also and the test firing had by some miracle been on target. We searched the bodies for documents finding a few items and collected their weapons and ammunition. Just then the helicopters arrived, requesting us to pop smoke. We threw a yellow smoke grenade, informed the helicopter of the color and quickly boarded it as it hovered one foot off the ground.

During the public debriefing session we informed the full team and several guests of our original twelve KIAs and the additional two confirmed KIAs resulting from our practice strike. We passed the documents and weapons we recovered to the Marine intelligence team that had come to our debriefing. The Marines had been there because it was their area of operation that we had been working. One of the marines, a Captain, upon examining our document told us that the two guys that our lucky shot got were members of the artillery group which was part of the 2nd NVA Division. He also said that it was their unit that had been firing the rockets at the Da Nang Air Base.

During the private debriefing following the public one, the major asked for additional feedback. Uncle Bob brought up about it being a good idea to blast any area we were going to use as an extraction LZ, just in case. As we were wrapping up Ducky said, "It was just bad luck that Terry and Lt. Washington got hit in that rocket attack but at least we got some payback by getting a couple of guys from the unit that hit us. And hopefully the other twelve gooks we got were part of that unit too." This caused a round of cheers from the guys. The major closed out the meeting by telling us that he and Ducky would remain here when we returned to the P.I., and that the second group would be coming in on the same plane we were leaving on tomorrow.

* * *

May 13, 2018
On the minibus between Matala and Hersonissos, Crete

Ron said, "Did that answer your question about our first time in Vietnam, Joan?"

"All too well." was her response.

General Straight stood up, walked over to where Ron was sitting, laid his hand on Ron's shoulder and said, "I never did get to thank you for saving my life that first night there. When the rockets hit, I too was going to jump into the same trench as Terry and Nick Washington. But for some reason I followed you to the other trench, which more than likely, saved my life."

Ron looked up at the General and with tears in his eyes said, "Terry and I had been real close, but losing him that first night hardened me and took away much of the fear for the rest of the time we were there. It made me realize that it was all fate and pure luck if we lived or died. Given all the area on the air base and the majority of the rockets hitting the landing strip area, the odds for that one rocket to go right into the trench where they were was astronomical. It also made me think that from that night forward I was just waiting for my number to come up. So there was no use worrying about dying because it was a sure thing. I guess our luck just held out long enough, George."

General George Straight responded. "About time someone called me George. We are no longer in the service and we sure as hell are friends by now. I don't know about the rest of you, but I sure could use something to drink. A lot of something to drink! As soon as the bus gets back to the hotel, let's go tie one on."

CHAPTER 8
May 14, 2018
Santorini, Greece

The whole group was looking forward to today's excursion to Santorini. They went to the Iraklion harbor to catch the morning high-speed ferry to Santorini. The ferry takes less than two hours to make the trip. It was about 10:30 when they arrived on the dock at Fira. While many tourist take donkeys up to the city from the old port, the ferry landed at the newer port so the group took several taxis from the dock up a long series of winding switchbacks going up the caldera's side to the city of Fira and then on to Oia. Santorini is the largest island of a small, circular archipelago group of islands. The archipelago is basically what remnants of one large island after an enormous volcanic eruption destroyed it. Many believe that the volcanic destruction of the large island and the Minoan culture there at the time grew into the legend of Atlantis.

They toured the town and poked their heads into many of the little shops in Oia. Along one of the city's paths they were at the top of the caldera looking down into the mouth of the volcano that had turned the one island into several. They were enraptured as they looked off the edge, over beautiful white and blue buildings built along its steeply sloped sides, down to a remarkably beautiful sea. The island is one of the picture book scenic locations of Greece. They ate at a wonderful restaurant that had a view down the side of the caldera overlooking several beautiful boutique hotels with private mini-pools for their guests. They broke up into smaller groups and wandered around the caldera edge of the city until time to catch the ferry back to Crete.

The ferry left for the return trip, about 7 PM. On the ferry the group commandeered a cluster of tables and had gyros for supper as they discussed the wonders they saw on Santorini. As the conversation was winding down Mary asked General Straight about what happened after their first visit to Vietnam.

The General though for a moment and said, "I guess I should start from the time the rest of the team finished their On the Job Training in Vietnam."

* * *

August, 1968 ~ Clark AB, Philippine Islands
As told by George Straight

The last OJT group finished up August 15, 1968. Being the nice guy I am, I gave the airman the 16th off while I held a meeting with Captain Cummings and the NCOs. When I first built the organization composition,

78

the original plan was to have five operational teams each composed of ten airmen and one officer or NCO, but as we went through training and got more information from experienced behind the lines experts, we settled on operational teams of four. Each team to be led by an officer or NCO. However, we were extremely short of NCOs and officers, especially after the loss of Lt. Washington. In that meeting we had to pick six of the airman to become team leaders. The airman we chose were: Wild Bill, Ron, Steve Borns, Charles Cullum, Dwight Dillinger, and Steve Schmidt. I then sent a note off to my old boss General McConnell telling him that Detachment 11 was ready to go operational and to request his assistance in getting the very early promotions to sergeant for the seven new team leaders.

I saw, as soon as I walked into our operations center the next day, a message that came in during the night from General McConnell saying the promotions were on the way and the new sergeants would have a date of rank of September 1. He also gave me the first three target locations in North Vietnam and the dates that he wanted to use for the detachment's initial operations. I had Master Sergeant Briede suspend the evening training schedule and told him to round up the troops for a full unit meeting to be held at thirteen hundred hours.

At the meeting I explained how from now on we would continue to work with four man teams and that each team would be led by a sergeant or above. Then I announced the new sergeants. Apparently the unit agreed with our selections because there was a lot of well wishes and enthusiasm for those selected as team leaders. I posted the team assignments and gave the guys the rest of the day off to help celebrate their friends' promotions, knowing that the Little Brown Jug, the unit's favorite bar in Angeles, would be getting a lot of business this afternoon.

Reading the requirements General McConnell had sent for the first operations, I had decided that because of mission requirements, I would use two teams instead of just one. To go on the first mission, I picked my own team and Ron's team. Captain Cummings would remain at Clark in command during my absence and man the operations center. The following two missions would be Captain Cummings with SSgt Ellingson's teams and then MSgt Briede with Born's teams. Using the information I received about our targets, I put in a rush order for maps, aerial reconnaissance photographs, and the history of previous strikes on the same targets. As soon as that was done, I dragged the few guys that were still in the office with me to join the others at the Little Brown Jug celebrating our new sergeants.

While we were hoisting a few beers I got the team leaders for the next three missions together and told them to take the next morning off since I had a feeling it would be a long night for them. But I also told them to head over to Operations Center after lunch tomorrow so we could start planning our missions. After we had put in our appearance and had a few beers, "Jo Jo" Cummings and myself left to head back to base and check to see if, and when, we would get all of the information I had requested.

The next morning everything but the detailed aerial reconnaissance photos of the hill tops close to the targets had arrived. There was a stack of detailed topographic maps for the targets areas which had been flown in from Military Assistance Command, Vietnam, also known simply as MACV. The aerial reconnaissance photographs of the targets and the airstrike history from the Air Staff arrived shortly after 9 AM. An aerial reconnaissance mission for individual hills, away from the strike targets, had been tasked and reconnaissance planes would be dispatched to take the pictures when priority permitted.

MSgt Briede had put his carpentry skills to work when we first arrived and he had covered full 4x8 sheets of plywood with cork and mounted them on frames with wheels such that the bottoms of the horizontally mounted cork covered panels were two feet off the floor. He has made five of these movable operations planning boards and he rolled three into place along the front of the Operations Center. Each planning board was marked top and bottom - Top Secret. Bed sheets were tacked to the top of the boards so the classified contents could be covered if necessary. Even though the entire 6922nd operations center was secured for Top Secret material, our operations did not fall under the need to know requirement for the non-Detachment 11 personnel.

The three boards, one for each operation, were labeled with the operation names, Operation Sunny Virgin, Operation White Snow, and Operation Igloo Home. How MSgt Briede came up with these code names I have no idea, but having the word Virgin in our first operation may have been appropriate. The other two may have just been the heat getting to him. At the top right of each board was a neatly typed page containing the callsigns, frequencies, and authentication codes to be used during the operation; the names of the team members that would participate in the operation; and names, tasks, and phone numbers of all the members of the command team that would be remaining behind to coordinate the operation. Below that along the right edge was a page that was blank except for the title Support Assets. Below that page was one titled "Weather." Those pages would be filled in when the information became available. As the planning progressed these boards began to fill with details.

Operation Sunny Virgin was to be the bombing of a bridge over the Red River. To assist with this bombing, it was our objective to place battery powered VOR, which are a type of short-range radio navigation beacons, on the top of two hills. The VOR on one hill was to be located east of the target and another was to be placed on a hill southwest of the target. These were to facilitate multiple air strike packages coming from many different directions to merge into two large strike packages. Trailing behind each of the two merged strike packages would be an aerial reconnaissance aircraft to take pictures for Bomb Damage Assignment normally just referred to as BDA.

One team was to place each of the VORs and have them operational by oh-five-hundred hours the day of the strike. The teams would be extracted utilizing HH-3E, Air Rescue helicopters following the strike. One HH-3E and a helicopter gunship would be assigned to each merged strike package to assist in rescuing any downed pilots and to extract one of our teams. If a plane went down while over target, the HH-3E was to retrieve our team first so that our team could provide fire support and aid in the recovery of any downed pilot. Each strike package also had a FAC aircraft associated with it to provide anti-aircraft suppression aid and air cover support until the HH-3E and its gunship escort arrived.

The insertion was to be done right after sunset on the day before the strike was to launch. Each insertion was to be performed by a Huey flying out of Da Nang with an escort of two gunships.

After the team leaders did a thorough study of the maps, the two target hills were identified. The east VOR was to be placed on a small hill exactly ten kilometers due west of the target, the hill was in a perfect position and couldn't have been better placed if we had built the hill ourselves. The other VOR location was not quite as perfect but it fell well within our planning criteria. It was located 220 degrees from the target; perfect southwest is 225 degrees, so we were close but not perfect. The hill we would use was 15.1 kilometers from the target. Again not perfect but due to the highly cultivated nature of the area it was the best we could find without having an extraordinary high risk of exposure.

Now that we had VOR positions we could request an aerial reconnaissance run to get photographs to determine LZs. The communications with the reconnaissance group indicated we should get the pictures in two days weather permitting. The team leaders shifted to the other two operations just to pick the potential VOR locations so they could request photographs of the LZs earlier in the planning processes for the other two operations. That done, the team leaders then started other tasks associated with planning the first operation.

While the team leaders were building lists of the gear they would be packing, Ducky came in carrying a dirty pair of jungle boots to show me. The boots must have belonged to someone else because they looked as big as amphibious landing crafts. On the bottom of each boot was one-quarter-inch thick used motorcycle tire tread cut to the shape of a Ho Chi Minh sandal that Ducky had glued there. The shape didn't quite cover the whole bottom of the boot and Ducky explained it was because few Vietnamese had feet that large. He jokingly explained that one of the guys he had testing the boots was Jimmy Hebert who the guys had nicknamed Baby Huey because of his large size.

Ducky told me how he had gone off base to Angeles and purchased a couple of used motorcycle tires that weren't worn to the tread. He then took the used tires and several pairs of boots to a small shoe repair shop owned by an old retired PC. PC stood for Philippine Constabulary, a form of paramilitary policeman. The shoe shop owner had done a wonderful job and none of the guys who tested the boots had been able to damage the new soles. Ducky explained that they worked well but not quite as good as the original soles. The only minor problem was that they didn't work as well on wet slippery surfaces like on rocks in streams. But even with that drawback, they would work, and any footprints left behind would be far less noticeable in places we weren't supposed to be.

I asked Ducky if the shoe repair shop owner could be trusted. Ducky told me that the guy was a hard-core PC NCO and was just too old to work that job anymore. So if a fellow NCO asked, gave him a lot of work and a few extra Pesos, Philippine money, the guy would forget that the world was round much less gluing tires to a bunch of military boots. I told MSgt Briede to check the records and expedite the order for an extra pair of boots for everyone. Then draw some cash for Ducky's PC friend's work and some more for additional used tires. I told Ducky to prioritize the boot updates for the guys going in on the first operations.

Two mornings later we had the photographs for the potential LZs. We then picked the insertion and extraction LZs and a couple of alternates for each. During the examination Ron notice that a couple of the LZs we were choosing from were actually bomb craters formed by 500 pound bombs. Ron said, "Now we know how to have LZs made in the locations we need them. We can have one of the B52s 'accidentally on purpose' drop a load of those big bombs exactly where we want an LZ."

I told MSgt Briede to make a note of it and put it into our SOP for future reference. We ordered extra copies of the detailed maps for the insertion and extraction areas for team use and the team leaders then planned their routes and contingencies for getting to the target area and back to an LZ. Each team leader then briefed all of the other 13 team leaders on their detailed plans. Using the feedback from the group and knowledge from the other briefings, they reworked their plans which they then presented to their own teams.

The SOP for each operating team was to assign two alternate members that would take the place of any team member who may get sick or injured. The alternates would be part of the planning and any special training the operation teams underwent until the end of the operation. The SOP called for each member of a team, including alternates, to present their team's plan to all the units' team leaders, so that everyone knew their part of the plan as well as the whole plan in case of casualties.

All of our planning was done and reviewed again and again three days before the first operation was to take place. Two days before the operation the teams and their alternates transferred to Da Nang Air Base which would be our departure point for destinations in North Vietnam. My team would be composed of myself, Johnny, Jim Wiggins and Gus Rantz. Gus was my point man and Jim my drag. Ron's team was Harold, Chief Begay, and Dick Duggens with Chief as point and Harold walking drag. Both teams were 100% ready so the alternates would wait for us at Da Nang until after the mission and we would all go back to Clark together.

* * *

August 1968 ~ North Vietnam

On August 27, we loaded each team into its own Huey. The flight of the two troop transports, four gunships, and one FAC fixed wing aircraft would take off at dusk and fly together into North Vietnam. Flying Combat Air Patrol, or CAP, would to be a flight of F-105 Thunderchief fighter bombers that the FAC could call upon for assistance if required. At a point equidistant from both insertion LZs the flight would split with one troop transport and two gunships continuing on each team's LZ. The FAC and our CAP would linger in the general area, should they be required, until their fuel ran low at which point they would be replaced by others.

The helicopters danced at a few fake LZs before proceeding to the planned primary Landing Zone. We scanned the area using our eyeballs and our night vision gear, seeing nothing, we inserted. We jumped two feet to the ground and sprinted for the cover supplied at the edge of the clearing. The helicopters left us to go dance at a few more fake LZs before heading back. We stayed at the edge of the clearing a little longer than normal to listen. The sound of the departing helicopters had faded and all was still quiet, so Gus and Jim went back to cleanup the LZ and our path out so it would look like no helicopters had ever been there.

Before my team moved we sent the short code that we are safely down at the primary LZ. We then moved away from the LZ, clearing up our tracks as we went along. About 20 meters away we did another Stop, Look, and Listen, the second of many that night. With Gus and Johnny swapping point using the night vision gear, even with our frequent stops and a zigzag route, it only took us about three hours to reach the hilltop position for the VHF Omnidirectional Radio Range, or what we called VOR. We sent the code that we were in position, set up the southeast VOR site, and assumed a defensive stance to wait until just before 5 to turn on and test the VOR. At five minutes to 5 we turned on the VOR and radioed the current CAP on duty to check if the VOR was performing as planned. They acknowledged, so we used two of our claymores to set booby traps to protect the approaches to the VOR and started to our extraction LZ. We were there in about an hour and waited for the strike to come.

First through where the Wild Weasels taking out the radar controlled anti-aircraft defenses. Followed by the F-105s, from our position we could not see the hits but we sure could hear the explosions. Following the F-105s were some of the new F-111s, judging by how the ground shook even as far away as we were, the ordinance they used must have been the two 750 pound bombs that they could hold in their bomb bays.

As the bombs were doing their business, the radio announced that the HH-3E would be at our extraction point in minutes. We popped yellow smoke and soon the HH-3E's open rear ramp was a welcome sight as we literally ran right into the back of the helicopter. As soon as we were aboard one of the crewman handed me a headset. The pilot told me that one of the F-111s was having mechanical issues and was going down and we were on our way to pick up the crew.

The F-111 was brand new and had a unique feature of a detachable cockpit module. In emergencies, the crew remained in the cockpit and explosives detached the cockpit module from the aircraft. The whole module could then descend by parachute. The helicopter pilot informed me that we were to pick up the crew and blow-up anything that remained of the aircraft, or the crew module, into pieces so small they couldn't be picked up with tweezers.

We went for the cockpit module first, a parachute was exposed as it draped over some smaller tree tops so it was very easy to find. The problem was no radio contact had been received from the crew on the ground so we had to go in to get them. There was a suitable LZ just 20 meters from the module so getting in and out should be easy. The plan was my team would exit and the helicopter would lift to provide fire support. The HH-3E hovered and my team jumped out running directly to the module without taking the normal procedures we would use for a clandestine insertion, time was of the essence. The NVA had to know that a plane went down and were sure to be on their way. A helicopter gunship arrived and proceeded to spray 7.62×51mm caliber insecticide along likely approaches to the opposite side of the LZ we used just to keep the cockroaches away.

We popped the openings of the escape module and removed the unconscious crew. From the look of the module's position it must have hit a few trees on the way in and shaken up the crew. Jim and Gus each dragged a crew member out; I assisted the guys getting their charges into a fireman's carry position. Jim and Gus carried the crew back to the LZ while I ran along to cover them. Johnny remained behind to set some C4 to destroy the module. The HH-3E came back down and by the time we got the crewmen in to the helicopter, Johnny came running to the LZ like the hounds of hell were on his tail. His momentum was so fast that he couldn't stop until he hit the forward wall of the bay. From there he yelled NVA were approaching the module.

The helicopter quickly took off, with its crew passing Johnny's warning to the pilots and the gunship that company was coming. The ramp was still open as we lifted off and we could see the flash as the C4 blew-up the module. As we gained altitude you could hear small arms fire striking the sides of the thankfully armored HH-3E.

The HH-3E pilot passed word back to us through the crew-chief that the F-105s were going to take care of destroying the body of the F-111 and that there was not enough of the crew module left to waste a missile on. The F-111 crew members were in the care of a medically trained HH-3E crewman so we sat back and enjoyed the trip back to Da Nang. After a quick stop to drop the now conscious and very grateful F-111 crew at the hospital landing pad we landed back at the helicopter staging area.

Waiting when we landed was Ron, his team, and the alternates. The ten of us jumped into a truck that took us to the flight operations building where a C130 was available to take us back to Clark. During the flight back Ron told me that their mission ran as smooth as silk and they hadn't see any traces of the enemy at all. I think everyone of us slept like babies on the flight back.

At Clark waiting for us standing by the side of two M715 cargo/troop carriers were Ducky and Captain Cummings. After a lot of handshaking and backslapping, we loaded up and drove straight to our compound. We dumped our gear in the equipment shed and entered into the 6922nd Operation Building to get back to our secure Operations Center. We were filthy-dirty in sweat soaked camouflage fatigues and with our faces still covered in grease paint. That caused a few of the ditty-boppers taking code to miss a character or two as we walked past.

The second the door to our Operations Center closed Captain Cummings started to tell us the radio chatter about the strike. We would know for sure when we got Damage Assessment photographs tomorrow, but according to the pilots the strike was a big success, the bridge was badly damaged. Even with 12 different groups of aircraft coming in from multiple directions, because of the aid provided by the VORs, all aircraft arrived on site and joined together to perform a coordinated strike. The only loss was the F-111, but at this point they think that was due to a mechanical failure of the horizontal stabilizer, a known issue they had been fighting since that aircraft became operational in Vietnam. He also told us that we received a big thank you from the F-111 crew and that they were fine and had just had their bell rung due to impact of the module bouncing through the trees before hitting the ground.

General McConnell must have followed the progress of the mission from back in D.C. because a few minutes later we got a "Well Done" radio message from him, shortly followed by another from the MACV Air Staff.

For the next two hours the teams went through the SOP post-operation debriefing session. The team members each went through in detail what they thought went well and what didn't. After the debriefing I gave them the next two days off. Unfortunately I had a lot still to do so I didn't get to join them for the unwind festivities at the Little Brown Jug that night.

* * *

Using the feedback from Operation Sunny Virgin, Operation White Snow planning was finalized and the very next week it was activated. The strike was a success but this operation did not go quite as well as the first. One of the VORs went silent just as the attack flight packages passed the unit. It was no longer needed at that point, but the shutdown itself generated a lot of concern. The VOR that went offline was the one placed by Captain Cummings' team. Captain Cummings, backed up by his team, reported that they thought they had heard one of their claymore booby-traps go off. Since the strikes were passing over their location at that time, the sound of the jets made the report of the claymore difficult to hear. We assumed that the NVA had discovered the site and shut down the VOR, the claymore going off could have been an indicator that enemy personnel had entered the area. It also raised concern that the NVA were aware of us using the VORs and that they may begin to actively search the radio waves for other VORs. Two successful operations down, one to go.

Operation Igloo Home was not successful and the price was far too high. Given the feedback of the possible disabling of a VOR by the NVA it was decided that the VOR would not be activated until much closer to actual strike time and that the team would remain to guard the VOR until the strikes cleared that location. They were then to destroy the VOR with a timed explosive before leaving. Also since one of those locations actually had line of sight to the target, that team would remain on site and provide visual Bomb Damage Assessment before being picked up.

Things got a little screwed up early and it only got worse as time went on. One of the air strike packages was late leaving and was way behind schedule simply because a truck had broken down on the runway. MSgt Briede's team VOR was activated at the scheduled time and as the packages flew over it his team extracted with no issues but Born's teams had the VOR that required them to stick around and do BDA. With the late strike package and waiting around for them to perform their strike, the North Vietnamese Army had time to send troops to the VOR location and managed to get there before the team extracted. The HH-3E 'Jolly Green Giant' and the gunship were just getting to the extraction site as the NVA hit the team at the LZ. According to the report from the HH-3E and confirmed by the gunship, the team was overrun by the NVA in company strength, well over 120 had been trucked into the area and deployed against our 4 guys. The HH-3E broke off the rescue attempt when the pilot was wounded and the co-pilot saw all four of the team members were down with NVA by their bodies. The report from the FAC aircraft that controlled the fighters in the strike sent in against the NVA company that got our guys said that between the gunship and the fighter strikes, they were all but wiped out and all their vehicles destroyed.

What a waste, aerial BDA photographs showed the ammunition depot that was the target of the strike only suffered minor damage and there were no secondary explosions to indicate successful detonation of stored munitions. If that one package had not been late our guys should have been able to get out in time.

* * *

May 14, 2018
Ferry between Santorini and Crete

When George finished the story of our first official operations in Vietnam the group fell totally quiet except for the background ferry noises. The men were thinking of losing a friend and the girls thinking how something so little as a truck breaking down could have cost the lives of their husbands.

The subdued atmosphere from the ferry trip continued until the end of the evening meal when the raki was being poured. That's when Harold muttered, "It never happened." He then loudly continued, "Have I ever told you guys the story about when we were having a party on Malia beach and the bus load of all female English college student tourists showed up." As Harold continued to spin the tale the mood livened until everyone was once again laughing and kidding around.

CHAPTER 9
May 15, 2018
Fodele, Crete

Today's road trip took the group to Fodele via the village Dafnes where the Winery Douloufakis is located. After a short tour of the Winery the group went to the tasting room and sampled some excellent wines. The wines ranged from the dry Dafnios White to a super sweet Helios red. By the time the tasting was over the group all had their favorites. Kathy loved the Femina white and bought a case to take back. It was strange that most of the men preferred the sweet Helios dessert wine. When it was time to check out the group was totally amazed by the prices. The bottles ranged from three Euros to eight Euros for all but one of the wines. The most expensive was the Helios which had to age in the cask for ten years before it could be bottled, and that was only thirteen Euros.

As they were walking back to the bus, some not as straight as others, Harold, loaded down with two 12-bottle boxes of wine commented, "We better drink a lot of wine the next few days because there is no way I'll be able to get all of this into our suitcases.

Joan replied, "I guess I will just have to go shopping for more suitcases later this week."

When Harold began groaning loudly, and Ron asked, "Are those boxes too heavy for an old man like you? Or are you groaning because your wallet is so much lighter?"

Harold's response was just a much louder moan.

The group then went on to Fodele which was famous because it was the home of the Greek painter Δομήνικος Θεοτοκόπουλος (Doménikos Theotokópoulos), better known as El Greco. They visited the El Greco House and Museum and the nearby 11th century Church of the Annunciation of the Virgin Mary. From there they walked back to the village proper and visited a small taverna that had a sitting area along the bank of the stream that runs through the center of the small town.

As they sat down the owner of the taverna came running out and greeting the General like he was his long lost brother. Grinning like the Cheshire Cat he said, "Colonel Straight, do you remember me? I use to work on the base."

The General responded, "Sure, I remember you, Geórgios. How are you?"

The power of the General's memory amazed all the reunion attendees. You would expect that an employee on the base would remember the base commander, but you would not expect him to remember the name of one of well over a hundred civilian employees that had worked there, especially over 40 years later, but he did. When the General explained to Geórgios that we had all been stationed on the base and were here on Crete for a reunion Geórgios' grin got even bigger. He shook everyone's hand and dashed back into his taverna and came back with a tray containing a lot of small glasses and two large unmarked bottles of what else but ... raki. He explained that this was his home-made raki and he wanted to give everyone some to celebrate our reunion.

After several toasts to the reunion he sped back into his business and returned in about 15 minutes with eight different people each carrying two plates of different appetizers. As each person placed the plates on the tables he introduced each of the servers as members of his family. Following the family introductions Geórgios proudly started telling any of his fellow Fodele residents who walked by or even came close to the taverna that we were his "American family."

Between the wine tasting and the raki toasts everyone was feeling fairly mellow. The group was enjoying the appetizers while the speakers in the taverna's sitting area were softly playing Greek Bouzouki instrumental music but then the music shifted to American 60's and 70's hits. After a few songs the speakers began to play Sonny and Cher's "I Got You Babe" causing Mary to remember yesterday's conversation and say, "Poor Sonny died in North Vietnam, what ever happened to Cher, I mean Cheryl Borns?"

The General responded, "We had to stick with our cover story, and since we didn't have the body, we had to notify her that Steve had died when his plane crashed into the sea off the coast of the Philippines. I later learned that she had remarried and died 5 years ago of breast cancer."

Mary continued, "How sad. Did you contact her, Bill?"

Wild Bill replied, "Sadly, no. Two things got in the way of doing what I should have done. The first thing is that I am ashamed to say, after losing six friends out of forty-six that officially became Detachment 11 at Clark, most of us hardened ourselves with an 'It Never Happened' attitude. After a brief inebriated drowning of sorrows, the fallen were locked away in our memories and kept out of our, shall I say, 'active' minds. Secondly we were doing a lot of training for a new role we were going to start and we began spending more time in Vietnam. Let me tell you about what happened after those first missions."

* * *

November 1968 ~ Laos
As told by Wild Bill O'Rourke

After the experience gained during those first three operations we changed things up a little. We setup a forward command post at Da Nang Air Base. Operational planning was still done at Clark but things sometimes got a little too hectic to have everyone in the Philippines instead of already in Vietnam. Five teams were moved to Vietnam. One team was always on duty in the forward command post and the others on rotating shifts or standing by to deploy on a one hour notice. The other five teams staying in the Philippine Islands would train but one always remained on duty in the Command Center. Every two weeks the five teams at Clark would board a plane and swap the duty with the five teams at Da Nang. So thankfully most of us got to spend lots of time out of the field. But we were still training in the Philippines and only sometimes enjoying life in our off hours. But I must say compared to the Marines and Army grunts in Vietnam, we were living a life of ease.

We were getting an operation about once a week for most of September and October. The good thing was we got an equipment upgrade to the VOR. We could now set a timer which would not start the navigation system until we were safely away from the site and the same timer would trigger a demolition charge to destroy the VOR two hours after activation. We still switched it on as a test after setup, but only for a few seconds. Just long enough to get a confirmation it was working, but not long enough for the NVA to get a fix on the location and send troops. The other thing we changed was if we were required to do Bomb Damage Assessment we would send a third team that did the BDA from a site that was not near the VOR units. Using these new techniques we didn't suffer any more casualties.

We were getting great feedback on the job we were doing from General McConnell and the Air Force command structure in Washington, as well as from Military Assistance Command, Vietnam. But in the beginning of November the President called a moratorium on bombing in North Vietnam and the air war shifted to supply interdiction along the Ho Chi Minh Trail in Laos. Now our task shifted from setting VOR equipment with large-scale air operations to target acquisition, smaller scale air operations, and BDA reports. As a result of the task shift, we went from being inserted one night and extracted the next day to spending up to a week at a time in the field and a heck of a lot more moving around where we weren't supposed to be.

Before I go any further in telling you about our time in Laos, I don't want you to think that the Ho Chi Minh Trail was just one big road. It was not even one route but a tangled mess of trails, roads, paths, and waterways that comprised a whole network of transportation routes from North Vietnam through eastern and southern Laos. Some paths entered South Vietnam from Laos and others continued through Cambodia before entering Nam. There were many divergent paths exiting the main trail network going into South Vietnam along the entire length of the Trail. The Trail made expert use of multiple techniques to hide itself from the air. It used camouflage, underwater bridges, and the thick overhead jungle canopy to stay hidden. It would be our job to find the parts that were actively in use so that our air strikes would do more than just tear up the open countryside.

The Standard Operating Procedure would be to insert two teams at different locations in the same area, close enough to support each other if needed. We would insert in the late afternoon, move to a night hidey-hole, and come daylight we would find an ideal spot for an Observation Post. We would stay in the OP through the night. The job was to see if we could find the parts of the trail the NVA were using to move men and materiel into South Vietnam, and then call in airstrikes.

* * *

My team and Ron's team had the honor of the first trip into Laos. We were to set up on opposite sides of a ridge line north of a small village called Ban Co Bai. One team would watch along the Baanghiang River and the other team the valley on the opposite side of the ridge line. Ban Co Bai was just west-northwest of Dong Ha, which was the northernmost town in South Vietnam.

At that time my team was composed of three guys we haven't talked about yet. There was Barry Britain, a slow talking, lanky, brown haired guy from western Kentucky. Barry was my point man. On drag was a short, skinny, African-American, Leroy White who was from Chicago and our Blooper, the M79 Grenade Launcher, was Don Reinkens, a blond haired, blue-eyed, second-generation German from New York City who still had a little German accent to his English. Since both sides of that ridge line were blasted by a Rolling Thunder strike a few months previously, we were going to use LZs that were created or enlarged by bomb craters. Depending on what kind of traffic we saw in that area we could call in anything from something as small as a single gunship up to a big, multiple B-52 bombers, Arc Light strike.

Due to a heavy rainstorm, we almost had to abort our first Laos operation but under very marginal conditions we managed to insert just before dark. The rain was a bit of an aid since it covered our tracks as both teams moved up the ridge. We found a spot to do a Stop, Look and Listen and my team set up an ambush in the event we were being followed while Ron's team continued on up and over the ridge line. We took extra care to cover our trail as we moved away from our common path and proceeded another half kilometer to find a good hidey-hole for the night.

The next morning we found a good Observation Post with an excellent view of almost a full kilometer stretch of the Baanghiang River and a good view of the whole valley. We were doing sweeps utilizing our high power binoculars when Barry caught some movement by the river. It looked to be about a dozen troops carrying shovels in their hands with their rifles slung over their backs. They were coming out of a trail behind a small hill that led down to a tiny rice paddy close to the river.

Upon further inspection, I noticed that there was another rice paddy on the other side of the river about 100 meters upstream on the east side of the river. The NVA moved into the stream by the rice paddy and waded upstream with the water only coming up to mid-calf. Suddenly the water level jumped to waist level on the guy leading the group, they then started digging along the edge of the stream and putting the fill they extracted into a hole they just discovered the hard way. We had apparently found a unit that was repairing an underwater bridge crossing the river going from one rice paddy to the other.

I decided to wait to see if the bridge was going to get some use rather than calling in a strike on just a dozen workers. They worked on filling in the erosion the river had caused to their bridge for about eight hours. Before they left they placed a series of sticks with short white pieces of cloth on them that created markers for a somewhat curved lightning strike shaped path of the underwater bridge. By the time they were gone it was almost sundown.

The trail markers they placed would indicate that they expected traffic tonight so we did not move from our OP and planned on spending the night to watch for the traffic. During the day as they worked we had radioed in the coordinates of the bridge and the trails leading up to and away from the two rice patties. We also arranged for an air strike team to be on standby should we get some trail traffic that night. An hour after we pre-registered our request for a strike team, we received confirmation that there would be a FAC aircraft, two AC-130 gunships out of Ubon Air Force Base, and some F4's flying support on standby orbiting close by our area if we saw enough traffic on the trail to justify their use.

The AC-130 Spectre also known as the 'Super Spooky' was a modified version of the C-130 cargo aircraft equipped with four 7.62mm MXU-470 miniguns, four 20mm GE M-61 Gatling guns, night optical devices, infrared sensors, and a fire-control computer. It was just the aircraft to take out a convoy of trucks moving down a trail after dark. The infrared sensor should even be able to pick out the heat signatures of hot truck motors under a thin canopy of trees. So they would be able to track vehicles further along the trail, beyond where we would be able to see them from our OP.

About 2030 hours we begin to see brief flashes of light moving through gaps in the cover toward the underwater bridge we had targeted. We radioed in to tell the FAC that vehicles were approaching. We got word back that they were three minutes out and waiting for word to strike when the first truck had crossed the bridge. Our patience paid off, a few minutes later the first truck pulled into the rice paddy up to the edge of the bridge and stopped. Two men got out of the back of the tree branch camouflaged truck and proceeded to walk the length of the bridge side by side about a truck's width apart. They were double checking that the trucks would be able to cross.

They waved a flashlight to the lead truck and waited for it on the other side of the river. When the first of the trucks were just about across the river we called for the FAC to start the strike. The AC-130 arrived on site just as the first truck was passing the edge of the rice patty into the tree line on the opposite bank of the river. Three other trucks were still visible in the river crossing. The AC-130 began a banking turn so that the guns on the side of the plane pointed down at the trail and hell rained from the sky down onto the truck convoy. Something that looked like a slightly curved laser beam shot from the side of the plane to the lead truck that just exited the rice paddy. The laser beam effect was caused by the tracer rounds leaving the miniguns at such a high rate of fire that it seemed like a continuous line of light. The tree tops above the first truck exploded into the air as the 2,000 to 6,000 rounds per minute leaving each minigun ripped through the foliage.

One AC-130 started at the front of the convoy moving toward the rear. Meanwhile, the other AC-130 approaching from the opposite direction must have utilized their infrared gear to locate the rear of the convoy and moved forward. When the rounds began striking the water of the river it appeared as if the water was boiling. Trucks were almost disintegrating with the thousands of rounds tearing through them. There were several secondary explosions as the munitions that some trucks were carrying exploded in fireballs.

Nothing could have remained alive down there as each of the two AC-130s passed over the convoy twice while raining fire from the sky. We only had four trucks in our range of view but judging from the secondary explosions further back, the trail must have been made up of 10 to 15 trucks in the convoy.

The flight of planes left the area but the normal quiet of the night did not return as the trucks below crackled and burned. There were a few pops as rounds of ammunition carried by the drivers and escorts exploded in the fires. In radio communication with the departing FAC we were informed that the infrared systems indicated that there were actually 14 trucks and all were destroyed.

About two in the morning we saw flashlight beams coming down the trail from the same direction as the original repair workers. Cautiously two men came into view and proceeded to walk the route of destruction that had once been a convoy of trucks. Those two were followed by about ten more that moved to the end of the ill-fated convoy and began searching the remnants for survivors or anything still of value. We saw them stack about ten bodies or it could have been parts of bodies along the river bank, they had also gathered a few small piles of salvage. There wasn't much left of the drivers or the fourteen trucks in the convoy that was still usable.

I was tempted to call in another strike to get the trash pickers but I wanted to see if I could follow their flashlight beams back to where they came from. We kept a close watch as they departed. Every now and then I caught a quick flash of light in my night vision gear, just enough to trace the trail to the next ridge over about 200 meters south of our position. I marked the trail route on my map and waited for something else to happen. However the rest of the night was extremely quiet.

The next morning some Laotians with two teams of water buffalo and eight NVA soldiers arrived and they began to haul the wreckage from what remained of the trucks off and away from the trail. I let them work in peace hoping that they would think that the convoy just was unlucky and was spotted in the crossing by a roving air patrol rather than think there was a recon-team about. There was not any traffic on the trail for the remainder of the day. But the next morning proved that my hope had been false.

The next morning three NVA came into the rice field by the underwater bridge. Two took covering positions at the edge of the field and one stood right at the water's edge and began to scan the hill on both sides of the river with his binoculars. He was very patiently looking for us while we watched him. He was there about 30 minutes before he walked back up the trail. His security team quickly following him.

We then started seeing movement in several areas of the valley. It was obvious that there were a heck of a lot of people looking for us. Around noon several teams began crossing to the side of the river we were on. I radioed in that they were looking for us and warned Ron that we were being hunted. We were told to hunker down until we were sure they were headed our way and if so, to move to the other side of the ridge line for evacuation. Around four in the evening we heard some movement on the uphill side of our position. They were moving along the ridge line above us between our two teams.

We trusted our trail covering skills, our concealed location, and hoped the size of the area they were covering with only a limited number of troops to be our safety edge but luck was against us.

Leroy had the uphill sector as his area to cover. He had put the suppressor on his Mk22 pistol and had that lying next to him in easy reach. The NVA coming off the ridge line were making more noise than we made the first day of training. Crashing through the undergrowth and talking to each other. They were working in teams of two and depending on the terrain about 50 or 60 meters between each team, far enough apart that we could easily escape attention. Leroy got our attention, put down his CAR-

15 and picked up his Mk22. Two NVA wearing their green uniforms and pith helmets carrying their AK-47s at port arms walked right into our area. Leroy fired two quick shots at one and as he started to fall put two bullets into the other NVA. Both were instantly killed and their bodies falling down caused more noise than the shots from the silenced Mk22. If they had just been ten meters over they never would have seen us and they would have lived another day.

Everyone's ears were straining to hear if more NVA were approaching. We could hear them moving downhill on both sides of us but nothing else from the direction the pair had come from. We had packed up everything earlier when we saw them begin their hunt so I figured now would be a good time to move back behind their search line using the hole left by the two dead searchers. We quickly moved out using the path through the underbrush already cleared for us by the dead pair. We had to get as far away as we could before the others missed their friends. We had about eleven minutes before we heard the shouting when someone found the bodies. A single shot followed by another shot five seconds later echoed through the valley, it was more than likely their signal that we had been found. Now knowing where we were, they would be converging on our location as fast as they could get here.

We rapidly move up the ridge with me following closely behind Don Reinkens, as we were moving I frantically worked the radio calling for an emergency extradition from an LZ just a little downhill from Ron's location. We got an acknowledgment saying an extraction helicopter and some gunships were on the way to our position. Ron said he would set up an ambush point just outside of the LZ, they would stay there until we joined them to await the helicopter and air support before going the last few meters into the LZ.

Unfortunately our streak of bad luck continued. As we approached a small trail that ran along the ridge line we did a quick stop to be sure the trail was empty before we crossed. Not seeing anyone on the trail, we started across. Just as our last man entered the trail opening, rounding a bend in the trail was a squad of NVA. A split second later and they would not have seen him. Their point man was good and sprayed the trail with his AK-47 on full auto just as our drag, Leroy was exiting the trail. Leroy caught a round in his leg and went down. We opened fire to check their advance and Don blooped an M79 grenade right into the area where the NVA squad took cover. That held them in check for a while.

By now Barry had dragged Leroy into cover and hoisted the smaller Leroy onto his back in the fireman's carry. I continued to lay down fire while Barry hustled down the reverse slope toting the skinny Leroy like he was weightless. I ran through a 20 round clip in a heartbeat. I jumped to my feet and started to follow Barry as I reloaded. I knew that Don would cover me as I leapfrogged back a few meters to where I would in turn cover him as he withdrew. Don again managed to put an M79 right in the middle of our pursuers. How he got the shot through all the limbs of the trees to put it right on target I never knew, but he was darn good with the Blooper. I guess all the hours and thousands of rounds of ammunition we had burned through in training was paying off.

The last grenade gave us another short reprieve and allowed us to break contact with that group. But they say bad luck always runs in threes, we were well past number three and bad luck was still raising its ugly head. We came under intense fire from our flank. Apparently another group had been coming down the trail from the opposite direction as the first group. They left the trail and moved down hill to cut us off. Their plan or luck worked almost perfectly. As they opened up on us, Don and Barry both took multiple hits. The impact of the rounds pushed Don against a tree and his body jerked as round after round slammed into his already dead body. Barry, who was carrying Leroy, fell when he was hit; his forward momentum caused Leroy to sail through the air landing a few feet downhill.

A quick glance at what was left of his head told me that Barry was dead also. I was lucky that Don had not fallen but remained propped against that tree. Because he was still upright, his body was still drawing all the fire. I ran, dropping my CAR-15, scooped up Leroy in my arms, and ran as fast as I could toward Ron's team and the LZ. I zigzagged down the thin trail running as I had never run before. But I could hear the NVA were gaining on me. I remember leaping over a claymore pointing right up the trail I was running down. Two steps later something tripped me, sending me down to the ground as shots from the closely pursuing NVA started to strip the leaves from trees all around me.

I saw it was Harold that had tripped me as I passed over his ambush position. The NVA thinking they were chasing one man encumbered by carrying another were chasing me at full speed and had bunched up along the trail slowed to the speed of their leading man. A large number of them were exposed on the trail when Harold fired the claymore. Hundreds of ball bearing projectiles smashed into the tightly packed pursuers and both sides of the trail. The firing of the claymore was the signal for the rest of Ron's team to open fire. They mowed down the remaining NVA that were in their sights. The others quickly fell back and took cover before they started returning fire.

I could hear the helicopters approaching the LZ. Ron and his team had taken up positions along the ground across the trail just at the edge of the LZ. We were taking fire for several minutes when the gunships opened up on the NVA. One gunship was packing a minigun and it began to pour a stream of lead into the NVA that were firing on us. The other gunship worked its guns in the area along the ridge line trail and back towards us.

I picked Leroy back up and started moving towards the LZ where the helicopter was now waiting. I put Leroy on board then climbed in myself. My heart was still pounding as loud as timpani drums playing the "1812 Overture." And no matter how hard I tried to suck in air, it just didn't seem like enough. I finally pulled my Mk22 to assist the door gunner of the helicopter cover Ron's team's fallback to the LZ. As I looked back I saw Ron running like Dennis Weaver playing Chester on the old TV show "Gunsmoke" hobbling along with one leg rather stiff. Harold and Chief were dragging Dick Duggens between them as they ran to the helicopter.

With everyone aboard we took off as the gunships continued to fire into the NVA troops that had been chasing us. The second we were in the air I turned my attention to giving first aid to Leroy. However he was already dead. Apparently he had caught another round in his side when we were hit on our flank. I had been carrying a dead man my entire run to the LZ. Harold was caring for Ron's wound, while Chief worked on Dick. Dick had a chest wound that was starting to bubble. I moved to Dick's head and talked to him while Chief did what he could to keep pressure on his chest.

After I had told Dick over and over again that he was going to be OK, and that he was going to have to hang in there for just a while longer, we landed at the medical emergency landing pad at the Dong Ha Combat Base and Airfield called Camp Spillman. There were medics and an ambulance waiting to whisk our wounded off to the base medical facilities. While they were loading Dick, Ron with Harold's help had limped to the ambulance and he rode off with Dick. Harold, Chief and I walked back to the helicopter to thank the crew and tell them we would stick around here to stay with our buddies and find our own way back to Da Nang.

I got on the radio with Major Straight who was at the command post in Da Nang, while Chief and Harold helped a couple of marines put Leroy into a body bag. The major told us to keep Leroy with us and he would be on a C130 to come get us in an hour or two.

Harold and Chief stayed with Leroy and our gear while I went in to check on Ron and Dick. Ron had already been sewn up and was lying on his side in a bed with a silly look on his face as I entered the ward he was in. They had given him a shot for the pain but he was still functioning enough to tell me the doctor said it was a minor scratch that only took 10 stitches but that he would be stiff for a while. He asked about Dick but I didn't know anything since he was still in surgery.

I was sitting with Ron when Major Straight came into the ward. He talked to Ron for a little while then went to talk to the doctors to see how Dick was doing. He came back about 20 minutes later when Ron asked him about Dick he just shook his bowed head and mumbled they lost him. He asked Ron if he needed to stay there or was he ready to travel. Ron said, "Let's get the hell out of hell."

* * *

About two hours later, Ron with a fresh shot of joy juice for the plane ride, was checked out of the hospital and we loaded on a C130 with the two body bags and what was left of our two teams. While we were flying back Major Straight was in communication with the commander of the marine detachment at Camp Spillman. He arranged for a marine reconnaissance force to go back and see if they could recover Don's and Barry's bodies. We later learn that they flew in a recon the very next day but the bodies were gone when they arrived.

When we arrived at Clark the first thing we did was get Ron checked into the base hospital and after we got cleaned up, we headed to the compound for a debriefing session. About halfway through the debriefing session what had happened finally got through my thick head. I had to quickly grab a nearby trash can and began to throw-up all of the food that I had eaten during the last two years. The smell got to Chief and he too started shaking and losing his lunch into a different trash can. That put an end to the debriefing session. The major said we could finish this up tomorrow and had a couple of the guys that were hanging around the Operations Center take us back to the barracks. He also slipped Uncle Bob, who had been there during the debriefing, a couple of bucks telling him to go buy a case or two of beer and to keep us busy for a while.

The next morning we all went to see Ron. He was doing fine and the doctors said he would be discharged tomorrow after they changed his bandage. When we went back to the compound, the Major was locked in his office on the phone to Washington. He stuck his head out long enough to tell us we would have our full official debrief after Ron was discharged from the Hospital.

* * *

May 15, 2018
Fodele, Crete

At this point Wild Bill fell silent. Kathy looked at Ron with both anger and concern in her eyes. But the anger was the stronger of the emotions at the time and she slapped him quite hard on his arm. "You never, ever told me you were wounded! You said that scar was from a motorcycle accident!"
Ron took the slap and just shook his head. With a huge grin on his face Harold poked Ron on his other arm and said, "Come on, Ron. Tell everybody where you were shot!"

Ron pursed his lips, still shaking his head while he gave Harold a look that could peel the paint off of a battleship. Laughing now, Harold wouldn't let it go. "Tell everybody where you were shot."

"OK, dammit! During the fight I was lying on the ground trying to get my body as low as it could possibly be. But you know even as skinny as I was back then, there is one part of the body that sticks up higher than the rest when you are lying on your belly."

Laughing to beat the band, Harold asked, "What was sticking up that got shot?"

Seeing Harold laugh, Ron could no longer hold in his laughter either. "OK, OK, you bastard. Attention everybody, I got shot in the ass!"

Seeing Ron's grinning embarrassment and Harold's obvious mirth everyone else, including Kathy started laughing with them. Harold was laughing so hard he was crying. Everyone had just about regained their composure, when Ron struck back by speaking loud enough for everyone to hear. "Harold, I don't remember if I ever thanked you for giving me first aid that day. After all, it was your soft, warm hand firmly pressing onto my bottom that stopped the initial bleeding and made me all better."

Then making exaggerated air kisses towards Harold, he said, "You know now that you mentioned it, my old wound is starting to hurt a little. Do you want to put your soft, warm hands back to work and make me all better again?"

That started everyone laughing once again. Ron and Harold continued picking on each other for the remainder of the ride back to the hotel and for the rest of the night.

CHAPTER 10
May 16, 2018
Hersonissos, Crete

There was a barbecue scheduled on the reunion agenda tonight at the General's home, but nothing scheduled for during the day. At a late breakfast the gang decided that today would be another lazy beach day. Harold immediately picked up where he left off last night by picking on Ron.

"Perhaps we should walk to the beach on the west side of the breakwater. There is a nude beach there and I know everyone wants to see Ron's butt scar."

Wild Bill decided to gang up on Ron too. "No thanks, who would want to see an old fat man like him nude. Yuck! Now maybe if we could talk the girls into joining the rest of the young *turistas* walking around the nude beach area, it might be worth the trip."

That earned Bill a dirty look from Mary. "No way boys, this old schoolmarm is going to keep some of her clothing on. But I am not opposed to going up to change into my modest swimming attire and reconvening this meeting on the beach."

The group commandeered their normal cluster of chairs; the ladies were in a row of chaise lounges while the five guys sat in chairs around a table under the thatched roof of a beach hut. A few minutes later Georgios their ever-present Greek waiter arrived and asked them what they would like to drink.

When Georgios asked Harold what he wanted, Harold was a little distracted because his eyes were following a young oriental lady walking along the water's edge. He just mumbled, "*Kor beer nueng keaw krap.*"

Georgios being a very good waiter at a large international hotel could take orders in, Greek, English, German, Dutch and Russian, but this phrase was beyond his comprehension. "Excuse me, please, Mister Harold. What did you say?"

The young distraction was far enough down the beach that Harold's attention had returned and he thought back to what he had actually said. "Oops. Sorry, Georgios. I asked for a beer, but I think I asked in Thai instead of English."

The General was as sharp eyed as Harold and softly said, "She did look like she was from Thailand, didn't she, Harold?"

Joan Vinter said, "I never heard you speak in Thai before. I guess that young lady in her red, skimpy bikini changed your blood flow enough to wake up some dormant brain cells. When were you in Thailand, Harold?"

"That would have been around Christmas, 1968. Would you like to hear the story?"

* * *

December 1968 ~ Da Nang, South Vietnam
As told by Harold Vinter

We were spending lots of time in Laos fighting what we called the "Truck Body Count War." After the debacle of the first operation our luck changed for a while. For six weeks we always had two teams operating in Laos, with operations ranging from three days to seven days. It was pretty much the same - hide and watch. We must have called in over 75 air strikes during that time, the majority involved trucks. We did have two big finds, one was an infiltration route Way Station, and the other was a transfer station.

The North Vietnamese Army troops, for the most part, walked along the Ho Chi Minh Trail all the way from their recruiting bases in the north to their areas of operation in South Vietnam. They would average about 10 to 20 miles a day, and at the end of a day's march they would spend the night and rest in what we called Way Stations. The Way Stations had everything the moving units would need; barracks, kitchens, first aid stations, and even some permanently stationed troops to maintain the trails and support the units moving through. It was MSgt. Ray Briede's team that found a large Way Station which contained two full companies of in transit troops and over 50 full time support personnel. That night the Way Station was blasted by a whole flight of B52 bombers. After the strike the team heard lots of commotion down in the Way Station but when dawn came and Ray did the BDA, there was not a building standing and no one to be seen.

The other big find was a transfer station. A transfer station was a terminus point for truck traffic where the trucks were unloaded and the supplies transferred to bicycles or human porters to be carried further south. When Ducky's team found it, they were in the process of unloading seven trucks and transferring the supplies to over a hundred porters using a mixture of bicycles and backpacks. That strike was done by several flights of Navy fighters that were operating from an aircraft carrier. The Navy fighter bombers dropped a combination of High Explosives and Napalm, destroying all the trucks, most of the bicycles and a lot of human porters.

* * *

It was the week before Christmas, Dwight Dillinger's team and Ducky's team were operating in Laos. After we lost the four men during our first trip into Laos the teams had shifted around. Wild Bill had taken over Major Straight's team so the major could spend more time administering the unit and less time in the field. To keep the primary jobs distributed properly, Johnny who had been in the Major's team was now on Uncle Bob's team. Now that Ron was off injured status and back on active duty, our team was back up to full strength with the addition of Sam Talbert, our friend from basic. Our team along with Uncle Bob's team was on standby. We were lounging around the tent while Sam bitched, as usual, about eating Vietnamese food instead of the good grub the chow hall was serving. Some people have absolutely no taste. Captain Cummings ran to the tent flap yelling for us to grab our gear because we had a rescue mission.

As we loaded up, Captain Cummings gave us a quick update. "We had just gotten a radio message from our contact in the 6994th Security Squadron; one of their EC-47 aircraft has taken anti-aircraft fire while operating in an area of Laos code named Steel Tiger, northeast of Saravane. They are trying to keep it in the air as long as they can and are headed out of Laos and south toward Hue."

There were two helicopters landing on the Pad by our command post. Our team loaded on one helicopter and Uncle Bob's loaded on the other Huey. Our orders depended on whether the plane crashed or not, should the plane go down, we were to rescue the crew and destroy all the sensitive equipment on the plane, if not just return to base.

We were in the air and headed into the direction that the EC-47 would be going if they could just keep it in the air. Ron got on the intercom with the helicopter's pilot and was passing him information on the EC-47's status as he received it from Captain Cummings. A few minutes later we were notified the EC-47 had finally crash-landed and was 24 nautical miles southwest of Hue Phu Bai.

The reason our group was dispatched for this rescue mission, rather than some other unit, was because of our security clearances and the classified mission of the EC-47. The EC-47 was a World War II era DC-3 based aircraft that was modified for use by the United States Air Force Security Service. Yes, the same SIGNIT organization that our unit was associated with. The function of the EC-47 was to locate and fix the positions of low-powered enemy transmitters. It was also to gather the intelligence from these transmissions and make it available to the local command authority for immediate action. The plane had ARDF, Airborne Radio Direction Finding, equipment. It also had a sophisticated computer that could compensate for the Doppler effect of a moving airplane and still pinpoint the location of a transmitter. Since low-powered transmitters are practically line-of-sight broadcasts, their transmissions were not strong enough for antennas like the AN/FLR-9 elephant cage antenna we had at Clark, in the Philippines, to pick up, so the EC-47s would fly around looking for weak radio signals.

During the flight Ron communicated with Uncle Bob and discussed the plan for both teams to secure the Landing Zone. Once the LZ was secure, Johnny, who had brought extra C4 explosives, would detach from Bob's team and go with Ron's team to the crash site. He would rig the EC-47 with explosives to ensure all the classified equipment would be destroyed while Ron's team would retrieve the crew and escort them to the LZ.

The rice patty being used as the LZ was large enough for both helicopters to approach at the same time. The location was well placed since it was only about 200 meters from the crash site. Both teams exited their helicopters with Bob's team heading for the far side of the paddy and Ron's team heading for the side of the paddy closest to the downed plane. Rather than remaining sitting targets the helicopters lifted off and remained close enough for their door gunners to provide some air support.

With the LZ secure, Bob's team spread out enough so that just three of them could cover the parameter. Our team plus Johnny moved with all haste to the actual crash site. We were just steps away from the rice paddy LZ when we heard the roar of low flying jets screaming over our location. Great, we now had air support should we need it.

As we neared the crash site we could hear people moving around and talking. So rather than just dashing in and getting shot by our own people we took cover and Ron shouted, "Hold your fire, we are USAFSS fellow ditty-boppers here to take you home. OK?"

Still unsure of us there was a call from the plane, "Say the password and advance to be recognized."

Ron got off the ground, raised his hands, and started slowly moving forward saying, "Hell, nobody told us your password but, there is no gravity, Keesler sucks!" This caused a laugh to be heard from someone at the crash site and he could be heard telling his fellow crew members to hold their fire. Once Ron was within arms range of the crew, he started getting his back slapped and treated like a conquering hero. We found that the crew was all out of the plane and several had taken up guard positions around the plane with the rest huddled around three crew members laying on the ground. A TSgt crew member was telling a Captain that only a fellow ditty-bopper from Keesler would have known to use the term ditty-bopper and Kessler's gravity situation as a password.

Ron took a closer look at the three guys on the ground and saw that two were dead and one badly injured. Ron told a major that was a member of the operations crew that our team would set charges to destroy the equipment in the plane. The major told Ron to come with him. The major led Ron and Johnny into the plane. The major pointed to the classified equipment and picked up a dark blue B4 bag, similar to a cloth suitcase, telling Ron that it contained the classified documents for the flight. He grabbed the B4 bag and he also pointed out a large box of fliers, telling Ron to scatter those around the plane and the crash site.

The box contained a lot of psychological warfare leaflets. The cover story used should they get into trouble, like now, was that the plane had been dropping off these leaflets. The leaflet was nicely printed on two sides, one side in Vietnamese and one in Laotian which said:

PASSPORT

To: North Vietnamese Soldiers Living in Laos.

You have the opportunity to escape death and live in safety and peace. The Lao Royal Government and its people will welcome and treat you as brothers. Please show this passport to any LAO soldier or civilian.

Tong Tu Lenh,
Commander in Chief of Lao Military Forces

Ron stuffed three of them into one of his pants cargo pockets as souvenirs.

Once out of the plane Ron told the major to gather his men, take the wounded and dead and to follow Chief and Sam back to the LZ. Ron quickly scattered the leaflets around the area and joined me in a rather compressed defensive perimeter around the plane while Johnny was busy in the plane setting charges.

A few minutes later Uncle Bob radioed Ron that five healthy and two KIA had been loaded onto one of the helicopters and that the wounded crewman, two from our team and three from his were on the Hueys but they had to extract now since they were starting to take small arms fire. He told us another Huey was on the way in to pick up the three of us left behind to blow the plane.

The Forward Air Controller, FAC, flying above us gave us a heads up that a large force was close to our location and that he would try to disturb their movement long enough for us to blow the plane and get the hell out of there. The pair of F104s that had been flying above us dove to drop napalm canisters on the approaching enemy. They made two more runs expending lethal devices and firing their 20 mm cannons into the jungle between us and the men in their black pajamas. Apparently their shooting wasn't enough to totally deter the Cong headed this way. The FAC told us that our current guardian angels had run out of toys and another couple fast movers were on the way to assist. Then he gave us the bad news, the Cong would get to the LZ before the helicopter that was due to pick us up. He suggested that we blow the plane and move north away from the site toward another LZ about two kilometers away.

Johnny came out of the plane trailing a thin wire behind him. Ron spun his finger in the air and pointed north. Johnny followed Ron and me to the edge of some thick undergrowth. Johnny finger signed for us to wait so he could blow the plane. We took defensive positions with a few trees between us and the plane. Good thing too, apparently Johnny, as usual, was a little over enthusiastic with his use of C4 and when the plane blew the concussion nearly knocked the trees we were hiding behind down. One was leaning over and another badly leaning tree was the only thing stopping the first line of trees from falling on us.

Grinning like the pyrotechnic manic he is, Johnny waived for us to get the hell out of there. Before we left, we used the debris from the tree Johnny knocked down to cover our trail as we moved away from the crash site. We started moving north towards the landing zone the FAC had given us with Johnny walking point, me on drag and Ron in the middle keeping continuous contact with the FAC that was orbiting above, so that he would know exactly where we were.

We had only traveled about fifty meters when we heard more jets coming our way. The FAC warned Ron that we may want to get our heads down. Not one second after Ron had warned us to hit the ground, we were bouncing in the air from the concussions caused by the bombs hitting what was left of the plane. I guess they didn't trust Johnny's already thorough job of blasting the classified equipment because they were dropping some really big ordinance on what was left of the plane. I sure hope they managed to get a few of the nasty little bastards that were dogging our trail when they hit the plane.

We had traveled halfway to the next Landing Zone when the FAC warned us away from that one too, saying there was already Viet Cong setting up an ambush at that site. He said to standby while he scouted out another potential LZ for us. Ron flipped a mental coin and pointed to the west. I moved a few more steps up the path we had been on until I got to an area with heavy vegetation residue on the ground. I walked backwards then, using the exact depressions in the tracks I left behind thereby setting a false trail.

I fluffed up the vegetation Johnny and Ron had disturbed when they shifted direction to hide our new path. I cleaned up our trail and caught up with Ron and Johnny about ten meters further along. About fifteen minutes later the FAC came back on the air to get our position and tell us there was another LZ about five kilometers to the west-north-west of our location. We shifted direction to head to that local and had gotten about halfway when we again got word that the LZ was already covered. I was beginning to wonder if we had landed in the middle of all the black clad, pajama wearing bastards in Southeast Asia.

Ron shifted us back to the west with the FAC alternating between calling more strikes on the hornets we had stirred up and looking for a usable LZ for us. The game of fox and hound continued for the entire day. Shortly before dusk we came upon a stream where we could refill our canteens. Ron dutifully reminded us to add the Halazone Water Purification Tablets to our canteens. The original water in our canteens had been long gone an hour ago. Not thinking we would be spending the night in the bush when we grabbed our gear we only had rations for one day packed. We moved a little away from the steam and hunkered down for our evening repast. The FAC radioed that they would send a helicopter for us come first light and that since he was very low on fuel another FAC would be replacing him soon should we require help during the night.

Because we had been on standby we had just been eating Vietnamese food for the last two days, the rations we carried were nothing but cooked rice balls spiced with some veggies, and what today you would call, Huy Fong Chili Garlic Sauce. The rice balls were wrapped in leaves so that nothing we left behind, including what came out of our behinds, would be associated with Americans. We rested there about an hour and broke out the night vision equipment and continued on our westward trek.

By dawn we had covered about fifteen kilometers when we stopped to figure out where the hell we were. We ate what was left of our food and finally got a bearing on a couple of hills so we could get our approximate location. We had only a few minutes of early morning light from the eastern ski when the sky darkened with ominous black storm clouds. We got into radio contact with operations and were told that everything was grounded due to the extremely bad weather coming through. And it more than likely would be another 24 hours before anything could get to us.

To add insult to injury, the second they told us it would be another day the sky opened up. The rain was coming down like it was being pushed from a high pressure fire hose. The wind picked up to about 45 miles per hour and added to our misery. We moved towards a ridge line where we hoped we would be able to find some shelter from the storm for the day. The only good thing was that if we were having so much trouble seeing where the heck we were going, the VC wouldn't be able to see much either and that the rain would wash away any trail we would be leaving behind.

An hour or so later we reached the ridge line, before we moved higher we stopped at a now rain swollen stream to refill our canteens, then we moved up the slope looking for a little shelter. We found a spot with overhanging rocks and good thick cover all around. With the high winds and pouring rain we didn't need to do too much to cover our tracks into the hidey-hole. We radioed in our position and our plans to stay here for the day, we warned control that we were going to turn off the radio to conserve battery power but would check in every two hours and we settled in for the long wet wait.

We spent a very long miserable day and night waiting. We didn't speak out loud but used our hand code to communicate with each other. You can just guess what the conversations were about, yep, food. Ron kept signing about having a nice cold San Miguel beer and Johnny about a three inch thick, medium rare, T-bone steak. Me – I wanted some chocolate ice cream. We may not have been talking aloud but our stomachs sure were gurgling loud enough to be heard across the valley.

Come dawn, we powered up the radio and were immediately in touch with control. Captain Cummings informed us that the rest of our teams were back safe and sound at Da Nang and that the EC-47 crew was currently at Clark getting a little R&R. And he thankfully told us that there was a FAC and helicopter coming our way to pull us out.

A few minutes later the Forward Air Controller came online and told us there was a good LZ about half a kilometer from our location. We headed that way and when we were a hundred meters out the FAC said to hold where we were. He then had the gunship that accompanied our ride blast away at the LZ to be sure it was not being watched. Nothing stirred so we went to the clearing posthaste, threw a purple smoke grenade and confirmed its color with the helicopter which scooped us up and brought three very hungry guys back to Da Nang.

We were two steps into the command tent when I spotted an open box of c-rations. I was faster than the other two and had a can of peaches half opened before Ron or Johnny had even put down their weapons.

As I wolfed down the peaches, Captain Cummings told us to get cleaned up and he would take us over to one of the main base mess halls. We quickly shed our wet clothes and went off to get some hot American food. On the drive the Captain told us the major on the EC-47 crew and Major Straight have been spending a lot of time together at Clark. He told us how Major Faigon was very appreciative of how we arrived just in time to save their bacon. The point was definitely driven home by the small arms fire that was hitting their helicopter as they were lifting out of the LZ. And when he found out that you guys had been left behind so his team could escape he became, as Major Straight told me, very emotional. I have been fielding calls from Major Faigon asking about you guys ever few hours.

After a rather filling meal we headed back to the command center to join up with the rest of the teams. The eight of us and Captain Cummings were just finishing up the after action debriefing when our scrambled telephone rang. The Captain spoke on the phone for about 15 minutes and returned to the briefing and told us that the call was from Major Straight and he had some good news for us.

It seemed Major Faigon told Major Straight that his crew was about to leave for two weeks of Rest and Relaxation in Bangkok. But with them now in the Philippines, he had eight R&R chits they could not use and offered them to the eight guys that came and got them out. Cummings went on to explain that Major Straight was very happy to relieve Major Faigon of his R&R passes. So in two days we would get to leave for two weeks R&R in Bangkok.

We were all screaming and yelling so loud that they could have heard us in Hanoi. The Captain suggested that we go to the base PX and buy ourselves a couple sets of civilian clothes and a full 1505 uniform. I lamented to the captain that I hadn't brought any money with me to Vietnam and only had about $5 in MPC, that is, Military Payment Certificates, the currency used by the American military in Vietnam.

The captain excused himself for a few minutes and went to his tent. He came back with $2,500 in MPC. He told us $100 was for our uniforms and personal supplies that had been lost, wink, wink, and $300 for each of us. He told in detail that the $300 was a loan from the unit and that we would need to replay it over the next few paydays. He went on to explain how the hotel room expenses would be covered by some chits we would receive tomorrow, and that we would be able to exchange the MPC for Baht, Thai currency, before we left for Bangkok. I never came so close to kissing a captain before.

* * *

Two days later the eight of us were in our new 1505s complete with blue overseas cap and new dress shoes. Our chevrons of rank were hastily sewn on, but passable. Each of us was armed with a new AWOL bag packed with two sets of civilian clothes and toiletries and a few had even purchased cameras. We exchanged the MPC for Baht and loaded on a commercial airliner for Bangkok.

The whole passenger section of the airliner was packed with guys going on R&R to Bangkok. It is a wonder the wings didn't blow off the plane as we left the ground. Everyone was screaming, cheering and overflowing with joy. The plane was met on the ground well away from the terminal building by four buses and eight U.S. Army NCOs wearing chrome helmets and MP armbands.

We were herded onto the buses and taken to a briefing given by an Army Major. After an hour of being told what to do and not do, and how to behave ourselves, we were told that we would be assigned to buses that would take us to our hotels. The Army Major must have told us 10 to 15 times that today was December 24 and that on January 5 at 10:00 we were to be waiting at the hotel we had been assigned where buses would be waiting to take us back to the airport. If we were not there waiting to board the bus the minute it arrived, we would be considered deserters and court-martialed.

He gave us the date, times, and threats one more time before he dismissed us to check a bulletin board for which bus we were to board. The eight of us boarded a bus to take us to the White Elephant Hotel. We knew we arrived when we stopped next to a blinking neon sign that had large English letters proclaiming its name and an animated White Elephant that appeared to be walking through a green jungle background as two set of legs alternately blinked. The Hotel was constructed of white painted cinder blocks with a window air-conditioning unit sticking out of every window of the second, third, and top fourth floors. Above the fourth floor was a faded, green, canvas covering over an outdoor garden bar with a green hedge wall ringing the sides.

We checked in at the front desk and handed in our chits. The desk-clerk told us that we could also charge up to 100 baht per person for room service per day and it would be covered by the chits. The exchange rate was 20.8 baht to the dollar and for $5.00 per meal, not counting drinks; we would be able to eat very well on just room service. We were told that instead of room service we could use the 100 baht at the rooftop restaurant and bar. We all planned on meeting in 30 minutes in civvies on the rooftop to get something to eat and plan our evening. Since we had to share rooms, we all paired up, Ron and I bunked together.

We got together on the roof and had a steak dinner with baked potatoes and green beans washed down by a few Singha beers. Our waiter, Gan, was a very personable young man who spoke English particularly well. He wasted no time telling us that he could get anything we wanted, American cigarettes, Scotch Whiskey, or Thai girls. He told us that the infamous Patpong Street with all the go-go bars and massage parlors was just three blocks north of the hotel. He also gave us one very, very good suggestion. He said that many G. I.s got robbed and that we should only take enough money for one day any time we left the hotel and that the hotel would give us receipts for any money that they would keep for us in the hotel safe. We decided since it was Christmas Eve we should stick together tonight and head to Patpong Street and celebrate being alive. We charged the meal and beers to our room service tab and each only used 45 of our 100 baht daily balance. We all slipped Gan a few baht in cash and after stopping at the desk to drop off our extra cash, we walked off as a group to Patpong Street.

Patpong was a blaze of colored light and it had a variety of small booths running down the center of the street selling everything from beautiful silk neckties to cheap gaudy plastic toys. On both sides of the street where shops, bars, restaurants and massage parlors. In front of each was a barker trying to lure you into their establishment. We settled on a well lit bar where we could hear the music of Sonny and Cher blaring into the street. I suggested we go have a drink to remember our Sonny and we entered the bar.

In the center of the large room was a long oval bar. Behind the bar was a raised stage. On the stage were about 20 girls dressed in a variety of miniskirts, shorts and bathing suits, each with a big number printed on cardboard pinned to their tops. We all squeezed into one red vinyl booth along the back wall. A waiter came over and we ordered Singha beer, before the waiter left eight girls came up to us asking if we wanted company. The waiter hovered waiting to take extra orders for the girls.

Uncle Bob said, "Thanks for the offer ladies but tonight we are drinking to lost friends. Shoo! And waiter if you want to get a good tip tonight, tell all the girls to stay away from us and be sure to instantly replace every empty or near empty beer bottle on this table."

Before the waiter left Ron innocently asked, "What are the numbers for on the girls?"

The waiter responded before he scurried off for the beers, "If you see girl you want. Tell me her number and I get her for you." This caused all the guys to break up laughing and Ron to turn a brilliant shade of red.

When the beers arrived I raised mine and said, "To Steve 'Sonny' Borns, a fallen warrior."

By the time we saluted all of our fallen friends, one or more times, we were very drunk. At one point during the night Ron had looked at his watch and wished us all a Merry Christmas. To which we once again drank a few toasts. Around 3 AM we paid our bill, which I am sure our waiter padded a little, and we all headed back to the hotel.

We were all hanging on to each up to remain standing when we entered the hotel lobby. I remember Uncle Bob walking right into a small pond with a fountain they had in the center of the lobby. He said something about not having dry feet since we arrived in June. When he sat down in the shallow water around the fountain the hotel manager began to yell at us to get him out of there. Three of us got him up and carried him to his room.

We all had a late Christmas lunch on the roof. Most of the residents of the hotel were GIs and the hotel restaurant had a full turkey meal with the works ready for us. All of Christmas day we stayed together except for a short trip to a Thai Telephone Company building where we could make long distance calls to our families back home. It was early in the morning back home but I don't think any of our families minded being disturbed by those phone calls. Following the phone calls we went back to the hotel roof bar and stayed with our other "family" that Christmas day. We had not gone out shopping but we did buy each other Christmas presents - Singha beers. All and all we had a wonderful relaxing Christmas with our family. The family we knew we could trust with our lives.

New Year's Eve and News Year's Day were totally different stories that I will never tell, because I don't remember them at all. So it never happened.

For the rest of our time there, we stuck together in twos and threes and enjoyed our time in Bangkok, sightseeing, shopping for gifts to ship back to our families back home, and enjoying the delights of Patpong Street.

* * *

May 16, 2018
Hersonissos, Crete

For the first time since they arrived Harold noticed Ron's hands were shaking. Then it finally dawned on him that Ron was using the old hand code. It had been a while since he had used it so it took him a few seconds to translate what Ron was signing, "Shut up you fool before our wives kill us."

Aloud Harold said, "During my time in Bangkok, I learned how to say three important phrases in Thai, 'Thank you', 'a beer, please' and 'where is the bathroom?'"

Before Joan or any of the ladies could ask Harold anything more about the delights of Patpong Street, he stood up and rattled off a string of Thai.

"That means, where is the bathroom." Whereupon he beat a hasty retreat back to the hotel lobby so he wouldn't need to answer any questions.

CHAPTER 11
May 16, 2018
Karteros, Crete

That evening the minibus brought the group to General Straight's home in Karteros which was just a little east of the Iraklion airport. He lived in a beautiful two story home just off of the beach. The building was white stucco with the famous Greek dark blue doors and shutters on each window. The General met the bus in a large circular drive in front of the house.

Kathy wowed, "Your home is beautiful! If it were not for the traditional blue accents this house looks like it should be in old California and not on Crete. And I love the way you have it landscaped."

"My late wife was an architect originally from San Diego and loved the Spanish Mission style homes. Won't you all come in and I will give you the five drachma tour."

The General showed them through the house but when they went into his office the guys stopped the rather rapid tour right there. The office was on the second floor and as you entered the room opposite from the door there was a wall with two large windows that looked out to the sea. The wall with the door was all bookcases made of the same red oak as a desk which faced the windows. There was a high back red leather desk chair and two matching captain chairs facing the desk. But what got the guys attention was the wall between the windows looking out to the beach. In the center of the wall was a large picture of Detachment 11 with everyone in full battle dress. They had their faces striped with grease paint, wearing camouflage uniforms, and boonie hats. They were all holding their weapons in a variety of casual manners. In the center of the first row was the General.

The General said, "We took that the first full exercise we had in the Philippines. I had to have it touched up to blow it up that big and to brighten up the colors. The original was from an 8x10 inch print I had in my office at NSA. The original photograph was classified which was why you were never given one back then. In tubes on the desk are 24x30 inch copies for each of you. I was going to pass them out the last day of the reunion but go ahead and grab one now."

Until he mentioned their own copies, the guys were all looking at the picture on the wall finding themselves and their buddies. Now they all went to the desk and took their copy thanking the General.

"Let's go out to the back patio and have a few drinks while we look over the pictures."

The back patio was a large twenty-foot deep space that ran the length of the house. It was completely covered with trellises which were totally overgrown by four interwoven bougainvillea vines planted in huge clay amphorae in the corners of the patio. The amphorae were replicas of the five foot tall ones found at Knossos. Against the house was a bar and an outdoor kitchen. Busy in the kitchen were two Greek men, our minibus driver, Niko and his father Manoli. Manoli had worked at the chow hall on the base. The General stepped behind the bar saying, "I will get the first round, after that you will need to get your own. Name your poison."

After the lamb kabob meal the group sat around looking at multiple copies of the Detachment 11 group photo showing their wives the people they had talked about in the stories they told the last few days.

Ron asked, "This is great, General. But I have a question for you. After Crete I had lost track of everyone because I lost my address book along with my luggage on the return trip from Crete, how the heck did you get our addresses?"

"Can you keep a secret? Oh yea, you guys are good at that. I had some old paperwork from the unit that had your social security numbers; of course you remember that social security numbers replaced your original Air Force serial numbers in the early 70s. I have a friend who retired from upper management at Social Security, I asked him to pull the addresses on file for you. He broke some rules but when I told him whose addresses I wanted, he readily agreed. As a matter of fact, he says if you ever need him, he still owes you guys all the beer you can drink."

That caused a few "I'm curious." looks from the guys.

"It was Captain Tyree. You should remember him from Laos."

Harold asked, "Was that the pilot we snatched from the Pathet Lao?"

"Yes."

Joan leaned forward and said, "I have to hear about this."

The General said, "It was January 1969 when I went with Ron and Uncle Bob's teams to get Major Tyree."

* * *

January 1969 ~ Da Nang, South Vietnam
As told by General George Straight

I was on the phone with the planner I worked with at MACV. We were setting up another "Truck Body Count War" scouting operation into the Steel Tiger area of Laos when Lieutenant Colonel Riggs asked me to hold on for a second. When he came back on the line he apologized for the delay and said he had just gotten word that a McDonnell F-101 Voodoo Reconnaissance Aircraft that was taking pictures of LZ for next week's operation area had sustained damaged and just crashed. He said that there has been no word from the pilot, a Captain Tyree.

Judging by the aircraft type and name, I knew that it was my best friend from my Air Force Academy days, Paul Tyree. So I got all the information I could and told Lieutenant Colonel Riggs that I was shifting the location of today's planned operation to the area where the F-101 was expected to have gone down.

The second I got off the phone I called Ron and Uncle Bob to the operations tent and we did some quick planning for a new operations area. During the planning I decided that I was going to go in with the teams. The helicopters we had scheduled for today's insertion would be at the landing pad in 15 minutes. So I had Ducky take care of filing our operation changes with the transports, support gunships and FAC while I geared up to go in with Ron's team.

* * *

We made several passes over the still smoking crash site. The canopy was blown so I knew that Paul had ejected and judging from what remained of the plane, it had been traveling toward the southeast when it went down. We shifted the search area to the northwest trying to find where Paul could have come down after ejecting. The helicopter's pilot had real sharp eyes and he noticed some badly disturbed tree tops and took another pass over the area. We started taking small arms fire when we went lower to get a better look. But before we left, we spotted several armed men and what we thought was a poorly bundled parachute.

Rather than landing in two places like we normally did, we all landed in a clearing about four kilometers from the site where we saw the parachute. We headed into the direction of a hill that should have a pretty good view of the entire area. We knew the enemy was in the area so we took extra care with our noise abatement and trail cleaning protocols.

With Chief walking point we arrived at the crest of the hill which did indeed have a very good view of the area where we spotted the parachute. The teams took up defensive positions and we began to do a thorough visual reconnaissance of the area. Several small groups of armed men were spotted moving around. They were not wearing uniforms of any type and judging by the mixed arms they were carrying, they were Pathet Lao and not NVA. The Pathet Lao were a communist political movement in armed opposition to the current Laotian government and were closely aligned with North Vietnam.

Come nightfall we left our location on the hill top and worked our way to the spot where Paul had come down. There was no one there when we arrived but by the light of the three-quarters moon coming thru the damaged tree tops, we could easily see the ground had been trampled by a lot of people. We were just about to leave when Chief signaled us that he had found something. He showed us one semi-clear track from a boot. None of the other tracks were boots so we knew that Paul was on his feet at one point.

I am not sure how Chief did it but with the aid of his night vision equipment and the filtered light of the moon he was able to track the boot prints. We moved off following the trail for about a kilometer when during one of our Stop, Look and Listen pauses we heard someone talking in a normal tone of voice around the bend in the trail. We all quickly exited the trail and took up defensive positions. The voices were not moving so we knew they were probably settled in for the night where they were.

Gus Rantz, Uncle Bob's point man, put on his night vision equipment and slowly belly crawled to where he could see who was ahead of us. Twenty minutes later he returned and hand signaled us that the talking we heard was a three man team watching the trail which continued over the hill and that there was a large camp just on the other side of the hill.

We shifted further off the trail and took a roundabout route to a spot on a different hill where we had a view into the camp. The camp looked like a permanent site that had several huts near a stream. The camp had several large trees growing in it, providing excellent cover to prevent it from being seen from the air. There were two guards walking around the camp and one that was standing still next to what appeared to be one long and one short, wide bamboo ladders lying on the ground. The guards were talking and acting very relaxed so they had no idea we were in the area. A few minutes later a person approached the stationary guard spoke for a few minutes and knelt down looking at what we at first though was the short ladder. He started talking down to the ladder and got up laughing. He then opened his pants and began to relieve himself through the ladder. A string of English cuss words came up from what we now knew was a hole in the ground covered by a bamboo gate. The two Pathet Lao laughed and the visitor moved away from the guard and walked back to one of the huts.

We had found an English speaking captive and assumed it was Paul. We took another good look around the camp and backed down the hill and a distance away from the camp to do some planning. The first thing we did was radio in the location of the camp telling operations that they had a prisoner. There were too many people in the camp for our small group to attack but we knew we had to do something before they took Paul from this camp to someplace from which we would not be able to extract him.

We made our plan, set up a hell of a lot of air support for first light and moved our positions to wait for dawn. Ever since our first mission in North Vietnam when we rescued the crew of a downed aircraft we never had any issues getting any air support we ever needed. But this time when they found out we were going in for a captured pilot the air support we requested was more than doubled. Just as the sun was starting to lighten the eastern sky a shot was heard followed ten seconds later by a second shot. The shots appeared to come from the next valley to the east of the camp. The camp came alive; they came scurrying out of the huts like ants from a disturbed nest.

One man in what appeared to looked like a somewhat green uniform started yelling and pointing. Minutes later, the vast majority of the camp personnel jogged from the camp down a trail heading toward the sounds of the shots. Nine guards remained in the camp. One guard was by the prisoner and eight guards were in pairs of two around the parameter.

About twenty minutes later there was the sound of a claymore mine exploding in the next valley. A minute after that was the roar of ten fighters popping up over a high ridge a kilometer to the east. They began to blast the valley the Pathet Lao had gone into in response to the shots fired earlier. Apparently the Air Force had pulled out all stops to rescue one of their own captured pilots because another wave of planes appeared over the ridge and headed for the valley but at the last-minute they alter course slightly and napalmed both sides of the hill between the camp and the next valley where all the action was taking place..

At the sound of the first bombs from the air strike the two guards on west side of the camp collapsed. The other guards didn't see anything because their attention was towards the sounds of the airstrike. Less than a second after the first two guards fell, the guards on the north side of the camp also went down. The only sound heard was the plop of two M79 Grenade Launchers firing, rapidly followed by explosions that took down the remaining four parameter guards. At the blast from the grenades I, Ron, Harold, and Sam charged into the camp from the east. Uncle Bob, Johnny, and Butch entered from the north. Harold and Butch were firing shots into the bodies of the downed parameter guards make sure they stayed dead while the rest of us opened up on the lone guard by the prisoner. He fell after being hit multiple times by a wall of CAR-15 rounds fired from two sides.

All the guards in the camp were killed in less than twenty seconds. The first four by the silenced Mk22s fired from positions close to the camp that we had spent hours crawling to before dawn. The first two phases of the plan had worked well. The first phase was Chief and Gus moving to the next valley setting a few booby traps using claymores with trip wires across the trails set well into the valley. After setting the booby traps they moved to positions where they would be able to see into the valley and call in the air strikes. The claymore firing gave away the fact the Pathet Lao reaction force was in the valley responding to the two shot alarm signal we had learned about in earlier operations. An alarm conveniently sounded by Gus, not the local bad guys that had been taken out the night before by Chief and Gus. The claymore blast was the signal for Chief to call in the waiting aircraft.

The second phase of taking out the remaining guards in the camp was now done, so we moved to phase three. Johnny quickly began to set detcord and plastique explosives to blow a landing zone in the smaller trees on the side of the camp. Ron and I moved to get Paul out of the hole while the other five took up defensive positions to take care of any Pathet Lao who may be coming in from any remote guard posts.

Assisting our five guards watching the parameter were two AC130s hosing down the jungle and trails approaching the camp. We got a very battered Paul out of the hole. I had to use the long bamboo ladder and climb down to assist Paul out. It appeared that they had used Paul as a punching bag to take out all of their frustrations for past airstrikes. His eyes were swollen shut and his head caked with dried blood.

Johnny yelled, "Fire in the hole!" We all hit the dirt, five seconds later a loud boom, and the tall thin trees that were in the new LZ were all down and scattered pointing out from the center. The downed trees looked like someone had dropped a handful of uncooked spaghetti on the kitchen counter. While Ron was taking care of Paul, I called in the HH-3Es that were standing by to pick us up.

We loaded Paul onto the helicopter then the rest of the team piled in behind us. Another HH-3E went to pick up Gus and Chief. They didn't have a clear LZ so they were lifted out utilizing a jungle perpetrator dropped from the HH-3E and hoisted back up to the hovering helicopter.

The first aid specialist on the HH-3E was taking care of Paul. I knelt next to him and told him he stunk worse than he did the first time he had ever gotten drunk as a Cadet Fourth-class at the Academy. Paul managed to open one swollen eye just enough to look at who was telling him he stank. He finally recognized me through the face paint, the resultant smile caused a cut to reopen on his bottom lip. "Is that you, Georgie?"

"Yea, you know I am getting tired of getting your ass out of trouble."

Paul smiled again but at that point the morphine the first aid specialist had given him kicked in and he fell asleep. As we were flying away another wave of planes were entering the area and they totally destroyed what remained of the camp.

The HH-3E first aid specialist told me the captain was not too bad. It felt like he had a few cracked ribs and had the stuffing beaten out of him but no other penetrating wounds. Nothing was too critical, so we flew the helicopter back to Da Nang rather than stopping at a closer aid station.

When we landed at Da Nang greeting us was a whole bunch of pilots who kept thanking us, beating us on our backs, promising that anytime we would ever need them – they'd be there. Several even offering to treat us to all the beer we could drink for the rest of our lives. It wasn't too often that a pilot gets rescued once captured and that good news spread through the grapevine quickly.

We went back to operations for our debriefing but I was pulled out of the briefing so many times to take phone calls that I told Ducky to finish it without me. One of the calls had me leaving for the base airstrip to catch a C130 to Saigon to report on the mission directly to the Air Force big honchos from MACV and Tan Son Nhut Air Base.

At that meeting, it was the second time I had to turn down offers for metals for members of a unit that was not officially in Vietnam. But I did come back with thirty-two more chits for R&Rs, sixteen in Hawaii, and eight each in Japan and Bangkok. I almost felt bad that the guys that had earned them weren't the guys who would get to take the R&Rs. But they had just come back from one and I knew they would not mind seeing the rest of the team enjoy the fruits of their labor.

When I got back I found that they didn't totally go without rewards. Piled up in the command tent were twenty-two cases of American beer and two cases of Jim Beam Bourbon Whiskey. Ducky told me he had to practically point a gun at some pilots that came by with steaks and other food that the guys couldn't eat because of our Vietnamese only food diet while we were on standby. But he let them leave the beer and booze, because we could take it back with us later.

I went and saw Paul in the Hospital. He was no longer doped up and managed a painful smile when he saw me. He was pretty mummified with bandages around his head covering much of his face with just gaps for his eyes and mouth. He must have thanked me ten times before he asked me what in the heck I was doing in Laos looking like a real soldier. He laughed when I told him that if I told him the truth, I would have to give him back to the Pathet Lao so they could kill him for me.

After a while a stern nurse major with a face that would stop a Mac truck chased me out of the room.

* * *

May 16, 2018
Karteros, Crete

The General finished his story be saying, "As I left the room Paul said he owed me big time and I could collect a favor anytime I ever needed it. Getting all of your addresses from Social Security was that favor."

The General excused himself for a minute and came back with a dusty bottle of Jim Beam Bourbon with several pieces of the paper label and cap seal missing. He placed the bottle on the table and went to the bar and returned with a tray of small raki glasses.

"I kept one of the bottles from the cases we got that day. I have had it with me for all these years. I think now would be a good time to drink it. I hope it is still good after all these years and all the miles that it has traveled. At least it is well aged."

He poured the entire bottle into the glasses normally used for raki. We all raised our glasses and drank after the General said, "To the most successful operation ever conducted by Detachment 11."

The General started laughing when he looked around at everyone's faces after drinking the shot. "I guess that fifty year old bourbon didn't age as well as it should have, the top must have leaked."

Harold came back with, "Good thing that we aged better than that bottle of bourbon did."

CHAPTER 12
May 17, 2018
The Island of Dia, Greece

In the morning the group boarded a 187 foot, three masted sailing yacht at the hotel's marina. The yacht was owned by a wealthy friend of the General who loaned the yacht and crew to him for the day. They sailed off into the morning sun and visited the island of Spinalonga. Spinalonga was not always an island. Before the Venetian occupation, it had been a peninsula. However, it was manually separated from the coast when they built a fort there. The fort was converted to a leper colony in 1903 and was still used as such until 1957.

After they toured the fortress/leper colony, they sailed to the island of Dia. Dia was on the tour itinerary because there is a good view of the island from the old Iraklion Air Station and from the city of Iraklion. From those vantage points, the island resembles a sleeping dragon or lizard. So naturally almost everyone stationed at IAS always called it Dragon Island.

On Dragon Island they had a lunch of pork steak cooked over an open fire, grilled vegetable kabobs and a Greek salad. The yacht pulled away from the island and anchored about 25 meters offshore so the group could go swimming in the beautiful, clear blue water. The yacht's owner, Aris Markopoulos who had worked on the base when the group was there, supplied a wonderfully stocked bar for the group's use. So by three o'clock, everyone was just sitting around on the deck, well lubricated and relaxed, enjoying being millionaires for the day.

As they were lounging around drinking, Joan noticed an ant crawling on her arm. She said, "How in the world did an ant get on my arm in the middle of the Mediterranean Sea? Ugh ... I hate ants."

This triggered a memory in Harold's mind as he replied, "Remember, dear, that the big boat here does spend most of its time at a dock attached to land."

The memory flash also triggered Harold's mischievous sense of humor, "Ron, why don't you tell us what you think of ants."

Ron's voice was almost a growl when he shouted his answer, "Ants and leeches are the two worst things God ever created!! I hate, hate, hate, the miserable beasts!"

Getting himself back under control, Ron continued, "Knowing you Harold, I guess you won't leave me alone until I tell them about why I hate ants, but I should tell everyone the full story behind it all."

* * *

January 1969 ~ Cambodia
As told by Ron Lafayette

In mid-January of 1969 the team's emphasis shifted from Laos to Cambodia. Richard Nixon had successfully campaigned on a pledge of "peace with honor" and was to take office in just a few days. So he was looking at peace negotiations as a way to get us out of Vietnam, but meanwhile the U.S. troop level was approaching close to half a million servicemen in Vietnam. The intelligence we were getting out of MACV was that even though we were conducting almost 200 airstrikes a day along the Ho Chi Minh Trail, it was still estimated that there were 10,000 NVA supply trucks en route along the trail at any given time. So it didn't look like we would honorably be leaving for home anytime soon.

Operation Igloo White was just starting in Laos, the leadership hoped that it would lead to better intelligence for the air interdiction war in that area. Operation Igloo White was a covert operation that utilized electronic sensors, computers, and communications relay aircraft in an attempt to automate intelligence collection. The system would analyze the information gathered from the sensors and then assist in guiding the strike aircraft to their targets. The system utilized a combination of munitions, audio, and motion sensing devices which were air dropped along suspected infiltration routes. Specialized aircraft would receive signals from these sensors and forward the information to a collection center which would coordinate the air strikes. The hope was with this system in place, Air Force and Navy planes would not need to rely solely upon luck and aerial reconnaissance to find and hit the supply trucks along the trail. And as our politicians were always saying there was never, never, never anyone like us actually on the ground giving good real-time information. So in reality they were attempting to automate what our teams had been doing quite successfully but on a much larger scale.

Unfortunately, the news of our rescue of a downed pilot from a Pathet Lao camp was rapidly becoming public knowledge, so it was time for us to get out of the limelight. While the information that our unit was supplying MACV was excellent, we were only a small unit and it was decided that our operations shift from the "Truck Body Count War" in Laos to finding the major staging areas in Cambodia.

The powers from on high decided that our group would be an excellent way to prototype a modified Igloo White program for Cambodia. We would rectify some of the shortcomings of the system by physically placing some of the sensors along known infiltration routes rather than relying upon the randomness of simply airdropping them. By physically placing them we would eliminate several problems caused by the airdrop. They would be placed along trails that were known to have been used for NVA resupply. Also less physical damage to the units, almost 20% of the airdropped devices never functioned. With our teams doing the manual placement of units, they would be placed where they would provide the best coverage without exposing them to be easily found by the NVA.

* * *

We had not yet received a shipment of the sensors so the initial operations were scouting missions only. My team was once again working with Uncle Bob's team. A study of aerial reconnaissance photography of an area of Cambodia around Svay Rieng suggested it as a potential portion of the Ho Chi Minh Trail complex. The terrain around Svay Rieng, which was less than 70 miles west-northwest of Saigon, was much different than the hilly terrain we were working in Laos. Here the ground was much flatter with more swampy jungle area and rice paddies and the local population was much denser. The examination of some aerial photography revealed a well maintained trail through a marshy region along the Stoeng Basak River, southwest of Savy Rieng. We had inserted during a light, steady rain at night in a rice paddy two kilometers from the suspected trail route. We then moved closer to the river to find cover for the night. The next morning we went exploring and found a trail loaded with lots of Ho Chi Minh sandal and bicycle tire tracks. The tracks were fresh and definitely made after last night's rain. My team found a good hidey-hole in dense foliage that had a view of the trail and settled down to watch what kind of traffic the trail was getting. Uncle Bob's team moved further south paralleling the trail, documenting the trail's path for future reference.

Shortly after dusk we detected more movement on the trail. It started out with just two NVA in their green uniforms wearing pith helmets. About five minutes later we started seeing bicycles, lots and lots of bicycles. We counted over a hundred bicycles moving in clusters of ten to fifteen with each cluster separated by ten to twenty uniformed NVA troops. We had definitely found an active part of the Ho Chi Minh Trail.

When we first sighted the movement we radioed Uncle Bob and gave him a heads up that traffic was headed his way. He responded that he would move to a safe area and keep his eyes peeled.

Later that night we saw another group, slightly smaller than the first, also moving down the trail. Two hours before dawn we packed up and went to meet up with Uncle Bob's team. We were passing through a relatively open area along the bank of the river, about fifty meters away from the trail, when we heard more movement coming down the trail. We took what cover we could find to wait for them to pass. Unfortunately, one of the contingents of NVA troops decided to take a break, and moved off the trail to an area not more than twenty meters from our location. The early morning dawn was giving just enough light that we could not move without giving away our location.

It was then that I started feeling movement on and in my pants. It wasn't a good feeling, but ants. Apparently when I took cover I didn't notice that there was a large ant nest not more than a foot from where I was lying. It took all the willpower that I had not to jump up and do anything to get the ants off of me. Ever so slowly, I moved my hand to the area where I felt the movement and started to squish the ants crawling in my pants. Wrong thing to do! The ones that didn't die on the first squish attempt now started to bite me. I kept squishing, they kept biting. I was biting my own lips to keep from yelling with the burning pain of multiple ants biting me on my legs and in my groin area.

After what seemed like a week and a half of agony, the NVA finished their fifteen minute break and moved back down the trail. The second they were out of site, I started crawling, at a very high rate of speed, to the river. I crawled into the river, pulled down my pants and began to frantically get the remaining ants off me. In my mind I was screaming and cursing all ants, and the son-of-a-bitch that put buttons rather than zippers on our camouflage pants. I remember thinking that perhaps a zipper could stop the little beasts from crawling into anyone's pants.

Harold came to check on me and when I hand signed what had happened he damn near blew himself up in his attempt to keep himself from laughing, he knew laughing out loud would be the same as telling all the NVA in the world where we were. His body was shaking and his face went from a smile to a grimace as he fought not to make any noise laughing. If he would have laughed out loud I think I would have saved the NVA a bullet and shot him then and there. I was not in the best of moods at that point.

We got out the open area and resumed our movement south to link up with Uncle Bob. It was a good thing that Chief was on point and not me. I was spending more time scratching the ant bites than watching where I was going. The teams united about thirty minutes later and we cautiously moved south until we started to approach a heavily wooded area. Before we even got close we could smell the fires and hear the noise of a large encampment. Judging by the smoke we could see and the amount of noise being made there must have been over 200 people in the camp.

Chief crept up closer and found a view through the foliage; he watched the area for a little while and returned to the team. He reported that the encampment was a staging area. He could see several huts in a highly used area with well-defined trails between them; it even included several large covered sleeping shelters.

We noted the position on our maps and moved back north, away from the camp. We traveled about two kilometers and radioed in the enemy's position and enough grid points to allow mapping of the trail's locations.

We quickly left the area before anyone else headed for the base area stumbled upon us. When we were far enough away we radioed for extraction. Thirty minutes later we were headed back to Tan Son Nhut Air Base. We were in the air for only a minute or two when the jolly green giant's pilot told us we had to divert to check on a downed Huey. Someone had sent a mayday radio call and then they had gone off the air.

We could see unfriendly movement on the ground headed toward where the Huey would have gone down. It took us less than ten minutes to find the wreckage. As we passed over the crash site, we saw some movement and went lower to check it out.

There were two people in U.S. uniforms on the ground by the helicopter, one laying on the ground and the other frantically waving his arms in the air. As we approached to land, the side of our helicopter was raked by large caliber machine gun fire. The pilot broke off his approach and climbed to get out of the deadly hail of fire.

Since we couldn't go down there and still be in condition to lift off again, the pilot decided to land us in a clearing about a kilometer away from the crash site and send us to bring back the crash survivors. The pilot took off again saying he would get on the horn and get us some air support. We know that the downed aircraft survivors didn't have long since we had already seen NVA headed in that direction. Both teams got off the helicopter in a big hurry and started heading for the crash site. After we were about a hundred meters from the landing zone, Uncle Bob's team moved off towards where the emplacement of the heavy machine gun that had hit our helicopter was located, while my team headed to get the survivors.

As we were approaching the site we took extra precaution in case someone else had beaten us there. I peeked through the foliage and got a good look at who we were going to get. I was surprised to see it was our old friend, Major Wayne Phillips from the Green Beret training school. It flashed through my mind how he had called us a bunch of Boy Scouts, and my attitude got the better of me. Between the itching going on in my crotch area from the ant bites and his attitude towards us, my mind caused me to make another bad decision. Instead of announcing myself before entering the area, I told my team to stay down and wait while I continued a stealthy crawling approach. I was only five meters from him when I shouted, "BOO!"

He twirled around with fear making his eyes as big as saucers, but his training kicked in and he let loose with a three round burst from his M16. Luckily, the burst went well above my head. I then quickly yelled his name before continuing. "Wayne, hold your fire."

Hearing his first name he instantly knew that it was a friend and not the NVA scaring him and he stopped firing. I reinforced this by continuing, "Major Phillips please hold your fire."

I slowly raised myself from the tall grass close enough for him to see the stitching on my uniform. Upon seeing that someone had gotten that close to him without him noticing he blurted, "Holy Shit! Where the fuck did you come from?!"

"We are here to take you to an LZ safe enough to get a rescue chopper in to get you, and anyone else, out of here."

"Am I glad to see you. Only Sergeant Smith and I survived the crash."

I signaled for the rest of the team to come in. We didn't have enough personnel to take the bodies as well as the wounded out so we decided to leave the bodies and we would radio to have a much larger relief force come in later to get them. Harold and Sam grabbed Sergeant Smith and we moved out back towards the LZ where we had landed. We hadn't gone but a few meters when we heard the blast of a M79 grenade explosion, quickly followed by a lot of small arms fire. We heard another blast, this time from an M-26 hand grenade and then quiet. I got on the radio to check on Uncle Bob but he told me his team had taken out two 12.7 mm machine gun crews and a few of their friends and it is now OK for the jolly green giant to come back and get us out of here.

Rather than carry the wounded Sergeant, we went back to the crash site to wait for the helicopter to return to pick up my team and the two live Green Berets. The helicopter told us that a Green Beret relief force was on the way to the crash site to pick up the bodies and destroy what was left of the crashed Huey.

We loaded onto the helicopter, made a quick stop to pick up Uncle Bob's team, and we were winging it back to Tán Son Nhut. We had just crossed the Cambodia-Vietnam border when the helicopter started filling with smoke. The pilot notified us that apparently we didn't go totally without damage when we were hit during our first approach, and that we needed to make an emergency landing. We all grabbed on to something in case the landing wasn't too smooth. The pilot did manage to put us down safe and sound in a rice paddy area before he cut the power. Because the engine was still smoking we all exited the helicopter moved twenty-five meters away and took up defensive positions while we waited for another helicopter.

The position we occupied was along a highly vegetated raised strip of land between two rice paddies. The helicopter flight crew took care of the wounded Green Beret Sergeant while the rest of us spread out and covered all points of the compass.

The Major left his position and came close to me when he heard me on the radio. I was on with the Green Beret relief force that went to pick up the bodies. They told us they had to temporarily abort because the site was swarming with NVA. The look that passed between Major Phillips and I said that apparently we had gotten out of there just in time. The nod and smile he gave me was more than likely the only thanks I was going to get from him. The relief force was going to wait for air support to blast the NVA away from the crash site before going in for the bodies. Mean while we waited for another evacuation helicopter and an even bigger helicopter to come to lift ours out and bring it back for repair.

Harold, who had taken up a position close to me, couldn't pass up the opportunity to give Major Phillips a poke. He said, "Good thing the Boy Scouts were around. Huh, Major?"

You could almost see the wheels turning in the major's head as he started thinking real hard about his rescuers. His eyes widened as he finally noticed our uniforms had black Air Force winged chevrons instead of Army stripes. He thought about the fact that I had called him by his first name and started to put two and two together.

"Do I know you?"

I didn't say a thing, but Harold couldn't leave it alone and as he moved away to find a better defensive position and he started very softly singing the little ditty we marched to while we were at Fort Bragg.

Everywhere we go
People want to know
Who we are,
So we tell them.
We are the Boy Scouts,
Mighty, Mighty Boy Scouts...

The major looked down, put his face into his hands, and shook his head - no. He then said, "Oh God. You guys are from that Air Force unit that took a class at Fort Bragg."

He recovered his composure and trying to reclaim his pride, he said, "No wonder you could sneak up on me. Apparently you learned something when you attended my school."

He just stared at me but I only gave a very noncommittal head shake, and didn't say a word to confirm or deny his suspicions. His stare was broken when the sound of small arms fire and the ping of ricochets bounding off of the downed helicopter attracted his attention.

I got on the radio to report that we were under fire and to get some air support over here right now. We didn't give our position away but let them ping away at the empty helicopter from the tree line on the far side of the rice paddy with downed craft. A minute or two later two NVA exited the tree line into the other rice paddy on the opposite side of the wooded area where we were hiding. We withheld fire until they were three quarters across the paddy and a much larger group had exited the tree line following their point men across the paddy. The sound of almost simultaneous "bloops" coming from Johnny's and Sam's grenade launchers was the trigger that cause everyone to open fire. The first rounds from our CAR-15s cut down the two closest point men and then fire was shifted to those still standing after the two M79 grenades had blasted the large group of NVA that had already exited the tree line.

Only a few that had entered the rice paddy managed to make it back to the cover of the trees. But apparently they had friends that hadn't entered the rice paddy yet and we started taking fire from them. From the trees by the patty on the helicopter side a lot of fire shifted from the helicopter itself to our location. They were on at least two sides of us and it looked as if we were trapped in the middle.

Uncle Bob and I both had the same idea as we both sent our point men to make sure that they couldn't flank us by approaching through the edges of the strip of land between two rice paddies. They couldn't approach us easily through the rice fields without being cut to pieces but we couldn't escape either. So far we were lucky and only receiving small arms fire. I was thankful that they hadn't bought along any mortars.

After the initial high volume of fire, things quieted down to where we were only receiving sporadic incoming fire. That got me nervous thinking that they were maneuvering to flank us, so I signaled for Sam to drop a few M79s along the raised approaches between the paddies. I had guessed right, the scream that resulted from Sam's grenade confirmed my nervous feelings. Johnny's grenades on the other side got the same results. Of course that caused a lot more fire to erupt from both tree lines headed in our direction. The firing intensified but not enough for me not to hear the approach of helicopters.

I was immediately on the radio giving our position and the positions of the approaching enemy. I popped a green smoke grenade to visually identify our position, confirmed color with the helicopters, and told them to open up along both tree lines and the 25 meters either side of us on the raised approaches to our location. A combination of rocket and machine gun fire chewed up the area behind the tree lines on both sides of our position. The incoming fire remained heavy for only a few more minutes before slowing and finally stopping.

I heard some moaning coming from the spot where we were taking care of the wounded sergeant and went to investigate. The crew member of our jolly green giant that was taking care of the Sergeant had been hit. I started to take care of him. The Green Beret Sergeant pushed himself up a little and asked how the crewman was doing. It was the first time I had gotten a good look at him. I searched my memory and came up with a name and said, "He'll be O.K. How are you doing, Smitty? What sin did you commit to still be stuck with Major Phillips after Bragg?"

He was faster on the uptake than the major had been and responded, "Obviously a very grievous one. Well, if it isn't the Zoomie jackrabbit that passed the major on the welcome run."

I put my finger to my lips and said, "Shhhh. Just like Sergeant Brown said when you first noticed him. You don't know me."

Smitty smiled and just shook his head. By then the helicopter pilot had come to help me with his crew member. I patted the wounded crewman, thanked the pilot and the crewman for their efforts and started talking to the FAC that had appeared overhead. He told me that it looked like our NVA friends had left the party and there was a whole flock of helicopters loaded with Army grunts going to make a few landings to try to cut the NVA off before they hightailed it back across the border. He also told me that a dustoff medevac was on the way for our wounded and that we were to return aboard one of the helicopters that were bringing in the relief force.

I went to brief Uncle Bob on the relief status when I found him kneeling by Sam. Sam had been shot in the knee. Uncle Bob had already cut off Sam's pants and was finishing the application a pressure bandage to Sam's still untanned, overly white leg. Sam looked up at me and was obviously in pain but he still made a wisecrack by saying next time he would be sure to take cover behind a thicker tree. I informed them that a medevac was on the way.

Uncle Bob gave Sam a shot for the pain and I was assuring Sam that he was going to be O.K. Just then Gus came running up and informed us that Butch had been killed. He had taken a round in the throat and would be going back with us in a body bag. The medevac arrived minutes before the rest of the relief force. We loaded, Sam, Smitty and the wounded crewman on helicopter and stayed with Butch.

The relief force came in on a flight of ten Hueys. Our teams, Butch, and the downed jolly green giant's crew boarded the relief force helicopters and flew back to Tan Son Nhut. We were met at Tan Son Nhut by Captain Cummings. I briefed him about our casualties and on who we had rescued. I told him how the major thought he knew who we were but not what we were doing there. He said that he would take care of it and visit Smitty in the hospital to secure his assistance in keeping Major Phillips in the dark.

Uncle Bob's helicopter landed a few minutes after mine. He informed the Captain that he and his team were going to take care of Butch and then go to the hospital to see Sam.

As I was talking with Captain Cummings, the ant bites were causing me to do a lot of excessive itching. He was nice enough not to say anything at first but finally asked me what was causing my "discomfort." When I told him about the ants he sympathized and said my team was to go with him to the hospital and while I got the ant bites taken care of, he and the rest of the team would check on Sam and Smitty.

* * *

May 17, 2018
The Island of Dia, Greece

At this point in the story Harold was miming scratching his crotch and laughing out loud. Harold asked Kathy, "Does Ron still scratch his crotch all the time? Or has he finally become a gentleman?"

"Oh, he is a gentleman now. So much of a gentleman that he will refill my wine glass for me."

Ron got up from the forward part of the deck where everyone but Harold was lounging saying, "I'll get you another glass of wine, Dear."

But as Ron passed Harold, who was still miming scratching, he pushed Harold over the side of the boat. After a huge splash Harold popped back up to the surface with a look of rage on his face.

Ron only smiled down at Harold telling him that he threw him into the water for his own good. "Judging by the way you were scratching, because of my vast experience, I had to assume that you were covered in ants. And I have learned the best way to get them off is in the water. Oh, by the way you can swim, can't you?"

Harold's response was a big smile and to wave one hand out of the water at Ron in an all too familiar finger configuration. Everyone broke into loud laughter as Ron departed in a great show of running in slow-motion to get Kathy another glass of wine.

CHAPTER 13
May 18, 2018
Chania, Crete, Greece

Today's excursion was to Chania. Chania is the second largest city on Crete located approximately 90 miles west of Iraklion. Touring the city is like a trip in a time machine to a new modern city built around the core of the old city which centers on the harbor. The old city, at one point, was also surrounded by a wall like Iraklion and there are still some sections of the wall found in parts of the city. But, the historical influence can best be seen in the harbor area from the old lighthouse, at the entrance to the large Venetian shipyard buildings dominating the waterfront view. Because it gets far more rain than Iraklion, the city streetscapes have a lot more containerized green and flowering plants enhancing the views of the picturesque buildings dating from the Venetian and Turkish occupation times.

The group was dropped off to wander around the old town while the General and Wild Bill took the minibus to the Naval Support Activity Souda Bay. Wild Bill was to pick up a few supplies and the General was going to pick up a prescription at the clinic, one of the benefits of being retired military. NSA Souda Bay is collocated on the Hellenic Air Force Base by the village of Mouzouras just about 10 miles outside the city. They quickly finished their errands and rejoined the group for lunch at a taverna on the promenade along the waterfront.

They were enjoying a nice breeze off the water while they waited for their lunch to be delivered when Mary asked, "Did you guys get everything you went for on base?"

The General said, "While Bill was at the PX, I went to the clinic to pick up my blood pressure and cholesterol medicine. But I only got back to the PX in time to help Bill load his purchases into the bus. We loaded a ton of stuff so I assume Bill got everything on the list and perhaps a bit more."

Wild Bill said, "Yes, and I even picked up a couple of bottles of bourbon for the beach tonight. I had to get my bourbon prescription filled too, ya' know."

Mary chimed in with, "Bill does need his prescription filled a little too often, perhaps he over medicates. When we go out for a meal or to the American Legion Hall, he doesn't signal for a waitress, he yells for a nurse demanding his medication."

Johnny chuckled and said, "I hope your nurses are as cute as Sam's was."

Wild Bill's response was, "I don't remember her, was she good looking?"

Johnny thought for a moment and began telling the group more about their time in Vietnam, "You don't remember Nurse Cutie Pie? I remember it like it was yesterday."

* * *

March 1969 ~ Cambodia
As told by Johnny Porter

Because of our emphasis being shifted from Laos to Cambodia, our in-country forward command post moved from Da Nang to Tan Son Nhut Air Base, so we got to spend a lot of time with Sam while he was in the hospital. One of the reasons I visited him so often was the fact that he had a very cute little nurse. She was a Captain who was about 5'5" short, slim, with dark brown hair, and a chest that threatened to pop the buttons off any uniform she wore.

Sam stayed in the hospital a lot longer than normal because the doctors couldn't decide if he had a million dollar wound or a twenty dollar wound. If we ever got metals, the million dollar wound would give him a medal, a trip back to the states, and a medical discharge. The twenty dollar wound would only give him the Purple Heart medal and he would have to stay in Vietnam to finish his tour.

The X-rays they took were inconclusive and they had to wait until a specialist came in from the United States to make the decision. After a couple weeks the super surgeon finally made it to Tan Son Nhut. Several of us were visiting Sam when they took him off for the specialist's examination. He was gone for almost an hour before they rolled him back into the ward where we were waiting. He was breathing hard, his face was a bright red and he was covered in sweat. We quizzed him on his status the second he was back in his bed. Sam's response was that the specialist that examined him was a sadist the way he poked, prodded and twisted his leg around. He said it hurt so bad that he thought he was going to die. Gus and Harold were mad as hell about Sam's examination causing him so much pain. They were just about to go looking for the doctor to give him an opportunity to experience first hand some other doctor's bedside manner while he healed from a bad betting. The angry villagers were about to light their torches and start searching for Dr. Frankenstein when the Specialist and Nurse Cutie Pie walked into the ward.

One thing you can say for that doctor, he was observant. One look at the pain on Sam's face and the way the rest of us were looking at him, he quickly apologized to Sam. "I'm sorry that I caused you pain, but I had to see the extent of injury and the only way to do that was to move your leg. It is good that your friends are here, so you can say goodbye. Tomorrow I am having you shipped back to where I normally work, Walter Reed Hospital.

I'll do the necessary surgery there to fix your knee, and it should give you back 90% to 98% mobility. But I am afraid that after the surgery and extensive physical therapy, you will in all likelihood be given a medical discharge from the military."

Without another word or waiting for Sam to reply, he just turned around and walked out the ward. The news that he was not going to be a cripple washed the pain right out of his mind. Everyone was so glad for Sam that we got a little too noisy and Nurse Cutie Pie had to return to Sam's bed and chase us out of the hospital. Although she was cute and a good nurse to Sam, I think we all hoped we would never see her again in the line of duty.

We got back to the forward command post and spread the good news about Sam to the rest of the teams. That was when we got the bad news. Master Sergeant Briede's team had been spotted by the NVA. By the time the evacuation helicopter had gotten there they had been in a running firefight for almost thirty minutes. Unfortunately as a result the sergeant and Michel Boyd had been killed in action.

With two teams now shorthanded Major Straight had to re-balance the teams once again. He did so with the goal in mind of keeping what was left of MSgt Briede's team together. He transferred me to Ron's team to replace Sam, and Uncle Bob's team would now be him, Gus, and the two guys remaining from MSgt Briede's team, "Good Time Charlie" Lee and Dan Wilson.

* * *

During the end of January and the whole month of February we had been mapping and placing sensors along sections of the Ho Chi Minh Trail in Cambodia, other than data being collected for future analysis, nothing was being done with the intelligence we were gathering. But things changed March 17, 1969 when President Nixon authorized Operation Menu, the secret bombing of Cambodia by B-52s, targeting North Vietnamese supply sanctuaries located along the border of Vietnam.

Now Detachment 11 was tasked with revisiting sections of the Trail we had visited and mapped before, this time to replace the batteries and reset sensors if necessary and to verify that the staging areas we had located were still in operation. It was one of the first times that all the teams were in Vietnam at the same time. All eight of the remaining teams were deployed into Cambodia; no one remained in the Philippines, because even the command center team lead by Major Straight was in the field. Depending on how dangerous the area we were working was, we would either deploy a single team or two teams. It only took eight days and all the sensors we had placed the month before, plus a few more we added, were back online. The data was being collected by the specialized aircraft and sent to a computerized command center where all data, from both sensors and other sources, like us, was compiled and analyzed.

Air Force command wanted to be sure at least one of the targets for the first strikes was a guaranteed provable success. That is why even though the analysis selected the staging area that we had discovered near Svay Rieng, Cambodia as a target, it was decided that it should be scouted one more time to confirm it was still in use. We were also to perform Bomb Damage Assessment, BDA, after the B52 strike. Since it was Uncle Bob's team and Ron's team that made the initial discovery, we were chosen to recheck the site.

Svay Rieng is located in a section of Cambodia called the Parrot's Beak that juts into South Vietnam. South Vietnam surrounds this section of Cambodia on three sides, the north, east and south. In the area we would be working, traveling from southwest to northeast, it was only about 20 miles across. Though not condoned, aircraft had taken this 'shortcut' across the Parrot's Beak from one section of Vietnam to another quite often in the past. Major Phillips' helicopter had been taking this shortcut when it was shot down. So our plan was to make use of this 'shortcut' as a cover for our insertion. One tight cluster of helicopters containing our insertion bird used the 'shortcut', but on the way through it dropped down and landed our teams. Shortly after, another cluster of helicopters took the same path over the Parrot's Beak, when this cluster passed over our landing zone, our helicopter would take off and join the second cluster to exit the area.

The insertion took place at dusk. We quickly secured the landing zone while the helicopter waited for the second group to pass. The second our bird was in the air we cleaned up any disturbance we had made in the LZ area and got away from there as quickly as possible. We had traveled just a little way when the clouds started rolling in. We had good cover where we were so decided to hold up until it started to rain or at least until the clouds got thick enough to hide us from the light of the three-quarters moon. The wait was not long, in about 20 minutes it started to pour.

Rain was our friend, it covered any noise we made, it lowered visibility reducing the possibility of us being seen, as well as, washing away any tracks we would leave behind. Luck was with us, the rain continued long enough for us to reach our objective, an area of dense foliage along the river about three hundred yards from the staging area. The rain stopped but the clouds still blocked out the light of the moon. Uncle Bob decided that we should not waste the opportunity of utilizing the complete darkness to scout the staging area. The teams set up a defensive area while Gus and Chief stripped off all of their gear but their Mk22 silenced pistols and their night vision equipment. The two of them proceeded to slowly and silently approach the staging area.

As they were getting close they saw two perimeter guards casually walking a patrol with their weapons slung from their shoulders. They have never had to worry about intruders before so they had become sloppy. Chief and Gus got close enough to get a good eye full and safely returned to our hiding area. They reported that the trees of the area had been thinned to the point that there were just enough trees to stop the area from being seen from the air but open enough to allow for a very large staging area. They had seen a bicycle parking area that contained close to 250 bicycles already loaded, piled high with supplies leaving only enough room for the 'driver' to push rather than ride the bicycle. They had also seen many huts and entrances to bunkers. By one of the bunkers they had seen close to twenty men sleeping in the cleared areas next to the opening. They did not see nearly enough men to push all the bicycles they had spotted, so the majority of the porters must be out of sight sleeping in the bunkers with only a few claustrophobic ones sleeping at the entrances.

We had enough information, so we decided to move away from the site while it was still very dark. Shortly before dawn we had gotten two kilometers away and radioed in our findings. We had just found a spot with good cover when the word came back to find a deep hole to hide in because there was a flight of B52s on the way to give the NVA staging area a few 500 pound eggs for breakfast and they were only fifteen minutes from the target area. We frantically dug holes and prayed that the bombers would be on target and not drop a few kilometers off target where we were hiding.

We had just finished frantically digging shallow holes when Uncle Bob pointed at the sky that now had just enough light to show us the contrail cloud vapor trails forming behind the passage of the big bombers. We tried to make ourselves as small as possible in our holes. I peeked over the edge of my hole and thought I could see the string of bombs falling from the B52s. Then I saw the flashes of light coming from the encampment area, quickly followed by the sounds of the explosions. The concussions caused by the blasts actually traveled the 2 kilometers through the earth to us and physically caused me to lift off the ground. I was bouncing around like a pair of dice thrown by an over enthusiastic Vegas gambler at a craps table.

When I stopped bouncing around, I again looked back towards the encampment. I could see a lot of smoke and debris in the air and I could also hear secondary explosions from some of the supplies they had been ferrying into South Vietnam or from some that had been stored at the staging area. Having experienced the concussive might of the bombs this far away, I could only guess what hell the NVA were experiencing first hand.

We radioed in that the airstrike had been right on the money and received orders to do a BDA report. I didn't like the idea of moving back into the area that had so many NVA in it, but as Alfred Lord Tennyson said in his poem "The Charge of the Light Brigade",

Theirs not to reason why,
Theirs but to do and die
Into the valley of Death
Rode the six hundred.

Unfortunately it was not really a valley and there was no high ground we could use to survey the damage from a distance so we had to move back into the area of the encampment. We were well over halfway there when we heard a loud movement in front of us. Stumbling out of the cover came an NVA soldier. His helmet was gone, blood was running out of his eyes and ears and both of his arms were clutching his belly. He saw us, stopped, fell to his knees, and keeled over. We had seen the same bloody eyes and ears before on corpses that had experienced high concussive damage when we were in Laos.

Uncle Bob approached our visitor and started to check him over. The fall had caused his arms to move away from his belly and his bloody intestines were now hanging loose from his wound. It was obvious that he did not have long to live. There was nothing we could do for him. Uncle Bob took out his first aid kit and removed four morphine syrettes. While it was no longer normal practice to have morphine in an IFAK, Individual First Aid Kit, we were working without the benefit of having a medic, so we were a little more prepared than most grunts. Uncle Bob gave the poor NVA all four syrettes and let him go peacefully rather than leaving him there to die while looking at his own guts. Uncle Bob did a quick search and removed a few papers from the NVA body.

As we move closer to the encampment we stopped often to do a Stop, Look, and Listen. Seeing and hearing nothing we went closer and closer until we actually entered what was left of the encampment. The place was deserted; apparently anyone who had survived the bombing had gotten the heck out of there before another wave of bombers came over to finish the job. There was not much to see but large craters and bits and pieces of bicycles and what may have been people. We did find what was left of several bunkers and tents but nothing survived the contents that had poured out of the B52 bomb bays. We didn't want to waste any time, we planned on only taking a quick look-see and a few photographs and get the hell out of there as soon as possible. While taking the photographs we came upon some documents that were blowing in the wind near what was left of one of the larger huts. When Gus showed Uncle Bob one of the pages had a map on it, we altered our time schedule and spent another five minutes to gather what documents we could find. While we did that Uncle Bob shot a second roll of film of the bomb damage. Then we got the hell out of there before anyone returned to the camp.

We went to a LZ that was at a bend in the river about three kilometers from what was left of the staging area, took up defensive positions in the tree line at the edge of the clearing, and waited for our dusk pick up. I had just checked my watch for the one thousandth time and it was only 1400 hours and extraction was not until 1800. It was then that we heard the sound of loud splashing coming from up river. By the amount of noise being made there was more than likely over a hundred men moving down river towards us.

Uncle Bob was just about to radio in for an emergency evacuation at an alternative LZ when we heard the trumpet call of an elephant. Abandoning all semblances of standard operating procedures we all turned to look at what was approaching. A herd of elephants was walking towards where we were hiding. Nobody knew what the hell to do. Fingers were flying – Run? Stay? What? The elephants were moving slowly and mainly on the opposite bank so Uncle Bob signed back, "stay - no - move."

We all watched in awe as 11 adult elephants and one baby elephant proceeded to approach where we were. Two of the larger ones that were in the front of the group stopped and faced the trees where we were hiding, their ears spread open and they keep a good watch on us as the others approached. As I watched them come toward us, lots of questions were running through my mind: Would they charge, would my CAR-15 stop something that size, would they be afraid and stop at the sound of firing, would I be able to outrun one of them through these trees, when should I start running? ...

Thankfully, once the rest of the herd passed by, and were well pass our location, the two guardians turned and followed the herd. I quickly looked around at the rest of the guys and saw a mixture of emotions on their faces. Chief had a grin from ear to ear, obviously overjoyed by what he saw. Uncle Bob showed fear and relief, perhaps questioning his call to stay and not get out of there sooner. Ron's head was tilted to the side with a look like "what the hell was that." But Harold's face puzzled me the most, it was almost like he had seen this all before and relieved that the elephants weren't pink this time.

After exchanging quiet grins, knowing that we would have lots to talk about when we got back, we resumed our defensive positions and waited for our extraction. At a few minutes past the scheduled 1800 we heard several helicopters approaching. Uncle Bob tossed a red smoke grenade into the clearing as he chatted with one of the pilots of the evacuation flight. We loaded up and were back at the forward command center getting our debriefing by 1830.

Our feedback report, the rolls of film from the BDA and documents we had gathered were packaged up and sent to MACV intelligence for analysis. The next day Major Straight called us into the sandbag covered

Quonset hut we were using as our forward command post to pass on the congratulations on the job we had done from Air Force command, including one from the Air Force Chief of Staff. They were very impressed with the quality of our BDA and especially that we had actually gotten photographs taken from within the still smoking remains of the staging area. The debriefing paused when the Major had to take a call from MACV.

We chatted among ourselves while the major was on the phone. We all turned to look at him on the phone when the major started to yell at whoever he was talking to. We quieted down enough for us all to hear, "The next time, why in the hell don't you get your own stupid ass on a helicopter and do it your f'n self!!!" The Major slammed the phone back down and with a face as red as a beet stormed out of the hut.

We stood there for a while wondering what to do next.

The phone rang again, this time Ducky was responding to whoever was on the line.

"I'm sorry you were disconnected, Sir."

...

"I'm sorry, Sir, he stepped out of the office, Sir."

...

"No, I don't know when he will return, Sir."

...

It then sounded like Ducky decided to pull someone's tail a little, "I am not sure where he went, Sir. But since he had just recently gotten off the phone with the Air Force Chief of Staff, General McConnell, who was complimenting him on our last mission, he might have gone to pass on the General's 'well done' to the men who performed our last mission, Sir."

...

"I'll be sure to tell him, Sir."

...

Ducky hung up the phone and made an obscene gesture to it and chuckling said, "Boy, that guy sure was mad at the start of that conversation but changed his tune at the end."

We waited about 15 minutes until the major came back in. "I'm sorry about that guys, I had to cool off a bit before I could speak in a normal tone of voice. It seems as if the A-Holes at MACV were very pleased with the documents and photos. The documents had some real good intelligence on other staging areas and the amount of supplies and number of troops passing through that one. But that stupid Army major I was just talking to started bitching at me that you guys didn't explore the area long enough to get an exact body count. The G'damn idiot actually wanted to know why you didn't dig down into the destroyed bunkers and count the bodies."

We were flabbergasted and were about to explain about getting out of there before the survivors realized another wave of bombers wasn't coming right away and returned to their camp, but Major Straight raised his hand to stop our protest. He said, "Don't worry. I know, no need to explain to me. It is just that some R.A.M.F.'s don't have the sense they were born with. To them it is more important to look good to their bosses than to reduce the risk of others who actually put their lives on the line."

As he continued speaking his face started getting redder and the volume of his conversation louder until he shouted "The G'damn idiot!". He paused, took a deep breath before continuing, "Sorry again guys. I need more time to cool off. Why don't you guys take the rest of the day off and go to the BX and bring us back some nice cold beers."

Before we left Ducky told the major about the conversation he just had with MACV. "Ducky, you didn't actually tell him General McConnell called personally?"

Sheepishly, Ducky replied, "Well.... it sure did splash some really cold water on that hot headed bastard. It kind of took the steam right out of his yelling at me to get you on the phone right away, Sir."

The major starting to laugh but trying to keep a straight face he said, "I get to call majors, hot-headed bastards, not you Ducky. You are to call them by their proper rank and name, 'Major Bastards'. Go get lots of beer, guys! We are all taking the rest of the day off."

Laughing Ducky said, "Excuse me, sir. Just how many cases of beer did you need, Major Bass, oops, I mean Major Straight?"

Major Straight totally lost all control and laughed out loud. He handed Uncle Bob a stack of MPC he had taken from his wallet and said, "Get one dented can of warm beer for Airman Basic Ducky and about 20 cases of beer for the other 31 of us in camp today. I said LOTS of beer."

* * *

May 18, 2018
Chania, Crete, Greece

The waiter just happened to be passing our table as Johnny said, "LOTS of beer." So he asked, "Eight more beers?"

The timing was perfect so after a quick scan of his table mates, Johnny replied in Greek, "Ναι, οκτώ μπύρες."

They were halfway through that round of beers when Mary asked, "How did Sam's operation go?"

The General said, "Sam actually wrote a letter telling us that the operation was a success and after six weeks of physical therapy it was determined that he had gotten 99% of the flexibility back in his knee. Then he actually apologized to us that when given the option of a medical discharge or coming back to rejoin us, that he had taken the medical discharge. I had written back that he made the correct choice. Sam and I actually continued to exchange letters and Christmas cards. After he was discharged he went home, got his degree from Stanford in medicine and went on to become a pediatrician and absolutely loved his job. His son wrote me that Sam had worked until the day he died. He passed away of a heart attack one night in his own bed, that was a little over two years ago."

Johnny raised his beer and said, "To the fallen."

Toasting, they all echoed, "To the fallen."

CHAPTER 14
May 19, 2018
Frangokastello, Crete, Greece

On today's agenda was a ride to the south coast of Crete to Frangokastello. The reunion group was going to have lunch at a beach side taverna owned by Kostas who is the brother of their minibus driver, Niko. Kostas had arranged for a special barbecue meal and a private tour of the Frangokastello Fort given by his wife Christina, the administrator for the historical site.

After a two hour picturesque drive, they arrived at the taverna and were warmly greeted by Kostas and Christina. When Kostas was introducing himself and his wife, the group was a little taken aback by his accent. He spoke English with a distinctive Texas Twang. When Kathy remarked on his accent he explained that he attended Angelo State University in San Angelo, Texas. The General expanded by telling them that when he was stationed at Goodfellow Air Force Base in San Angelo, Kostas had stayed with him while he attended the university there.

Because lunch would not be ready for a while, Christina took the group to the Frangokastello Fort. Since Christina was the administrator, the tour was well beyond the ordinary. She took them into places where the public is not normally allowed and she was extremely knowledgeable on the history of the site. She told the group the Venetians built the fortress in 1374 to protect the area from pirate raids and the local population. She had lots of little antidotes on the construction about how at night the local Cretans, who were not yet subjugated by the invading Venetian, would tear down portions of the construction built during the day.

It was originally called the Castle of Saint Nikitas by the Venetians but, as a sign of disrespect it was called Frangokastello by the locals which means the Castle of the Franks (Venetians). The fort was constructed before the widespread use of cannons so it was built using just stone walls rather that earthen ramparts like the fortifications built around Iraklion and Chania. It is also different from the major city fortifications in that it is rectangular with square towers on each corner, and was not meant to encompass and protect an entire city, but to provide a strong point for the defending garrison. The fortress did not see much action against the Arab pirates but did see a lot of action against the Cretans. It initially was built by the Venetians to suppress the locals, but following the Turkish invasion it was then used by the Turks for the same purpose. In the 1820s it was the location of a major uprising of the Cretans against the Turks.

She told the group how in May 17, 1828, just 210 years and two days ago, 600 Cretans occupied the fort and were attacked by over 8000 Turks. The Turks managed to enter the fort after killing over half of the defenders.

She told them how to this day the locals still see a ghost army of the defending Cretans, who had not been buried after the fort fell, move through the area and enter the sea. But today, we were too late to see the ghosts, called the Drossoulites, or Dew Men in English, because they only appear when there is heavy morning dew.

After the tour the group got something they were not expecting. They were treated to Texas style barbecue, ribs, corn on the cob, and baked beans, quite different than the Greek meals they had been having. They were sitting on the beautiful white sand beach talking about the fort's ghost story when Harold said, "The fort's defenders might not be walking around in the morning dew if they would have had Johnny around to help them."

Laughing, he said, "Johnny has lots of experience making really cool defensive toys."

Joan asked, "What do you mean?"

"Let me tell you about the time we got stuck in a fort along the Vietnam/Cambodian border."

* * *

March 1969 ~ Vietnam/Cambodia Border
As told by Harold Vinter

Our team had been working inside northeast Cambodia along the border by the Vietnam highlands. We had just spent five exhausting days setting sensors and replacing batteries in ones that we had planted on previous visits. The section of Cambodia where we were working was a lot less densely populated than the Parrot's Beak, so things were not quite as intense as some of our earlier incursions. We were scheduled to stay two more days but there was a bad weather front coming in which could cause problems with a helicopter extraction so we left early.

The helicopter we were in was just coming up to the border when we took ground fire from several heavy machine guns. Sitting in the back, we didn't know this until we heard several of the nasty sounding cerchunks as rounds hit someplace around the motor cowling. At the sound, everyone's eyes and ears went into hyper-tense mode. Eyes were roaming the inside of the machine to see if anyone was hurt or if smoke could be seen. Ears were listening for any change in the sound of the helicopter's engine and for more cerchunks. The pilot started some very dramatic evasive maneuvers throwing everyone around. The Huey crew chief who was acting as the left side door gunner was perhaps a little too relaxed. When the violent maneuvers began, if he hadn't been strapped in with a monkey harness he would have flown out the side of the helicopter..

This particular bird had been equipped with two M60 7.62mm machine guns, one in each side door. The M60s were suspended using bungee cords rather than mounted on swiveling mounts. The bungee mounted weapons allowed for increased firing angles, but in this case, the added maneuverability of firing angles caused the problem. As the crew chief started to fall, instinctively he grabbed the closest thing around - his gun, causing the M60 to fire a few rounds. But his fall also caused the angle of fire to be up at the most extreme possible angle, and one or two of the bullets must have hit the helicopter's rotors. The damage brought about by the accidental firing resulted in a disruption of a smooth airflow over the blades causing the helicopter to begin to violently shake.

By now we were over the border and the pilot headed for the first safe landing site he could find, which was a fire base located on a hilltop about five kilometers from the border. The FSB, fire support base, we landed at was brand new and still in the early stages of establishing its defenses. Only six howitzers were in place, not all the bunkers were complete, there was only one row of concertina barbed wire fencing, and the defensive minefield was not yet in place. Luckily the helicopter pads are usually one of the first things the engineers build. The bird landed safely but the pilot wasn't about to take off again until he got his machine repaired. After a long, loud "conversation" with his crew chief about shooting down his own bird, the pilot was on the radio checking on getting us another helicopter to bring us back to Tan Son Nhut, but bad news, a severe weather front was just about on us, so they were grounding all flights until the weather improved.

Ron was checking in with the camp management when 82mm mortar rounds started landing in the FSB's perimeter. One of the NVA mortar-man was either highly skilled or super lucky because the first mortar round landed practically on top of one of the six 105 millimeter howitzers that were the primary reason for the base's existence. The blast flipped the 375 pound cannon on its side and took out five members of its crew, but thankfully didn't cause any secondary explosions. Three other rounds in the first salvo fell on other sections of the FSB. One was not too far from the helicopter landing pad.

Chief, Johnny and I were waiting for Ron near the helicopter, but when the mortar rounds began to pop, we ran like hell to a nearby bunker. The bunker we entered was filled to capacity. Besides us, there was our helicopter crew, and several army engineers that were working on the construction of the fire base's defenses. It was standing room only, but no one was complaining as several more salvos of four mortar rounds struck the base. One round hit extremely close to our bunker and the bunker filled with dust shaken through the, "oh, I wish it was a hell of a lot thicker", roof. The smell of the bunker went from stale, musky sweat to dusty outhouse. Apparently someone in the bunker literally had the poop scared out of them.

The shelling lasted about four or five minutes when two of the base's howitzers opened up in counter-battery fire mode. The NVA gunners let fly with one more salvo then ceased fire to make a hasty exit before our guns could zero in on their location. No one moved for several more minutes just to make sure the firing had stopped.

We emerged from our crowded, stinky bunker and looked around the camp. The smoke of several small fires was hanging in the air as more and more heads started popping out of the holes they were hiding in. Shouts were heard as officers and noncoms hustled troops to strengthen the perimeters defenses or to take care of the injured. One of the officers saw us emerge from the bunker looking a little lost and pointed toward the west yelling for us to take up defensive positions close to one of the 50 caliber machine gun emplacements on that wall.

The base had been caught flat footed and unprepared for that daytime mortar attack. The defenses were not yet finished and lots of personnel were in the open or working on the defenses, so there were a large number of casualties streaming towards the aid station. We were shortly joined by Ron who had been in the command center when the barrage started. He had stuck around long enough to be politely asked to have our team augment the defenses on the southwest perimeter since it was the weakest area of the defenses. Knowing that the fixed machine gun emplacement was a mortar magnet, the rest of us quickly got away from it and headed to our newly assigned position on the southwest side of the camp.

We merged in with the other defenders along the perimeter waiting to see if the mortar attack was a prelude to a ground attack against the base, or just a harassment shelling. As we waited Ron filled us in on the information he had gathered while in the command center. It seems that the base suffered ten killed, including five members of the now out of commission howitzer, and twenty-one wounded. This was extremely heavy casualties considering the entire fire base was only manned by an infantry company of about 140 men along with 25 engineers, 75 members of the artillery component and less than 60 other personnel, bringing the entire fire base's complement to fewer than 300. So we had suffered an over ten percent casualty rate in the attack.

We had just gotten ourselves situated when the weatherman decided to make matters worse. The sky opened up and a heavy downpour began to turn our little trench defense into a flooded canal. The heavy rain was not helping with visibility either. Combining that with the strong winds whipping up the foliage, out past the cleared free fire area around the base, made for a very nervous time.

Due to weight limitations we were not packing much ammunition so Ron sent Johnny and Chief back to get us a few claymores, hand grenades, and enough ammo for our CAR-15s to make sure they remained operating as guns and did not revert to being only clubs. We needed the ammo just in case we need to beat off a prolonged attack. When they returned they passed out the munitions. The two of them crawled out of the trench to place the 4 claymore they had obtained well in front of our positions. They crawled back through what was quickly becoming a sea of mud and we began a long wet wait to see what would develop.

At 1600 the local infantry company sent out a patrol, but they had not even made it past the cleared area around the base before they came under heavy fire, taking several casualties. The base artillery quickly started shelling the area the fire came from and the enemy fire from the tree line fell rapidly back to zero. The howitzers then fired several rounds of smoke to cover the patrol's return to base before they resumed firing High Explosive rounds, into that area of the tree line. The patrol returned to the base with another three casualties, including two KIA. One more percent of the base defenders were out of action.

Things quieted down until dark. About an hour after full darkness, word was passed down the line that we were to have a mad minute the second the big guns fired illumination rounds. A "mad minute" was used to describe a minute when everyone would fire their weapons into the vegetation line area at the edge of the cleared free fire zone around the fire base. It is intended to flush out infiltrators or catch the enemy in areas which could provide potential concealment for staging an attack.

Everyone listened intently for the gun commander to yell "fire". When he did so, we all fired our weapons into the tree line on full auto. Our team used ammunition conservation and only ripped off two 20 round clips before we stopped firing. One of the illumination rounds which contained a parachute flare lighted up the area before our position, giving us ample time to survey the ground before us and the tree line as the slowly descending flare wildly swung around in the heavy winds.

At a bellowed "cease fire" command, the mad minute ended with a few sporadic shots fired by trigger happy GIs at a few shadows that danced in the fading light of the wind swept flares. As the rain and stiff winds swept the pungent smell of the cordite from all the expended gunpowder from the camp, things became quiet once again, a least for a little while.

Word came down the line for every other man to stay on the line and to rotate every four hours so we could all get some sleep. It sounded easier than it was to get any real rest. We were kept awake by the sounds of the howitzers intermittently firing illumination rounds, interspersed with the blasts in and around the base from the NVA mortar shells. The NVA mortar team would fire eight or twelve shots then move to some other position before the howitzer counter-battery fire could find them, as soon as they would move to a new spot they would fire another couple of salvos and move again. One of the mortar attacks did score a hit on the helicopter we arrived on, making it a candidate for the junk yard, rather than a maintenance yard. It was far too noisy and dangerous to catch any sleep. We were used to the danger of living in enemy territory, but it wasn't the same as all of this noise and the randomness of incoming mortar rounds. When we were in enemy territory it was always very quiet and any noise could mean trouble, here it was constant noise and danger.

Morning brought no relief from the weather; we were still in the grips of the storm. No relief flights would be landing anytime soon, not even medevac for the overflowing aid station that had to expand into a neighboring bunker. Another six men added to the wounded at the expanded aid station and two others died during last night's shelling. Chief also passed on the bad news that our night-vision gear was out of service from being submerged too long in the canal that was our fighting trench and he couldn't get it working even after replacing the batteries.

Everyone in camp was busy digging in deeper and adding to the defenses of the base. Johnny and Chief disappeared into the camp and twenty minutes later Johnny came back rolling a sloshing partially full 55 gallon barrel of aviation gas. It was what was left over after it had been used to refuel our now badly damaged helicopter. He was followed closely behind by Chief with his arms full carrying two large boxes of laundry detergent and another claymore mine.

When Johnny saw the questioning look on our faces, pointing he said, "This is for right above the portion of the hill right down there, by the steep drop off. There is a big blind spot there where anyone could hide and not be seen from the base."

He took off the top of the barrel and mixed in the laundry detergent to thicken the fuel into a foo-gas mixture. He wrapped a small chunk of the C4 he always seemed to be carrying around with some detonating cord, lowered it into the barrel, and recapped it with a length of the detonation wiring coming out the top. He and Chief rolled the dangerous mixture directly above the blind spot Johnny had pointed out. They dug a small trench and used some rocks to stop the barrel from moving in the heavy winds and placed some small scrub grass to hide it from the view of anyone outside the base. He then spliced the wiring from the explosives he had placed in the drum into the same firing mechanism as a claymore. They aimed the claymore at the drum and ran the wire from the claymore's firing trigger back to our trench. Now when that claymore fired, it would rip open the barrel at the same time as the C4 inside would explode, igniting the thickened fuel. Anyone on the other side of the blast and in the blind spot below it would be blanketed by a rain of the burning foo-gas mixture.

Ron and I watched as they created their little surprise for anyone who attempted to use the blind spot. When they returned I told Johnny and

Chief they were nasty, devious bastards. Then I patted them on the back saying, "Atta-boy!"

The rest of the day, not spent hiding from mortar rounds, was spent filling sandbags and reinforcing our area of the perimeter line. On one of his foraging missions Johnny came back with a dozen M14 mines. The M14 had been in use since 1955 and was known better by its nickname, the toe popper. This mine only had an ounce of explosive in it and was meant more to wound and maim rather than kill. The mine was tiny, only 2.2 inches in diameter and less than 2 inches deep, so it was extremely easy to plant and difficult to find. During the cover of a particularly heavy downpour, Johnny crawled out to the barbed wire guarding the base. He did the obvious of adding a few tin cans with rocks in them to the wire so if someone moved the wire the rocks would make a noise and alert the defenders. This was extremely old school and a trick known by all the NVA sappers. The NVA sappers were elite commando units trained to approach highly defended locations, disable the defenses and inflict heavy damage on the defenders using a variety of explosive devices. The twist Johnny added was he hid the toe popper mines in front of the wire in the most likely path a sapper would use to approach and disable the tin can and rock alarms. Surprise Sapper! We aren't as dumb as we acted. Now instead of the noise from the tin can alerting us, the blast of the toe popper would. Johnny made careful notes of where he placed the tiny mines so we could retrieve them before we left the camp. It is not a good idea to leave unknown mines around your base defenses.

Having done just about all we could to strengthen our defenses, we waited for an attack since it was bound to come tonight, if it came at all. The forecast was for the weather to clear tomorrow and I am sure the NVA knew that as well as we did. So if they wanted to attack the base before its defenses were completed and without the possibility of air support, tonight was the night it had to happen.

During the day, the howitzers fired H&I missions. H&I stood for Harassment and Interdiction, these were when the artillery fired on suspected and probable areas where the enemy might hide or use for mortar tube firing positions. They are used to keep the NVA from getting too comfortable and exploiting good positions. As night fell the H&I missions were intermixed with firing illumination rounds. It would be another long sleepless night.

At about 8 PM there was a blast in the wire on our side of the base, one of Johnny's toe poppers had been tripped. When our team started firing toward the wire, everybody else along the entire base's perimeter opened up too. The howitzers shifted from their H&I mission to firing illumination rounds such that all sides of the perimeter fire free zone were lighted. There were several sappers caught in the lights. While there were a few on the other sides of the fire base, most were on the western side. The illumination flares pinned the sappers down like butterflies in a display case. The sappers that were seen didn't last long with the entire base blasting away; however one on the northwestern side did manage to blast a gap into the barbed wire with a satchel charge before he was killed.

Now that their sappers had been exposed, firing began coming from the tree line on the north and east sides of the base at the same time as the NVA started to mortar the base from several locations. Most of their effort seemed to be directed at the artillery but one of their mortars concentrated on blasting the defensive emplacements on the western perimeter. The 50 caliber machine gun on that side was the primary target receiving over 10 rounds before it took a direct hit. That was the gun the team had originally been assigned to protect when we first arrived, before Ron had us shifted away from the machine gun to the southwest defenses.

The NVA mortar team had put all of the practice from the earlier shelling and multiple firing locations to good use because they had the artillery firing pits zeroed in. The howitzer crews were too busy dodging flying chunks of scrap metal to return counter-battery fire or fire illumination rounds. Thankfully the fire support base's mortar team was well trained and they began to fire illumination rounds. And good thing too, because the NVA had started to advance in from the tree line in the north and east. The fire from that side of the base became almost deafening. The night was lit with the crisscrossing of tracer rounds, all reddish orange going out and mainly greenish coming in from NVA automatic weapons, but a few reddish orange from their smaller arms too.

Then we heard another one of Johnny's toe poppers going off to our front. We again started firing to our front rather than worrying about what was going on behind us. Johnny fumbled with his blooper for a few seconds and managed to get off an illumination round. What the small flare revealed scared the living daylights out of me.

The NVA had made use of the attack on the other side of the camp as a diversion. With the big guns out of service due to the mortar attack and our mortars busy lighting up the north east, the NVA, under the cover of darkness, were advancing from the west in strength. The leading edge of the assault was just getting to the barbed wire. The toe popper gave us enough advanced warning that the NVA had not yet gotten past the wire before they were spotted. Now others on the western side of the base opened fire, catching the advancing enemy in the open. But they were close and soon there were more charges going off opening gaps in the concertina barbed wire fence.

The height of the hill the base camp was built on and the slippery mud of the rain washed denuded earth more than likely saved the camp perimeter from being breached right then. The steepness slowed the advance just long enough for the concentrated full automatic fire from the defenders and the claymores to render well over 25% casualties to the attacking force, but they kept coming. Just as things were getting touch and go, the base's infantry squad that was being held in reserve was committed to the defense of the western side. Their added fire power drove what remained of the enemy attacking force back.

Johnny, who had been putting his blooper to excellent use lobbing grenades into the gaps in the wire, noticed a lot of NVA were not withdrawing completely but evading into the blind spot he had so thoughtfully defended with the foo-gas. He picked up the M57 firing device he had rigged to fire both the claymore and C4 ignition charge in the foo-gas barrel. He gave us a warning that he was going to fire it so we could take cover ... just in case he had been too enthusiastic with the C4.

Of course, I couldn't help myself and continued to watch what happened. There was a double loud explosion, one from the mine and one from the small amount of C4 in the barrel. The concussion wave and most the 700 steel balls packed inside the claymore started moving forward in an explosive blast at close to 4000 feet per second, smashed into the barrel. The barrel was shredded and flew over the edge and down the side of the steep drop off. The blast of the small C4 charge in the barrel ignited the napalm like thickened aviation fuel in the barrel creating a firestorm that rained down into the blind spot where the enemy had fled.

There were screams coming from the area where the flaming foo-gas landed. Suddenly two of hidden NVA who had not died in the initial rain of fire began running away from their cover with the thick gooey mixture still burning on their uniforms and bare skin. I am not sure if I was being kind or cruel for not shooting them as they fled flaming, but I did pity them.

Apparently Ron too watched because all he said was, "Damn, Johnny, that turned the little blind spot into a spot in the seventh circle of hell."

Unfortunately the flash totally ruined what little night vision I had and I couldn't see what was going on in the rest of the attack area for a minute or two. But there was only sporadic firing from the base defenders and no return fire coming from attackers. But to be sure the blind spot had been completely cleared, Ron and Johnny both skillfully tossed hand grenades over the side of the ledge where the barrel had been.

The Second Lieutenant who had led the reserves in the charge to reinforce the western defenses came by counting each defender he passed and taping every fifth man on the shoulder telling them to move to fill in the gaps on the western side of the base where we had taken the most casualties. I was one of the fifth men tapped so I moved away from the team to take up a position in about the center of the western defense line.

Just as I took a good defensive position, alone in a two-man position in a chest deep pit three quarters rain filled hole, the firing resumed.

Apparently the NVA had rallied and were making a second attack on the west side. This time all their mortars fired rounds concentrating on the trenches and firing pits of the western defenses. They then shifted their attention back to the howitzers before the gunners could emerge from their hiding spots and start counter-battery fire. My night vision had returned and I concentrated my fire on the closest advancing NVA. I was distracted when the Second Lieutenant that had pulled me from the rest of the team came crawling up and joined me in the two man pit.

I had not had time to check my ammo status so I switched from full automatic to single fire and made use of the illumination flares to choose my targets, firing at a slow steady rate rather than blazing away a full clip at a time on automatic. The LT must have known his ammo count because he was practically melting his barrel as fast as he was changing clips. The base mortar team had switched from the M83 Illuminating, parachute flare, rounds to High Explosive rounds, and together with the reinforced perimeter defenders, we proved too much for the NVA to handle and they started to withdraw, again with heavy losses.

The LT tapped me and asked for a couple more clips for his M16 since he was out. After a quick pat down to check my ammo level, I handed him two and told him to slow down and single fire because I only had two more clips left. If looks could kill, the look he gave me when I TOLD HIM to slow down was enough to put me in a hospital for the rest of my life.

The rain was down to a slow drizzle, the wind down to a mild breeze, and I could hear jets and helicopters headed our way, so life was once again good. We were still receiving occasional shots from the tree line but the incoming mortar fire had stopped. I finally had enough time to take a second look at my firing pit partner. What I saw shocked me; he looked like he was a freshman in high school, not old enough to be in the military, much less an officer. Then I even noticed that he was wearing nice shiny brass emblems of rank, and though wet and filthy now, his green utility uniform had showed signs of having been freshly starched in the very recent past before he jumped into my rain filled firing pit hole. He was breathing with a respiration rate that seemed to be well over a hundred breaths a minute.

We had two seconds of comradeship and shared a smile of relief before he ruined it all. The idiot then told me to "Go out there and get a body count."

There were still shots coming in from the tree line and I know that there had to be more than a few of the many bodies scattered out in front of us playing possum. I didn't hide any of my feeling when I flat out said, "Ain't no f'n way! If I go out there now, the first body I will count would be my own!"

His eyes rapidly jumped to where my name tag would be and to my arm where my rank insignia would have been, but ever since the time we saved the Green Beret Major in Cambodia we no longer wore anything at all on our uniforms.

He then yelled at me, his voice breaking as he did so, "I order you to go get a body count!"

"Like I said before, ain't no f'n way. Go do it yourself, you idiot."

"I said it's an order."

Emphatically shaking my head no, "I sure as hell am not going out there to take a G'damn body count. That can wait until in the morning."

With a face as red as a desert sunset he yelled, "You coward, I'll see you when I get back."

He then yelled up and down the line to hold your fire, and told the defenders he was going out there before the lines. He proceeded to climb out of the fighting pit and crawl down the hill to begin taking a body count. Not more than two minutes later I hear some shots and the young lieutenant yelling, "Medic! Medic! Medic!"

Cursing the stupid fool under my breath, I knew what I had to do. Leaving my CAR-15 behind, I pulled out my Mk22, checked I had a full clip, a round chambered, and the safety off, before I proceeded down the hill to go help the idiot. I inch wormed my way towards the place I thought I had heard the call come from. I was slowly advancing with my finger on the trigger ready to shoot anything that moved that wasn't the Lieutenant. I found him lying on his side with both of his hands clamped over a profusely bleeding thigh wound.

He looked at me and was about to say something when I put the index finger of my left hand to my lips and quietly shushed him. At least he was smart enough not to make any more noise. We had both heard movement a little downhill from us. With a muffled "put, put" I fired two silenced rounds into an NVA that had been playing possum and was more than likely, the one that had shot the LT.

I didn't want to stay out here and find any more surprises so I started to drag the LT back up the hill. He moaned when I had to drag him over some exposed jagged rocks, but it was the best path with the most cover, and at this point I was so mad, I would have dragged him naked through a mile of broken glass not to expose my position.

When I was close enough to the firing line, I softly said, "Friend coming through with a wounded dumb-ass second lieutenant."

I waited until my presence was acknowledged before slowly proceeding. I sure didn't want to live through this fire fight only to be shot by a fellow American. I got him behind some sandbags and a medic arrived to help me attend to his wound.

The lieutenant looked at me and said, "Thanks for coming to get me, but I am still going to bust your ass for not obeying orders."

I continued helping the medic bandage his leg, took some morphine from the medic's kit. Showed the shot to the medic and when he nodded, I asked the lieutenant,

"Do you even know who the hell I am?"

He again gave a quick glance to where my name tag and rank should be displayed.

I smiled, gave the LT the morphine shot and said, "Good. He's all yours, doc."

I went back to my fighting pit, retrieved my CAR-15 and headed back to rejoin the team. The second I saw Ron, I told him to get on the horn and get us the hell out of here PDQ and it is extremely important we do it NOW. He cocked his head with a questioning look but without saying a word he snatched up our radio, requesting the boss to do whatever he could to be sure we were on the first non-medevac flight out of there.

* * *

May 19, 2018
Frangokastello, Crete, Greece

At this point the General interrupted Harold's story. Displaying a very grave face he said, "Harold, do you mean to say I was suppose to have had you court-martialed for disobeying a direct order?"

Harold gave us a mischievous smiled, "Oh, no, sir. I don't believe my name ever appeared on any charges. Though I might have disobeyed ... ummm ... I mean misinterpreted one or perhaps two orders during my time in the military."

The General began to laugh hard now. "That's only because he didn't know who the hell you were. Of course if he did, I would have gone to see him personally to explain about your personality defects and talk him out of filing charges. Then I would have come back and shot you ... ummm ... I mean given you a shot of bourbon and thanked you for saving his dumb ass."

"O.K. everybody back to the bus. Let's get back to the hotel before Niko needs to drive back through those mountains at night."

CHAPTER 15
May 20, 2018
Rethymno, Crete, Greece

Today the group planned on a drive to Rethymno to do a little shopping and sightseeing, but a better opportunity had presented itself. The General learned that the sailing yacht that had taken us to Dia was going to a shipyard in Rethymno for minor repairs. The General asked Aris, the boat's owner, if the group could hitch a ride. The tour got even better when the General learned that the yacht would not be sailing back until just after dark. There would be spectacular scenery on the way back watching the lights of the island pass by as they sailed back under the stars.

The group got box lunches from the hotel and enjoyed a light meal as they sailed to Rethymno. The yacht dropped them off at the harbor then proceeded to the shipyard. They went off sightseeing and to do a little shopping. The General took them to a ceramics workshop where he had ordered some customized German regimental style steins to be made. The shop owner was very apologetic that they were not ready yet. It seems that the steins' lids had arrived late from the supplier in Germany. He brought out one of the almost finished steins. The group was a little shocked to see the sample.

It was a full liter size, liquid-pearl white, ceramic stein. On one side of the stein was the Air Force Security Service emblem surrounded by a raised laurel wreath motif. The Air Force Security Service emblem was a shield divided into four components. The design had on the upper left a green and yellow globe on a blue field, the upper right a yellow lightning bolt on a red field, the lower right a small white sword and shield on a blue field, and the lower left a blue wing on a yellow field, below the full shield is a scrolled banner saying USAF Security Service. That side of the stein also had a raised scroll below the laurel wreath with the unit's motto "Freedom through Vigilance" printed in gold. The other side had a raised jungle motif with a circle in the center. The circle had three lines of raised text painted in gold. The lines were "6922nd Security Group", "Detachment 11" and, "Southeast Asia 1968-1969".

He also showed the General one of the unattached lids. It was gold with a 100 mm statue cluster at the center with four GIs in combat gear wearing boonie hats. He said the German lid maker had done a remarkably detailed job on the sculpture, and you can even see the faces and weapons of the men in the picture. He produced the pictures he had used to create the lid sculpture. One was a picture of Ron, Harold, Johnny and Chief in full combat gear walking out of a tent. The General explained he had taken that picture of the team as they were leaving on a mission from Tan Son Nhut. The General then passed the lid around to the group. Kathy must have moved her stare from the lid sculpture to Ron's face and back at least five times before she passed the lid to Joan saying to Ron, "It sure does look exactly like you must have back then, before the gray hair, wrinkles, and your beer belly."

Chuckling Ron said, "Back then I never thought I would live long enough to ever have gray hair and wrinkles. I also never thought my six-pack abs would turn into a full keg. General, this is marvelous. Will we be able to order one made for ourselves?"

Smiling the General replied, "No, you can't have one made. I already planned on giving all four of you a set of six to take home. And I am keeping a set of twelve for my bar at home. And I will email you all a digital version of all the other photographs of the group that I have."

After the lid was examined by everyone it was returned to the ceramics shop owner. He apologized once again that steins were not yet ready but he promised that they would be ready for pickup in two days. The General told him they would swing by in two days around 4 o'clock to pick them up and to please have them safely packaged for international shipping in boxes of six each.

The group did a little more shopping, and then had a nice seafood supper at one of the restaurants along the waterfront under old Venetian Fortress, Fortezza. After supper they went to the dock to await the yacht. It showed up about ten minutes later, just as the last reds and purples of the setting sun were fading to black. They boarded and opened one of the bottles of wine they had bought in Rethymno. By the time they had maneuvered out of the harbor the sun was down and the lights of the city were coming on.

The yacht went about a half a kilometer north of the island so they could get a better view of the night lit city. The Fortress Fortezza walls and the stone lighthouse at the harbor entrance were illuminated by large lights along their bases giving them a golden glow. The effect coupled with the multicolored lights of the old city between the golden glow of the Venetian relics was quite spectacular. They sailed along enjoying the sights rather than speaking.

Looking up at a sky filled with stars Johnny softly said, "I miss seeing all the stars in the night sky. There is far too much light pollution in Miami to see more than a few of the brightest stars."

The group agreed and reverted to silence when Joan poured the last bit of wine from the bottle, not quite filling her glass. She stood saying, "I'll go get another bottle of wine but I hope there aren't any ants on board like the last trip. After hearing Ron's tail of getting bit by all those ants I am afraid of them more than ever. Of course Harold couldn't miss the opportunity. "Ron, now that you have told the story about the ants why don't you tell us why you hate leeches too."

"By now I know better than to fight you on these things, Harold. But like I said when I talked about the ants, I hate them. But, I hate leeches just as much, if not more than ants."

* * *

April 1969 ~ Cambodia
As told by Ron Lafayette

It was about mid-April and we were still staging out of Tan Son Nhut setting and maintaining the sensors along the Ho Chi Minh Trail in Cambodia. We were in a swampy area northwest of the Parrot's Beak working with Wild Bill's team. There was a sector where none of the sensors had picked up any activity for a long time.

We were checking the sensors to see if they had failed or if the activity that had been along this section had shifted to another branch of the trail. We were finding nothing wrong with the sensors and were just replacing the batteries when word came down that there was possible activity north of where we were working. We finished replacing batteries in the area where we were, then headed north along a raised wooded island between two swampy areas, I am not sure what this type of area is called in Cambodia, but back home in Louisiana, we would call it a chenier.

We discovered a trail heading north that had not been used in a few weeks, but because of the hard packed earth of the trail, along with the signs of manually cut back vegetation along the edges of the path, at one time this trail was the location for lots of traffic. It was obvious that the trail was not currently in use since we found lots of large complex spider webs across the trail. It takes a while for spider webs that complex to be created and enhanced upon by the area's giant wood spider, the Nephila Maculata. While not the biggest spider in the world, these things can reach over seven and a half inches from toe to toe. And I remember having seen one of its webs almost fifteen feet by five feet and strong enough to have captured a small animal. The ones we were seeing along the trail were not close to that large but big enough to have taken several weeks to create. Just to be sure we placed a few sensors along what had once been a well used route and continued north with my team following Bill's.

We stayed off the main path by moving along the chenier on the west side of the trail, you could tell the chenier was getting narrower, because in order to stay out of a swampy area we were being forced closer to the trail. We crossed to another chenier by wading almost waist deep for fifteen meters through some slimy green water. On the other side of the depression the ground again rose to above water level and the undergrowth began to thin.

Once we hit dry land again, looking down, I noticed that there were several leeches clinging to my jungle boots and fatigue pants. I pulled my knife and flicked them off as we took a short breather. I wasn't the only one. Chief was doing the same thing. He said, "We don't have these on the reservation in Arizona. And I think I like our rattlesnakes a lot better than these blood suckers. You can keep this damn swamp shit; give me the high deserts of the Diné any day."

I asked him what he meant by high deserts of the Diné. He thought for a minute. "Have you seen some of the western movies when they are in the desert with lots of plateaus and rocky hills all around?

"Yep. Just like the area I passed through with my family when we went to the Grand Canyon. One of the places I saw like that was called Monument Valley."

"Exactly, Monument Valley is on our reservation. And Diné is how we refer to ourselves; it translates to 'The People'."

Our conversation was interrupted by Wild Bill calling an end to the break and getting us back on our way. We traveled another five kilometers north and during a Stop, Look and Listen we faintly heard some talking coming from our front. Wild Bill hand signed a warning to the team in case anyone hadn't heard it.

After the losses it had taken in Laos, Wild Bill's team had Jim Adams on point, Dave Thrasher on drag, with Don Reinkens as the blooper. Jim was leading us up to this point and asked Wild Bill what he wanted to do, wait here or continue forward. Wild Bill looked at his watch, saw that we were in a well covered area, and signed for us to hunker down here for the night.

Through the night we had not heard any more talking or movement so first thing in the morning we again moved north paralleling the trail we were following. We had not gone more than 250 meters when the trail we had been tracking dead ended at the intersection of another trail, this one had lots of fresh tracks. We placed two sensors on new trail on both sides of the intersection.

Wild Bill and I had a quick conversation and it was decided that I would take my team east, he would take his team west, and we would join back up at last night's bivouac. We moved out with Chief leading the way as usual. The thinness of the undergrowth allowed us to make relatively good time and we had covered about four kilometers, placing a few sensors as we went along. when we heard movement from the trail. We went to ground in some thicker vegetation and waited to see what would be passing on the trail.

We watched a point man pass followed less than a minute later by fourteen NVA regulars in their green uniforms, these with red collar tabs, along with the green pith helmets. Next was a large group of fully laden bicycles, followed by another fourteen NVA regulars. It looked like we had found the active section of the Ho Chi Minh once again. We had good cover so I decided to remain here a while to see how dense the traffic along the trail was. While we waited I reported back to our command post and warned Wild Bill of what we had seen.

About an hour later I overheard the report Wild Bill was sending back to command. His team had found a staging area. He reported that there was a large area with camouflage netting already in place to protect it from aerial view, in the area were several huts and bunkers, as well as, a large bicycle park that currently had thirty-seven bicycles parked in it and it was undoubtedly the destination of the group that my team had reported earlier.

Captain Cummings, who was in the forward command post at Tan Son Nhut, told us to fall back to where we had spent last night and to stand by for orders. A B52 bombing raid would be laid on for the staging area for some time tonight. Both of our teams acknowledged the orders and headed back.

We joined back up just as the sun was setting. Since there was going to be a bombing run tonight we decided we better dig in just in case the B52s were not 100% on target. Some interesting points about B52 raids, the big bombers flew in at 20,000 feet or higher, had a target area which was about a quarter of a square kilometer in size, and had the task to precision bomb the target. When the bombs fell from those great heights towards the target area the only thing precision about it was the fact that 100% of the bombs hit the ground, though not necessarily in the target area.

About 0200 hours those of us who were asleep were rudely awakened by the B52s pounding on the doors of the staging area Wild Bill's team had found. The first few blasts were way too close to us for comfort. To tell how far away from us the strike was hitting, we used the old trick of telling how far away lightning was striking by counting the number of seconds between the flash of the lightning and the sound of the thunder. It takes approximately five seconds for the sound of the thunder to travel one mile, so if you see a flash of lightning and count fifteen seconds until you hear the thunder, you need to divide by five to determine the storm is roughly three miles away. We were about two miles from the staging area so we hoped to count to ten between the time of seeing the bombs' explosive flash in the sky and hearing the boom of the blast. But as the first strikes hit we were only counting to three. The blasts were loud enough to cause deafness and the concussion waves were shaking the ground under us far too much. As the strike continued, luckily the count between flash and boom was increasing instead of decreasing, but it never got past seven before the strike ended. So we had to assume that the strike fell way too short.

We stayed put but radioed in our belief that the strike missed the staging area and were told to go check if it did or not. Not the kind of thing you want to do after you have just stirred up an ant nest. Before we left our night camp we played gardener, we filled in the holes we had dug, transplanting some greenery and covering the fresh dirt with a mulch of other dead vegetation. It was not the best job in the world but it would do if someone just glanced this way from the direction of the trail.

Wild Bill's team again took lead as we headed back towards the location of the staging area. We went much more cautiously this time. When we got to the newly discovered trail we only went another half kilometer towards the base camp before we set up to just watch the trail for a while. There was no activity for the hour that we waited there, before we moved closer to the staging area. We did come across many bomb craters but no enemy. When we were closer to the staging area, we went and set up an ambush then waited while Jim Adams crawled ahead to check on the staging area. About an hour later he returned and reported that there was no damage to the camp but it had been abandoned. There went a hundred thousand dollars worth of bombs for nothing. Bill took no joy in reporting that back to the powers on high.

About fifteen minutes later word came back for us to stick around to see if the staging area would stay abandoned or if they would return again. My guess was that they would return since they left the camouflage netting in place. But 'when' was the big question. Since the failed air strike had been to the southeast of the camp we decided that would be a safer place to hide in that direction while we waited for activity. Our hope was that human nature would come into play, and the NVA would not want to move into an area that had just been heavily bombed.

Wrong!

We had moved into the bombed out area looking for a place to spend the night, when we heard someone coming towards us from the west. Through the underbrush we could see a line of about fifteen NVA walking abreast with about a ten meter gap between each, and they were coming our way. They were moving slow as they searched the area they were passing. Then two possibilities came to me, either they were looking for whoever had spotted their camp or perhaps they were actively searching the target area for any ordinance that had not detonated. They could build a lot of booby-traps with the explosive removed from one 500lb bomb dud.

We fell back before they spotted us. We moved away from contact by paralleling the trail that went to the staging area, we shifted to increasing our distance from the trail when we could hear talking coming from that direction. We moved back all the way to the northbound path that we had followed before we had gotten into this mess. There we turned back to the south. Judging by all the noise we heard coming from the trail there was a lot of people making use of it, most making their way back to the staging area. We moved passed our night camp and continued moving until we crossed through the swampy water where we had picked up the leeches. It was past dark when we finally got to some heavy undergrowth that we could use for cover and held up for the night. Before settling down for the night we did check for any leeches but this time we had been lucky and not gotten any on us.

The next morning we were just about to have our breakfast when we heard a lot of noise coming from the crossing between the two cheniers. We quickly and quietly repacked the food we were about to have and took up defensive positions. A large NVA group was moving across the ford and down the unused trail. We remained quietly in place since several NVA remained at the crossing. They must have had no idea we were in the area judging by the casual way they sat around talking without posting any guards.

In about twenty minutes a lot more noise could be heard coming from the other chenier, heading in our direction. Chief signed he was going to look at what was happening. He returned with the news that the NVA were bring up a lot of logs and judging by the way they were digging along the edge of the crossing it looked like they were building a bridge or damming up the crossing so they could fill it in and make a shallower ford to cross the watery gap between the cheniers.

That meant they would be there for quite a while and it was time to make our exit before we were discovered. We couldn't move north because of the activity in the bombed out area, most likely the source for all the timber they were using in their construction work, we couldn't move east because we would have to cross the trail where they were building the crossing and we couldn't move south just yet because of the large group of NVA that had moved that way earlier. So that left only west into the slimy green water swamp. The plan was to move a little west, then cut back to the firmer ground after we had gone some distance south, and move to a clear spot we could use for an extraction.

It was a lot easier said than done. We moved west into the watery swamp, moving extremely slowly when we started to make sure we didn't make too much noise as we moved through the water. When we started the water was to our knees but gradually became deeper and deeper between the widely separated trees. And the bottom softer and softer, our boots were sinking past the ankle with each step making it take more and more energy to just extract your foot from one hole to move it into another. In about twenty meters we were chest high in the yucky green slimy water. Thankfully it didn't get much deeper than that though we did all manage to step in a depression or two and there was not one of us who was not covered head to toe in the green slime and leeches. But we had to keep moving because there was no option to stop or turn back. It took us almost an hour and a half to move about a half kilometer from the chenier, about the least amount of distance where we could be sure we would not be easily seen.

Finally we cut back towards the south; it looked to be about another half kilometer to the tree line indicating firmer land that way. We had to pass through a slightly deeper area where only our heads were above water but finally after another 2 hours we managed to hit the higher ground. That had to be the longest and hardest traveling I have ever done. The weight of my gear, now filled with water, combined with the extra energy required to extract our feet from the sticky bottom mud, and the arm strain of holding our weapons and radios high to keep them as dry as possible made for a task that I would never want to repeat.

Once we got to dry land and found a spot with good cover we all collapsed, but before we could rest we cleaned our weapons as best we could given the wet condition of our gear. Everything in our packs was soaking wet, our native food ruined. Here is where having good sealed C-Rations would have been better than carting around Vietnamese food. After all the energy we expended something to eat would have been wonderful and at this point I didn't care if my poop would smell American or Vietnamese.

I had been so preoccupied with cleaning my guns and wanting something to eat that I had briefly forgotten all about the damn leeches all over my body. They were everywhere! I looked over at Chief and even noticed them on his face. UCK! But I had one more thing to do before I could get them off me. I had to radio in and get us the hell out of there. But neither my primary modified PRC-64 nor my team's backup AN/URC-64 radios enjoyed their swim and neither was working. Luckily Bill had gotten his PRC-64 to work after taking it apart and changing the battery.

We were told that extraction would not be for another three hours and it would coincide with another B52 strike on the staging area. Now we had time to get the damn leeches off our bodies. You just can't pull them off of you, if you do parts of the leech will remain under your skin and you will get an infection. Some G. I.'s used one of two main ways to remove them, burn them off with a hot cigarette or put mosquito repellent on it then remove it. Neither way is without danger though. Either of those ways can cause the leech to regurgitate when it suffers the pain of the burn or the chemical reaction to the repellent. The wound containing the regurgitation can get infected, so the suggested way to remove one without suffering the blood loss of waiting until it gets full and just falls off is to gently pull the skin near the sucker taught, then place your other hand next to the leech and slide one of your fingernails underneath the sucker causing it to extract itself from the wound. Then you flick it off before the leech attempts to reattach itself.

My team stayed on guard while Bill's stripped down and removed the leeches off each other. The teams swapped tasks and I finally got to get the damn things off me. We all removed those that we could get to ourselves than worked on each other. Chief and Johnny teamed up and I was unlucky enough to get Harold to help me. Every time he flicked one off he would take the time to squash it before moving on to the next one. It was kind of disgusting to see it explode then see the black-red mashed remains of the creatures. It might not have been so bad if Harold would not have been making sound effects every time he removed one and humming "Pop Goes the Weasel" while he worked. Of course he was always on the word 'Pop' when he would squash a leech.

Bill came back and told us to saddle up because the extraction helicopter was just fifteen minutes out. He pointed to the sky where the contrails from the B52s could be seen approaching. The extract helicopter would be getting here just minutes after the bombs fell. They told us that there had been a typing error in last night's strike orders, a single digit mistyped in the coordinates that caused them to miss the target. At least this time we were further away and the plan was for us to do a BDA from the air utilizing the extraction helicopter.

From our position the bombs looked like they were on target but we would find out soon. We loaded on the chopper and flew towards the staging area. Bill decided to get a little payback on the NVA that made us move into the water, he directed the helicopter to fly over the ford where they were working on the crossing. As we passed over, we dropped all the hand grenades we had and shot up the area with our small arms. Hopefully even if we had not killed any, we at least forced them into the water so they would get the attention of a leech or two. We all hoped that payback would be a bitch.

The B52 strike had been on target this time. The camouflage netting had been blown down so we got a good look at what remained of the area. All that could be seen was a lot of bomb craters, the still smoking rubble of the huts, and one or two lucky NVA staggering around the parameter. Since the strike was during the day, there was no telling how many had been in the staging area when it was hit but if they were in the camp, the odds were they didn't live through it.

We took one or two photos, not knowing if they would even come out since the camera had been underwater for quite a while during our stroll through the green water. When we got back to Tan Son Nhut, Captain Cummings sent us all to the aid station to get the leech wounds checked out. Good thing too. I was having a little trouble hearing on the flight back but I just thought it was caused by all the racket when we shot up the ford, but it turned out that there was a leech in my ear canal that was so swollen from being engorged with my blood that it was stuck in there. I will never forget the squishing sound and the warm gush of liquid when the doctor put a little too much pressure on the hemostats he used to get the damn, now squished, creature out of my ear.

At least he didn't make the 'squish', 'uck', 'ker-plop', 'squirt', 'splat', sound effects Harold made. After a massive shot of "just in case" penicillin we all headed back to the teams' hootches for a debriefing. Of course Harold was humming "Pop Goes the Weasel" and didn't stop until I threatened to examine his ear canal for leeches using my kabar knife.

* * *

May 20, 2018
At sea between Rethymno and Hersonissos, Crete, Greece

The look on Kathy's face was enough to see that any more talk of leeches was going to cause her to christen the deck of the yacht with something other than champagne. Joan had poured the last of the second bottle of wine while Ron was telling the leech story. She gave Harold a kick and told him to get another bottle.

Harold, being very efficient, returned with three bottles of wine and the corkscrew rather than just bring back one opened bottle. Of course right before he pulled out the cork he started humming "Pop Goes the Weasel" and timed the pop of the cork's removal to correspond with the 'Pop' in the song's lyrics. This got a laugh from everyone but Ron, who mimed pulling out his knife and going after Harold.

CHAPTER 16
May 21, 2018
Hersonissos, Crete, Greece

Everyone had gathered at the beach after lunch and assumed their normal positions, the guys sitting around a table and the girls on chaise lounges within a few feet of the table. There were a couple of conversations going, with everyone chatting away about several topics at once. One of the conversations turned to the time when Johnny lived in Hersonissos. This topic caught the attention of the whole group when Johnny told about the time he and several others friends from base had a barbecue on the beach and several Swedish flight attendants joined the party.

When Johnny noticed he had the girl's attention too he explained, "Before I tell you what happened please note that none of the other guys here were at this party, so you girls can't hold them liable for anything that occurred."

Pointing down the beach, "We were over there by a resort next to this one; of course neither resort was there back then. The sandy area of the beach ended, and it was the beginning of a very rocky area that ran down the coast for over a hundred yards."

He pointed to a section where there was now a part of a resort building. "I use to live in a small house about 300 steps from the beach and had brought my small barbecue grill from the house down to the beach for a party. There were just four of us from the base, a large ice chest full of beer; a steak for each of us and a couple cans of beans."

Harold said, "Enough of the chatter, get to the good stuff and tell us about the Swedish stewardesses."

This earned Harold a kick from Joan's sandy foot.

Johnny continued, "Eight people were walking down the beach and when they got to us they remarked on how great the steaks smelled. There were two guys, who we later learned were the pilot and copilot, and six nice looking young women, the stewardesses, all from a Scandinavian Airlines charter flight from Stockholm that was on a layover for the day. Being the red-blooded American bachelor youths that we were, we invited them to join us for a few beers."

"I was rooming with Joe Blinn then, he had not been in Detachment 11 but he had been stationed in the Philippines when we were there. He and I ran back to our house to grab a lot more food and another case of beer. Joe even grabbed his camera, a radio, a thin blanket, and a couple more towels. When we got back with the radio and food, the party really began."

"We were listening to A-farts, playing some great music from Chicago, Three Dog Night, Rod Stewart, and Carole King."

When Johnny noticed a shocked and questioning look on Kathy's face, he quickly added, "Sorry, A-farts was what we called AFTRS, the American Forces Radio and Television Service, we had a small radio and television station on the base that was run by the military to keep us poor GIs stationed overseas entertained. Where was I? Oh, yeah."

"The party was in full swing when Joe and I talked two of the stewardesses into taking a walk with us to a great spot to take photographs. There were some places along the rocky part of the beach just a short walk away where the rocks had eroded away creating rock bridges. The rock bridges created a great photo locale because with someone standing on the bridge, you could get a picture with them and the rocks, along with beautiful blue water in front, under, and behind them."

"One of the girls took off her sunglasses for a picture and they fell in the water. Since Joe had the camera, I was the gallant gentleman that jumped into the water to dive down and retrieve her glasses. The water was crystal clear and the depth to the bottom was quite deceiving. I had to go about 6 feet under to get the glasses. When I retrieved them, I threaded water and held the glasses up for the stewardess to get but she misjudged how far she had to lean over to take them from me and fell into the water right on top of me. Spitting and sputtering we got back to the surface, she didn't look too happy at that moment but I couldn't help laughing my head off. She was even more unhappy when I told her we would have to swim all the way back to the sandy area of the beach before we had a place to get out of the water."

"Her attitude turned around when I told her at least she got to go swimming while she was on Crete. She took off the shoes that had luckily not fallen off when she took the plunge, handed them to me, and we began the swim back to the sandy beach where the party was. When we got to the beach, I handed her one of the towels we had brought from the house. Rather than taking the towel then, she just started taking off all her wet clothes right in front of everyone. When she was completely naked she took the towel from my hand and began to dry her hair, leaving the rest of herself exposed"

"The Swedes acted as if nothing was amiss, but us Americans were all wide eyed and just gaping at her very attractive busty nude body. When another of the stewardesses asked how the water was and our nude mermaid responded great, they all started shucking their clothes and headed for the water. Soon all twelve of us were buck naked and swimming in the warm water."

"It was a great day, but now I can't even remember any of their names. I did get a souvenir though. The next morning when my mermaid left, she couldn't find her bra. I found it the next day on the floor behind the sofa. I kept that souvenir as a trophy until I went back to the states."

Mary then stood up and playfully punched Bill on the arm telling us that all you GIs are the same. Bill's reply was, "Why get mad at me now, I never met the Swedish stewardesses. And the way I met you was almost the same. Besides - I got to keep all your clothes AND YOU as my souvenirs."

That caused Mary to put both her hands around the back of his neck and give him a kiss. After a good laugh the group talked a little more about other souvenirs they had from Crete. At one point Harold asked, "Did anybody else keep any of the souvenirs we picked up from a certain airline we ran into during our time in Cambodia?"

The guys became real quiet and gave quick questioning glances to each other, the girls, and the General before anyone spoke up. Ron sheepishly said, "I still have a souvenir coin and the modified shotgun I picked up from a certain Air America plane."

Looking at the General, Johnny said, "I still have my 1966 British Gold Sovereign coin from it too. General, perhaps there is something we should have told you about a long time ago. We did leave out a few things from one of our after actions reports."

Johnny then went on to tell the story to the General and the rest of the group

* * *

May 1969 ~ Cambodia
As told by Johnny Porter

I believe it was early May when Bill's team and Ron's team paired up again to work an area northeast of Phnom Penh. We had been out in the boonies for three of a four day mission when at dawn we got a radio message to head, post-haste, to some coordinates about five kilometers from where we were and to look for a downed plane. We traveled far faster than we should when moving through enemy territory, so it didn't take us too long to arrive at the coordinates given. There was nothing to be seen but there was a faint odor of smoke in the air. The wind was very calm but what little of it there was came from the north, so we headed that way.

We had traveled about a kilometer when we came upon a lot of fresh leaves and branches on the jungle floor. Looking up we could see some damage to the tree tops so we followed the debris further north and found the wreckage of a white Douglas DC-4 with Air America printed on the fuselage and an American flag on the tail. Bill's team took up covering fire positions while our team carefully approached the wreckage. From the outside there was no sign that the plane had taken enemy fire, although there were scorch marks around both of the engines that were on the wing that had once been on the left side of the plane. Both wings had come off as it descended through the trees on its way to the ground and the front crew compartment had smashed in upon impact.

Ron and Harold moved to defensible positions on the exterior of the plane while Chief and I, using all our combined strength, finally managed to pry open the aft cabin door enough to enter the plane's passenger compartment. The interior was modified to have an area for freight in the back and passenger seating in the front. But it was not a pretty sight inside the plane; the crash had caused some cargo that was stored towards the aft of the plane to be propelled forwarded tearing up the seating area of the plane. There had been two passengers dressed in plain olive-drab fatigue uniforms but with no insignia of any kind, both still strapped to their seats but both were dead and their bodies badly mutilated by flying debris from the interior of the craft. One of them had even been completely decapitated and was also missing his left arm.

After double checking to be sure the non-decapitated passenger was indeed dead we moved towards the front of the craft to check on the crew. Against the bulkhead we found the missing arm still handcuffed to a briefcase that had opened during the crash. Spilling from the open case were several small bags. One of the bags had opened and there were gold coins scattered around the floor by the case. We took a quick questioning look at each other and I pointed towards the forward area of the plane. With an appearance of great reluctance, Chief sighed and we continued to the crew compartment. We found three severely battered crew members there and even a quick glance showed that all had died during the crash.

I told Chief, "Let's go tell Ron what we found."

On the way out Chief stopped and scooped up a handful of the exposed coins stuffing them into his pocket saying, "Finders – Keepers."

On the way out, I noticed that the other passenger still had a briefcase handcuffed to his arm too. We left everything else the way we found it. Once outside we told Ron about what we saw and he radioed in a report. After a few minutes Ron signaled Bill's team to join us by the plane and updated both teams on the orders he received. We were told to defend the plane at all costs until help arrived and that we could expect to be relieved in a few hours.

The "at all costs" portion of the order did not sit well with any of us. We had never really been combat troops, it was always our mission to go undetected and avoid contact. We were not armed well enough nor did we carry enough ammunition for any kind of prolonged fire fight. We were supposed to look and run, not stay and fight. Luckily the plane had crashed at night so maybe no one would be actively searching for the downed aircraft. However, just as we had followed the smell of smoke and a debris field to this location, any curious unfriendly natives might do the same.

Ron told Chief and Harold to go back in and find anything we could use to help in our defense of the plane. He pointed out a few likely approaches telling me to deploy both teams' claymores and then use any other explosives we had left to prepare an area on the thinly treed north side of the plane where he could blast a landing zone when the relief arrived. The others created a rather loose square parameter around the plane, Ron and Wild Bill took opposite corners with Jim and Chief on the other corners. I was to stay on the north side of the box so I could blow the landing zone when the time arrived. We began to dig in and camouflage our positions with downed tree limbs and parts of the plane wreckage.

Chief went to strip the weapons and ammunition from the crew members while Harold searched the cargo area. There was food, paper, a mimeograph machine with supplies, other office equipment, and a few goodies we could use. The goodies included: two M16's, an unopened ammo can full of 5.56×45mm NATO bullets that would fit our Colt CAR-15 Commando assault carbines, a box containing one hundred 12-gauge 2-3/4" shells with a nine-pellet load of buffered double-aught buckshot, and one very oddly modified 12-gauge shotgun.

None of us had ever seen a shotgun like this before. It was a 12-gauge Belgium made Browning Automatic 5, usually called an Auto-5, which is a recoil-operated semi-automatic shotgun. The modification was that it had a 15 round banana clip attached to the bottom of the action, so instead of shells being fed into the bottom of the action and stored in a tubular magazine, they went directly from the clip into the chamber. The barrel and the stock of the gun had been shortened a little bit making it look even more unique.

Chief returned with 5 web belts each containing a holstered M1911 and pouch with two spare .45 ACP clips. The two of them hauled their finds out of the plane to be distributed to the teams. Harold was always teasing Ron that he was a terrible shot, so he gave him the shotgun and shells. He teased him saying that perhaps he could hit something with a shotgun. The two M16s went to Chief and Jim Adams whom I thought were the two best marksmen, and a .45 to the others. We opened the ammo can and distributed the Mil-Spec 10-round stripper clip mounted rounds to everyone. Due to weight limitations, we did not carry that many clips of ammo but at least now, if given time, we could reload our spent magazines.

We refilled everyone's canteens with some water stored in the plane, and passed out some C-Rations also found in the plane. We were due to have been extracted this morning, so we were all short of food. Once that was distributed, Dave helped me finish rigging the explosives we were using to create the LZ, then to prepare my defensive position.

Thankfully all was quiet for well over an hour before our luck went bad. We heard them coming well before we saw them. They were coming from the south, the same way we arrived, apparently they had seen the very fresh tracks from our Ho Chi Minh sandal soled boots and thought there were other NVA or Viet Cong waiting at the crash site. I could not think of any other reason they would have called out announcing themselves before entering the area. I guess they didn't want to get shot by their own side, but surprise! As the batch of ten NVA entered the area of the perimeter covered by Ron, Harold, and Chief, that side of our defensive square opened up on them.

While Chief and Harold fired with their CAR-15s, Ron blasted away with the shotgun we had found. The shots from the CAR-15s sounded like small pops compared to the loud boom – boom – booms coming from the semi-automatic shotgun. As the three-round controlled fire bursts from Chief and Harold were taking down four individuals, the wall of double-aught buckshot delivered by Ron's new toy mowed down five of them and knocked the sixth off of his feet causing him to fly four feet back down the path they had entered by. The enemy had not even gotten off one shot. I don't think anyone was more surprised by the results than Ron. After he had fired the last shell in the clip he just stared at the gun for a few seconds before setting it down to pick up his still fully loaded CAR-15.

All the firing just took a few seconds, but everyone remained in position to see if the group we had just ambushed had any friends close by. After seven or eight minutes of no action, Ron went forward to check the enemy to be sure none of them were playing possum. He went back up the path they had entered by until he was out of sight for two or three minutes before returning. With a very worried look on his face he waved for Harold to come join him.

Ron and Harold stripped the NVA of all their arms and ammunition. They also searched the bodies and removed all documents they could find. Returning to the group they distributed the captured AK-47s and ammunition, giving us all another backup weapon. They even passed out a few of the seldom seen Chinese Type 23 Stick Grenades they had found on one corpse. Ron gave me an RPG launcher and bag of rockets. Then he told us the bad news. The one that had been blasted back down the path had gotten away, there was a blood trail so he was wounded but he was still capable of hightailing it down the path and to be gone before Ron went to search.

Wild Bill radioed in that we had been located and asked for some fast moving air support to get to us ASAP. He also checked and found out the relief force was still assembling and the current ETA to our location was two hours. Not what we wanted to hear. In two hours all the NVA and their local friends that heard the shooting could be at our location. And this time just seeing friendly looking footprints wouldn't fool them.

We got another hour's reprieve to strengthen our positions before things heated up again. But by now we had a Forward Air Controller flying over us and he had a couple of jets waiting to come to our assistance. We had spoken directly to the FAC and confirmed that he had our exact position registered so he would be able to bring in support and hopefully not hit us.

This time they came in from two sides in a pincer movement. One group was slow crawling their way to our position from the north side of the plane where we were going to make our landing zone and the other group from the southerly path they used before. The group that was approaching from the north was moving slowly and stealthily as they sneaked towards the plane, while the southerly group was making some noise to divert our attention from the north.

Jim had spotted movement earlier so Wild Bill and I were not distracted by the diversion from the south. They had picked the wrong side to use to sneak up on us, the one we had already rigged with explosives to create the landing zone. I signed to Jim and Bill to hold their fire until I set off the explosives.

By now the south side was starting to receive small arms fire from the diversionary group. I waited until the little bastards trying to sneak up on us had traveled well into the area planned for the LZ before setting off the explosives. BAM! All the C4 and detcord, I had set, went off at once. The explosives were rigged so that the outer trees would fall away from the LZ and the inner trees were rigged with more explosives so they would be blown into smaller pieces to allow the helicopters to land the relief force. This meant that the larger blasts were right where the enemy was approaching. The blasts themselves must have gotten a few of them and the falling trees and flying splinters perhaps caused even more casualties.

I thought it was a good plan but perhaps it wasn't; now their approach was shrouded with dust and smoke from the explosives and the entire area was now covered with limbs and branches of trees they could use for cover. Jim and Bill were firing away using their CAR-15s but I used my blooper and then the RPG to negate the tree branch cover I had provided them. Don's east side of the plane was not presently under attack so he assisted me by firing his M79 grenade launcher into the LZ area also.

Ron was on the horn to the FAC, requesting that the jets napalm the southerly approach and do a second pass using guns only on the northerly LZ approach. That way they could come a little closer using guns rather than if they used napalm and we wouldn't be setting our LZ on fire. The FAC quickly relayed our request and a pair of F-100s, that was our air cover, lined up side by side for their bomb run. Ron yelled for us to get our heads down, streaking in low the jets dropped their white phosphorus and napalm bombs.

The blasts caused by the white phosphorus and napalm was a sight to behold. When it first hits there is a blast with white smoke and lots of streaming smoke tentacles almost looking like an upside down jellyfish. That is followed by the rolling, billowing red fire and black smoke of the napalm, cooking everything in its path. Thankfully they dropped the napalm far enough away to leave a good 25 meters separation between us and the rolling fire. It was a perfect pass, close enough to catch any troops staging for an attack against the south side and far enough away to prevent us from becoming crispy critters. But, a little too far away to remove all the NVA on that side, so Ron, Harold, and Chief were still exchanging shots with the few that managed to move close enough to our position to escape the napalm.

Even over all the firing coming from my side of the defensive box, I could still hear the distinctive shotgun booms as Ron ran through another 15 round clip of double-aught, mowing down all the grass, weeds, small trees and NVA that were in front of him. However, the NVA on my side of the plane that had survived the creation of our LZ along with some that had been initially out of the blast area were now starting to pour heavy fire into our positions.

I fired every round I had for the blooper and all the RPGs we captured from the first attack. I was hearing Jim and Wild Bill firing the captured AK-47s instead of their CAR-15s so they must have gone through every loaded magazine that they had for their CAR-15s and switched weapons. Then I heard the pair of F-100s approaching and ducked a little deeper down into my fighting hole. With a screaming loud roar they were over us firing all four of their 20 mm Pontiac M39A1 revolver cannons. They were dead on target pulverizing everything in their path. The bullets from the M39A1 are just slightly smaller than a U.S. nickel and over three inches in length. The F-100s' gun pass broke the NVA that were approaching from the north and those that survived broke cover to run back the way they had come.

Other than the ringing in my ears from all the previous loud bangs, things became suddenly quiet. No one was shooting and the jets were far enough away to only be a distant rumble, even the FAC's little propeller plane was on the far end of his figure 8 holding pattern. Then I started to hear all the clicks associated with everyone reloading the magazines for their CAR-15s using the spare Military Specification, Mil-Spec, 10-round stripper clips we found in the plane. I heard an "Ouch! God-Damn-Stripper-Clips!" coming from one of our fighting holes telling me that someone pinched some skin loading the rounds into their clips. I had used that exact same phrase for the exact same reason more than once myself. I could hear Wild Bill on the radio thanking the F-100 pilots for the assistance, just as Ron yelled out for everyone to call out their status. Everyone responded except

Chief. Instantly, Harold was out his hole and running to check on Chief. Harold passed the word that Chief was alive but was unconscious and it looks like he was bleeding heavily from a long shallow cut along the side of his head. Dave joined Harold and the two of them carried Chief into the downed plane, shifted around a little of the cargo and laid him between the boxes of paper and office supplies in the back of the plane to provide him with a shield.

Dave was one of five people that had taken an emergency first aid course back at Eglin AFB when the rest of us were practicing calling in airstrikes, so he stayed with Chief to see what he could do to stop the bleeding. Harold returned to the line to continue reloading his magazines and waiting to see if the NVA would return.

From the hole next to mine Jim Adams whispered, "I sure was glad that I had the AK-47 as a backup piece. I fired every magazine I had for my carbine and emptied both my MK22 and the .45 before I picked up that damn AK-47. I didn't hear you use yours, do you have any extra clips for the AK-47?"

Since I had spent most of my time firing the blooper and the RPG, I had not fired too many rounds from my CAR-15 so I tossed him all the AK-47 ammo I had except for the one clip still in the weapon. Wild Bill was off the radio now and having heard the exchange between Jim and me, he proceeded to crawl to each person, checking their status and distributing Chief's remaining rounds. We were down to about 100 rounds each. He was about to go out and see if he could retrieve some more ammunition for the AK-47s from the nearby dead NVA but he had not crawled but a few feet past our line when he started to receive fire. Discretion being the better part of valor, he quickly returned to his hole. It looked like we would have to get by with what we had left or start throwing rocks. He passed the word around to get off full auto and to only fire three shot bursts; we still had almost another hour to go before the relief force got here.

The NVA troops were still out there, but their attack having been busted by the explosives in the new LZ and the air strikes must have sorely depleted their numbers. If they knew how short we were on ammo they would attack again. Now there was only sporadic firing from both sides just to keep the other side pinned down. This went on for about a half hour. I was thinking that we were lucky they hadn't gotten any more reinforcements and didn't have any mortars with them or we would be in deep dodo. Stupid thing to think about!

I no sooner had the ill-omen thought than firing picked up a little and I heard the thump of a mortar firing shortly followed by the boom of the blast. Between the thump and the boom Bill had yelled, "Incoming!"

Thankfully the round landed way long, it went crashing into the far end of the newly made LZ. We all scrunched a little lower in our holes waiting for the next shoe to drop. I could hear Bill yelling into the radio to have our air support fry the SOBs with the mortar and giving the FAC approximate location of the mortar crew. The second round was a lot closer but still a little long. Then their third round fell a little short. Oh, oh – they now had us bracketed and it would start to rain shrapnel real soon.

Round four landed right on the cockpit of the wrecked plane spraying the area with not only pieces of the mortar bomb but also with chunks of metal from the plane. The next round was to the right of the hit on the plane very close to Don's fighting hole. But before the mortar team could get off another round, rockets fired from blue and white helicopters started hitting in the general vicinity of the mortar team's firing location. It was an extremely strange site coming towards us from the direction of Thailand, a flight of six helicopters all painted with the blue and white colors of Air American instead of the normal olive drab colored military helicopters I expected to see. Two of the six helicopters were sporting rocket launchers and one of them had thankfully taken out the mortar just as it was about to take us out.

As the two gunships gave covering fire each of the other four helicopters did a quick hover over the landing zone dropping off four men each. Some rushed off to clear the other end of the LZ and some joined us in a perimeter around the plane. A few minutes after the helicopters that dropped off the troop lifted off, the fast movers came in at treetop level. A flight of eight fighter bombers were clearing a large area around us leaving us on a small island in the middle of a man-made hell of flaming napalm. That put an end to any threats for a while so we came out of our holes.

Wild Bill went to talk to the man in tiger-stripe camouflage fatigues that appeared to be passing orders to some members of the relief force. As a couple of tiger-stripes ran into the plane wreckage, Ron went to check on our teams beginning with Don to see if he was OK after the close hit. He was still several feet from Don's position when he stopped, bent over with his hands on his shotgun, the shotgun lying across his knees, and his head down below his waist. He paused there for a little while, straightened up and moved to kneel by the fighting hole.

Slowly straightening up, Ron started walking back towards us shaking his head, with a more gravelly than normal voice he said, "That last one cut Don in half. I'm going to check on Chief."

As Ron approached the door of the aircraft, a tiger-striped trooper with no insignia of any kind on his uniform broke off talking with Bill and blocked Ron from entering the plane saying, "You can't go in there. It's classified."

Ron's quick angry response was, "Fuck you! One of my men died protecting this thing, and two of my men are in there right now so get the hell out of my way!"

Just then the two tiger-stripes that had gone in earlier came out carrying two briefcases. The tiger-stripe leader that was barring Ron's way saw his team and moved away from the plane's door and departed with the briefcase toters. Ron entered and a few minutes later he came out and told us Chief was still unconscious but the bleeding had stopped.

Tiger-stripe leader approached and this time acted a little more like a fellow comrade in arms and said, "I'm sorry for your loss. As soon as we can place some charges to destroy the plane, I'll call the choppers back in and get us the hell out of Dodge."

True to his word a little while later all six of the blue and white helicopters returned, the first in was one of the gunship Hueys, four tiger-stripes bearing the two briefcases jumped on that one while the other gunship hovered and kept a steady stream of M60 rounds chewing up the jungle around us. On the next ship down we loaded Chief, Dave, and a few more tiger-stripes. The rest of us loaded on the remaining helicopters with Don's body loaded on the second gunship which was the last ship out the LZ. When we were about a quarter of a kilometer away, the wreckage exploded leaving nothing but smoke, a clearing in the jungle, and bad memories.

The Air America helicopters brought us to a small unrecognizable base someplace in Thailand. There was an Air Force C130 parked there with the ramp down and a medical team waiting for Chief. After pointing to the C130, the Air America tiger-stripe troops disappeared into a building on the base without saying a word to us. The six of us with the help of the medical team carried Chief and Don's body to the waiting plane. As we were carrying Chief aboard he woke up with a jerk and tried to sit up on the stretcher, one of the medics gently pushed him back down telling him to remain still. With a quick look around he saw Harold walking beside him and asked, "What the hell happened?"

Harold was quick with a reply, "The NVA tried to scalp you but your head was too hard."

On the flight back to Tan Son Nhut the medics gave Chief a quick exam waving a small flashlight in his eyes like some sort of magic wand, and then they gave him a giant shot of antibiotics saying he would be OK but they wanted him to go the hospital for observation in case he had a concussion. As the medic turned to put his gear away, Chief dug in his pocket and handed Harold something as he whispered in his ear.

We were met by a military ambulance when we landed. Harold, Ron and I went with Chief to the hospital while Wild Bill, Dave and Jim accompanied Don to the Mortuary Affairs unit.

Being rather naive and innocent, that afternoon at the debriefing I asked Major Straight why an airline like Air America would have gunships and troops. I was a little taken aback by his response that Air America was mainly a front for the CIA and apparently they had something on the plane they wanted to recover.

We explained about seeing the two briefcases and the sacks of gold coins that at least one of them contained. After the debriefing we were reminded that everything we saw was confidential and to keep our mouths shut. We then went to the hospital to visit Chief and tell him what happened. When he decided to take a nap the rest of us departed back for our camp.

Two days later Chief came back to the team area. He and Harold huddled together for a few minutes before calling Ron's and Wild Bills teams together. Chief gave each of us a gold coin saying they were souvenirs from our last mission. Jim brought up the fact that the CIA might come looking for the missing coins. Chief's response to that was, "Heck, there were coins all around that open briefcase, if anyone asks, no we don't have any coins and they must have blown them up along with the plane. Besides, they owe us for stopping the other little buggers from taking it all. I say Finders-Keepers."

With a smile, Ron added, "Ain't no way I am giving back that shotgun. If they ask if we took anything I believe the proper response is ...?"

Harold quickly finished the sentence for Ron, "It never happened."

* * *

May 21, 2018
Hersonissos, Crete, Greece

After he told the story Johnny stopped and looked questioning at the General. The General thought back for a little while and said, "You know I really hated giving that "hold at all cost" order but that came from very high up the military food chain. And after all we did and suffered, I never did hear anything from anybody in the CIA about that operation. Not even a thank you for saving their bacon, much less any questions about missing money. So ... it never happened."

Then Kathy spoke up, "So that is where you got that monstrosity of a shotgun. I remember asking a few times but you kept changing the subject every time I did. And you know I saw that coin in the safe deposit box when I picked up the passports for this trip. At the time I got curious and looked up how much the coin was worth. The website said depending on condition they could be worth around $400."

Wild Bill looked at Mary, hunched his shoulders to await the punches he knew would be coming and said, "At least one of the souvenirs from my time in the military is worth something."

Mary instantly remembered the earlier conversation when Bill had said she was one of his souvenirs from Crete. As she playfully slapped him on his hunched shoulders she asked, "Just ONE of your souvenirs is worth something?"

CHAPTER 17
May 22, 2018
Between Rethymno and Hersonissos, Crete, Greece

After a leisurely morning and a light lunch at the hotel, the group took a ride through the Arkadian gorges to the Arkadi Monastery which was 23 kilometers outside of Rethymno. No one is sure when the first monastery at that site was first built, but it underwent a major restoration during the 16th century. As the group walked toward the entrance of the monastery from their minibus, the General remarked that this place always reminded him of the Alamo, just a little in its appearance but a lot more in a small piece of its history. Surrounding the church the monastery walls resemble a fortress with the four walls ranging from 67 to 78 meters in length. Along the inside walls were the monks' cells and other buildings, such as, the supply rooms, workrooms and refectory.

The monastery became a national sanctuary in honor of the Cretan resistance during the Cretan revolt of 1866. One of many revolts the Cretans waged against the Ottoman Empire took place that year. In November, the monastery sheltered close to a thousand people of which 325 were men, but less than 260 of them armed and the rest were women and children. An army of 15,000 Ottomans, supported by approximately 30 cannons, besieged the outnumbered Cretans. The Cretans held out for two days but the artillery proved too much for the walls and the defenses were breached the second day. After room to room fighting and a lack of ammunition by the isolated Cretan defenders, all appeared loss. The defenders were using one of the safer rooms as a powder magazine and that was were the majority of the women and children were hiding. As a last desperate act of defiance on the order of the monastery's abbot, the powder magazine was blown-up by one of the Cretan defenders.

After the smoke had cleared and the final defenders fell, less than 120 of the almost one thousand Monastery inhabitants survived only to go into captivity. The estimate of Turkish losses was approximately 1500. Much like the American Alamo, while the battle was a defeat for the Cretans. the local and worldwide reactions to the massacre's outrage were far-reaching. Some say it may have even led to the enactment of what is known as the Organic Law which gave the Cretan Christians equal control of local administration under the Ottoman rule.

After the tour they picked up the now completed unit steins in Rethymno and were on the bus back to their hotel when the conversation shifted back to the tour of the monastery. Kathy was commenting on the General's remark that the monastery reminded him of the Alamo. "I think that having so many people die rather than surrendering is rather sad."

Ron's response was, "Sometimes surrender is not an option. It was not when we were in Vietnam. There are times in a soldier's life when it is necessary to be willing to put your life on the line for others."

Ron paused for thought then asked, "Isn't today May 22nd?"

After he got a positive response he continued, "I just remembered something. Our unit's Alamo was today, forty-nine years ago, on May 22, 1969."

* * *

May 22, 1969 ~ Cambodia
As told by Ron Lafayette

After all the casualties we suffered, Detachment 11 was down thirty percent from its original strength, with just eight full strength teams, so the unit was reorganized yet again. Captain Cummings gave his team to Wild Bill. After the reorganization we had seven combat teams and a new command team that would be Major Straight, Captain Cummings, Chief and Bob Berringer. This would allow the major and captain to focus on getting us some replacements and finally catching up on all the paperwork that never seemed to end. Chief and Bob were both on limited duty because of their minor wounds, so they would be assigned to the command posts as the radio operators. What was left of Wild Bill's old team was divided between me and Ducky. Jim Adams was temporarily transferred to my team as point man and Dave went to replace Bob on Ducky's team.

Four full teams in Vietnam would be working out of Tan Son Nhut while three teams got to stand down at Clark Air Base in the Philippines. The command group would work on getting us replacements but it would be split with an officer and an enlisted man at each Clark and Tan Son Nhut. On May 22, 1969, the team leaders in Vietnam were me, Wild Bill, Dwight Dillinger, and Steve Schmidt. Enjoying themselves drinking San Miguel beer at Clark were Charles Cullum's, now Technical Sergeant 'Uncle Bob' Ellingson's, and the recently promoted Master Sergeant 'Ducky' Brown's teams. With two of our original NCOs both getting well-earned promotions; they would be having a real good time at The Little Brown Jug for the promotion party.

Dwight Dillinger's and Steve Schmidt's teams were working in an area of Cambodia east of the Vietnam highlands. It was the second day of their patrol when they missed their morning status report. This was not totally usual, it was monsoon season and there had been some very heavy thunderstorms rolling through the area.

Major Straight, following protocol, arranged for a prop-driven Forward Air Controller plane to go to the area where the teams should be so it could relay any radio communications. It would assist the team's communications if atmospherics were bad or if their long range radios weren't working. With a FAC flying close, they should be able to use their short-range emergency radios if necessary.

Just in case they missed their noon status report or they had not at least gotten in contact with the orbiting FAC, the major told Bill and I to get our teams ready to fly out to go look for our missing friends. The major also sent one of the sensor gathering planes in to take readings in the area they should be working so he could use the information on which sensors were working to help us locate them.

Noon came and still no word from them. We had a pretty good idea where they should be based according to the patrol's mission plan and the readings from the sensors they had put back on line. None of the motion sensors that they put on line the first day of their mission showed any movement so we could even guess which way they were headed. We chose a clearing just short of the last sensor that had been activated as our LZ.

We took two Hueys with my team in one and Bill's in another. That way we figured we could double our search area from the air before we had to get on the ground. Before we did our insertion we over flew the mission's planned route twice. Seeing nothing, we faked a few landings away from our actual LZ before we finally hit the ground. The helicopters would do one more sweep of the area and a few more fake insertions before heading back.

We quickly moved away from the LZ and tested our radio communications with the forward operations center. We had no problem communicating with the Major which only heightened my sense of dread. If the teams had gotten into trouble, running in blind would only get us into trouble too, so we began our search with even more caution than we normally did. We began by going to the trail where the teams had been working on the sensors. My team led the way with Bill's behind us, keeping a 200 meter distance between the two teams.

We followed the trail to the last activated sensor and had not found any indications of trouble. We found the last sensor placed the evening before, so after moving up the trail for a ways we did not see any additional sensors or signs that Dwight or Steve have passed. So we assumed that they quit for the night at this point. While we still had enough light to see, I decided to look for the hidey-hole they had used last night. The jungle got denser towards the north so we headed that way. Once we got into the thick cover I waited for Bill's team to catch up. We found lots of good hidey-hole spots that were possibilities but not the one used by the missing teams, I selected the best one for us to go back to once it got dark. There was only an hour of daylight remaining so Bill and I decided to search for another hour then rejoin to spend the night together. We split up to continue our search, Bill's team going back down the direction we had come from and my team paralleling the trail towards where, according to the mission plan, the missing teams should be heading.

Just before it got too dark to see Jim found a muddy area on a narrow trail with lots of recent activity. There were a lot of Ho Chi Minh sandal tracks, but you could tell by the number and variety of impressions that a lot more than eight people had moved through here quickly and they had not bothered covering their tracks. Supporting the suspicion that they were moving quickly, was that most of the tracks were light and the strides farther apart than would be made by someone moving slowly carrying a heavy backpack. I sure wished Chief could have been there, he would have been able to tell me a lot more about what took place just by looking at the tracks. But it was getting too dark to continue so we headed back to the hidey-hole and unless Bill found something we would continue to follow this trail tomorrow. We settled in for the night after reporting back to the major.

Bill and I discussed the tracks we saw and decided that perhaps we should split up to continue our search at first light – my team would follow the trail we found and Bill's would continue looking for any other sign of our missing teams. At first light we resumed our search, planning to join up again around noon. This time Bill searched the south side of the trail from where the sensors were placed.

My team went directly back to where we found the trail of the rapidly moving, lightly loaded tracks. The trail was extremely easy to follow but we took extreme caution so as not to run into whoever made these tracks. We had followed the tracks about an hour when we came upon a lot of shell casings. There had been a brief but intense firefight here, so I checked in with Bill. His team had not found anything and the information on a fire fight caused him to abandon his search and to rejoin us.

We continued to follow the trail but now we did it paralleling the trail instead of on it. From earlier examinations of the trail we estimated about twenty to thirty people were moving down the trail. It would be a darn good idea not to run into that large of a group without warning so the distance between our point man, Jim and the team widened larger than it normally did. After about a kilometer we found more evidence of pursuit. This time we saw the results of a claymore blast. The undergrowth was shredded and there were blood trails and signs of bodies being moved. We were definitely on the right path now. Apparently someone on Dwight or Steve's team set a claymore booby-trap to take out a few overzealous pursuers, and judging by the amount of blood on the ground it worked. A little further away we found four temporary graves.

We radioed the information in and asked the major to get some more air assets into the sky and scout the area in front of us. We continued paralleling the trail but pausing often for brief 'Stop, Look and Listens'. We had only moved another 250 meters when during one of our pauses we heard someone talking. The rest of the team held position while Jim crawled closer to investigate. He returned a few minutes later and signed that there were two NVA taking care of three wounded comrades.

After a quick debate with myself, I decided to go around them, rather than over their dead bodies. I noted their position so that at next contact I could tell Bill to be sure he skirted their position too. We continued to follow the trail, at the next pause we were far enough away that I could radio Bill the location of the wounded NVA. He responded that he had just gotten to the claymore ambush site so the warning was well timed.

We slowed our advance for Bill to catch up. The slowdown allowed us to scout a little more thoroughly and find a section of the trail that split into two paths before rejoining just about fifteen meters further on. On one path there were six sets of prints and five of the six had the exact same tire tread design as the faux Ho Chi Minh sandal soles as my boots so it seems we had indeed found five or six members of the missing teams. Upon another examination of the other path we found prints with varying tire tread designs for twelve people. So now we knew what type of odds we were facing, at least until more of their friends joined the hunt.

When Bill caught up with us I filled him in on our track counts. We radioed in our position and that we were going to try to make a dash up the trail to try to close the gap that separated us from them. We then proceed to do something very dangerous and stupid, but our guys were in trouble. We alternately ran then fast walked right up the trail for close to two hours. While we took a short break we received a radio message that the FAC had seen activity but he couldn't be sure which group, but the activity was only about five kilometers from our current position.

After we got the radio message, I looked at Bill and the rest of the guys and though not a word was said or even signed, everyone agreed we had to take some more risks and jogged for the next five kilometers.

Here is where all those nice long runs with Ducky in training really paid off, for the last two hours we had been running ten minutes fast walking five, and repeating; now we had another 5 kilometers to run. More than once during the last two hours I was singing Ducky's cadence in my head and would have bet my last dollar several of the other guys were too. We had gone just two of the five kilometers when we heard firing in the distance. You could hear the distinct difference in the sound of AK-47s and those of the CAR-15s. The AK-47s were on full rock and roll while the CAR-15s were firing in short bursts or single shot.

We paused to catch our breaths and see if we could raise the FAC to get some air support for our guys. However our timing was bad, the FAC had just left to refuel and his replacement would not be on site for another fifteen to twenty minutes. That meant we were on our own. Bill pointed towards the sound of the gun fire and we all started running again.

The sounds of the fire fight were not moving, so we rapidly closed the gap. We were approaching a hill and by the sounds we could tell the CAR-15s were definitely up on a small hill and the AK-47s from positions to the east and south of the hill. We paused to make a quick plan, my team would wrap around to the south of the hill behind the enemy and Bill's would do the same for the eastern side. Since I had further to go to get into position, the signal to spring our flanking attack would be Johnny's blooper firing.

We quickly but quietly made our way around to about fifteen meters behind the positions the NVA were firing from. I sent Johnny and Jim to a spot behind the furthermost point of the NVA firing line – telling Johnny to do his thing as soon as he saw Jim take position. At the sound of the bloop and before the sound of the M79 exploding, we opened up on the enemy's rear.

From my position I could see the backs of two NVA. On this mission I had taken the modified shotgun I had liberated from the Air America crash instead of my normal CAR-15. When Johnny fired, I had the first of my two targets in my sights; I fired three blasts at one and quickly shifted to the second target firing another three doses of double-aught buckshot at that one. After my second burst I got up, charging to their positions to double-check that they were down for the count, I had not taken more than two steps when I realized that sure was a stupid thing to do and dove back down to the ground. Good thing one small part of my mind was still working and halted my advance, because as I hit the ground I saw foliage at my chest height in front of me get shredded. To this day and in nightmares, I still think that I even heard the whiz and felt the breeze of the rounds as they passed over my prone body.

I quickly gathered what was left of my wits and visually checked the two targets from where I was - both were down but one moved. I fired another two shells at what was the moving target. All movement stopped after the jerks cause by the impacts as both blasts hit him. Now I could finally swing my attention to the rest of the fight going on around me. There were a few sporadic shots fired by an AK-47 from Bill's side of the hill answered by a long burst from an CAR-15. Then quiet.

Strangely enough we had still never made any kind of password or signal to alert other teams of our presence. The loud reports made by the shotgun made any noise conservation from my position useless so I decided to loudly sing the first line of Ducky's cadence as a sign to Dwight's and Steve's teams that there were friends out here and hoped to avoid a friendly fire incident.

To my "Be kind to your web footed friends" came a response from the hill, "For that duck may be somebody's mother."

When my shouts didn't draw any more fire, I yelled for Jim and Harold to check the bodies and take a look around to be sure we were alone. I got to my feet and approached the hill where I was warmly greeted by Eric Larsen, the point man for Dwight's team. "God, are we ever glad to see you guys! We got jumped at our night's campsite. Dwight and Steve were killed by a grenade when they first attacked and the rest of us had to run like hell. Unfortunately we had not yet re-loaded our packs up so we had to abandon most of our gear, including the backup radios, when we evaded. We have been running ever since, but Jerry and Moose were wounded and couldn't run any longer so we decided to make our last stand here."

"There is a FAC on the way here now and perhaps he can find us a clearing to use as a landing zone. All of this shooting has bound to have attracted a lot of unwanted attention, so get your guys ready to move and we'll blow this pop stand."

I got back on the radio and notified the Major that we had found the teams and their status. He proceeded to tell me to do the exact same thing that I had just told Eric, great minds must think alike. In three minutes we were ready to move, the FAC was not yet on site but movement in any direction was a lot better than staying here. We had not passed any sizable clearings on the way here so I decided we should leave the trail they had been following, cut at about ninety degrees towards the north, a direction they would assume we would not go, and use maximum trail concealment to make it a little harder for anyone to know which way we were headed.

Bill's team laid a false trail back the way we had originally came in from while my team lead what was left of the other two teams out of the area. Bill's team, once they set the false trail, would follow behind the rest of us and clean up the trail we all left.

We had gotten in touch with the new FAC and he vectored us towards a landing zone he had found to the north. Helicopters were on their way to meet us, so things were starting to look up. But like Robert Burns said in his poem, "The best laid schemes o' mice an' men / Gang aft a-gley." We had covered about half of the distance to the LZ when we were discovered by an NVA patrol. Our point man, Jim Adams, was a heck of a lot better than theirs and he managed to kill both of them before they had even brought their weapons to bear. But it was too late - we were once again in contact with a much larger force.

The NVA were between us and the LZ, word passed down the line to shift directions, everybody but my team started towards the east. My team had our hands busy slowing down the newly discovered enemy. As he fell back Johnny paused to put the blooper to work by dropping grenades into the advancing enemy. I took cover behind a small mound made thanks to a tree's roots and proceeded to mow down the jungle in front of me, emptying a whole fifteen round clip from my shotgun. Harold moved into position a little behind me to the right, immediately setting up a claymore to cover our next 'advance to the rear.'

Wild Bill got in touch with the FAC to find us another LZ and get some air support to cover our retreat. The FAC replied that fast movers were on the way and two mikes out. A mike was radio shorthand talk for a minute. I heard the conversation between Bill and the FAC and threw a purple smoke grenade to both hinder the NVA's view and to mark our location. I confirmed the color of the smoke with the FAC and told him to have the jets smash anything north of the smoke.

Bill's team, took up positions, getting ready to support my team as we fell back, about twenty-five meters to the southeast and set up an ambush at the far side of an area with thin undergrowth. The other two teams, carrying the wounded, continued towards the new LZ. Bill's crew had just gotten into position when my team, except Harold, broke contact and ran like scared jackrabbits back to the south a little rather than towards the east on the same track that the others had taken. Harold waited until the NVA broke cover and started to advance to fire the claymore. He didn't even wait to see the results of the widespread destruction caused by the flight of 700 steel ball bearings before he was up on his feet and dashing back with the rest of my team.

The results of claymore was enough to hold up the NVA advance just long enough for a pair of U.S. Air National Guard F100s to begin a strafing run of the area north of the smoke marker we had used. The strafing run was shortly followed by another pair of F100s who proceeded to napalm torch a wide area just a tad north of the line taken by the strafing F100s. That should have taken care of the trailing NVA but a few had gotten up to the location of the smoke grenade and escaped the wrath of the Air National Guard fighters.

My team ran right past Bill's without slowing down or acknowledging them in any way, no use giving up the location of a perfectly good ambush by being civil and saying "howdy partner." Admittedly we were moving a lot slower than our top speed, it seems like we had run the entire day and even with the adrenaline surging through our veins we were pooped and slowing down. We kept going for another fifty meters and found a small rise we could use as our next defensive position to cover Wild Bill's team as they dropped back. I could barely breathe much less tell the guys where to take positions, but the team didn't really need any instructions and each man took a position with good cover and a wide field of fire. It would be a few minutes before we would be quite enough to have any element of surprise on an advancing enemy because we were all breathing so hard and puffing like the Little Engine That Could.

Even though I had a full clip in my shotgun I managed to find the time to use all of the loose buckshot shells I had left to reload the two shotgun clips I had emptied. I didn't have enough shells to fill the second clip, I was down to 42 rounds and I knew we didn't have any more claymores left. I waved my arms to get the attention of the other guys and signed to them to report on ammo status.

Johnny told me he was down to four grenades for the blooper and one hundred rounds for his CAR-15. Jim was down to sixty rounds and two fragmentation grenades. Harold was the same as Jim. None had told me the status of their handguns but I don't think we had used any so far on this mission so everyone would have the standard 24 rounds counting those in the gun and the two spare clips. I had no idea how long it would be before we would be able to get out of here so I signed for us to go into ammo conservation mode and no longer use full auto.

I was finally getting my breath under control when I heard Bill's team pop their claymore then open fire with everything else. After only a few seconds of intense fire the shooting tapered off to nothing. After three minutes Bill's team came through our position but Ted Boxer, Bill's point, was being carried between Merlin Veller and Ronnie Newman. Bill dropped down besides me and gave me a quick update. "They ran right into our ambush and got severely punished again. At least four KIA and a couple wounded. I hung around and they didn't seem too keen on advancing again. Ted took one in the side and it doesn't look fatal but we need to get him out of here ASAP before he bleeds out."

I told Bill, "The LZ should only be about a half klick from here. Get your guys back there and set up a perimeter for the LZ and update Major Straight on our status. I'll stay here for a few minutes to see if they finally work up the nerve to continue following us."

Bill then ran away to catch up with his team while my team waited. Apparently the enemy was getting a little smarter, after running into two ambushes they were not tricked by a third. They didn't even get into the thinner undergrowth at the base of the hill we were taking cover on. They started firing from the thick brush trying to draw our counter fire. A pattern quickly became apparent, firing from three locations followed by a pause and more firing from three different locations. Either there were only three of them left or the three to our front were a diversion as they tried to flank us. I signed for Jim and Harold the two outer people in our mini-ambush to watch our flanks and for Johnny to fall back and watch our rear while I kept the front diversion busy. I fired off a blast from my shotgun, rolled a few meters to my right and then fired off several rounds from my Mk22 without the silencer in place.

When I heard Jim open fire from his position on the north side of the hill, I knew my guess of them trying to flank us was right. I fired off a few shots from my shotgun to keep the three guys to my front heads down, and then ran over to back up Jim, who was by now receiving heavy fire. I got to Jim's position just as he was changing clips. Harold must have read my mind because he moved to take my old position. Johnny turned the NVA's flanking attack by opening fire on their flank. He had shifted from the south side of the hill where he had been covering our rear and managed to slide into position on their eastern flank. Nothing is as great as flanking someone trying to flank you. When he opened up they quit firing and evaporated back into the heavy undergrowth leaving two more of their comrades behind.

I frantically waved to Harold to get his attention and pointed east signaling that we should continue our retreat to the LZ. I hadn't even noticed that Jim was slow in getting up and I started to move away. I must have gone twenty steps when I checked my six and noticed that Jim had not followed me. I ran back and found that Jim had been shot in the head as he was changing clips. With a curse on the NVA that were following us, I slung the shotgun across my chest, scooped up Jim's body, and with him in the fireman's carry position started jogging back to rejoin with the rest of the team.

Jim weighed a lot more than I did and every step I took was a major fight with exhaustion and I stumbled several times as I moved to join the others, but I was not going to leave Jim behind while I could still put one foot in front of another. Harold and Johnny waited for me and Jim to catch up with them about fifty meters back. When Harold saw me staggering with Jim over my shoulders he ran to me to help. Harold was by far the strongest of the three of us remaining and he took over carrying our friend so he could go back home.

When we were approaching the LZ, I whistled a few bars of Stars and Stripes Forever, the tune to Ducky's cadence. When we got a few bars whistled back we entered the LZ. I dropped exhausted to the ground next to Bill. He told me four helicopters were on the way in and due to arrive here in five minutes. I gave him a weak nod of acknowledgment and moved away to a position to cover the LZ. The LZ was large enough for two helicopters to land at once. The wounded were to the east side of the LZ with what was left of Dwight's and Steve's teams. After Harold took Jim's body to wait with them for extraction he moved into position to cover the perimeter with what was left of our teams.

When we heard the ever so sweet sound of the helicopters coming in to land, we knew salvation was at hand. We popped and confirmed yellow smoke and two of the helicopters landed while the other two fired their M60s into the jungle around the clearing. While Bill and my teams watched the perimeter, Dwight and another loaded the wounded and Jim on the helicopters. The rest of the members of Dwight's and Steve's teams loaded up too. They were just about to take off when all hell broke loose.

The NVA must have had this LZ under observation for quite a while, because they had a mortar team that had the clearing zeroed in. Almost simultaneously four 82mm mortar rounds landed in the center of the LZ. One round directly on one of the helicopters and others scattered around the center. The direct hit caused one of the helicopters to explode and pieces of the exploding machine totally ruined the other helicopter. One of the blades became a flying scythe slicing into the cockpit of the other, killing the crew instantly. It then dropped the fifteen feet of height it had gained and crashed to the ground exploding into flames. No one aboard survived the fiery wreckage of the two helicopters.

More mortar rounds began to fall into the already devastated remains of the helicopters but they paid for their success. The FAC had seen where the rounds originated from and vectored two of the F100s still providing us support to the location. The mortars went silent as several napalm bombs turned their mortar firing pit into a barbeque pit.

Then the six of us on the LZ perimeter came under heavy small arms fire. Apparently we had run right into an ambush ourselves. They even were sneaky enough to not spring it until we had all entered the LZ. We were taking fire from three sides, every direction except the one we had entered from and I am sure that the group that had herded us into this LZ was busy taking up positions to close the gap.

Things were not looking good at all. If one of the pilots of the helicopters had the nerve to come down into this hot LZ they would come under extremely heavy fire and odds of all six of us and the helicopter and crew making it off the ground were not very favorable. On the positive side, the mortars were no longer raining communist scrap metal down on our positions, we had a FAC providing interface for the close air support, a couple of F100s on site, and I hoped more on the way. So the tough call we had to decide on was trying to make a break now or wait until air support could put down enough fire power to raise our odds.

Bill, the FAC, and the pilots of the helicopters and F100s were all on the same radio frequency so I quickly asked the questions to allow us to make a big decision. I knew that the F100s on site had to be low on munitions about now since they had been doing continuous strafing runs on the enemy around us. I was not too sure about the willingness of the helicopter pilots to come into such a hot LZ especially after watching the crews of two other helicopters being killed. So I asked the FAC, "Is more air support on the way and how long?"

The FAC's answer gave me some hope and upped our odds of getting out of this alive. More support was on the way including an AC130 which had the firepower and capability to provide us with excellent support for a long time. The FAC said that we must have some big pull with someone high up in the Air Force to get one of the AC130s to fly here during the daylight hours, not to mention the number of fast moving jets that were on the way. I said a quick "Thank God" to myself for having the Major pulling all the strings he could, of course his reputation of having saved flight crews of downed planes helped a lot.

I got a quick confirmation from Bill and told our air assets we would stay down here and let the Air Force take care of us for a while. When I said that, I heard a heavy sigh of relief come over the airwaves, which must have come from one of the chopper pilots. That sigh told me that while ready to put their lives on the line to try and get us out they were grateful that they didn't have to do it right now.

Bill said we should pull back closer to the now smoldering helicopter wreckage to allow us to lessen the size of our perimeter and let the air support get in a lot closer, not to mention that we would have a little more cover both from the smoke and what was left of the destroyed aircraft shells. I concurred and we all started scooting our way back from the foliage we were hiding in towards the wreckage. We had managed to pull back a little when I heard a scream come from Ronnie Newman. I was closest to him so I changed directions and started heading his way.

When I got to Ronnie I saw that he had taken a couple of hits to the side of his body. I grabbed his belt and started dragging him back with me. I had managed to get him a few feet when Merlin Veller appeared and began to help me drag Ronnie. It was a close call because the side of the perimeter that had just been emptied by the three of us heaved upwards blasted by a 500 pounder dropped a little short by a newly arriving F105. The concussion of the big bomb caused the three of us to roll a good fifteen feet from where we were when the bomb hit. Ronnie and Merlin were now both unconscious and I was seeing stars and it sounded like I was at the bottom of a well.

I am not sure how long it was before Harold, Johnny and Bill showed up. Harold slapped me back to my senses and yelled that the gooks were starting to get close enough to enter the LZ. I yelled, "Big bomb hole!" pointing to where the 500 bomb had landed. Bill quickly got my idea and with Harold dragging Merlin and Johnny dragging Ronnie we headed toward the bomb crater. Unfortunately as we were moving Ronnie was hit again, this time fatally but Johnny continued to drag him with us to the crater. Bill was on the horn to the FAC telling him our plan, yelled into the radio, "Leave the new big ass crater alone, but kill everything else in a 100 mile area!"

Not the best radio procedure in the world but the FAC got the idea, as soon as we made it to the lip of the crater; all the aircraft that had anything left to shoot or throw began to plaster the LZ and everything around it.

Once we got in the hole Bill threw a red smoke grenade above the rim of our hole and notified the FAC to help in keeping our location visible to the air support flight crews. We sure didn't need another 500lb. bomb falling into our hole.

As we moved the unconscious Merlin and Ronnie's body to the center of the bottom of the hole and with the four of us around them ready to blast the head off of anyone else that got close enough to look into our hole, we made sure that our heads stayed below the rim and out of the path of the lethal projectiles flying all around us. At this point I had no idea of time or of what kind of support we had above us, but there was a continuous roar of sound from the screaming of jets passing over, bombs exploding, and the buzz-saw sound of the AC130's mini-guns.

I think we all tried to make ourselves as small as possible but even so both Johnny and Bill took minor wounds from pieces of junk buzzing through the air around us. Bill had a long deep gash on his forearm and Johnny a nasty cut on his calf. As I was slapping a compression pad on Bill our eyes met and we both said our wordless good-byes to each other. Our mind-meld was broken when Harold yelled at the top of his lungs, "This never fuckin' happened!"

And for some strange reason Bill and I both laughed aloud like maniacs. I tried to keep the gallows humor out of my reply by correcting Harold in a very poor, fake upper crust English accent. "Harold, you need to use correct tense when speaking proper English."

I then yelled, "This ain't fuckin' happening!"

It was immediately echoed by Bill, Johnny, and Harold, "This ain't fuckin' happening!"

Their shout was echoed by a loud explosion of another 500 pound bomb that caused us to bounce off the bottom of the hole before gravity won the fight with the shock wave and we fell back to the ground. That ended our brief escape from reality and I finished securing the bandage around Bill's arm. Johnny was taking care of his own leg so I went to check on Merlin, but he was still in la-la land, I tried to get him back to consciousness by slapping him lightly a few times but to no avail.

My ears were ringing loudly so I could barely hear the FAC trying to contact us on the radio. I keyed the radio and yelled, "What!? Repeat!"

The FAC was checking that we were still alive and gave me the best news I had ever heard, the enemy was withdrawing, beaten by the air support and a helicopter was coming in to get us. We started to get ready, Johnny said he was OK enough to make it on his own, so I got in position to pick up Ronnie and Harold got ready to carry the heavier Merlin.

Just as the helicopter came to a few feet from the edge of the crater, I put Ronnie over my shoulder and sprinted for our ticket out of here. I was followed by Johnny, then Bill, and finally by Harold carrying Merlin. I got

187

Ronnie on the floor of the chopper, helped Bill and Johnny into the ride and had just mounted myself when we came back under fire. Apparently not all of the NVA had run from the air attack. Harold and Merlin went down just inches from the helicopter. I jumped back off, took Merlin off of Harold and not so gently threw a now very bloody Merlin on top of Ronnie and reached back down for Harold.

I knew Harold was alive, but hurt, because he was having trouble getting up and kept yelling over and over about the NVA being the offspring of female dogs. He had been shot in the top of his right thigh, one inch higher and it would have been in his ass. I grabbed him by his shirt back and hauled him off the ground and pushed him onto the helicopter. With the aid of lots of adrenaline, I leaped up to the only open spot of the helicopter's floor. The helicopter crew chief was yelling for the pilot to, "Go! Go! Go!"

I could hear bullets slamming into the helicopter's body as we took off. I looked down and saw Bill checking for Merlin's pulse. He looked up at me and shook his head. Out of the sixteen members of Detachment 11 that had gone into Cambodia for this mission, only four of us got out alive, and I was the only person not wounded. I chased that though out of my mind and bend down to aid Harold. Just as I started to do so, the helicopter pilot performed a radical maneuver to dodge a line of tracers he saw appear right in front of us. I lost my balance and fell out of the helicopter.

It is strange what you think of during times like these. I pictured myself painting DIPUTS with reversed characters on my hand so that I could then hit my forehead with my hand and it would transfer the imprint STUPID onto my head. Then I thought about preparing to hit the ground but by then it was far too late. Luckily I didn't hit ground, but began crashing through the limbs of a tree. I then hit the ground knees first, and the momentum remaining caused me to roll downhill about twenty feet into an open clearing. I guess I was lucky since we were passing over a ridge line so the fall from the chopper was only about twenty-five feet and the relatively softer tree limbs absorbed most of the momentum of my fall on the way down. A minute later and it would have been a fatal fall of more than a hundred feet.

I was told later that Harold started yelling at the pilot to go back. If the pilot even heard him, he must have thought Harold nuts so he kept going. Somehow Harold got to his feet and tapped the pilot on the shoulder with the barrel of his Mk22, lifted the headphones off of one ear and told him "Go back! Your rotten driving caused one of your passengers to go skydiving."

The pilot gave Harold one of those looks that said, "Are you totally out of your mind?"

"Go back! Your maneuvering caused Ron to fall out, back at that ridgeline!"

The pilot then took a quick glance at Harold's face and the pistol in his hand and decided to return to see what happened to me. He told the door-gunner to get the machine gun that he had dodged earlier and they headed back to see if I had even survived the fall.

I wanted to get up and signal the helicopter but when I tried the pain in my knees nearly caused me to black out. I managed a weak wave when the helicopter returned; the first pass was at high speed as the door-gunner fought a duel with the machine gun that had caused the problem in the first place. The helicopter zigged and zagged faster than the NVA 12.7 mm machine gun could swing around and stay on target, so the helicopter's gunner won the duel and the machine gun went silent.

Luckily I had rolled into a clearing large enough for one helicopter to enter. The helicopter came back around and hovered long enough for the door-gunner to jump down and push me up into the chopper. He had not been too careful in how it did it and I banged my injured knees causing so much pain that all I saw was a bright flash of lightning through my skull and I passed out.

I didn't come back to reality until I woke up in a hospital bed and the first thing I recognized was Major Straight sitting in a chair next to my bed. He was sitting bent over, elbows on his knees and his face buried in his hands. I managed to croak "Good morning." through a very dry throat.

At first the sound startled him but he quickly gained control, wiped his eyes with his hands, and looked over to me and said, "Good middle of the night. It is almost 11:30 PM so it is not officially morning yet."

I managed a weak smile at the detailed correction and asked, "I remember getting back on the helicopter but how are my men?"

He gave a smile and nod before replying, "It is great to hear you think of your team before you even ask about yourself. Harold, Johnny and Bill are all here in the hospital with you, just a little farther down the ward. They are all going to be OK, but you four are the only ones to make it back alive."

"You got out of surgery about 3 hours ago, the doctor said that you would be OK and be able to walk again but may require some physical therapy."

That was when I finally looked down at my legs and saw that I had casts on both legs from just above my ankle to the middle of my thighs. I didn't say anything for a while as my drug hazed mind replayed everything that happened the last few days in fast forward mode. After the replay I realized that it was a miracle that any of us were still alive. Then I had almost another two full seconds of semi-clear thought before the pain started to work its way through the drugs. With tears of pain both physical and mental coming down my face I managed to say, "I'm glad that they are OK and I am sorry, Major, that I couldn't bring everybody back for you. Could you chase away the son of a bitch that keeps stabbing me in the knees with ice picks and then give me some water please?"

The major reached over to a bedside table and placed the straw sticking out of an olive-drab tin cup to my lips so I could take a sip. He then said, "I know you tried and gave it your all. It was just not in the cards, the mortars hitting the helicopters just as they were taking off was just plain bad luck. Let me go get the nurse to get you something for the pain."

He stood up, walked away and returned a few minutes later with a six foot tall guy in olive drab fatigues carrying something on a metal tray. The giant fooled with something beside me and magically the additional happy juice he gave me kicked in and I was out like a light once again.

The next time I came back to my senses it was Bill in the chair.

"How ya doin', Ron?"

I thought about it for a few seconds before I managed to say, "Too doped up to tell. How are you and the rest of the guys doing?"

He slightly raised a bandaged arm in a sling. "I'm not too bad. Johnny and Harold are doing fine also. Johnny's leg is fine and we figured that the bullet that hit Harold must have gone through Merlin before it went into him because his wound was less than a half-inch deep. He's already been discharged and back at the barracks packing our gear. We are all being shipped back to the hospital at Clark tomorrow."

"I might as well tell you, while you are still doped up, the rest of the bad news. When we went off to look for Dwight and Steve's teams, the guys in Ducky, Uncle Bob and Charles Cullum's teams, to a man, all volunteered to come to Vietnam and help in the search. So everybody at Clark, but Captain Cummings and Bob who stayed back to man the radio, geared up and headed here to help out. But the C130 they were on had some kind of a problem and crashed into the South China Sea between Clark and here. They have not found any survivors but they are still looking."

All I could do at that news was close my eyes and fight not to start crying. I lost that fight. I looked back at Bill and I saw the tears running down his face too. We both remained quiet not saying or moving for several minutes. Magically the olive drab clad giant with the metal tray reappeared. He chased Bill back to his own bed and gave me another shot of happy juice.

The next thing I coherently remembered was awakening again and the olive drab giant had turned into a cute Philippine girl in a starched white nurse's uniform giving me a sip of water. She told me they were cutting back on my drugs and to let her know if the pain got to be too much to bear. I laid there the rest of the day reliving the last mission over, and over, and over, again, trying to figure out what I could have done to change the outcome. What if I had turned right instead of left? What if we had gone to another LZ? Through the hospital window I could see that it was dark when the Major came to see me.

"Hi, Ron. Welcome back to the Philippines. Bill said that he told you about the guys that had been at Clark. They have called off the search and there were no survivors. Let me get the rest of the official business out of the way first."

He looked around then quietly said, "Remember everything we have done is still classified. If anyone asks, the official cover story is that you, Bill, Johnny, and Harold were in an automobile accident. Everybody else we lost was on a training exercise when their plane crashed. Got it?"

I nodded; he took another quick look around making sure no one was close before he continued. "I just got off the horn with General McConnell. They are disbanding Detachment 11. He is stepping down as Chief of Staff, but before he leaves office he will see to it that everyone still in Detachment 11 gets a promotion, and we are officially now attached to the 6931st Security Group. We will all be stationed at Iraklion Air Station on the island of Crete in Greece doing something totally different. The doctor said that in another two weeks you can travel by wheelchair or on crutches. As soon as you are mobile and can travel, you'll get a two week leave at home before going to Crete. As far as Detachment 11 is concerned, we were never in Vietnam, we never saw combat, and we were always here in the Philippines. OK?"

I said, "I know. It never happened."

He continued briefing me on what was going to happen, "You four will travel as a group back to San Francisco. Once there, Bill will see to helping Johnny get on his plane and Harold will get you on your plane home, and then go home himself. I'll arrange for you to have all the flight details and you'll get to telephone your parents to meet you at the airport. If you have any medical issues when you get home or an emergency have your parents take to you to the VA Hospital in New Orleans or to the medical facilities at Alvin Callender Naval Air Station. You are also expected to get an examination halfway through your leave at home at the Alvin Callender medical facilities. In a day or two, someone will supply you with the orders and flight schedules to get you to Crete. Any questions?"

"What will we do in Crete, sir?"

"I was stationed there once before, what we will do is have fun. It is one of the best postings in the Air Force. The rest of us will be leaving directly for Crete early next week and I will figure out what we will be doing as far as work is concerned once I get there."

* * *

May 22, 2018
Between Rethymno and Hersonissos, Crete, Greece

The bus hit a big hole in the road and brought Ron back to the present. He looked over at Kathy and there were tears running down her face. Ron and Kathy were at the back of the minibus and everyone was looking back over their seats at him as he told his story. Ron looked at their faces and every eye that looked back at him had a watery gleam.

But leave it to Harold to tear everybody's mind away from what they were thinking by saying, "It never happened! I'm not sure where we are going to eat tonight, but there better be lots of booze there. And NO we are not going to talk about me almost being shot in the butt like Ron."

CHAPTER 18
May 23, 2018
Malia, Crete, Greece

It was the last day of the reunion and the participants would be leaving tomorrow for their homes. The reunion group had spent the last night staying up late chatting and laughing in front of the huge outdoor fireplace behind the resort and got off to a late start, but by noon they were all sitting in a new taverna that had an excellent view of Malia beach from a covered outdoor dining area.

The conversation was light and centered around passing out physical and email addresses and discussing seeing each other back in the States. During the reunion they had all renewed or created new friendships that would last the rest of their lives. It was during the "let's get together again" conversation that Kathy asked, "Why didn't you guys keep communicating all the years you were apart after your time in the military?"

Harold confessed, "I have to say that was my fault. Except for General Straight and Major Cummings, we had all entered the service within a few weeks of each other, so except for those two and Bill, who was going to be a lifer too, we were all going to be discharged about the same time. As it was getting close to time for me, Bob, Johnny, Chief, and Ron to get discharged, none of us were sure where we would be living once we got out. Ron was going to take his discharge here on Crete and I would be the first one to actually go home. I had planned on staying with my widowed mother so the plan was that they would all write to me at my mom's home once they got settled and I would consolidate and distribute everybody's addresses around to the guys. But fate intervened, it was about three months later that I had finally received everybody's new addresses, but I had not yet distributed them when there was a bad fire that destroyed my mom's house, along with my address book containing all the addresses. I was away interviewing for a job, and my mom was killed in the fire. I was not in the best mental place for a while. I just took the insurance money and moved to Silverton where I would be starting a new job soon. I confess I just left and I screwed up by not following through. I am so sorry, guys."

Ron put his arm on Harold's shoulder and said, "I am very sorry about your mom, buddy." After a second Ron removed his arm and gave Harold a light punch on the arm as he said, "That punch is for screwing up and losing the addresses. But at least I got a forty-five plus year break without having to put up with any of your bullshit. Brothers forgive brothers for screwing up. Right, gang?"

To a chorus of agreements and promises that they would keep in touch from now on, the conversation shifted around to visiting each other when they got back. Kathy had just arranged with Harold and Joan for them to come to visit them the coming fall in Lake Charles and was warning them about the rather wet greeting they would receive from Ron's over friendly, lick happy dog.

Harold said, "I love dogs, so a few wet dog kisses in greeting wouldn't bother me in the least, but I draw the line at Ron licking my face. But I am sure that even that greeting would be a lot better than the greeting we got when we left the Philippines and were in the San Francisco airport."

Joan asked Harold to explain.

* * *

June 1969 ~ San Francisco Airport
As told by Harold Vinter

The General, Captain Cummings, Chief and Bob left a couple of weeks before we did. When Ron was in condition to travel, the four of us left the Philippines wearing our uniforms on a commercial airliner chartered by the Air Force. We flew from Clark to Hawaii to refuel then on to the public terminal of the San Francisco airport where everyone would catch regularly scheduled commercial airline flights to their final destinations. Because of the casts on Ron's legs the four of us were the last to get off the flight; we all still had a long wait for our connecting flights so we decided to get something to eat. After a meal consumed with real, instead of reconstituted milk, served by a real round-eyed woman, we were finally splitting up. Ron and I from one terminal, and Bill and Johnny from another terminal, we shook hands saying we would be seeing each other in two weeks and headed off on our leaves.

This was back in the days before all the TSA security crap we have now and there were not any restrictions as to where people could go in the terminal. I was walking and Ron was bouncing along on his crutches when we were approaching a bunch of hippies grouped together by the side of a walkway between the terminals. As we came near, one of the hippies pointed at us and the others looked our way and moved to block our path, then they started shouting at us calling us 'warmongers,' 'baby killers,' and several words that even I would not say in the company of ladies. One even pointed at the casts on Ron's legs and told him that he had gotten what he deserved for killing babies.

My temper was reaching the boiling stage at that point so when one of them threw a small water balloon filled with red liquid on our uniforms, I lost it. I punched the bastard right in the nose, knocking him down on his ass. Another one of the hippies pushed me while I was looking down and cursing at the balloon throwing idiot I had just decked. A third grabbed me from behind but quickly let go when Ron used one of his crutches to bash him in the back of the head. At this point there was lots of screaming and cursing going on as Ron and I faced down the rest of the pack. There had been a couple of policemen not far from the group of hippies and they soon showed up to break up the impending riot.

I was shouting about the idiot throwing the balloon with the die and they were shouting about us hitting two of them. So the cops decided to start arresting people, but instead of the hippies, they arrested Ron and me for hitting them. With me supporting Ron because they took away his crutches, we were hauled off to the road. There we had to wait for a patty wagon to come get us because with Ron's knees in his casts, they couldn't get both of us into the back of a patrol car. A half hour later we were finally driven to the local police lockup.

Ron was leaning on me when a police sergeant started talking to one of the arresting officers that had traveled with us from the airport. I was still burning up and every other word I said started with an F. As an older police sergeant approached us, Ron told me to shut up, and he would do the talking. Before the policeman said a word, Ron told him we wanted to press charges against the hippies that attacked us at the airport and attempted murder charges against the one that threw the balloon that we think may have had dangerous chemicals in it.

The police sergeant looked at us; a smile appeared on his face that vanished before he quickly turned on the arresting officer and asked if someone had thrown a balloon containing chemicals at these men before the altercation became physical. The arresting officer said yes but that he knew that it only contained red food coloring. Ron quickly inserted that we were greatly outnumbered by our attackers and didn't know what was in the balloon, other than the fact that it was reacting with our uniform where it splashed on us, we saw red and thought it was blood. The police sergeant told the other officer that we had a valid case to claim self-defense. He then told the officer to give Ron back his crutches, take us back to the airport and stay with us until we got on our flights home. The police sergeant turned back to us winked and whispered that he had been in the Air Force too and wished us a safe trip home.

When we got back to the airport we found out we had missed our flights but we could re-booked on a later one. I had calmed down a lot by then and I told the cop we didn't have any U. S. coins on us and bummed some change from the police officer that had arrested us so we could call home and notify our families about the change in arrival times.

* * *

May 23, 2018
Malia, Crete, Greece

195

When Harold finished the story everyone was laughing that Harold had gotten the cop to pay for our calls home, long distance telephone calls from payphones cost a couple of dollars which was not cheap back then.

A brief conversation ensued about cell phones for a while before it shifted back to Malia and how when we were here before, the only place we could go to get a drink close to the beach was Mike's. Mary then started talking about her and Bill's wedding reception being at Mike's. After the conversation about Bill and Mary's wedding the conversation changed direction once again when Joan said she now knew what we did during our time in Southeast Asia but what did we do here on Crete.

Bill said, "Besides drinking on the beach and chasing girls, not very much."

Everyone laughed at that, but Bill continued, "All kidding aside, we were re-trained to do radio signals intelligence work to assist the National Security Agency, NSA, and that is all any of us will ever tell you about our jobs here."

The General smiled and quickly changed the conversation again by telling the girls that we worked hard when we were here. He went on to explain that when he got here he had received his promotion to Lieutenant Colonel and had been assigned as the assistant base commander. However when Colonel Altman, the base commander, went home on emergency leave just three days after his arrival, he became the temporary base commander. Colonel Altman did not return so he became the base commander.

The General continued his story about their time on Crete.

* * *

June 1969 ~ Iraklion Air Station
As told by George Straight

General McConnell, the Air Force Chief of Staff, knew he was going to officially retire the end of July so he did everything he could to clean up all the loose ends that were lying around, and Detachment 11 was one of those loose ends. The Detachment had lots of successes but the large losses we took at the end of May spelled doom for the unit. Everything the unit had done remained classified Top Secret Codeword protected and hidden in files that would more than likely never see the light of day again. He did what he could for those of us who survived by pushing through a promotion for each of us and arranging for our transfer to Iraklion Air Station. The records of Detachment 11 were edited with large chunks being expunged for classification purposes, and when you read what remained, it looked like no one from Detachment 11 had ever left Clark Air Base except on training flights to other Philippine islands, and that the unit had a very unlucky history of training accidents. The last 'unlucky' accident occurred on May 22, 1969 when a C130 flying from Clark Air Base on a training mission crashed killing twenty-two members of Detachment 11. Only two bodies were recovered from the crash to be sent home, Merlin Veller and Ronald Newman, the two friends that Ron and Bill's teams had gotten out of Cambodia.

So officially, at least as far as unclassified records are concerned, of the forty-six people that started Detachment 11 and arrived in the Philippines, eight were transferred to the 6931st Security Group, one was discharged for medical reasons and thirty-seven died in 'training accidents' or car crashes. Officially we were, more than likely, the most unlucky unit in the history of the U. S. Air Force. That is strange when you consider if you look into the official records of MACV, which missed General McConnell's purge, you find mention of the unit and more than twenty commendations for meritorious action and great praise for the intelligence it gathered.

When I learned of our being disbanded and transferred to Iraklion Air Station, IAS, I had to send in recommendations on what to do with an ex-Green Beret, now an Air Force Major, four Sergeants and two Staff Sergeants who could move unseen through a jungle but who had never really finished a training school preparing them to do the normal work for the currently open slots at IAS. IAS is one of those few bases where the people stationed there do whatever they can to extending their tours. In many cases the airman assigned there right from tech school, keep volunteering to stay there, and never leave until it is time for their discharge from the military, so the openings available were rather limited.

There was a perfect slot for Major Cummings in base support where he would oversee many of the support aspects for the base except for the SIGNET intelligence operations. The other six openings available were for four Morse code operators and two radio printer operators. The men all knew Morse code so training on the new process they would have to use at the 6931st would be relatively easy. Before we even left the Philippines I had Chief and Bob work with one of the Morse code specialist NCOs at the 6922nd compound. As soon as Johnny and Bill were released by the base hospital they too started to work with a training NCO. Harold was assigned to work with one of the radio printer specialist when he was discharged from the hospital, but Ron would have to wait until he was on Crete to learn his new job as a radio printer specialist.

In order to support a 24/7 mission at IAS the SIGNET operations personnel were divided into five groups. A small group was on the day staff and mostly only worked a normal Monday to Friday shift. The majority of the others were split into four groups called Flights. Each flight would work four days on a swing shift, from 4 PM to midnight, then have twenty-four hours off; work four mid-shifts from midnight to 8 AM followed by twenty-four hours off; then four day shifts from 8 AM to 4 PM; then they got to have almost four days off before they began the cycle again. This allowed for there to always be one flight on duty 24/7. Chief and Bob were assigned to Able Flight and the others to Dog Flight.

I had their new supervisors report back to me on how they were doing and all were performing extremely well. My responsibilities as base commander kept me rather busy but I remember one night when I couldn't sleep and decided to do an unannounced visit to base operations. Dog Flight was working a mid-shift when I walked into operations. I checked in with the flight commander and started walking the aisles. I first ran into Johnny and Bill, they were sitting next to each other and holding a quiet conversation. What amazed me was they were both typing the characters associated with the Morse code they were listening to, and judging by the speed of their typing it was coming in at about 30 or more words per minute. They never looked at their keyboards, they had their radio headsets tilted to listen to the Morse code with one ear and the other ear off so they could hold a conversation with each other. Bill notice me and their conversation shifted to include me all while never missing a character they were typing.

I mentioned that I thought that they were taking to this jobs like ducks to water, Bill winked and said it was a lot easier than watching one hundred directions at once like they did for their last job. He never mentioned what their last job was; none of the guys did, as far as the other people they worked with were concerned, they were just transfers from doing this exact same job at Clark for the 6922nd. Since it was a Saturday and the last day of their mid-shift, they had 24 hours off coming up, I invited them to my quarters for a mid-day shift break breakfast party.

I moved off and went to find Ron and Harold. I found Harold first; he was talking to an airman first class, apparently fresh from training in the U. S. and working his first shift in operations. Harold was instructing him to go around to all the other operation area positions and ask for an EMHO report. Harold was explaining that he was to take a clipboard and write down each operator's name, rank, and ask them if they had an EMHO. Harold saw me standing there listening to him. He didn't stop until he had completed his instruction and never changed expressions when he told the rookie to start with the base commander who was standing right behind him. The poor airman Harold was talking to jumped two feet in the air and managed to stammer out, "Pardon me Colonel, do you have an EMHO?"

I replied, "Negative. Why don't you start asking the linguist in the back of operations before doing the other sections. Be patient and wait if you must, but be sure they are not busy before you ask them. Carry on."

The airman quickly checked the name tag on my uniform, wrote down my rank and name and "Negative" next to it. He then moved off to continue asking others about their EMHO. As soon as he got out of hearing range, I shook my head, started laughing, and asked Harold when he was going to tell the rookie that he was asking people if they had an Early Morning Hard On?

"It is a great way to introduce new guys to everybody on flight. And if he is so dumb as to not know what he is doing by the time he finishes – I'll get him to do it every mid-shift until he does. Thanks for playing along major, oops, I mean colonel."

"Slow night, Harold?"

"Yes, we only have about twenty sites up and working now, during the days we can get up to forty or more."

At that point Ron joined the conversation. I asked them about what they were doing and found that Harold was moving into a small apartment in Malia and spending most of his time on the beach while Ron was looking for a place in Iraklion and spending a lot of time with a couple of the locals. As the three of us were chatting I had sat down at a workstation and had my feet up on the desk

I don't remember where our conversation roamed to then but I remember we were joking around laughing rather loudly when I heard someone behind me say, "Hey! Keep it down and at least look like you are working. I heard the old man had been seen walking around earlier."

Before I stood up I told Ron and Harold to warn me if they see the old man around. Harold in a loud mock stage whisper said, "Colonel, look out, there is an old 'lifer' behind you!"

I stood up and turned. TSgt Smith was a short, black, stocky man but when he saw who Ron and Harold were talking to, he shrank to about two-foot-tall and turned the most beautiful shade of mahogany.

"How are you doing, Tech Sergeant Smith? I was just about to invite these two reprobates that work for you over to my quarters for breakfast after they get off work. Why don't you join us and we can discuss how us old men can keep these young punks in line." Harold and Ron broke out laughing and so did TSgt Smith when I patted him on the shoulder and said, "Watch out for these guys, I think they can be sneaky sometimes. See you at breakfast. OK?"

As I was leaving I turned to TSgt Smith and gave him one last request, "Oh, when the rookie comes around and takes your EMHO report you may want to respond that you had an EMHO but lost it."

* * *

May 23, 2018
Malia, Crete, Greece

Everyone at the table was laughing when the General finished his story. The General concluded his story about the early days by telling everyone that while there was lots of kidding around and fun times, the mission always took first priority and he was proud of the work of all the people assigned to the 6931st Security Group.

The conversation shifted around to how the guys spend most of their time when off duty. Ron told about his preference to hang out in Iraklion's Lion's Square with his local Greek friends during the day and at the old Piper Disco in the basement of the Astoria Hotel at night. Harold talked mainly about riding his motorcycle around the island and hanging out in Malia. Bill's story told about how he met Mary and their time on base. Johnny reminisced about shifting between Iraklion and Malia where he knew there would always be one of his friends around.

George told everybody about what happened to Joseph "Jo Jo" Cummings and how they had stayed friends and were close all the way up to when Jo Jo suffered a heart attack last year. He also told them about his effort to track down Chief and Bob to get them to come to the reunion and finding out they had both been victims of cancer.

The last piece of news coming from the General about the other Detachment 11 alumni of Iraklion Air Station put a damper on the conversation for a while. But the reminiscing brightened up and went on until the General said that he would have to go back home to change and get a few things ready for that night's farewell dinner.

* * *

May 23, 2018
Hersonissos, Crete, Greece

At 7 PM the group had once again gathered in the same hotel meeting room that the initial welcoming dinner took place. The table was laid out the same with the extra place setting on a black placemat. Everyone was decked out in the dressiest clothing they had taken on the vacation. Joan had even gotten Harold to wear a new dress shirt and slacks that she had purchased for him during one of her shopping trips to Iraklion.

They once again started their meal with a toast to the fallen. This time it was not just the guy whose throats constricted but the women as well, since they now knew the stories behind their husband's friends represented by the empty place setting.

The General, who was finally starting to be called George by everyone, began by thanking them for coming and asking if they had a good time. There were a chorus of agreements and thank you's. He then proceeded to tell them about something that he had hinted to during the opening dinner.

George said, "Before the reunion I had talked to friends at the Pentagon and my son, the congressman, had talked to a few of his friends. I want to let you know, now that the exploits of Detachment 11 are no longer classified, I can have your service records amended with what you actually did during your time in Southeast Asia. All of the survivors will qualify to receive Purple Heart medals and at least Bronze Stars for heroic or meritorious achievement or service. I think that several of you will receive a Silver Star instead of a Bronze Star. Though, in my opinion, you actually deserve higher than that."

Ron then asked, "What about the others who are not here tonight?"

"I'm not really sure about them since I only filled in the paperwork for you guys. I would have to go back and review files to research the information for everyone else before I could submit their papers too."

Ron responded, "I can't speak for the others but I have been telling my children and grandchildren our cover story for so long, that in my mind and theirs, the cover story is the truth. To come back and change all of that now may not serve any purpose except to tell them that I have been lying to them. For many years I suffered nightmares and daymares about what I did and saw. But, I managed for the most part to keep it all bottled up within me by telling myself the same thing that I said to myself every day we were in Southeast Asia, "it never happened." I am too old now for a few pieces of metal attached to some cloth to change anything. So please, if you could, don't include me in any amended paperwork. I didn't do what I did there for any medals or recognition, I did it for my friends at this table and for the friends represented by that black place setting."

Harold then chimed in, "I feel the same, please excuse me as well. And opening that can of worms for the others not here, may just cause the reawakening of memories of lost that had been suppressed over time by the families of the fallen. Not to mention how angry they might be with the military for lying to them and not telling them sooner."

The whole table came to the same consensus. Bill did take a little bit longer to think about the better bar at the VFW hall before he too agreed.

George said, "OK, guys. It is too late to have it all reclassified but I can withdraw the paperwork for the metals and without the publicity their approval would generate, as far as the rest of the world is concerned – IT NEVER HAPPENED."

GLOSSARY OF ACRONYMS

A1C	Airman First Class (E3)
AB	Air Base or Airman Basic
AFB	Air Force Base
AFJROTC	Air Force Junior Reserve Officer Training Corps
AFRTS	American Forces Radio and Television Service
ARDF	Airborne Radio Direction Finding
AS	Air Station
AWOL	Absent Without Leave
BDA	Bomb Damage Assessment
CAP	Combat Air Patrol
COMINT	Communications Intelligence
COMSEC	Communications Security
EMHO	Early Morning Expletive
ETA	Estimated Time of Arrival
FAC	Forward Air Controller
FNG	Expletive New Guy
FSB	Fire Support Base
FSC	Sergeant First Class (E7)
H&I	Harassment and Interdiction
HE	High Explosives
IAS	Iraklion Air Station
IFAK	Individual First Aid Kit
KIA	Killed in Action
LT	Lieutenant
LZ	Landing Zone
MACV	Military Assistance Command, Vietnam
mm	Millimeter
MSgt	Master Sergeant (E7)
NCO	Non-Commissioned Officer
NSA	National Security Agency or Naval Support Activity
NVA	North Vietnamese Army
OC	Operations Center
OJT	On the Job Training
OP	Observation Post
PC	Philippine Constabulary
PDQ	Pretty Damn Quick
PI	Philippine Islands
PT	Physical Training
PX	Post Exchange (store)
R&R	Rest and Relaxation
RAMF	Rear Area Expletive Expletive

RPG	Rocket Propelled Grenade
Sgt	Sergeant (E4)
SIGNIT	Signals Intelligence
SOP	Standard Operating Procedures
SSgt	Staff Sergeant (E5)
TI	Training Instructor
TSA	Transportation Security Administration
TSgt	Technical Sergeant (E6)
USAFE	United States Air Forces in Europe
USAFSS	United States Air Force Security Service
VC	Viet Cong
VFW	Veterans of Foreign Wars of the US
VOR	VHF Omnidirectional Radio Range (radio beacon)

ABOUT THE AUTHOR

Ronald (Ron) Tell served in the United States Air Force from 1968 to 1972. After his basic training and technical schools, he was stationed as part of USAFSS at Clark Air Force Base on the Philippine Islands with the 6922nd Security Wing and at Iraklion Air Station, Crete, Greece with the 6931st Security Group. He was honorably discharged as a Staff Sergeant from the service while in Crete where he remained until finances caused him to return to his home in New Orleans, Louisiana. Ron used the G.I. bill to continue his education receiving a BBS degree (Bachelor of Business Studies not the other BS) from Tulane University and an MBA from Washington State University. Ron worked for IBM for 37 years as a repairman, Systems Engineer, Consultant, Instructor, Global Content Manager, Consulting Education Specialist, and Conference Specialist until his retirement in 2010. He currently resides south of Lake Charles, Louisiana with his wife, Kathy, and his dog, Coal.

It Never Happened

36999389R00117

Made in the USA
Columbia, SC
28 November 2018